"A brilliant, brave, whip-smart n
takes on the truths and absurditie
politics and murder. It's filled to t.. _____
ter characters who reveal much about humanity, history, hubris, religion, and
love. *University of Lost Causes* would make a fantastic movie."
—Richard Taylor B.A., Retired Professor of Creative Writing, Carleton University, and author of *House Inside the Waves: Domesticity, Art and the Surfing Life*

"Larry McCloskey's passion for understanding the complexities of human
nature and relationships either draws people to him like a magnet or repels
those who fear being exposed. The characters in this book cannot escape his
astute mind and heart. The revelations of the dark and the light of human
nature as experienced through the intriguing characters and their relationships to themselves, others, and the world will keep you connected to them
long after you finish reading. I feel like I know Larry's characters personally. I laughed and I cried with them; and I learned from their mistakes, fears,
and willingness to be vulnerable and open to life. This is one of my favourite
books of all time."
—Susan Prosser, R.N., B.Sc.N., M.A., Registered Psychotherapist, and author
of *Growing Home: A Lifetime of Self-Awareness and Transformation*

"The chaos of modern times has been concentrated and distilled into university campuses around the globe. The effect has been akin to watching a thousand kittens chasing the moving lights thrown by a bright revolving disco
ball. Larry McCloskey's *University of Lost Causes* resonates deeply with the
unanticipated creativity and dark humor that *Catch-22* reflected for earlier
generations."
—Dr. John A. Meissner, C. Psych

"As a recovering professor of thirty-five years, I can say that *University of Lost
Causes* captures the absurdity of university life that no one sees, and no one
else believes, unless they have been there. A wild and unfortunately accurate
peek behind the curtain of what I have long called 'heir ejumukashin.'"
—Richard Sparks, Ed.D., Professor Emeritus, School of Education, Mt. St.
Joseph University

"With creativity, wit, and keen insight, Larry McCloskey has woven an engrossing tale of colorful characters and unexpected plot twists. Equal parts comedy, parody, and tragedy, *University of Lost Causes* shines a spotlight on present-day university politics and the disconcerting trend in higher education to discard that which in the past has helped to provide purpose and meaning to young people universities purport to serve. This is a read that will engage your mind and stir your heart."

—Chris Barrett, B. Eng., National Director of The Navigators of Canada

ACKNOWLEDGEMENTS

A heartfelt thank you to: Cara Lipsett, Richard and Dale Taylor, Don Cumming, Patrick McCloskey, Donna McCloskey, John Meissner, Susan Prosser, Chris Bickford, Richard Sparks, Chris Barrett, and Marina and Larry Willard.

ALSO BY LARRY J. MCCLOSKEY

Fiction Award Winner:
University of Lost Causes (Word Guild Best Manuscript, 2023)

Nonfiction Award Winners:
Lament for Spilt Porter (Word Guild Best Book, 2019)
Inarticulate Speech of the Heart (Word Guild Best Manuscript, 2021)

Young Adult Fiction:
Murder at Summerhouse, Tom Thomson's Last Paddle, Murder Fit for a King, Unspoken, The Dog Who Cried Snake, A Christmas Dragon

UNIVERSITY OF
LOST
CAUSES

LARRY J. M^C CLOSKEY

UNIVERSITY OF LOST CAUSES
Copyright ©2024 Larry J. McCloskey

978-1-998815-15-9 Soft Cover
978-1-998815-16-6 E-book

Published by:
Castle Quay Books
Burlington, Ontario
Tel: (416) 573-3249
E-mail: info@castlequaybooks.com | www.castlequaybooks.com

Edited by Marina Hofman Willard PhD
Cover and book interior design by Burst Impressions
Printed in Canada

For Library of Congress Cataloging Information please contact the publisher

For Library and Archives Canada Cataloguing in Publication Information please contact the publisher

Dedicated to students, staff, faculty, and the still salvageable university

AUTHOR'S NOTE

Despite what my protagonist might say, I love universities, and mostly those who populate them. But, in channeling Machiavelli in recent years, much of the university sector has chosen to be feared rather than loved. University life used to be a time for trekking into the deep weeds of discovery—both of oneself and the infinite possibilities of learning—an exploratory reprieve away from the coarseness of the world. With rigorous application over a challenging period of trial and error, one's study of objective truths led to an informed, evolving, and dynamic point of view and sense of self.

But the intellectual safe space of university experience of past generations has been subverted by a metaphoric safe-space obsession over perceived threats and correct thinking in a world too dangerous for individual exploration. Danger requires direction, which the modern university is only too willing to give, and often insist upon. Better go with the motto of the University of Bologna (the first university in the world, in continuous existence since 1088): *Alma Mater Studiorum*, Nourishing Mother of Studies.

Ideology is borrowed thinking, antithetical to what universities used to stand for and were conceived to do. In its closed loop, self-replicating fashion, the university modus operandi is often unhinged and one-sidedly political at the expense of relevance, utility, and inspiration. And, most important, this ubiquitous progressive bias comes at the expense of impressionable students who need to figure it out for themselves.

University of Lost Causes is fiction, is satire, has humor tending towards farce, and in combining the trendy idea of dystopian fiction with my quirky brand of farce (the novel is set in the near, postsecondary dystopian future), I've coined the term *farcetopian*. Still, in Shakespearean tradition, the farcetopian fool may convey a message. Writers Albert Camus, Tim O'Brien, Henry James, and others have written variations of this truism: "The art of fiction is to take truth and tell a lie in order to tell a greater truth." My purpose is not to offend but to expose—with absurdity alternatively packaged as fanciful, commonplace, exaggerated, or understated—the inner machinations of university dysfunction towards the possibility for renewal. Solving a mystery and having fun are also on the docket.

The great satirist Jonathan Swift created a sensation when he wrote "A Modest Proposal for Preventing the Children of Poor People from Being a Burthen to Their Parents or Country and for Making Them Beneficial to the Publick." In this essay, Swift advised impoverished Irish parents to sell their wee babies to the rich for culinary consumption. The sensation was not from his modest call for the consumption of babies, but rather from the immodest reforms Swift argued Britain must make to its heartless Irish policy. The British public understood that Swift was not advocating eating babies, that his satiric hyperbole had purpose, and that the real sensation was his audacious call for change.

The year was 1729. The public understood. Swift was not cancelled.

—Larry McCloskey

 Larry McCloskey completed two graduate degrees before founding and serving as Director of the Paul Menton Centre for Students with Disabilities, Carleton University, for over three decades. Not understanding the concept of retirement, he then qualified as a Social Work Psychotherapist, as well as ratcheted up his writing ritual. Not understanding the concept of rest, he rounds out his day torturously running with his two eager dogs. Teaching Larry the concept of play are his amazing daughters, wife, and most instructive, three wondrous grand-daughters

University politics makes me pine for the relative peace of the Middle East.
—Henry Kissinger, former Secretary of State, after a stint at Harvard

And when asked, "Why are university politics so fierce?" Kissinger responded, "Because the stakes are so small."

Place and Time: St. Jude's University, a midsized private, once-Catholic institution of higher learning, somewhere in New England, sometime into the wacky near future.

INTRODUCTION

All psychological pain can be derived from not
being able to reconcile the world as it is
from what we would have it be.
—Anonymous psychiatrist, obviously intending
to teach me a lesson

I have a dilemma. I'm an avoidant sod with an unavoidable metaphoric wedgie. I have to move my apolitical posterior and stand up to the maelstrom of university politics, pain in the ass as that may be. Worse, I have to be discreet and diplomatic, tempering my bull-in-the-china-shop tendencies. The four horse-persons are coming for me in my non-equestrian electric wheelchair. And worse than worse, the unidentified they, of *they say* fame, are coming for my beloved work crew stranded on our island of the misfits. I—who cannot walk—have to outrun those who want to take down civilization in the name of fairness and virtue.

I once was heralded as among the oppressed. Not my assessment, but a widely held view from university folk who divide the world between armed camps. I could have held court while holding sway, indignantly claiming crimes against humanity, if not for that thing about being human. I just couldn't or, as colleague Luna says, wouldn't go with the flow. And being antithetical to flow, I'm salmon-like, flailing upstream to my inevitable demise. Which qualifies me as an oppressor, I guess. Nice to finally achieve an identity.

Though not yet fact, there is no doubt we are being rejigged, reworked, and restructured; could be shut down and replaced by more progressive people. Been close to this before, and never sweated it before, never sweated much of anything, but something is different this time. Flaky as feelings might make me, something is really up, something really not good, and I can feel it with every ounce of my unfeeling body.

Somehow, I need to protect the Center, my peeps, and our students against the machinations of this place, which is becoming weirder every day. I need to move head and spirit with stealth and cunning, even if physical movement is denied.

Paralysis is not necessarily stasis. It no longer haunts me, hasn't for years. Surprising what you can do without if you do without. Still, my dreams are far removed from the unmoving carcass that inhabits this bed. I dream about movement, always movement, not vague and effervescent, but as it was in the flesh, with a vividness I don't indulge thinking about during waking hours. Which is strange because when I could move, besides actively chasing women, I mostly moved to the couch. Only self-indulgence moved me. I worked as little as possible and pursued pleasure as much as I could get away with.

Until I was hugged into life—and yes, there is a story there—with the revelation of simple. In the mix of all the complexity in which we live and breathe there really is only one thing, one move, one response that matters. The human touch—with feeling fingers or not—is *it*, is our only it, is our meaning and mission, even if contrary to every aspect of university functioning.

So we have to choose. Either we play politics, or we hug someone into existence. That stark, that simple, that which either elevates or diminishes.

University life and how it plays out in the progressive world does not elevate. Case in point: today's meeting could change everything, and my peeps are worried. Luna and my brother Iggy will work, worry, and scheme, but I just don't have it in me. I should worry, I suppose, but am oppressed by UIS (unbounded indolence syndrome). Crisis, this crisis, should move me, but it just seems the stakes are so small. I'll let them wring their hands while I merely resolve to flow upstream. It is enough, and it is an enough that will require everything I have. These are my thoughts in darkness, in bed, in this moment with false dawn verging on first light, waiting for Brenda, my attendant and lover, her lovely presence soon to grace this space. I will drift off again, prisoner to a thousand pillows, as I move through time and across the universe, fending off attacks, defeating villains, and alleviating the many vicissitudes of the people for whom I would lay down my life, or least hug into one worth living.

As sincerely as I can muster,
Phelim O'Neill

CHAPTER ONE

Some of the animals remembered—or thought they
remembered—that the Sixth Commandment decreed,
"No animal shall kill any other animal."
And though no one cared to mention it in the hearing
of the pigs or the dogs, it was felt that the killings which
had taken place did not square with this.
—George Orwell

Four hours later, Halloween morning, Phelim's bedroom

My long-suffering attendant, Brenda, has me sitting up in bed trying to shake off the cobwebs, and she'll be back in a minute with strong coffee in my trusty mug, replete with paper straw. She's thrown a bathrobe over my rhinoceros belly because there's some problem with school so she had to bring her eight-year-old daughter, Pearl. Pearl always hangs back at first, feigning disinterest before sliding into the room and asking a question or ten. Brenda shoos her out for most of the morning routine—well, midmorning routine, since, as alluded to, I am pathologically lazy. Pearl always inches back in with an intense look of nonchalance and a slew of questions and answers waiting to be born. Not that she'll admit it. I feel like reversing the question-and-answer sequence today.

"Hey Pearl, is that a green dress you have on today?"

No answer.

"Can't remember the last time you didn't wear either pink or purple."

No answer.

"Have you switched your favorite colors or something?"

No answer, but she is moving toward the foot of the bed.

"Guess there's nothing wrong with switching favorite colors."

Brenda returns, and together we place my fingers around the handle of my coffee mug. She then admonishes her daughter with a single word, "Pearl."

Pearl knows this is a warning to leave the room, but she practices selective hearing. Once she reaches the foot of the bed, my dog Zigo gets up, stretches, and leans over to receive Pearl's hand on his ears. Zigo's tail crashes into her face as he turns around and faces Brenda. Pearl giggles as Zigo jumps off the bed and follows Brenda to the kitchen for his morning gruel.

"Hum," I ponder.

"What?" Pearl erupts, curiosity displacing nonchalance.

"Well, it's just that I'm surprised Zigo recognizes you, since you're not wearing your favorite colors. Don't think he's ever seen you wearing green."

Big breath, hand on hip, said with absolute confidence, "Everyone knows that dogs are color-blind."

"Is that what you learned at university today?"

Exasperation. "I don't go to university yet. I'm in the third grade, which you know."

"What's the difference?" I ask and realize I really don't know the answer.

Pearl thinks about this. She is always thinking, and her responses, all her responses are deliberate and serious. The more important the pronouncement, the more air she exhales, "In the third grade you have to do what the teacher tells you, and in university you get to do whatever you want."

Good answer, I think. "Hey, what's that book under your green arm?"

Pearl adjusts her glasses and sighs, having mastered the art of exasperation. "You should know since you gave it to me." She holds the book with outstretched arms for all to see.

"Ah, right, *The Big Book of Dinosaurs*, a classic. So, when you grow up do you want to work looking for dinosaur bones and researching stuff, you know, like a—"

"Paleontologist," she enunciates with the confidence of, well, a paleontologist.

Brenda walks back in the room and gives Pearl a dismissive glance.

"Before you leave, Professor Pearl, do you have any questions for me?"

Pearl shakes her head and starts out of the room, but then she turns and asks, "How come you work at a university and you don't even know what a paleontologist is?"

I gotta admit, I like this kid. "Well, it's because I work at a university that I don't know what a paleontologist is."

Pearl considers this, serious and thoughtful, as she always is. "I am definitely not going to go to university."

I really like this kid.

I also really like my work peeps who are terrified about today's meeting. It was rescheduled from nine a.m. to eleven a.m. because of my affliction. Been allowing sympathetic speculation around what that might mean for thirty years, and it is rarely challenged. Still, some people keep trying to schedule me for nine a.m. meetings, knowing my attendance is unlikely. I guess people feel good, accommodating, compassionate even, about making a change from what they knew would never be for what was always going to happen.

Our Center has been shamed for having insufficient Diversity, Inclusion, and Equity, whose acronym, under present circumstances, fittingly is DIE. Not sure if that means students or staff; could be both. Never mind that the majority of my staff and all our students were well within DIE parameters five minutes ago. And if that isn't enough, it has come to people's attention that we require students registering for inclusion at our Center for Students with Disabilities to actually have a disability. Our office, created to help students with disabilities, has always required students to provide a letter from a doctor to prove they have a disability, but in the new woke world that practice is deemed insufficiently inclusive. There is a movement afoot to forgo such arcane practices and simply and without question believe poor, oppressed students. Always. Not always believing is to place our staff among the oppressors. Today's meeting is ostensibly about making damn sure we do something about it, without the infamous *it* ever being defined. Our Center is lauded internationally for innovative programs and includes every disability and humanoid variation under the sun, but that is not enough. Not knowing that is not enough is more than enough: we are to be made an example of.

All of which is funny for anyone with a perverse sense of humor. No one was more surprised than I was that our Center became famous. The short version is we did real stuff for real people who needed help to succeed. They started to succeed and then succeeded in ever increasing numbers. In the early days before our center became the Center, I had an office with some regulars visiting on a daily basis because they didn't quite fit in anywhere else. I once heard a faculty member—taking an elevator up one flight of stairs—refer to my office as "island of the misfits." Sitting and being at a lower level—both physically and metaphorically—he hadn't noticed my presence which I reminded him of with a mighty belch before blocking his exit from the elevator. Oddly, "island of the misfits" appealed to me, and once I informed the gang, my misfit friends adopted this kitschy term. We didn't kid ourselves about inclusion then, just as we don't pretend that bandying the term today neutralizes the reality of, say, blindness, schizophrenia, or quadriplegia. It's one thing to reside in this chair; it's quite another to listen to someone—whose knowledge of disability and life is theoretical and aspirational—tell you that that their notion of *inclusion* excludes the prejudices of other, less enlightened people. And, most offensive, they offer the caveat that if they were in charge, with all their progressive ways and access to other people's money, they'd fix all the deficiencies and liberate us from our unenlightened, non-defective selves. How nice.

As our Center's reputation grew, and I became a sort of ad hoc national spokesman for getting students with disabilities the stuff they need to succeed, I often felt like a fraud. I knew less and did less than people assumed and gave me credit for. It took me a couple decades to figure out that not doing much is still a couple notches up from what most people do who inhabit the hallowed quarters of higher education. It finally dawned on me that at least I am an honest fraud, and my fraudster accomplishments pale in comparison to the people who do the real work in our Center.

Being apolitically avowed, I've always been amused by university politics. My mantra has been to never take too seriously people who take themselves too seriously. But something has changed. I am no longer content to be coy, ironic, amused, and bemused. I'm not getting serious, growing up, or any of those horrible things, but I'm also not willing to remain static. I want to move even if I have to do it sitting still. The world has moved all around me, taking with it most of what I thought was decent, in the name of higher, stronger, wiser. In other words, wokeness.

Iggy—brother, not to be confused with dog Zigo—and Luna—colleague extraordinaire—will agonize about strategy and their frustration over my inability to see the need to agonize and strategize. But neither agony nor strategy will work. Mostly, I think our purpose in life is to take in, look, and listen. No strategy, no agony, that simple. As mentioned, I like simple. Did I mention that I'm lazy as sin?

I shouldn't take advantage of this fact, but the fascinating combo of laziness and university politics has made me a creature of avoidance, to be avoided. Laid-back indifference seems a good way to mask intentions, but the thing is, I do have some fight in me. Timing will be tricky, and the landscape seems to both change every day and revert to what was with delightful predictability. Meanwhile, Iggy and Luna suffer. I could say it hurts me more than it hurts them. But in the university world reminiscent of Madame Bovary, wherein left is right and up is down, I am determined to fight the flow and tell the truth, even if packaged in my kitschy, corny take on life.

Brenda comes back in, all business today. In that other life, the one that slipped away on the night of my accident, I would have been oblivious to the obvious. I was for exteriors, frivolity, basically what appealed to my pecker at any given moment. I would not have seen Brenda, and I would not have allowed her to see me. My mask was impenetrable then. I would have squandered the opportunity to have a family of two or ten, which to my everlasting astonishment turns out to be what I want most of all. I wasted that life, but Brenda is here now, and though we have an uncertain future, we have a nice arrangement with potential for more.

"What's Pearl up to?" I ask.

"Oh, you know her, reading. She asked if I could hand her one of your books from high up on a shelf that probably hasn't been opened in thirty years."

"What book?"

"*The Complete Book of Auto Mechanics.*"

"Makes sense."

"Yup, that's my girl. Now, first thing, we're going to roll you over so I can see your backside."

"Naughty."

"Did you get Bill to check your skin in the last few days?"

"Nope. He once said that these sheets make my ass look fat, so I'm kinda shy."

"You really don't want to spend a week on your stomach again." With a big, practiced heave and strategic lift of the sheets, I am on my belly, ass pointing north.

Brenda does a thorough inspection, and I luxuriate in that space between wakefulness and the eternal pull toward slumber. Brenda says she needs to treat my skin, and she leaves the room to get something.

I appreciate Brenda, the conscientious attendant, but I especially appreciate that we are more than a business arrangement. My morning routine with Brenda takes longer than with other attendants, except for those times when Pearl is around.

We are not so much an item as a thing, though what that thing is is not clear. Yet. Still, it endures, and it feels good. Mostly, she and I can talk, really talk. Apparently, laziness is an appropriate bedfellow for listening skills. An attendant/lover relationship is discouraged and unlikely as hell, for many reasons. But for us, talk became cuddling, and yes—unlikely as it may seem—sex. What? How? Sorry, but my determination to tell truth does not go that far. A gentleman never tells. There are clinical books that will itemize what and how disability and sex can become bedfellows, but they will not tell you anything about me and Brenda. Suffice to say, intimacy is not prescribed, sex is not predictable—well, not good sex at least—and friendship might just be the most important ingredient in a good relationship because it involves seeing and being seen. Scary concept to be avoided by most. On a planet of eight billion, on an insignificant speck of the universe for a life that is over in the blink of an eye, we rarely see and are seen. And people think I have the dysfunction. Interesting.

Brenda in full utilitarian mode admonishes me for letting my skin get so close to breakdown, and I am drifting, floating on a thousand pillows, promising myself I will listen to Brenda if she ever stops talking about my negligent habits. Through the din I hear Pearl's name, something about her difficulty relating to eight-year-old kids who do not read books on auto mechanics.

I force myself to resurface, vaguely thinking that Pearl could probably better relate to paleontologists. "Brenda, promise you'll let Pearl keep all her quirky ways."

"Okay, so what do you mean by that?"

"She has inexhaustible curiosity and blistering drive, and I don't want her to lose that."

I can feel Brenda's smile through the silence. "She likes you, you know."

"What's not to like?"

"Did I tell you she said something interesting the other day. Something like, when Phelim stops kidding, which is almost never, he's the only adult who doesn't treat me like a baby."

I really like that kid. Brenda can feel my smile through the silence.

CHAPTER TWO

Halloween, at the Center for Students with Disabilities,
our Island of the Misfits

The mosh pit that is our Center is in full tumult. A 10:35 a.m. arrival is early for me, due in no small part to Brenda not being available for post-attendant naked cuddling. The waiting area is overflowing; interns scurry to meet frantic students, and staff—with a tad less enthusiasm but more skill—greet their next appointment. No amount of carrying students off to appointments seems to diminish the number of students wanting to get appointments. Front desk staff are students working for that minimum wage under the supervision of a force of nature we call Edie. Her name means "prosperous in war," and in happily dealing with our many, many students and solving their many, many crises, she is. There isn't one in a thousand who could attend to our battleground with prosperity as the outcome, but Edie does just that every day. Her uber happiness is balanced by being seriously wacky, making her my exemplary employee.

"Hey, boss, admit it. You're here early because you couldn't bear life without me!" Edie says with faux drama-queen histrionics. Then she is gone to calm a student employee who has just made a student un-calm, for which there has been wailing and gnashing of teeth. Edie's declarations of love and well-trodden innuendos enrich my life this and every day, for no particular reason. As one of her main peeps I give back as much as I take—that is, once she gets a few minutes reprieve from reception at crisis central. And in calmly attending to the un-calm between bawdy barbs, she is magnificent. My peep of peeps until my dying days.

It is the very end of October, midterms in full flight, November blahs encroaching, with winter blues on the horizon, and a theoretical Christmas break too far away to give relief. The next three days, remnants of a Christian tradition that is no more, were unceremoniously canceled some years back—unceremonious cancellation having to do with removing the scaffolding of civilization without thought to its replacement. Substituting the word *utopia* doesn't do it. Nietzsche, an atheist, predicted that the leveling and stripping of Christian civilization would lead to pernicious and unintended consequences. But he was a moldy old white guy, so give him a pass.

Halloween was mostly canceled a dozen or so years after protests at Yale inspired postsecondary enlightenment across the country. Twenty-five percent of our students wear masks—medical that is, and not of the Halloween variety—years after Covid has waned, for fear, for protection, for an identity with which modern people silently scream, *I exist.*

No one dares appropriate cultural icons like Mickey Mouse or Bart Simpson anymore. Rather than trick or treat like savages on city streets far removed from parental prying eyes, kids are taught to passively revere all other cultures and to disparage their own. Without knowing what one's cultural heritage is, it is difficult to know what one is disparaging, but that doesn't discourage enlightened people. All Saints' Day, November 1, once celebrating those who have achieved spiritual maturity, and All Souls' Day, November 2, once commemorating the souls of the faithfully departed, drowsily pass, somnambulist captives to the woke nightmare that has descended upon us. This world without rules or context, which promises as a human right what can never be delivered to mere humans, creates anxiety and depression. Without knowing any of this, it is why students come to talk to me every day. They so desperately want something but cannot begin to articulate what it might be. Life for our many, many students is tragic, unfair, and in need of immediate correction. Many come to me with demands for correction if only I will listen. I do listen and gently try to suggest that in the correction mix, introspection might offer surprising results.

Luna and Iggy usually pounce, but neither thought I'd arrive at such an unlikely hour, so neither is ready to greet me. I pass Luna's open door and notice she and Iggy in full strategic flight, so I continue as if there is an option not to engage. Iggy emerges first, running as he always does, with Luna a few quick wheel rotations behind. I stop in front of my office until my transponder clicks the door unlocked.

"We don't have much time," Iggy begins,

"to fill you in on the options we have come up with," Luna finishes, her rotating sport wheelchair flashing in the brilliant morning light.

I call them Frick and Frack when I'm not calling them Ying and Yang. Either way a dynamo duo, gratefully indentured to keep the world from seeing the obvious: that I'm lazy. Poor things don't realize I'm okay with my affliction.

"I'm early," I protest.

"Hey, good morning," David says, sticking his head into my office, "Let me know what you think about my suggestions on website changes when you get a chance." Another devotee to shielding the world from seeing the obvious in me.

Lucy, full-time student, part-time front desk minimum wage wizard stands at my open door waiting to be noticed. "The Special Adviser to the President's EA wants you to call. Do you need the number?"

"Nay, it's all up here," I say, lifting and leaning my coffee mug in the direction of my head.

Iggy's eyes betray acute anxiety. "I'll close the door," he says, springing up.

"We don't have enough time; we should start walking," Luna cautions.

"We have all the time in the world," I say, with my trademark silly grin.

"Phelim, this is serious, and we really should be on time."

"I'm never on time, and if I suddenly change my lifetime habit, people will think I'm running scared."

"You should be scared," Luna admonishes. "We're in trouble."

"Really? Starving is trouble, Ebola is trouble, and tsunamis are trouble, but this … not so much trouble as annoying."

"Phelim, they might take us apart."

"You need to take this seriously."

"Okay, so how's this?" I ask, with my best, Finest Hour Winston Churchill pose.

"You are *so* frustrating," Luna exclaims. She of Spanish name is of Chinese origin, where she contracted polio as a toddler decades after it was eradicated in North America. Luna is the hardest-working person on the planet, making me the most frustrating.

"That's true actually," I say, appealing to Iggy. "I'd pay attention to that girl if I was you."

"I do," Iggy responds, "And so should—"

"So whaddya got?"

Iggy pounces. "The way we see it, we've got to write a statement about pulling together a committee with all stakeholders so that we can come up with a policy to balance the human rights directive with our need to objectively assess who actually has a disability."

"And if you propose it today," Luna emphasizes, "it can seem like a proactive move instead of a chickenshit reaction."

"I get that," I say, not wanting to prematurely cut up what has been so carefully conjured.

"We've written some notes, a draft paper actually, which could be edited into a full position paper by the end of the day."

"Hum, one problem," I say, in a soft voice, which catches their attention, and they wait for me to finish the sentence: "we don't actually believe in putting in place the human rights directive that would surely flow from the position paper of the stakeholder committee culminating in the grand policy of compliance, do we?"

"No, but we have to be strategic," Luna argues, and Iggy agrees.

The door opens, and David says that we should go. Luna asks David what he thinks about their strategic plan, and being the opposite of moi in the frustration department, he says, "Oh yes, it's a good strategic plan."

"Bet you say that to all the boys," I say, leaning back to stretch my back and correct my awful posture, a practice of every ten minutes or so these thirty-five years and counting.

"You are so frustrating," Luna says, a catch-phrase practice said every ten minutes or so for these fifteen years and counting.

"You are so right," I say, and then, "Let's take our time, talk hockey, express our mutual admiration, exchange recipes, arrive fashionably late, and see what befalls us. Then over drinks tonight maybe we'll come up with something, or not."

Luna and Iggy look at each other, worried and anxious. "Told you," she says.

Followed by Iggy's "He really is so frustrating."

"Yes, but you do love me," I punctuate our closing line, and we are off.

Three guys from the attendant program are waiting along the corridor near the Center reception, reasons unknown, earlier than any one of them is usually up, and yet here they are as a gang. Coordinating their collective earlier than normal morning routine must have created a scheduling stir among attendants, so something is up. I'd be mildly curious if not for the fact that someone will frantically let me know what is up soon enough. I like these guys, little shites that they are, and I lift my unfeeling hand to slap their equally unfeeling limbs, as if we have just scored the winning goal in game seven of the playoffs. They know me, and they know better than to try to explain what the problem is as we high-five our fictitious goal, me in full flight, off to an important meeting to change the world for the betterment of personkind. Luc is a mid-level quad, Ben a few notches higher on the spinal column, and Doug has cerebral palsy, so we share a life that moves slowly and places us on display, always. I won't tell them that the prospect of getting older and being in a chair adds up to the kitschy contradictory combo of perpetual exposure and complete invisibility.

I lead Luna and Iggy down the long narrow corridor to the elevator. As always, the sound of Kevin precedes the sight of him. His erratic driving, due to an endearing mixture of spasticity and inattention, means the sound of his chair hitting the walls gives us forewarning to duck for cover. I slow and drift from my center position to as close to the wall as I can manage. Kevin sees me, and though we are friends all these years, he frantically tries to steer toward the other wall. Which he does, but rather than squeeze closer to the wall, he hits it and bounces back beyond the center of the corridor, where I just happen to be trying to slip past.

This is not a unique event. The long narrow corridor of about a hundred feet has an equally long continuous black smudge on both sides, recording the many years that Kevin, and more accurately, his chairs have graced our corridors. Our chairs hit, with Kevin doing a mighty full-body flinch—half nerves, half spasm—as ever, not quite believing what mischief his driving has gotten him into. I anticipate our habitual collision and slow, so no damage, except possibly to Kevin's self-esteem, as ever. Poor thing. Being beyond the middle of the lane, it is incumbent upon Kevin to back up, which he eventually figures out, to no avail. Somehow our wheelchair controls are entangled, and neither of us can move. When Kevin gets flustered, he gets more spasmodic and is more prone to do the exact thing that exacerbates the present problem.

His swearing is legendary, his frustration palpable, to which I simply say, "Wait."

"This d-d-damn—"

"Wait." This time with authority, and then looking over my shoulder, "Iggy." Who, being a quick study, sees the entanglement and reaches over with a lift of Kevin's controls for the fix.

"Oh," says Kevin, unaccustomed to things working out, "oh."

I understand when he says "oh" because of our long years of banter, but to most people everything Kevin says is incomprehensible. Neither hearing nor listening contributes to people's incomprehension. Not caring completes the uncomprehending trifecta.

Then, as a face-saving exit, Kevin mutters, "P-p-papist bastard," to my comprehending, slightly amused departing backside.

The single elevator that services our floor is slow this time of day. Young, fully functioning bipeds often stand for ten minutes to take the elevator up or down one floor. I never question or make faces at those who unnecessarily clog the elevator. I always smile or exchange pleasantries, secure in the knowledge that there are people on this earth who can challenge me for the title of world's laziest person.

"Should I go ahead? Do you want me to let them know that you are stuck at the elevator?" Iggy fusses and fidgets.

"Nay," I say, perfectly content to be late for all occasions, whether preventable or not.

"But it's already eleven a.m.," he counters.

"And the Special Adviser to the President always gives you a dirty look when you come in late," Luna adds.

"She just admires my consistency."

Iggy swears mostly to himself, and Luna says, "You are so frustrating."

"Ain't it the truth," I say, agreeably.

The concept of sneaking into a meeting in progress does not apply to an entourage of misfits led by a 250-pound quadriplegic in a squeaky electric wheelchair of equal weight followed by a completely unnecessary and yet kitschy companion dog, Zigo. Besides, the effort and desire to sneak is not in me. Luna and Iggy die a thousand deaths under silent scrutiny as we enter, whereas I glory in the profound silliness of this and, well, all of life's silliness.

To my perverse mind, the holy moment is equal parts holy and humor. Taking life seriously can be toxic.

The SAP gives us a withering glance (having perfected the art of withering) and continues talking. Nine times out of ten at meetings, she is the only one talking. Luna and Iggy scurry, trying to be and remain small. Zigo wags his tail, and I sit up in my chair and stretch my spine, canine pal and I unwilling to wither under withering intent.

The SAP's strategy of ignoring us, thereby reinforcing our collective insignificance, becomes problematic once I try to find a place to park at the back of the room. Most chairs are occupied, and those that remain empty lie scattered across my path. Iggy jumps to clear two chairs away while I ram two more and pivot around to face the front of the room. The ensuing high-pitched screech is painful and long, which I alone find amusing. Well, not exactly true, since the commotion causes an extra wag from my loyal canine. Zigo then rolls over, hoping to a get a belly rub, to no avail.

The SAP stops, almost speaks with annoyance, but it probably occurs to her that not clearing obstacles for a quadriplegic is a no-no for those holding progressive views, even for one you detest and want to exclude. She of withering glance withers. In equal proportion, my grin expands.

The SAP's attention shifts back to business, and she continues, "St. Jude's was never going to be satisfied simply being progressive …."

A little context. St. Jude's is not just any university, though we seem determined to accelerate efforts at being the best at being just like everyone else. We were conceived and born a Catholic university of necessity, in response to the need to educate and provide health care to any and all citizens of our fair city. This concept was acted upon, and later reflected in our charter, to provide educational opportunities to the poor, with specific emphasis on serving Native Americans. This singular feature, a first in American history, grew from the work of a convent first established in 1759. Twenty years earlier, Samson Wolf, the first Native American ordained minister, of the Mohegan tribe, cofounded the Indian Charity School. The convent and Samson Wolf pooled resources to run the school, which was very successful, and consequently ran out of funds after its first few years.

A small party was organized and went to Britain to raise funds. But interest in Native Americans not doing what wealthy Britons expected them to do did not garner much interest, and insufficient funds were raised to continue the school. For reasons unknown, the party traveled to Montreal, intending to continue south to New England. Somehow a connection was made with the Gray Nuns, a Roman Catholic order founded by Marie-Marguerite, Canada's first candidate for sainthood, in that city in 1737. The order's first ministry was feeding the poor, which quickly spawned a hospice for the sick and elderly and, interestingly at a time when no one else cared, included looking after children who had been abandoned by their parents, especially children with disabilities. Though the Gray Nuns, also known as the Sisters of Charity, were not formally recognized until 1775, and though they more than had their hands full doing charity work in Montreal, a small group of nuns agreed to move to New England to run the Indian Charity School.

It is hard for people to get their heads around this fact today, but early on, the Gray Nuns didn't just contribute to education and later health care; they were the only game in town. In 1864, in continuing the spirit of altruism bolstered by concrete actions, the Gray Nuns gave most of their adjoining land, some 380 acres, for the establishment of St. Jude's University. The convent only kept thirty acres, just enough land for the nuns to continue their school and indulge in their passion for gardening, which doubled as a means to feed themselves and the poor. Though thirty acres seemed a paltry amount of land in 1864, as the core of the city grew around it during the ensuing decades, the garden property with its one solitary residence building seemed to grow in size as well as exponentially in value.

Of course, the history of St. Jude's, particularly its early education of Native Americans, has been desecrated in recent years. A key point lost sight of is this: for a time, St. Jude's was not a lost cause. The school's history does not refute American racist history in relation to Native Americans, but does reveal that a pocket of enlightenment—in deeds, not virtue signaling—can exist as the spectacular exception to the general societal pattern. History is what happened, not what we assume or would like to believe happened.

Over the objections of prominent Native American elders, the singular contribution of St. Jude's to American history has been turned into a singular narrative of colonialism, racism, genocide, and murder. The narrative, created and sustained by St. Jude's faculty, has been amplified in the media, despite playing seriously fast and loose with the facts. And the elders, whom we are told to treat with deference and respect, were sidelined and ignored (for their own good, poor things). When unaccounted graves of Indigenous children were suspected to be on the sites of former residential schools in Canada, it was taken as fact that much worse had happened at St. Jude's. Falsehoods were fully and enthusiastically embraced and a revisionist narrative greater than truth came to prevail.

St. Jude is the patron saint of lost causes. Seriously. Which conveniently parallels a forgotten and elemental fact of life: we are all lost causes if not for our redemptive commitment to others. In recent years, that reality has been expunged from all aspects of university life. St. Jude's, still a Catholic university on paper, has become aggressively atheist in its new progressive configuration. Any notion of spirituality has become a lost cause. Progressive thinking includes a moratorium on irony. We have become a lost cause unwilling to be found. Maybe our patron, Saint Jude, was a former student.

"Our revolutionary mental health strategy, which celebrates intersectionality and personal truth over diagnosis and medical model reductionism, is complete after extensive consultation with marginalized stakeholders, and we will be going to Senate by the end of the month, right, Tim?"

"Yes, and under your leadership, it is a super strategy!" Tim was conceived, born, and lives to serve the SAP. He is a member of her inner sanctum. He is among those few behind the wall of knowing and power. Hell, he is the guardian at the gate who takes the password and gives access to the queen. His passive aggression and hubris are legionary. Still, my view is that only those can hold sway whom we acknowledge as having sway, which if ignored, doesn't exist. Tim doesn't exist for me, which probably makes me so frustrating.

It should be mentioned that our SAP's full and proper title is Special Adviser to the President, Exceptional Student Experience. As you ponder that, it is worth noting her specialness presides over everything, her rule is absolute, and in fairness to her stature at St. Jude's, her recently acquired lofty title should be further lofty-ized into Empress for Life.

Interesting connotation to her SAP title acronym. I almost fell out of my chair when I first heard it. Webster's dictionary defines the word *sap* as 1. A body fluid (such as blood) essential to life, health or vigor. 2. A foolish gullible person. 3. Blackjack or Bludgeon. Our sap is the lifeblood of our university; our president is a foolish, gullible person; and the metaphoric instrument she wields to maintain power is a bludgeon, which Webster's further defines as "something used to attack or bully." All of which, from her pointed point of view, is graphically, picturesquely perfect.

In the old days, universities were run by presidents, who consulted with and sought permission from, first, the ever-vigilant senate then the more distant, nonacademic, but powerful Board of Governors. Not so these days. Our ivory tower is typical of the great change that has swept power from the academics into the burgeoning arms of the student service world in the name of equity, customer service, diversity, inclusion, student engagement, funding, marketing strategies, mental health, student satisfaction, and synergy. Okay, so kidding about the last one, but it does seem to be the word most often used when two parties compare notes on how to aspirationally advance all the notions that preceded it. Academic programs take a back seat to the multiplicity of student concerns in the modern university, with academics passively providing the vacuum for nonacademic synergistic ascendency. Basically, busybodies rule.

There were recently three, but there are now are six vice presidents in our gilded tower. Senior position creep is just one aspect of the great nonacademic takeover happening across the land. Sure, there's a president too, but he mostly waits for his instructions from the VPs, who all take their instructions from our SAP. Our token president and the six VPs have never existed a day outside of the unreality of university life that began when they were first-year undergraduate students a millennium ago. Rumor has it that the real world is filled with deplorables who do not appreciate the superior intellect that follows from having a PhD. Still, someone has to occasionally descend from the castle, cross the moat, and deal with the peons. Consequently, the real-world (exceptional) experience our SAP brought into her portfolio is treated with uber deference and respect. Her ability to read the woke tea leaves has made her the ultimate university influencer and therefore the most powerful personhood at St. Jude's. That power is exceptionally effective at exploiting the prevailing mood of the times. Radical opportunist equates to visionary in the exceptional world in which we almost live.

The university has structured itself in deference to unexceptional students' perception of their exceptional experience (which if so, is ubiquitous and therefore unexceptional) in order that students not assert their full and expanding rights, many entitlements, and propensity to take legal action, which would make for an unexceptional experience for the senior officers of the university. So indistinguishable senior university careerists compete to come up with synergistic innovations for managing and bribing students with tricks and party favors within the expanding student services cartel at St. Jude's. As such, it is simple math. Our SAP has the most party favors, and though no one cares about math anymore, she is the undisputed queen of the castle.

Universities live in fear. Fear of students and their fragile states, fear of parents of fragile students, fear of human rights bodies whose mission is to protect same said students, fear of not living up to daily claims of diversity, inclusion, and equity for all groups except for former oppressors, and fear of the media reporting any deficiencies on the part of the university to protect and provide the best student experience possible.

Word is, the next relevant Act of Congress, based on a recent Supreme Court ruling, is that human rights will be extended to a student's right to have an exceptional experience. As such, our SAP's Exceptional Student Experience title was extended to position our university as *the* progressive leader for this coming trend. Luna, Iggy, and all my peeps are seriously upset by this rumor, but predictably, I find it funny.

Of course, I have a distinct advantage over my peeps on the funny front, because I regularly meet Professor John Staffal for lunch and for beer. In addition to possibly being the last faculty member to actually speak his mind— about all subjects, at all times—he is the funniest man to have ever lived.

He is universally hated at this university, but then so am I, just less blatantly so. I know we are sitting ducks, watching the approaching tsunami from the shore, but I don't much care. The value of humor is at an all-time low, and I must admit that there is a certain perverse humorless logic to the progressive buzz that has infected this room, our university, the world. Kill that with which

LARRY J. MCCLOSKEY

people identify—family, community, God—and we are left with the politics of identity—me, myself, and I. The progressive trinity of self does not do stand-up—or in my case, sit-down—comedy. Protecting my peeps is going to be tough because challenging this woman's power is a sure route to defeat, as many others have found. I grin at the Special Adviser to the President, Exceptional Student Experience, seemingly in agreement with all her proclamations, a crazy compliant fool. Still, this old boy is not dead yet, and may have a trick or two up his unfeeling sleeve.

CHAPTER THREE

Decades earlier on the spinal cord unit, Rehabilitation Center

The meeting ends with a stern warning of coming change coupled with a sterner look in my direction. I'm not sure what else is said, because I rarely know what is said at meetings. Checking out at meetings while sitting in attendance with a frozen, compliant grin is a solid survival skill. But I didn't develop it at the university; I just refined what I'd learned years earlier.

I dissociate therefore I am, not dead. I was once close to death, desperately wanted to die but didn't, and in time didn't want to. Thirty-five years ago, I was an arrogant, irresponsible drunk who some people actually found charming. I lived for seduction and sex and, well, alcohol, too, with the former lit up by the latter. That is, while not exactly shy and retiring when sober, I was a pick-up-chick virtuoso when drunk. To this day, I don't fully understand how I did what I did and got what I got so easily and often. And yes, it raises the question, and no, I was not careful about what I wished for.

My intake was prodigious. A full bottle of any hard liquor or a case of beer, no problem. And then I'd wake up, treat a hangover with a midmorning beer, and back to business. I considered restraint to be drinking an early recovery beer slowly. So how was I able to drink all day and night? To this day, I'm not sure where my drinking tolerance came from, and I kind of wish I had it for people instead. Believe it or not, I was a carded athlete with Olympic potential. That's right, the world's laziest guy was good enough to earn a modest track income, while being fueled by not Gatorade, but Jameson. My twelve-years-younger brother, who runs marathons, still cannot talk about the waste of my potential, but I can and do. I was what I was, and only in taking responsibility for what I was, was I able to become who I am, whatever that is. I learned early on not to carry the specter of *the other* on your back, what you might have become, who you might have met, those children you might have had, the life you might have lived, which was yours for the living, if only you'd made different choices.

In high school, I set the state record for 400-meter hurdles, and though at university my potential for greatness was compromised, I still managed to hang in as a contender. After my third year at St. Jude's, I was offered a summer job in the university athletics department. There were parties; I was a fixture. Hookups were frequent, opportunity endless, and I was a six-foot-three-inch good-looking sports hero who just happened to be both the life of the party and, as mentioned, charming as hell when drunk.

One night in June—on my birthday, in fact—I drove my decrepit 1969 Volkswagen Beetle with bald tires fifty miles outside town to a big party at someone's parents' summer home.

I was on. Funny, irreverent, the conversationalist of choice, the guy who moved like a cat and was as a petable as a dog. All I needed was a focus, that is, a great-looking woman to pounce on, directing predictable charm toward predictable results.

The problem, if it can be considered a problem, was overchoice. The women, all university students, all seemingly unattached, outnumbered the men two to one, and besides, there were no other men like me. Only when I got sober did I realize that the lack of assertiveness, the shyness, the lack of killer instinct of the other guys was not due to terminal illness or congenital defect. It finally occurred to me with a thundering clap of the obvious that they were not like me because they were not drunk.

That night I was a social butterfly extraordinaire. By midway through the evening, I had about eight potentials, which is great for the ego but is antithetical to focus. Candice, who I was favoring, yawned a big unconscious declaration of intention to leave.

I left her with Dawn and returned to Jackie, who had impressed me as being wilder than wild. I had challenged her as unlikely to be as wild as me, which she took up, which impressed me further.

I left Jackie and said I would return once I thought of a worthy wild challenge.

I waited until Jackie's friend Tina left to get drinks, when I approached her and issued *the* challenge. What if you and I blow this pop stand, and as we are leaving, what if we find someone else to join us? Who, you say? Well, you don't know her, but that too is part of the challenge. To which she said she was in, and five minutes after approaching Candice, so was she. She giggled that she was not into women, to which I cooed, "All the better for me."

I remember these things, and I remember getting into the car after having finished a full twenty-four of Heineken, but after that my mind melts into a murky series of discordant images.

What happened next is not nearly as remarkable as the fact that I had successfully driven home in an equally drunken state many, many times before. And it must be said—even if verging on bragging—I was impervious to erectile dysfunction however much I drank. Usually whoever was in the car with me was almost as drunk as I was and didn't notice my erratic driving.

But these girls, while tipsy enough to be seduced, were not about to surrender their lives to a nutcase steering a sardine can off a cliff. Somehow, and thank God, a couple miles along the highway my hookup partners partnered up and demanded I turn around and drive slowly back to the party. I don't remember the conversation, the argument, or my charming counterargument, but I do distinctly recall feeling indignant as I pulled away and rattled back down the highway all by lonesome. *How dare they say my driving is unsafe?* was my last thought as an indignant, albeit charming, walking man. For all my history of drunk driving and virile performances under the influence, I succumbed to that age-old affliction of falling asleep at the wheel before veering off the highway at high speed and hitting an oak tree.

Tin hitting oak has predictable physics to contend with. The 1969 Volkswagen Beetle was never safe. Its funky, functional shape was prelude to maiming and death. It did not have those pesky seatbelt things, which ironically in my case probably saved my life, which I cursed for some months on the spinal cord unit of the rehab center. On impact, I sailed right through the front windshield—all six foot three inches of me—before landing over thirty feet away from the rusted accordion that had been my car. Visualizing a 1969 Volkswagen Beetle windshield and my six-foot-three-inch frame sitting in the driver's seat, the fact that I sailed through that space into space defies predictable physics. Still, somehow I folded, or squeezed through the windshield like toothpaste out of a tube and did not die.

I lay in a field for the rest of the night and would have died if not for the vigilance of a couple of early morning runners, who I also cursed for some months. When I woke up in hospital, I was a C-3 quadriplegic—which I'd not known existed—and was having heavy metal screws drilled into my head to fit me with steel rods, known as a halo, to stabilize my broken spinal column. The double irony was that the halo did not make me an angel, and while I was unable to feel below my shoulders, my face screamed in pain as doctors removed shards of glass and reassembled my disfigured mug with over 200 stitches. Below my shoulders, where I could no longer feel, I was unscathed by glass, though fully scathed by paralysis. Before the accident I heard I was good-looking on a daily basis. No one has ever accused me of being good-looking since the accident.

Even the pain of the ordeal and the loss of everything that had mattered to me in this life was less an obsession than my bloody-minded thirst for death. And yes, the thirst for death was even greater than my thirst for the two dozen cold beers that had been my daily consumption. To say I was angry and difficult to be around then is the understatement of the century. I wasn't sad; I didn't talk about loss; I rattled the doctors and nurses on the spinal cord unit with my blistering, all-consuming rage. And apparently, pussycat that I am, I scared people, all people. I wouldn't do rehabilitation. Occupational and physiotherapy was for chumps, all my schemes and blistering drive went into planning how to die at the first opportunity. And I had no patience to wait for an opportunity that was not of my own making.

LARRY J. MCCLOSKEY

I gunned around the ward in the electric wheelchair they strapped me into like a race car driver, except without the skill. I managed to upset everyone who worked or was a patient at the rehab center as well as anyone visiting. I was warned that they would take away my electric wheelchair if I didn't slow down, and I cursed and dared them to just try. I was pushing for a showdown, I was salivating for conflict, could taste death and destruction. I wanted war.

And then a seemingly innocuous thing happened. I developed a bedsore, which became infected, which was my fault for ignoring all warnings. The rehab physiatrist insisted on looking and said that my bedsore showed evidence of blood poisoning and ordered complete bedrest. She warned me that untreated bedsores can be serious and even cause death, which you might imagine I laughed at and beckoned the grim reaper even if by way of hole in my ass. But I made a miscalculation. She, chief physiatrist, rehabilitation specialist, and head honcho, was in charge and not afraid to use her authority. When she delivered her proclamation, I was in full prone position on my stomach where she said I would remain, without a minute otherwise for two full weeks. I cursed and screamed that she couldn't do that, that I wanted out of the hospital, that I wouldn't submit to her stupid treatment, all of which she ignored and sternly told the nursing staff to stick to the treatment prescribed. I screamed for hours to the extreme annoyance of my three equally trapped new quadriplegic club members, until I was rolled in my bed to a private room with a door that could be closed, where I was left alone, freshly ensconced in my new quarters. And time stopped.

The thing about anger is, if it is generated by indignity, sooner or later you lose steam. Same for screaming obscenities. Truth is, no one wanted to hear me, including me. I was disgusted with life, with rehabilitation, and most of all, with myself. I didn't want to live with me anymore. Nursing staff and orderlies came to perform their requisite duties, but not in friendliness and camaraderie. I was nasty, and they had things on their mind other than the obnoxious nutcase intent on self-obliteration.

I was mostly estranged from my family and didn't encourage anyone to visit. And as for friends, the drunk that I was thought I had many more than the reality. I had beat out many guys trying for women that they really liked, for women I would soon dispose of, and having been disposed, former flings generally weren't inclined to come either. As for those few brave souls who did show up, they left quickly once I bit their heads off. I could not reconcile my present self with who I had been. It took me a while to figure out that my deep shame had more to do with who I had been as a drunk than who I had become as a quadriplegic.

I wasn't much of reader, didn't watch much TV, didn't have any hobbies. I had lived for physical sensation, pleasure, had always got what I wanted, was totally, spectacularly unprepared for the life that I had fallen into. I was a man untethered, without resources or will to find context or meaning in any aspect of a life that for mere survival was all-consuming. As much as I wanted death, I wanted to forget about me and my pathetic existence even more.

It came when least expected. Six days and nights in, I broke. We use the word despair commonly, but the full experience of its reality defies common understanding. Two weeks on full prone bed rest might as well have been a hundred years. I counted the hours between seconds, and the agonizingly slow passage of time did not lead anywhere. A complete dark numbness had displaced anger. At 4:12 a.m. on Thursday, August 27, I started to cry. And once started, I could not stop. Each sob felt like I was being physically and psychologically disemboweled.

And then the door slowly opened. Irene the night cleaner came in. She came in every night around the same time and tried to be friendly, but predictably I told her to leave me alone or pretended that I was asleep, which I never was. Irene was never offended and seemed to see right through me. No, not through me so much as into me, that place that I did not know, did not want to know, that filled me with disgust for not knowing. Each night into morning she would talk softly, ignoring my abuse and angry posturing, saying pleasant, sometimes insightful things which I chose to not hear.

On this night with my sobs in full flight she didn't say a word. Instead, she came straight to the bed and enveloped me in over three hundred pounds of a full-bodied, all-consuming hug. For at least fifteen minutes she simply and silently held me. I remember vaguely thinking that for all my sexual conquests I had never given or received contact like this, had not known of the *this* of which I had been missing. She then talked to me in her lyrical, hypnotic Caribbean accent in a way I had never experienced before. It's true I couldn't move, but more to the point, I didn't resist. I was overwhelmed by many emotions, especially gratitude, and for the first time since my accident, in some ways for the first time in my life, I felt what it is to be connected to another human being, even if that human being was a stranger.

For the longest time she murmured reassurances that I would find a life, that my life was not over, which I did not believe but was powerless to object to and did not even want her to stop saying. For the first time since my accident, I had a thought about a person other than myself, and I asked her about her family. She told me her father was Jamaican, and her mother, who was Haitian, practiced a wacky but insightful version of voodoo.

Through the veil of narcissism, pain, and numbness, I felt a glimmer of curiosity. She gave me some examples of wacky practices—involving bones and blood, I seem to recall—before saying that her mother was revered for imparting "the gift" to those who needed insight. She said she had learned something of the gift and asked if I wanted insight. When I meekly and weakly grunted in the affirmative, she told me she was going to pass on a great ancient secret, equal parts voodoo and mother's gift. She said she was not authorized to pass on this secret—for it was carefully guarded—but circumstances were desperate, and what she knew could change my life forever.

She said that we all have the power to be the best version of ourselves regardless of circumstances, and no one can take that power away from us. If not for the envelopment and comfort of hug in progress, she would have lost me with that pronouncement. She continued undeterred. She said that it is possible to access a part of our mind that can transport us, liberate us, create who we are from within and not how people see us from without. Despite lifetime cynicism about everything, at that moment I was unhinged and compliant. I was a broken child, a willing supplicant, so I took it all in and hungered for more. It took me years to figure out that the ancient secret (which sounded more like a new age cliche) had nothing to do with the veracity of the words, and everything to do with the belief of the listener. Her voice and warmth soothed me until the sun came up. When she said that she had to go, I had one question. "Did your mother's secret really work for people?"

"Yes," she assured me.

"Which people?" I asked.

"Slaves," she answered, and was gone.

CHAPTER FOUR

Back to Halloween in the present, Center for Students with Disabilities

Irene saved my life. I didn't know it at the time, though she knew exactly what she was doing. It's funny, in the vortex of the horror that this life can be, a kind word or gesture can make everything if not right, at least less horrible. A timely, slight crack into the darkness of despair can give us a moment's relief that can allow us to recalibrate, become reacquainted with the fact that we are human. That's something. A couple well-placed words or a gesture can help restore a life. And grasping and building on shards of brokenness is just what I did.

I searched, scrounged, ferreted for something to amuse or distract me from the paralysis of my body. I ferociously focused on life outside of the unfeeling carcass so as not to paralyze mind and spirit. And there's no better way to exit our inward-looking preoccupations than to try to comfort *nasty, brutish, and short* lives, the Hobbesian reality for most people on this planet. Best way to help other people is to not take ourselves too seriously. Best way to not take ourselves too seriously, especially if seriously paralyzed in four limbs, is to exit the screaming blather of the mob.

After Irene left my room, I slept for the first time since my accident. I dreamt about our family when I was a kid, when Iggy was a baby, when Mom and Dad were alive, when life seemed simple, and the future held unlimited promise—when the realizing of dreams was simply getting up from a chair and walking into the infinite bounty this life has to offer. Life was once passive and accessible. Waking to the reality of my condition was painful, but dreaming of my former life, the soaring of imagination that could take me away to another place whenever I wanted, was something to immerse myself in, not avoid. Perhaps not how a shrink would recommend processing loss, but I luxuriated without resentment in the way I would have lived my former life, if only the scales had fallen from my eyes earlier.

Yeah, Irene gave me the means of escape from the singularity of my lonely existence. That experience, coupled with working at the university for all my working life, has allowed me to become an exemplar of escape. During meetings and over time, I've crafted an uncanny talent for dissociation. My goofy grin has kept people thinking I'm scarily present when I'm really a million miles away on cloud nine of whatever fantasy I've conjured to get from this moment to the next. So while the goofy grin is the signature of complete absence, in the university you are never faulted for saying or doing nothing. It's only when you have an honest view or try to get something done that the sparks fly and murderous intent is revealed.

After the meeting, Luna and Iggy are all abuzz, equal parts fear and anticipation. There is never any good news at these cultish encounters, but Luna and Iggy are relieved because the much-anticipated directive to restructure and reduce staff at our Center was not made explicit. Watching the gallows being built is not enough; my two compatriots will hold out hope until the rope is placed around our collective neck and the lever is pulled. Even then, I'll be the wise guy and crack, "What's the worst that can happen, break my neck?"

My worrywart colleagues raise concerns, ask me many penetrating questions about the inevitable, but having just come back from a complicated and strategic failed attempt on Hitler's life at the Berghof in the Bavaria Alps, I am reluctant to talk. Five more minutes and Hitler would surely have come out for a walk with Blondi, his German shepherd, and I would have had him in my sights. And then it occurs to me this may be the idea I've been waiting for. Never mind focusing on a cure for freckles or cancer; I may have hit upon a formula for endless and juicy distraction. I need to dump my beloved peeps to flush out my writing plans. I need a setting where a creative genius can think without interruption, another meeting perhaps. And then that pesky, yet oddly beloved, voice again.

"…was clearly a threat, but then she didn't say anything else about us after that," Iggy agonizes.

"But you could tell by the look she gave us when we came in, and I saw it again when we left," Luna says, wheeling hard to keep up with Iggy, he fleet of foot, compared to my electric-chair fleetness. "And Phelim, it didn't help when you started to leave before she was finished talking."

"She said the meeting was over," I plead.

"But you knew taking that literally before she actually finished would seriously annoy her, didn't you?"

"Who, me?" I don't even turn around to feign seriousness.

"You do know she's good for her threat, right?" Luna often finishes a statement with a question in a pathetic attempt to make sure I'm listening.

We are traveling down the long corridor back to our Center, and I am about to answer yes to Luna's obvious question when I spot the love of my life, who is out of place in this place.

Sitting demurely in the middle of some twenty waiting students in our reception area is my Aunt Isobell. But before I can get to her, my path is cut off by some of my peeps who are anxiously waiting to hear the outcome of the meeting.

David stands expectantly, with arms outstretched. "Well?"

"How'd it go, boss?" asks Edie, leaning over the front desk, her favorite place for triaging our legions of stressed students. I note she's due for a Nobel Peace Prize, and that's just for putting up with me.

Farrah stands with her arms folded, a slight and worried smile on her face, too discreet to ask in public, but wanting to know the meeting outcome as much as anyone else.

Dr. Arthur, our dedicated, underpaid, aging bag of bones, resident psychologist and longtime friend, passes by with his Monty Python walk as a member of the Department of Redundancy Department, basically our shared nod to the absurdity of it all.

But my elderly aunt is the first order of business. Then I notice Aunt Isobell's companion, she of the same utilitarian modern nun business suit, but decidedly not of elderly Auntie ilk. Out of the corner of my eye I catch Iggy as he too notices her, and he too has the look of one whose mundane existence has been transformed by the unanticipated experience of beauty. Aunt Isobell's companion—a nun some fifty years younger—is as beautiful as any woman I've ever seen.

I wheel past my expectant peeps and exchange a hug with Aunt Isobell. "Bet you're surprised to see me," she giggles, as she turns to give Iggy, or Ignatius as she calls him, a hug.

"Surprised as hell, and delighted as heaven," I say, with sincerity.

"Yeah, really great," Iggy says to Auntie, while staring into the depths of Auntie's companion's eyes.

Aunt Isobell, who misses nothing, and whose observational acuity has only increased with age, notices Iggy's unintended stare and says, "Please let me introduce Sister Sandrine. She is on assignment from Mauritius for the next two years." Sister Sandrine nods and smiles ever so slightly, before Aunt Isobell continues, "Well, that was the plan, but now I don't know. Sister Sandrine only arrived at the convent two weeks ago, and today Mother Superior announced something that may change everything."

"What happened?" Iggy blurts, before looking around the reception area where we are gathered. In a low voice, he continues, "Guess this isn't the best place to talk."

"How about lunch?" I ask.

"Want me to order sandwiches, boss?" Edie asks, from behind me.

"You read my mind." Then to Aunt Isobell, "She does everything, you know."

"You got that right." Edie says, laughing.

Aunt Isobell responds, "I can tell."

"Come on," I motion, wheeling toward my office as Luna begins to explain the near horror and potential heartbreak of what happened at the meeting to expectant peeps. At least her catastrophic version.

Close to the door my transponder activates, the door clicks open, and we enter my working man's cave.

I go to the head of my meeting table and watch as Aunt Isobell and Sister Sandrine take their seats. Aunt Isobell still moves with perky purpose, and Sister Sandrine is as fluid as a ballet dancer, but decidedly more curvaceous. I vaguely wonder how shapeless gray tweed is able to reveal such sensual beauty.

I look up to where Edie and Barry share an office across the hall. I want to ask about sandwich delivery timing, but when wild Edie jumps onto shy and retiring Barry's lap and howls in the midst of a shared joke, I decide to leave lunch questions alone. Edie will take care of it.

"Love your office," Aunt Isobell always says of my eclectic mess. I occupy a big space, cluttered by over thirty years of junk, painted in dark fall colors, bucking the white-only walls policy prevalent throughout the rest of the university. We live in an old building no one is much interested in, so we are spared the fierce competition for chic modern glass and steel offices. It is universally agreed that our space and the work we do in it is uncool, uninspiring, and aesthetically unpleasing. We pride ourselves on being the exemplars of un-everything.

"Auntie, you look like you have something to say, so spill!"

"It's true," Aunt Isobell acknowledges, smiling before turning serious. "I'm afraid we're in a bit of a pickle."

"Which has probably happened many times, but I've never heard you say so. You do know we'll do whatever we can to help, don't you?" My Irene-inspired will-to-live revelation had a companion piece starring Aunt Isobell. She had mostly been a distant specter, a full-habit weirdo nun as far as we knew or cared about, growing up. But after my accident she showed up in my room, habit-less, not particularly nun-like—at least according to the stereotype I had conjured in my mind—and in addition to being supportive and warm, she was full of piss and vinegar, and biggest surprise, she was interesting as hell. She just was, and we became, to our mutual surprise, close friends.

Aunt Isobell nods in acknowledgment as Iggy jitters with nervous anticipation. "What is it, Auntie?"

I know better. Aunt Isobell always says what she wants to say when she is ready and not a second before.

"Well, as you know, a decision was made some time ago to eventually close the convent. There just aren't enough nuns left, and the ones who remain are old and infirm."

"But not you," Iggy interjects.

Aunt Isobell continues. "It's why we reached out to our sister convents in Southeast Asia, South America, and Africa. It's why Sister Sandrine is here and why we had hoped to entice others. We had hoped to renew our order with new, young blood. We thought we had two or three years at least to sort things out."

I smile as Iggy's eyes flash at the mention of young blood. We will later agree about our impression of Auntie's newest charge, and I'll easily embarrass Iggy with suggestive comments while pretending I'm so not like that. He's so easy, and I'm so bad.

"I had hoped that with the arrival of Sister Sandrine, and others to follow, we could make a case for strategic renewal of our order, even as we look after our sisters who want to live out their days where they have served for—in Sister Agnus's case—seventy-nine years. And she is not unique."

Not a popular notion today, but there is something to convent life, I ponder, and not for the first time. Since Auntie and I became close, I've spent a fair bit of time at the convent, and I've learned that nuns are not who people generally think they are. The old dolls are more content, have greater purpose, and live longer than just about any other group of people. Makes you wonder about the great freedom that we non-nun types have, and the lack of freedom they commit to in becoming a nun. Maybe unrestricted freedom and unlimited choice are not the formula for a life well lived. Maybe they choose, commit to shackles, because they know something. I have this thought about the great truths of life that we spend a lifetime searching for. What if great truths are both simple and right before our stubborn noses?

"But," and Aunt Isobell's face turns truly grave, "Mother Superior informed me just an hour ago that the convent has been sold. It hadn't even been listed on the real estate market. Maybe because several of our elderly nuns died last year, people began speculating that we would have to sell."

As we, that is, mostly Iggy, registers visible shock, Aunt Isobell's expression transforms from grave into the grave. "There's more. The price it sold for is more than twice as high as any of us thought possible, and apparently there is pressure to vacate the convent and agree to an earlier closing date."

"They can't do that," Iggy protests.

"Who bought it?" I ask.

"That is the strangest part. I asked the same question. But Mother Superior, with whom I have both a good working relationship and complete trust, says she is legally obliged not to disclose the name of the buyer."

"Odd, and why is that?" I ask.

"Even that, I am unable to determine," Aunt Isobell answers, with obvious discomfort.

"Doesn't add up," Iggy adds.

"Regardless," Aunt Isobell says, biting her lip, "they are determined, and Mother Superior says we need the proceeds from this sale, so there is no arguing otherwise. The fact is, not only is the price more than we anticipated, but there are several restrictions for selling the convent in its original charter that most buyers could never meet, but we are told the buyer has met them all."

I ponder Aunt Isobell's words before responding. "So with a very limited number of possible buyers, it seems all the more strange that the buyer's name is being withheld. The charter restrictions presumably exist out of concern for the integrity of the convent, which if satisfied, you'd think they would want publicized."

Aunt Isobell again bites her lip. "I know. Mother Superior says the buyer's name will be released, just not yet."

"Another problem," I note. "Practically speaking, how can the remaining nuns be placed that quickly, especially since many of them have serious health problems?"

"Apparently, they are the easy ones," Auntie answers. "For some years, our order has anticipated the demographic shift toward elderly nuns and is building a nursing home out west. We know it is close to completion, but we all falsely or foolishly hoped that we could be the exception and remain here. Mother Superior informed me that the facility will be completed by the sale date and frankly will need customers. The fact is, the nuns who will be difficult to place are us young and so far healthy ones for whom there has never been much of a plan." Aunt Isobell smiles at the reference to her mid-eighties self as young, before letting her perfect posture sag ever so little.

I have several questions, Iggy likely many more, but none of us speak as we contemplate the bad news. I have a thought, not yet fully formed, and am about to give preliminary utterance when Edie opens the door to give a ten-minute estimated time of arrival for lunch. "Auntie," I begin, "Can you and Sister Sandrine come to dinner tonight?"

Aunt Isobell looks at her younger colleague, who nods, and it is done.

Aunt Isobell is a creature of refinement, mostly, but she can surprise. She rises from her seat, smooths her gray suit and whispers, "Pit stop," before disappearing from my office and down the hall.

Without saying a word, Sister Sandrine gets up and follows Aunt Isobell. Iggy and I are straining not to miss a single frame from the poetry in motion before our eyes. So as not to sully the moment by acknowledging the obvious, I turn to Iggy and say in a slow, low voice, "You know, there may be a solution to their dilemma that involves some change on our part, but I suspect you'll like it."

Iggy gives me a deer-in-the-headlights look and says, "What in the world could that be?"

"We live in a big house that has three big bedrooms we don't use. If we cleaned up a bit and—"

"Phelim, that's frickin' brilliant, but I doubt ... I mean, they'd never—"

"Leave that to me. You know Auntie and I have an understanding, and well, after dinner tonight we can first ask the question and then press for the answer we want. In the meantime, I'm going to call Brenda and see if she can spruce up what we were going to have for dinner tonight."

"They'll never go for it, and would they even be allowed? I mean, I'd love it, but wouldn't it seem strange?"

"I've specialized in seeming strange my whole life, so we'll see. And in her own way, so has Aunt Isobell. I think we can pursue this with a clear conscience."

"What do you mean?"

"Meaning we love the old gal, so no ulterior motives—the fact that her companion is drop-dead gorgeous and shaped like an hourglass is merely a nice coincidence."

"Yeah, of course, goes without saying," Iggy mutters, as I smile to myself and let the dials in my devious wheelhouse churn.

CHAPTER FIVE

Same eventful day, mosh pit Center at the Center

The Special Adviser to the President's Executive Assistant (EA) has called twice. So far. I noticed but haven't bothered to listen to the messages. She also sent three urgent emails summoning me to meet with the SAP today at two p.m. I was further informed not to be late since she only has fifteen minutes. Since I keep both late and irregular hours, all my meetings with students are scheduled for the afternoon, which, after a two-hour lunch, begins at two p.m. In fairness to my uber late self, I do catch up on emails before this time. Front desk staff know that for all requests to meet in the morning, the stock answer is I am completely booked. Luna and Iggy are always in by eight a.m., so I like to think that we complement each other. Not sure I want to know what they like to think.

I call Maxi at 1:45 p.m., annoyed that my two-hour lunch has been cut short. I assertively explain that I cannot possibly meet until four p.m. Maxi responds with rising anger that the summons is not an option and that it would be wise for me to get over to the SAP's office right away. Now this might be considered a moment to back down, to grovel, to be wise, but unwisely, and yet characteristically, I opt for my inner wise guy.

"It's not that I won't, but I can't."

"She told me no excuses, so what do you propose I tell her?"

"Tell her the truth. Tell her I have a vulnerable student at two p.m. who might go into crisis if I try to reschedule. End of story." And it is. The current preoccupation in all universities is to be student-focused, to respond immediately to potential student crisis, to place student welfare above all else. Am I being opportunistic? Of course. Am I being a wee shite? Yes again. Is the student vulnerable, potentially in crisis? I'll find out in twelve minutes.

Our students have changed over the years. Numbers at our Center have exploded, mostly in the ever-expanding category of mental illness. Students are often both vulnerable and oddly determined to get whatever we've got, but even then, what we've got just as often won't address the real problem. They aren't faking, and I don't blame them, but I do my best to try to get to know them and bring them around to seeing how, in the mix, learning to help themselves is not something to ignore. I'm not against human rights, but the notion that everything is a human right is not helping twenty-year-olds figure out this life and where they might fit into it.

I have four students between two and four p.m., three with anxiety, one with depression. One young woman wants an exemption from going to class because she says it makes her anxious. I say we don't really have the power to do that. Most profs are no longer delivering lectures by teleconference, and not going to classes might diminish the experience of going to university. I ask a bit about her past, and she says that she was not particularly anxious in high school. She also says that she has been on cross-country and track teams but doesn't have time for running anymore now that she is grown up and in university. I suggest that she make room for daily exercise since it helps regulate anxiety, according to both research and her experience. She responds without a hint of irony that it's easy for me to say that, looking at or perhaps through my fat carcass sitting in an electric wheelchair. I refer her for assessment to Dr. A. It's easy to be cynical, but I feel for her, feel for all of them. Her life, those unfulfilled and many rights, wants and desires nibbling from the fringes, will not make life easy. With all my students, whether mild anxiety or severe disability, and especially those I get to know over time, I wonder how they will make their way in this world.

I receive the expected email, resummoning me to the Special Adviser to the President's office, this time for four p.m., a mere ten minutes hence. Without a word to any of my peeps, and especially with the intention of avoiding Luna and Iggy, I start to roll down the corridor to the elevator. So how is it that at that exact moment Luna and Iggy end up talking in the corridor and blocking my way? I do my best imitation of a delivery truck backing up, full volume and good enough to make Edie laugh and get a big thumbs-up. Since Edie never stops smiling, except to laugh, it is easy to see her as the picture of health, always. But her smile can't quite hide a puffiness, an unhealthy white pallor to her skin. I'll have to watch that, I decide. I deal with my own unhealthy white pallor by never looking in a mirror. Months ago, when Brenda held a mirror up to my face, it was the combination of appalling pallor and expiring follicles that cemented my anti-mirror resolve.

Neither Luna nor Iggy react to my beep-beep dump-truck-in-reverse imitation, which hurts, and for another ten seconds they continue with intense conversation. Intensity exchanged, Iggy turns to answer a student question and Luna wheels out of the way, but not before asking, "Where are you going?"

I feign innocence, "Who, me?"

"Well?"

But I've known Luna for over fifteen years and have a few tricks up my sleeve. "Sorry, nothing up, hate to disappoint." Then half turning and calling my brother by way of distraction, "Oh, Iggy, I've called Brenda, and she has agreed to make us a nice dinner. God love her, she even went to Francesca's and got fresh pasta. The gals will be there by 6:30 p.m."

"Great, how 'bout I pick up some dessert at Life of Pie?" In his present and rare state of Sister Sandrine happiness, I know he's easy to distract.

"Sure, but let Brenda know, or else she'll go shopping and get ingredients for a homemade dessert—and she really doesn't have time."

For all his energy and quickness, Iggy freezes blankly when faced with life-altering choices. I ask, "What do you think Aunt Isobell and Sister Sandrine would like?"

Poor guy seems truly perplexed before hesitantly suggesting, "Double chocolate brownies?"

"You got it, partner," I answer.

Iggy grins, and Luna scowls. With a look intended to convey self-satisfaction, I wheel past one uncomprehending brother and one close-to-comprehending friend and colleague.

As I'm waiting at the elevator—slowed at this time of day by multitudes needing an aid to walk down one floor—Mary emerges from the stairwell breathless and agitated. "Oh boy, we've gotta talk." Mary coordinates our Residence Attendant Service program for students with high-level physical disabilities, for which there is a history. Thirty-some years ago I was a student at this same, august institution. I wasn't much interested in much but needed something to get on with life after months in hospital. The university boasted that it was the most accessible university in the country, so I moved into residence and signed up for classes. But it wasn't, and I got stuck everywhere I went, couldn't make it to class most of the time, and only had limited access to an attendant, leaving 22½ hours each day I had to fend for myself. I didn't mind missing class, but I became interested in the few people who were fighting to make it through the day in a world that wasn't made for us. Still, the university said that accessibility was one of its core values and that it took immense pride in being the best. I mulled this over at Paddy's Pub one evening—where I do all my best mulling—and called a friend from high school who was a lowly and struggling lawyer. He happened to be free and arrived within thirty minutes, at which moment I said, "Have I got a deal for you," and the rest is history.

In front of a national audience—this before social media splintered all audiences into a thousand disparate parts—we sued the self-proclaimed most accessible university in the country, and I won a multimillion-dollar settlement, which might have been a happy ending if I hadn't opened my big mouth and said, "I've got a better idea." The settlement was turned over to the university, who matched my millions. Combined with a substantial private donation, this allowed us to create the disability center that I was to head—a job for life I think it's called. Our small center, which later grew into a sizable

Center, worked on practical little things that were a big deal for our students, which led to a set of precedents that became standards that were subsequently enshrined in legislation throughout the country, which naturally led to raising many more millions since those early days.

Today, half my day—okay, truth is, all my days are half days—are spent answering calls from across the country from those who think I know something about how to make their institution, town, or city accessible. Bottom line, though my boss and others hate me, I cannot be fired for fear of the national press once again taking up my cause. I wasn't exactly sure what the Special Adviser to the President wanted, but I knew that she knew there were limits to what she could do to me, which still left my peeps at the Center vulnerable. The air is electric with uncertainty and ripe for crime.

Mary waits for me to demand to know why we gotta talk, but I'm not going to bite. "Sorry, Mary, but I have to go. Tell me tomorrow."

As the elevator door opens and closes, she protests, "But, but, but—"

Maxi gives a dirty look as I sweep past into the Special Adviser to the President's office. Come to think of it, she's given me a dirty look every time she's seen me for the past eight years. I vaguely wonder what look she sees staring back from her mirror each morning. The Special Adviser to the President does not look up as I enter her palatial office. She continues, back to me, captive to her computer, so I look around her palatial office at photos of her palatial houses. It's hard to choose between her city mansion and the beach house at Martha's Vineyard. She appears in front of both houses, coiffed blond hair, designer clothes, same for exercise-designed body, a portrait of success for which I feel no jealousy. It is well known she comes from Boston money; that is, after marrying well, she divorced spectacularly well. And yet, for all the swirling privilege, I am about to be drawn and quartered over her sense of oppression.

Years earlier she was somewhat cordial, me being of an equity, oppressed group and all, but between her ambition and the fixed immutable grin on my unresponsive face, she's dispensed with any pretense of civility. Four p.m. is a late appointment for our beloved SAP, Exceptional Student Experience. The look on her face suggests bad oyster, so I expect her to come straight to the point. She almost says take a seat, catches herself and waves a hand to indicate where I should locate myself. Despite being slim and fit, she sits down heavily at a table across from where I wait and grin, grin and wait. She has the power, but I have the foreknowledge that I can outwait a cat's nine lives.

She often boasts to our lowly group of student service managers and directors that she is able to convince her senior management peers of anything because of her superior communication skills. I doubt that she includes discretion or sensitivity in her communication arsenal. I sit as if in nonverbal confrontation with Tolkien's Saruman the White for a full minute before either of us speak our first words. I'd have been happy to wait out the silence for our full scheduled fifteen minutes. I don't do awkward, but I've been known to inspire it.

"You have to make significant changes to your office, and it is important to do so soon."

She's made reference to needed changes several times recently, which I've pretended not to fully understand, so I expect this enlightenment to be unambiguous.

"I am instructing all my directors to make the same changes, so please don't tell me that your department should be exempted. As you know, diversity is the number-one goal of this university, so do not try to run interference on this one. If anything, as director of an equity office, you need to set an example. You have a history of voicing opposition to my suggestions, which I've never appreciated, so I need you to understand that this is not a suggestion but an expectation to be taken seriously."

It was a big deal for me to take anything seriously, but she did have a point about me voicing opposition to her "suggestions." Our esteemed SAP liked to vet her suggestions at director's meetings and to receive positive feedback from her colleagues, as she falsely called us. Problem was, the collegial spirit melted away as soon as anyone suggested her suggestion was a tad wanting. The list of directors willing to parrot support for all her proposed plans was long—unanimous, actually—and then there was me. In the eight years since she'd been SAP, I was the only one to ever suggest she think again. Like, for example, in response to her fetish for departmental name changes. She'd once been head honcho of Student Services—so straightforward even if boring—but then strategically reinvented herself as responsible for Exceptional Student Experience which netted her influence beyond a measly VP-ship. My very public comment was that an exceptional student experience didn't necessarily speak to the chances of graduating, which was the point of that experience, after all. The Student Affairs Office—whose name I always liked for the connotation of students having affairs—was changed to the Department of Student Compassion and Caring. I suggested that the ability to discipline students who cheat on exams might be compromised by an excess of compassion to the exclusion of consequence. The Equity Office was elevated to the Department of Progressive Race and Gender Communities for Diversity, Equity, and Inclusion (this terminology trifecta having swept the land without anyone agreeing on what it means). In response to the mental health tsunami of recent years, she created the Department of Mental Wellness, Self-Care, Mindfulness, and Life Balance. After the requisite oohs and ahs, I asked how a department sounding like a spa might help students with serious mental illness.

She strongly suggested to me—her suggestions were always strong—that we change our name from Center for Students with Disabilities to the more progressive Center for Accommodation and Disability Inclusion. I responded that at campuses where that change has been made, accommodations are regarded as entitlements for anyone who wants them, far beyond a basic need for a minority of students with documented disabilities to get a targeted number of required accommodations. Our mandate to accommodate is in response to legislation, not the need to feel good about including people regardless of disability. And I also told her, as I always do, which she never hears, that our Center does a great deal of student development work, which results in impressive graduation rates, so we are more than an Accommodation Center. The last time she suggested we change our name, I suggested the Center for Redundancy Center. Good old Smokey Albert, an elder from St. Jude's Indigenous American Center, roared with laughter until tears fell from his eyes while I grinned, and the rest of the SAP's minions remained serious, silent, and embarrassed for the spectacle that is moi. Murder hung in the air as the SAP plotted my demise.

I am expected to respond and quickly, in agreement with her direct directive. I pause, never quite sure what I'm going to say in these trying situations until I open my mouth. I don't lack emotional regulation exactly but do have a serious problem with social discretion. I also take perverse pleasure in anyone thinking themselves smart about thinking myself dumb. Depending on how you look at it, I either like to play mind games, am willing to match her mind games, or refuse to play mind games at all. I like to think the latter, with me as natural and innocent as Paleontologist Pearl.

When I see her winding up to remonstrate against my silence, I naively ask, "So are we talking about students or staff?"

"As I have repeatedly said, the university is too male and too pale, and we are determined to provide exemplary leadership for the American post-secondary sector and beyond. Both your staff and students need to reflect the reality of transformational diversity, equity, and inclusion that the Social Justice Committee has disseminated for the past two years, and now exists as university policy."

"Well, besides the fact that all our students have disabilities," I respond, "we have always made exceptional efforts to reach marginalized communities where disability may be less accepted than it is with us. But making sure people are aware doesn't mean we recruit students, which would undermine faculty's faith in our objective allocation of supports based on assessment and documentation."

"Not inclusive, not nearly enough. You of all people should know that designated groups are systemically disadvantaged and deserve far more resources and advantages than traditional students."

"It depends, and faculty trust requires we maintain objective—"

This time she holds up her arm like a traffic cop and cuts me off. "This is not faculty's domain. It is in my portfolio, where all equity decisions are made. I know your outdated views, and I am telling you the new paradigm of thinking, reflected in university policy, is to exceed marginal group representation in the population and achieve repertory equity. We will address the litany of past grievance while creating foundational future equity as has never been achieved."

She stops, expecting me to respond, as I revert to the silent grin for which I have become infuriatingly infamous. It is a curious moment. Our SAP has just revealed that she intends to achieve world hegemony through the manipulation of DEI. Not a surprise, but this may be—I have always worked towards, am committed to actual diversity, equity, and inclusion. But not her faux-aspirational, non-meritocratic version. We didn't adopt our moniker as island of the misfits because we were rebels; we did so precisely because we were and are excluded. We few are dangerous because in our excluded state we see what the SAP's minions refuse to see: the empress has no clothes. Our modest, inglorious efforts of past decades have included outsiders—their entire being and not just identity parts—and given them a chance. Our simple efforts are about people; her equity appropriation is about power. That dehumanized Machiavellian rendition—the one that has taken the country by storm—promises what can never be delivered and will be injurious to those who believe, while the purveyors of manipulation will never suffer the consequences of their actions.

My silence is disarming. She feigns adjusting her perfectly coiffed blond hair, pausing with deliberate effort to regulate rising anger. "You and all departments must actively recruit students from all marginalized groups, many of whom are experiencing mental illness as a result of the intersectionality of their marginalization."

I lean right and left in my chair, my habitual attempt to pull dreadful posture back from complete scoliosis and entropy. I know it is hopeless but opt for a minor, practical incursion into the SAP's reordering of the world. "The problem with intersectionality, the problem with arriving at mental illness as a result of one's membership in various groups, is that it doesn't tell us anything about a particular individual. Surely one's race, gender, and sexual orientation configuration doesn't necessarily equate to having mental illness. And if perception of oppression or self-assessment of disability is the new low bar for determining mental illness, how do we maintain any professional standard regarding assessment and diagnosis?"

"And that is where you and your outfit are hopelessly out of sync with progressive elements of the university community. Self-assessment is the future, not medical model stigma, and the future is now." This time she does not wait for my reaction but plows right on. "And that is not all. Your staff lacks transformational diversity, and this issue must be addressed."

"So, fire any hard-working staff who do not fit into an equity category?"

"The expectation is that a minimum of 80 percent of your staff conform to Equity Office guidelines within the next two months. Some offices will achieve 100 percent before that time. Exactly how that is accomplished is up to you as director. I expect a report on how you plan to accomplish my directive in the coming weeks."

I try to repress a smile as she reverts to the redundant Equity Office name over the mouthful it has become. "And the unions are okay with this?"

"Half of your staff are on contract, so they have no rights, and yes, as for the others, the union has agreed to this change. Displaced former union members will receive limited compensation, and contract workers will be paid out half of their remaining contract. The university is determined and will be fair to those displaced in the process."

In these moments of enlightened insanity, I rarely argue or even bother to comment. The antidote to madness is not talk. I need a plan, which my mind tries to formulate as our esteemed SAP finishes her diatribe. I know that half her bluster is frustration that she can neither scare me nor dangle anything in front of my nose that I want. She doesn't have the power over me that she does over all others, and it bugs her. Most of all, she is frustrated that she can't assign a handpicked assassin to bump me off.

Discussion of issues won't work. She isn't an ideologue as is the university norm. She is a strategic bloodlust opportunist willing to do what VPs and the president don't, won't, and shouldn't do. This willingness to do anything, among ideologues who do not know how to elevate aspiration into action, is the source of her ascendency and power. Oh, yeah, and she is ruthless. I know this and must find a way to work around, but not actively against, her very capable killer instinct. As she finishes with me, though still without a commitment from me, I am weightless on a thought cloud drifting back to Hitler at the Berghof.

This weightless drifting and current Hitler theme is my go-to means of avoidance. I keep telling myself that these escapist musings will crystallize into a literary work of genius, if I devote enough time to musing. The actual writing is a vague and distant detail, not to be faced as one engages in the conceptual phase of the creative process. So I kid myself.

Good ol' Adolf is walking his dog Blondi before dinner or perhaps before the nightly film. Even though he is a vegetarian, he always carries a few strips of meat to tempt and tantalize his loyal canine, control freak that he is. Blondi hangs by his side waiting for tender morsels, and Hitler laughs at her deference to his will. For all his outbursts and odd hours, Hitler seems to have some routine about his evening walk. So what if I litter the path with my own steak strips, leading Blondi from Hitler's side to where I wait just off the path, and aim my Luger straight at the murderous creep's heart? I'll keep a steak for

Blondi to shut her up but will pop her off too if need be. Ha! Not a bad plan for the twelve-year-old within.

Leaving the SAP's office, I notice that Maxi's bad oyster expression matches her boss's. Still, I am not deflated. In fact, I'm feeling good about oysters, believing the world to be mine. I decide I'm really going to have to give some thought to that other, non-Hitler plan, the one to save my Center and my peeps. It isn't going to be easy, but if I can take down Hitler, I'm pretty sure I can find a plan for the simpler SAP problem. Still, I can't think about it now. I have Aunt Isobell and Sister Sandrine to prepare for, and nothing is going to ruin that. Spoiler alert: not knowing what I am going to do about saving my peeps is never going to translate into doing what the SAP demands I do. Images of Aunt Isobell's childish giggle and Sister Sandrine's most un-child-like curves crowd out serious thoughts, save one: we have ourselves a contest.

CHAPTER SIX

All Hallows' Eve, at home

After which and throughout dinner, I think not at all. I don't think; therefore I am, and am grateful to be. Iggy, caring and anxious as he is, would have exploded after meeting the SAP. But he didn't have the divine intervention of Irene once upon a time. Not something you can coach someone into or through. Iggy just has to figure out how to live untethered to what happens to him. Me dispensing wisdom—at 250 pounds, tethered to a 250-pound wheelchair, paralyzed below but at least not above the neck—is kind of funny. Which is why I have these thoughts but rarely say them: life is a Shakespearean tragedy from cradle to grave, but, but, but, it is hauntingly beautiful, poignant, and not to be missed despite metaphoric sinkholes that litter our singular, bittersweet path.

Iggy is beaming, which, for someone who approaches life with dread, is a rare and refreshing sight. He doesn't relate to people easily, but to those few who are his friends, he is attentive and loyal to the grave. He and I usually consume a carb feast and several episodes of Netflix, so having company is a nice change to our rootless routine. Both of us are fond of Aunt Isobell, and Sister Sandrine is a riddle, wrapped in a mystery, inside an enigma, to quote Winston Churchill pondering Russia. The good sister sits erectly at her demure and visual best without looking Russian in the least. She seldom speaks, but when she does, we all listen. Scarcity will do that. Same for the way she dresses. Her dowdy, shapeless nun's suit titillates the imagination and draws attention to the prospect of what lies beneath. Less is more, and on both fronts, we want to know more. All the dowdiness and modesty in the world cannot hide her physical beauty. She is beauty itself.

"Well, this has been most pleasant," Aunt Isobell says, as she attacks her dessert, to Iggy's eternal gratification. She'd made sure to compliment Brenda on her excellent cooking and gracious hospitality earlier.

Sister Sandrine nods in sincere agreement, adding, "I can't remember when I've spent a more pleasant evening."

Brenda, who is becoming more beautiful every time I see her, wipes away a strand of her dark, luxurious mane and glows with satisfaction at pulling together a successful impromptu meal.

I begin slowly. "Well, I'm going to believe that you are being sincere, even as I hope it isn't true for your sake."

"Of course it's true," Aunt Isobell says, and Sister Sandrine agrees with a wide, unfathomable smile.

"So, that being the case," I say, with a tinge of the dramatic, "you wouldn't mind doing this again, and that being the additional case, you wouldn't mind if this is what we continue to do?"

I'm being coy, and the good sisters are understandably confused. "Meaning, dear sisters, you will soon have no place to live while we have plenty of room at the inn."

With emerging awareness, Aunt Isobell asks, "Are you serious, Phelim?"

"Never more," I say, as Iggy enthusiastically nods his head. "We have three large empty bedrooms, one on the third floor and another two on the second with Iggy, two of which have their own bathroom. With me decidedly hanging entirely on the first floor, we have more than enough room and would love the company. Truth is, there are only so many recipes and cleaning tips a couple guys can exchange."

"Well, I never ...," Aunt Isobell mutters.

Sister Sandrine gives a heartfelt, "You are most kind to even consider ...."

"Kind of self-centered," I answer. "Do you have any idea how bored and boring Iggy and I are here all by our lonesomes every evening?"

Just then Brenda comes in with Pearl, who is carrying a large, open book, which I take as my cue to continue, "And the ever-wonderful Brenda doesn't usually spend her evenings here, so if you move in, maybe you can convince me to convince Brenda and Pearl to do the same."

Brenda gives me a smile. She likes the idea, and our closeness cannot be denied. I return her smile and continue. "Please, our compliments to the chef, and, drum roll please for her able assistant, Alberta Einstein."

Brenda laughs, as Pearl registers extreme exasperation. "Albert Einstein was a boy and a physicist," Pearl intones, "not a girl in the third grade who hasn't decided what she is going to be."

"I thought he was a paleontologist."

"You don't believe that," Pearl correctly asserts. "You're just being silly, which you usually are."

"I am pretty silly, aren't I?" I both say and ask.

"Yes," Pearl answers decisively, at which point a piece of paper falls out of her large, open book.

"What's that?" I ask.

Pearl picks up the paper but is disinclined to show it to me.

Brenda says, "Go ahead."

With a sigh, she holds up the paper. Even without my reading glasses I can clearly see a likeness of me, tethered not to a wheelchair but to the living trunk and legs of a dinosaur. I am not a man in a wheelchair, I am a mer-osaur, dino-guy, Phelim-osaur, or some such. I can't quite access Pearl's expansive mind, but I like the subversive freedom of the image. And it looks like that hybrid being can really move.

"You can have it, if you like it," she says.

"I love it," I respond.

"Come on," Brenda whispers, as a barely perceptible smile registers on Pearl's stingy face.

"Hey, Pearl," I say, as the eight-year-old wizard is led away, "do you mind if I ask one question?"

Pearl does not answer—she never does when asked a silly adult and rhetorical question, as I have just done. She pushes her glasses up on her nose and waits.

"Do you think our Aunt Isobell and Sister Sandrine should move in with us?"

An unfair question to any kid, but Pearl is not just any kid.

She blows out air, her most expressive expression of exasperation. "Yes, of course they should. Everyone knows that."

Declaration delivered, Pearl pivots and exits with her mom, my daily attendant, my part-time lover and emergency cook. Brenda is shaking her head, never quite believing what her young daughter has just come up with. Again.

I turn to the assembled table and ask, "Any arguments?" In response, only silence and knowing smiles.

But then Aunt Isobell scrunches her face, which she always does when scrutinizing a problem. "Your offer is most generous, and I do love the company of my nephews of course, but where we live is actually determined by another problem."

"Oh?" both Iggy and I ask.

"Yes, well, it turns out Sister Sandrine and I share a trait, even separated by some fifty years." I love the twinkle in Aunt Isobell's eyes when she has a secret to tell or a rare tidbit of gossip to convey. "Can you guess?"

"You are both great beauties," I venture, which Iggy is thinking but will never say.

Sister Sandrine looks at me in a quizzical way, and Aunt Isobell giggles. "Well, I suppose you are including Sister Sandrine out of politeness, but you should know we are not so frivolous as to care about that. No, our trait—which both of you also share, by the way—is that we have a need to be useful."

"Which is why you've never retired," Iggy says.

"And why you never intend to," I finish.

"No, I don't, but unless we find worthy occupation, we will have to find and move to another convent, in another city. 'Course, the problem is, there simply aren't many convents left. Don't get me wrong, our order has looked out for me, and there are several retirement facilities I could go to ...." Aunt

Isobell grimaces and leaves unsaid that she isn't done yet and loves to mix it up with people of all ages, including youngsters like us.

I lean back in my chair, stretching my decrepit back, considering before saying, "Auntie, give me a day. I may have something."

"That too is very kind of you, but I wasn't trying to get you to create a project for us."

"No, I would never do that. We don't do make-work projects at the Center, and if I come up with something, I promise it will be both useful and without a moment of boredom."

We can hear Pearl and Brenda on the other side of the house answering the doorbell. It being All Hallows' Eve, and with me a bit of a monster as well as the guy who gives twice as much candy as anyone else, we are getting more trick-or-treats than all of our neighbors combined. That is, we compete for the very few subversive kids who defy stifling cultural norms and venture out on this fading fall occasion. There'll be a few egg-stained windows and a whole lot of kids with bellyaches tomorrow after engaging with our spooky, candy-laden house. I applaud both parties, yes even the egg throwers, because any kid who celebrates Halloween these days is to be celebrated. The practice of Halloween is now discouraged from all sides, with legislation coming that will make it illegal to appropriate voice, culture, or costume. I tried to interest Pearl in dressing up for Halloween earlier, but she said she went out last year and is now too mature for that kind of silliness. It occurs to me that I've got to find a way to get this kid a tad more interested in having plain old fun. Still, she is interested in answering the door along with Brenda and seems to enjoy plunking candy into waiting garbage bags held by expectant kids. And, she confessed to me when Brenda was out of earshot, she enjoys eating some of the candy too.

Abruptly the ever quiet and vigilant Sister Sandrine surprises us by speaking. I can't help wondering if she is uncomfortable with the thought of camping in our bachelorette abode. But no, the den of toxic masculinity does not scare her. "Your house is filled with old and fine stained glass, all of religious devotion. Some pieces are similar, some not. Can you explain their origin and how they came to be here?"

"Didn't Aunt Isobell tell you that Phelim is a bit of a medieval monk?" Iggy intones.

"This collection is somewhat more sumptuous than exists in a medieval monk's cell, where a single pane of glass was an indulgence," Sister Sandrine responds with a smile.

She can be playful, I think, though her overall demeanor is a confused mixture of tragic and calm. Something has happened to her, the calm being how she handles what happened to her. Except for a vague something, I have no idea.

I look at her and then around at the many stained-glass windows that grace the expansive open area of my kitchen, dining, and living rooms. There are about twenty, mostly large pieces, about half of them embedded into the walls, with others situated in front of lamps to show their full voluminous color in the evening light.

"After months in hospital in rooms with dull, white walls and gray moods," I reply, "I hungered for color. It felt like forever, but as soon as possible and even before my settlement, I bought a van and had it outfitted with hand controls to assist my limited dexterity, as well as a lift for my chair. Every day for months, I'd drive out of the city and down country lanes. About two hours from here is a tiny hamlet called Hastings. I came across the sale of what was left of an Anglican church that had been demolished. I couldn't get into the building where the sale was, but there was one arch-shaped stained glass piece outside to tempt people. The guy who worked there was lounging and smoking a cigarette at the doorway, and I asked him how many were left. He smirked and said all twelve of them, which as you can see are along the entire dining room wall into the living room. They were dirt cheap, and cutting through the walls to install them cost about ten times what I paid for them. The other pieces are from two Catholic churches, not sure where, both salvaged from fires, finding them the result of more long country drives to inaccessible auctions and antique stores over the years."

"Very interesting," Sister Sandrine responds as if she means it, before turning to Iggy. "And do you like your brother's unusual taste in decorating?"

"For years, Phelim piled his stained glass in one room, so it seemed like a strange obsession. I was away for few years, and when I came back, they were installed as you see them, and now I can't imagine this space without them. So compared to some of the goofy things my brother does, this is not bad."

"I just knew all those years ago that I had to find a way, when the time came, to make Aunt Isobell and Sister Sandrine feel at home. And with the sale and possible demolition of the convent, who knows, I might even get the chance to bring some pieces from your present to your future home."

Aunt Isobell bites her lip, "It could happen since we don't know who the actual buyer is or what they plan to do with the convent. I would hate to see the stained glass destroyed."

"I was kidding, Auntie, but I suppose if it comes to that, I would definitely buy some and happily install them in your rooms, in the location of your choosing."

"These pieces are far removed from the home I grew up in, but they are lovely," Sister Sandrine says with some mystery.

I want to ask about her home life but sense that this is not the time. Iggy likely thinks the same. Instead, I ask, "So, will you both move in, at least for the short term, and hopefully longer, if we can find you useful work here?"

"Well," Aunt Isobell begins, "I meant what I said about being in service to others, but there is also the little matter of us having to pay our own way. The convent gives us a small allowance, but not enough for us to go out on our own. Although it would be kind of fun to pretend we're teenagers leaving home, come to think of it." And she giggles, and I think as I often have in her later years, how wrong we were about her when we were kids and how bloody much fun she actually is. Then, becoming serious, she says, "No matter how generous your offer, we couldn't take advantage of your kindness for very long."

"I see your point," I respond. "Charity is just not your thing."

Aunt Isobell laughs. "You make a good point, but dispensing and being the recipient of charity are not the same thing."

"Only takes humility for them to be so," I counter.

"Oh, you are clever," Auntie retorts.

But I have a real thought and am determined not to let my dear old Aunt win easily. "You know, Auntie, whenever you visited in the past, you always spent time at the Center and always told me how much you enjoyed talking to students."

"That's true," Auntie acknowledges.

"And I've never told you this, but there is no one the students like talking to more than you and Edie, which is interesting because neither of you is a trained counselor." I pause to lean back, stretch, and savor the fact that I have everyone's attention. "Ever since the prolonged Covid episode, our students have become more fragile, constantly needing someone to talk to."

Iggy smiles and moves in his chair, sensing where I'm going with this.

"In fact, the need is so great our counselors cannot keep up, and I was about to hire, not one but two new ones. Iggy, Luna, and David do all kinds of work to get students accommodations, technology, and bursary funding, but right now what we need more than anything are people who can listen and talk to students and, when an opportunity presents itself, impart a little wisdom."

"Amen," Iggy says, a rarely used term from my atheist brother.

"But we aren't qualified," Aunt Isobell objects.

"No, you're more than qualified, just not credentialed. And, if I do say so, thank God. These students need someone to listen and give them some perspective, not a lot of psychobabble and validation for what may be holding them back."

"Wouldn't hiring us get you into trouble?" Sister Sandrine asks.

Iggy laughs. "My big brother is always in trouble and is never comfortable being out of it."

"It might get me into trouble," I admit, then—hitting upon the mother lode of wacky ideas—"but it just might get me out of trouble too."

And to the assemblage of surprised looks, I distract by calling for a toast to our dinner guests, whom I am now determined to transform into housemates and colleagues.

CHAPTER SEVEN

All Saints' Day, at the Center

Next day, I fly into action. Which is to say without getting up or getting to work any earlier, or even thinking much about what I am going to do until I start doing it, I ask Edie to contact Human Resources about setting up two new contract positions.

"Who are the new peeps, boss?"

"You wouldn't believe me if I told you."

"Try me."

"My eighty-five-year-old aunt and her fifty-years-younger colleague, both nuns and, worse, Catholics."

"You're right, I don't believe you, but I do like your aunt, and as for that other one, she's a looker. Makes you wonder why she's a nun, don't you think?"

"You'd have to ask her, and I have no doubt you will once she starts working here. Oh, and one more thing. I want us to use their names without using their 'Sister' title. I don't think the university environment would be particularly welcoming to nuns."

"Sure boss, I'll bet they'd have none of it. Ha!" Our perpetual jocular repartee, brilliant as it may be, doesn't require a response, and Edie continues. "But wasn't this joint started by nuns?" Without waiting for an answer, she says, "You better get going. You've got quite a crowd waiting for you."

Much as I try to cultivate an image of being a keener who is first to arrive and last to leave, no one believes my schtick, and they tend to cluster outside my office at the beginning of my limited available hours. Mary looks most frantic, so I decide to start with her. David and Farrah can wait.

But then something else intrudes into my normally ordered day. Edie has returned with a concerned look on her most expressive face. "Boss, Perry just dropped by. You know he'd never say so, but I think it might be important."

"Send him in, and tell Mary to give us a minute."

Perry appears at my doorway, a rare smile on his inscrutable face. Which on someone else might pass as lighthearted, but on Perry lighthearted is a mask for tragic.

He holds out a hand and warmly grips my withered palm and fingers. "I wanted to say goodbye. The Career Center is ending my contract early."

My silence is loud.

"Hey, don't look at me like that. It's fine. But I did want to thank you before leaving."

"Perry, this isn't right," I say, knowing he is the sacrificial beginning of a new progressive trend.

"I'll be fine." He smiles again, the second smile being something of a world record for this stoic guy. "Besides, I wasn't the only one, so don't feel sorry for me."

"What? Who else?"

"Our tech guy, Luke, and Cheryl, a career counselor."

"Luke I get, but why she of appropriate parts?"

"Apparently Cheryl once questioned and apparently wasn't sufficiently supportive of the university's new direction."

"Look, I've got a few people backed up just now, but I want us to talk, okay?"

"Sure, any time," Perry assures me, but I know better. My mind drifts as it does in these effervescent moments. Perry oversees our psychometric testing, a position we cost-share with the neighboring Career Center. He is smart, efficient, and conscientious, but doesn't have a permanent position, so easy pickings for the new regime. He is quiet, private, and while not exactly shy, clearly someone who carries shards from a life that has wounded and continues to do so. He is the embodiment of what used to be known as a tragic figure, though he does not curry that image.

He'd been here three years before I got the opportunity to ask him a seemingly innocuous question about his life. And he surprised me with his candor. He'd had a wife and a life and three kids. The middle child contracted something horrible and died, and as so often happens, so too did his family life. He'd been an aspiring novelist until then, but with work, wife, and three kids, writing only happened in fits and starts, most often punctuated by long periods of inactivity.

He and his wife lived together for a year after the tragedy, separate togetherness reinforced by a thousand self- and partner-inflicted wounds. A small part of him, through numbness and recrimination and depression, had hoped for reconciliation, picking up the pieces, especially for the two remaining children. But then she left, had a new relationship, and as he sank, lost himself, capitulated to the depths of despair, she announced that her new relationship, now fiance, had a new and better job in Texas, and they intended to move.

And what did Perry do from ground zero? He let them go and proceeded to work and despair and, surprisingly or inevitably, write. In fact, all of his newfound time, of which there was far too much, became devoted to a writing odyssey. Each evening, all weekend, holidays, as respite from sleepless nights, he wrote, rewrote, revised, finished, and then placed his completed manuscript on a pile, only to begin the next novel.

At the time of our discussion, he'd written ten full novels, each at least two hundred thousand words, none submitted anywhere for publication, thought he admitted to vaguely wanting them to be published. He'd written an inquiry letter to an agent once that had never been answered. And for the privilege of losing a child, his wife, and his two remaining kids, Perry had to pay support, which meant he had little to live on, which meant he had to relocate, and being a recluse by nature, he was drawn to the country, where he found a small log cabin a long commute away—which, if he was the least bit clued in to what he really needed, was the last thing he really needed. Which meant he mistakenly thought he really needed to suffer.

I think the bleakest hour I have ever heard described—and I've heard a few—was his bland description of disciplining himself to write during the Christmas holidays, weeks after his family's departure. He had no other family, friends, or people to remind him who he was, and having convinced himself that writing is a job that one must devote oneself to in order to earn the title *writer*, he decided to dress in a business suit, shirt, and tie in his tiny log cabin, without people and distractions, and write, exclusively to the point of insanity.

For some reason, as I heard Perry conjure this dreary image, all I could think about was whether he had a dog. I can't remember what he answered when I asked whether the dog too had died, whether he might have missed a career composing country and western songs. For the truly lonely, even the dog who died is better than the one you never had. I vaguely wondered if Irene might still be in the hugging business.

"Perry, when?"

"In a couple days."

"Damn. Okay, let me think about this—I'll come up with something. Let's get together soon."

"There's nothing to think about. I just wanted you to know I appreciate you getting me this job."

"There's lots to talk about. Promise me we'll get together before you leave."

"Sure," he agrees and is gone. Technically, he fulfills the obligation, but we never actually do. Talk, that is.

Our worst curse is the echo of an unfulfilled intention.

Mary comes through my revolving door and closes it behind us which is not like her. "Something serious?" I ask.

"Oh boy," Mary says, turning red and looking flustered.

I wait as she takes her sweet time looking uncharacteristically uncomfortable. She's worked for me for over ten years, so I give her my best it's-just-me look.

"I'm not sure how to tell you this, but there's a problem with Diesel and the guys."

Diesel is one of our attendants. She had hippie parents, which accounts for the both the name and a seriously weird upbringing. Apparently, her middle name is Axel, and combined with her last name, Ford, evokes quite an image. She is caring and flighty and has distinctive looks and body language that can and does stop cars. Most of our female attendants prefer to work with female students, but Diesel opts to work mostly with the guys. The "guys" are three of our students in the attendant program who hang out together and share a suite in residence. Come to think of it, they'd been waiting for me yesterday as I went to the SAP meeting. I would rather have talked to the guys than listened to tales of enhanced student experiences.

"I thought the guys liked Diesel."

"Yeah, they really like her."

"Okay, and whenever I run into her, she always goes out of her way to say how much she likes working with the guys."

"Oh yeah," Mary says, her neck and face turning ever changing intricate patterns of red.

"So what gives?"

"Do you remember after she started working here, she specifically asked to be assigned to the 'guys'?"

"I guess, and they asked for her, which is not surprising. They could be picky about attendants, so we thought it was a good arrangement."

"And do you remember when I told you that she was the only attendant to get perfect scores from her clients for all of last year?"

"Yeah," I answer suspiciously, trying to sound neutral.

"The only complaint she ever got was not from clients but from other attendants who said she spent too much time with the guys and didn't help out enough with the other clients."

"Okay, but the guys' care is heavy and doing three guys can take fair bit of time."

"Oh my goodness! That's exactly what the problem is. Well, not a problem for the guys or maybe not even for Diesel, but the problem is the guys with Diesel!"

"Mary, you're not making much sense."

Mary takes a deep breath, steels herself, and forces the words out of her mouth just as Edie silently opens the door behind her. "Diesel has been doing the guys, I mean doing their morning routine, and then doing the guys, I mean fellatio."

"Good for her, and especially good for them!" Edie booms as Mary recoils in horror.

Edie laughs, does a little celebratory dance, and then turns and motions to Barry across the hall, "Did you hear that?" Barry shakes his head no. Barry is a discreet guy, so *no* probably means *yes*, but no, he will not admit it across the very public hallway between us.

"Edie." One word is enough. She has almost free rein here and being the miracle worker she is with the students, her reign is well-deserved. Still, there are very occasional limits.

"Sorry, but you don't get good news like this every day." And howling with her infectious laughter to every corner of our little Center, she mimics herself, "I know, I know, 'shut your gob.'"

I'm split. I can think of many ways this could be a problem, but at the same time I can't help thinking that after a lifetime of deprivation, the guys have perhaps for once experienced the holy grail, and while I can never admit it, I find myself silently sharing Edie's exuberance.

I hold up a flaccid hand to Edie who is about to leave. "Wait." Then to Mary, "One question—well, one for now. How did you find this out?"

"Jessie walked in yesterday and thought she saw Diesel, you know, doing something incriminating."

"Isn't Ben a quad?" Edie asks.

I almost tell Edie that there is more to sex than physical sensation. But I don't, experience notwithstanding. No one has ever accused me of discretion, but I keep my own counsel, for once.

Then to Edie, "Take a peek outside and tell me if the guys have gathered and are waiting for me."

Edie leans back and looks out my door toward the reception area. "Hey, how'd you know?"

"Hunch," I say. "Mary, I'll call you later. Edie, escort the guys in please."

Mary leaves in full view of the guys who stream in and settle around my table.

We are often jocular, but today they're quiet, sheepish, uncertain. "To what do I owe this unexpected morning visit?"

Silence. I'm curious to know who is going to be the designated spokesperson.

Finally, Ben. "We saw Mary, so guess you know."

"Jessie made a big f-f-fuss yesterday. W-w-we knew she'd tattle-tell," Doug slurs. I haven't heard the term *tattle-tell* in forever and am amused. It characterizes the fellowship before me. They are young, naive, and in many ways endearing. Probably not the image they want to present to the world.

"Yeah, you guessed right. Now the question is, what do we do about it?"

Silence. They really need to work out the spokesperson role.

"Wh-wh-wh...," Doug begins, "why do we have to do a-a-anything about it?"

The "it" dangles, undefined, but not unknown.

"Well," I wind up, not sure where I'm going with this, "the university can be a cruel and unusual place, especially for young guys if there is any sniff of sexual impropriety with young women."

More silence. Then Luc who has not spoken: "But if she is all right with *it*"—more emphasis on the *it* word—"why isn't *it* all right?"

Now that's a good question, I think, the same one I would have asked if I was one of the guys.

I start to respond but stop. As I hesitate, Ben asks, "We get that you can't give us permission, but do you have to stop it?"

"I'm worried about the program, about Diesel, about you," I say pathetically, with uncertainty winning the day.

"You don't have to worry about us," Doug says.

"Diesel will never say we told her to do *it*," Ben says. "She said that if anyone ever asks, she'll tell them it was her idea."

"'Cause it was," Luc seconds.

"Yeah," Ben says, looking out my window, whimsically recalling, no doubt, a selection of *it*s.

"Hum," I say, stalling. "I need to look into this, and then we'll have to talk some more."

No one speaks or moves, so I say, "Sorry, guys, but I've got other people I have to see."

"Sure," Doug says, with the start of a spasm that goes through him every fifteen minutes or so, like an electric current.

"Okay," the others say, as they prepare to wheel out.

Doug is last to leave, and I can tell he hangs back to say something the other guys will not hear. "I n-n-n-never expected ...." When he is emotional his speech becomes more slurred. "I know it can't go on forever, b-b-but I might not ever g-g-get the chance ...."

It is a poignant moment, and although several responses to his unfinished sentence meander through my brain, I do not respond. I want to tell Doug that relationships will be plentiful, more meaningful and real, in a way that will make him look back and regard this little episode as frivolous and regrettable, but I cannot say that; don't believe it. Doug and the guys digest a measure of condescension every day and they don't need it from me.

I also understand the problem. While inner beauty may be more important than exteriors, few people ever see beyond the stutter, the spasm, the chair. For some, many, most people, secrets of the heart are never seen, never revealed. As the guys drift down the hall together, I decide to call Brenda and give her a virtual hug. *Ha!*, I think. *You're getting soft and mushy, O'Neill.*

Yeah, I answer back to myself, *Ain't it great.*

I ignore Mary's subsequent calls. I'm busy, will call her back, I reason. But I'm also conflicted, and being a creature of avoidance, I avoid. I'm late for a meeting, so later for Mary. Same for David and Farrah. I have people to see, emails to answer, but the office rule is everyone is put on hold every Wednesday at noon. The scheduled meeting is that important.

As I hurry out of my office, Edie steps forward and announces, "HR says contracts should be straightforward. Just call Hillary and confirm after your meeting."

"Thanks, honey."

"You're welcome, stud."

Luna and Iggy look up from deep conversation as I pass. Luna, who always has important questions about things that need answers, knows that I am unapproachable when going to this regularly scheduled Wednesday meeting.

Still, she conveys her need for an answer with a single word: "Later."

She knows I won't slow down to find out what later means, but I manage to half turn and say to Iggy, "Hey, contracts look good," before tearing down the corridor at warp speed.

Elevator takes five minutes, as it tends to do close to noon, carrying nineteen-year-olds up or down one floor. *Damn*, I think, *he's going to beat me this time*. Again, top speed, passing all walkers, and hoping no one steps into my path, considering the freight train of my chair and the heft it carries. I would hate to make someone into a quadriplegic.

I exit our old Wreck of the Hesperus building—a quirky quadriplegic scurrying across the quadrangle—to a cluster of four original fine limestone buildings built just after St. Jude's was founded. From my view, ours is surely one of the finest-looking campuses in the country. But once I have wheeled over cobblestone—beautiful, even if a bit bumpy in a chair—past masterfully built stone edifices, the new section of the university presents a diametrically opposed view. The new section is mostly accessible, but butt-ugly. In the postwar boom, universities grew quickly, which resulted in a dozen or so square, utilitarian, Stalinist-looking buildings notable for their exposed concrete pillars and walls. Apparently, architects thought this style kitschy and cool in the 1960s. St. Jude's is a campus of contrasts, and architecture is only one of the reasons.

I enter the Henderson building, soon to be renamed the Student's Safe Space for Social Engagement and Activism, and head to the Faculty Club. I don't know who Jackson Henderson was, but he was recently deemed imperative to erase from history. Tragic to be removed from casual obscurity into formal obscurity. Only after the Senate approved the name change, and it was ratified by the Board of Governors, did anyone bother to research why the building was named after the dead white dude in the first place. Turns out Jackson P. Henderson was an abolitionist, a Booker T. Washington predecessor, murdered because he was willing to resist racist orthodoxy of the day. *Oh well* was the response from the few who were privy to this information, *he's still a dead white guy, and besides, we really do like the progressive name chosen to blunt his existence.* So decision holds, cruel but fair. My bet is the building will continue to be called Henderson rather than the mouthful it officially has become, at least out of progressives' earshot.

Hard left turn past the receptionist who knows I do not need to be received and shown to my table. It is our regular table for these many years, and we have an ongoing competition to get to it first, but importantly, not a minute before noon. People watch and smile at our little competition as it unfolds each week. We are known as *characters*.

CHAPTER EIGHT

An All Saint's Day gathering of characters, at the Faculty Club

E specially John Staffal, professor of English literature. He is what is known as a controversial character. He writes quirky columns, does radio, television, and podcast interviews, and as celebrity and villain in his theatrical performances, reviews, and larger-than-life presence, he is combustible. His celebrity/villain status results from behavior that is histrionic and outrageous, without forgoing integrity and focus. He says what he means, and he means what he says. He doesn't bow down to ideologues, distrusts authority, thinks identity politics the end of the world, loves women to excess, disparages discretion, and views most of life as one loud, absurd belly laugh. Most noteworthy, he is a man completely, hopelessly, and treacherously out of step with the rest of the world. Especially, the modern world. Especially, especially, in the modern university, where he performs in this modern moment.

He either doesn't care or else does, and in caring or not is determined to aggravate people who have appropriated what universities used to be for what they have become. What they used to be is a place and time away, a reprieve from the coarseness of the world where an eager young mind could delight in the wonders of culture and civilization. What they have descended into is a form of tribalism, the very antithesis of the Enlightenment, Western civilization's greatest accomplishment. John has inspired students from the literary canon of civilization's greatest accomplishments for forty years.

But not only literature. Teaching the breadth of Western civilization and culture is John's mission, to which he brings an endless reservoir of passion and knowledge. But there is a fly in the ointment. The ascendency of progressive hegemony—the lurking nemesis of passion and knowledge—has infected universities. Though most people are simply deer-in-the-headlights passive participants, the players are ideologues, opportunists, social justice warriors, idealists, the purveyors of identity politics, cancel culture connoisseurs, disparagers of Western culture, my boss.

Conversely, John is the most entertaining and interesting person I have ever known. He is also the most dangerous person in the world to be friends with, and yet I value his friendship like no other. There is no other. John is singular, and as I swing around the corner to our table, he is already there.

"Yes, yes, yes!" John shouts, standing, knocking over his chair, disturbing most, entertaining some few others. He pumps his fist, turns to a waitress to complain that someone has knocked over his chair, shares a private joke, roars with laughter, slaps the waiter on the back, and orders a double Irish whisky (which is code for a more reasonable noontime Kilkenny beer), not because he wants it, he explains, but because he wants the waiter and the listening, watching assemblage to know that he has to pay tribute to his Celtic heritage. To which he has sparse claim, but that doesn't matter much to John. I am Irish, both sides back to the potato famine, a fact which, once learned, is the reason John and I became fast friends years earlier at Paddy's Pub, our other regular meeting place, at our other regular meeting time.

John seats his surprisingly agile three hundred pounds in his recently upturned chair, leans forward on his elbows, and says in a conspiratorial whisper, "Got some juicy gossip," and then sitting up straight, looking around, he loudly proclaims, "Just when I thought this place couldn't get any more corrupt."

Professor Mindy Flower, Chair of Climate Devastation Studies, and Randy Maitland, Professor of Gender Fluidity Studies, look up from deep conversation and a shallow bowl of soup, scowl in our direction, and resume talking. Both are on Senate, with Professor Flower recently proposing a new graduate program to be named Activists' Action Against Human Violence Upon the Earth. The Senate reception was positive, and the consensus is that the program name is appealing with its actionable guidance to future agents of change.

Not to be outdone, Professor Maitland presented the draft of a new university policy banning use of the words *male*, *female*, *boy*, and *girl*, among several thousand others. The draft boldly proposes that St. Jude's publish a "living" compendium of banned words and terms that can be regularly updated in dozens of languages as a display of hate speech regulation in action. Again, Senate reception was positive, with only minor discussion about practicalities. It was universally agreed that universities are above trivial considerations such as having enough uncensored diction left to be able to finish a sentence.

The professors thrust and parry their scowls of disapproval for the odious couple John and I have become, before turning back to their soup. We are a couple, aren't we, I think with a flash of the obvious. Luna and Iggy often warn me about the consequences of guilt by association, but I don't care. I do care about how my friendships might affect our Center, but for better or worse, I value loyalty over political considerations. I am loyal to John; he has a heart of gold and is loyal in return—a combination that allows for many questionable qualities. For all his questionable qualities, he comes from a good place, even if most gawkers cannot see past the John Staffal spectacle.

So how exactly does John draw such animus? Ah, let me count the ways. He is loudly critical of identity made political (channeling Martin Luther King's fight against immutable attribute prejudice), in a world of heightened, deeply invested identity politics. Especially universities. With great gusto and his signature belly laugh, John debates identity group leaders in venues where he cannot win. A recent debate with Oppressed Students Against Israeli Oppression comes to mind. He embraced a group of student activists, declaring all human beings to be equally racialized, equal in law and before God, advising them to ignore false dichotomous oppressor/oppressed labels which separate us. He turned from a woman he was debating and challenged the audience to be more than the sum of their personal attributes and political, religious, and cultural beliefs; he implored hostile members not to be limited or seek exceptionalism on the basis of dividing our essential wholeness. Most damning, some people in the audience began to favorably respond to him before he was declared a racist tyrant and the debate was over.

John has had several sexual harassment cases leveled against him for comments made in his lectures pertaining to works of literature that he has taught for forty years. Apparently, referring to Madame Bovary as an adulteress, calling Anna Karenina's beauty alluring, and pointing out that Becky Sharp is a social climber are misogynistic comments and worthy of dismissal. Most damning is John's loud, pervasive, and impassioned protest against the English department's decision to cease requiring students to take a course in Shakespeare in order to complete a degree in English literature. In the new paradigm of postsecondary enlightenment, students are required to take at least two core courses from the newly established Literature of Oppression canon. Judge a Book by Its Cover: Awakening from a Literature of Homogeneous, Heterosexual Tyranny is heavily recommended, along with Subjugated Ingenious People's Oral Literary Tradition Restored. Senate has approved a full Literature of Oppression degree specialty within the English Department to begin next year. Early interest is high, with expectation the new vibe will revitalize a dying department. The dead, white male lit thing has been deemed so oppressively yesterday. Though some of the old guard are stupefied by recent changes, most are mildly impressed by the transformation of the department from the mold of old to the drool of cool.

Still, without the support from any members of the English Department, John took the fight for Shakespeare to Senate where he made an impassioned, eloquent, belly-laugh-funny forty-five-minute speech, even if it was ultimately useless—except for the preservation of his own integrity and amusement. Among many literary references, John used a modern quote from an unlikely source. Vladimir Putin once commented on what elimination of Shakespeare says about the immolation of Western values and culture: "The fight for equality and against discrimination has turned into aggressive dogmatism, bordering on absurdity, when the works of the great authors of the past—such as Shakespeare—are no longer taught at schools or in universities because their ideas are believed to be backward. The classics are declared backward and ignorant of the importance of gender or race. In Hollywood, memos are distributed about proper storytelling and how many characters of what color or gender should be in a movie. This is even worse that the agitprop department of the Central Committee of the Communist Party of the Soviet Union." Ouch.

Having been assassinated and then convicted of war crimes in absentia, Putin is an unlikely and dangerous source to quote from. And for all his brutal, vainglorious ways during Russia's failed war with Ukraine, Putin's demise was rather anticlimactic. Though not particularly related to his Senate diatribe, John loved the retelling of Vladimir Putin's assassination, conceived and financed by disgruntled Russian oligarchs, and carried out by his lover, possibly second wife, and certainly mother of his three youngest children. Alina Kabaeva, former Olympic gymnastic champion, known as the "most flexible woman in Russia," managed to pierce Putin's complex web of security and knock him off with the oldest and simplest of methods: poison. Vladimir loved Alina's homemade American chili, and while recently visiting her in Switzerland, he accepted a proffered bowl without scrutiny and died within minutes. The oligarchs wanted Alina to return to Russia immediately and help legitimize the new regime. Alina adamantly refused, thus proving she is not the most flexible woman in Russia.

Even a provocative Putin tale, told with ribald humor, could not garner a heartbeat or singular response from Senators. Left screaming into the void to an audience of none in this and all endeavors, is my pasty white, pear-shaped, toxic male, though not yet dead, friend John.

Perhaps John's most impassioned plea for sanity in the wake of woke happened in another Senate diatribe in response to a unanimous vote (minus his), requiring all members of the St. Jude's community to submit to anti-racism, anti–white supremacy, anti-colonialism training for the entirely of the last week of May each and every year. St. Jude's is fulsomely committed institutionally to anti-everything in response to a high-profile case against police frisking, deemed police brutality—the first such commitment among postsecondary institutions in the country. St. Jude's is determined to become first in the wild woke west among progressive universities, whether or not that designation is regarded as positive or negative. Unsurprisingly, some somnolent senators expressed regret to John once they attended the self-flagellation week they had committed the institution to impose on all employees ad infinitum.

Still, for the truly enlightened, the signing ceremony called Pledge of Guilt (the ritual of hazing and apology to expunge said guilt), chanting and sweetgrass burning, slam poetry matches, drag-queen literary appreciation lectures, decolonialization simulation instruction, oppressor slap contests, and therapeutic crying workshops were all simply inspiring. It is rumored that John's resignation from Senate came in the same minute a communication canceling his membership in Senate was received. John's last speech to the stupefied Senators began with another quote, referencing another Russian exemplar, Joseph Stalin. "On the subject of mandatory training in a university, allow me to say, 'The production of souls is more important than the production of tanks.'" John's last Senatorial words were something like "I leave today finally and fully understanding that for my esteemed members of Senate, all essential, nonacademic matters in life remain, for all time, nonessential and academic."

John certainly has a minority of faculty members who support his outspoken diatribes, but they remain, invariably, silent for fear of retribution. It is one thing for John Staffal, who will never make full professor, to rant and rave, but they have the greater good to consider, that being the good that comes from keeping their job into great old age. Besides, the university is a credentialed world, and Professor Staffal—for all his popularity among some … well, actually many—never did get a PhD. Oh my!

John wheezes fiery mirth: "How can anyone ever teach anything worth knowing without a PhD?" Then, leaning into me or whoever he is talking to, "Little-known fact: Shakespeare, Tolstoy, and Dickens didn't actually have PhDs, which is why no one thinks those old white boys have anything to say anymore, I guess. Interesting caveat, most of the no-ones who think Shakespeare and company no longer have anything to say have never read the dead, disparaged trio. Ha!"

If John expected any support from the Vice President Academic, none was given, nor would any ever be forthcoming. Though responsible for academic integrity, he does not see himself interfering with the academic integrity of his fellow faculty members for whom academic integrity is nonexistent. Basically, he wants to keep people happy, faculty being inherently unhappy, and his pathological need to be loved by those who can never love is a recipe for capitulation on all fronts at all times.

Though an equal opportunity critic, John's righteous wrath is particularly pointed when addressing senior management of the university. John is a thorn in their sides, often opposing decisions to cut language departments or other traditional, unexciting departments that are yet to understand the progressive imperative that the center cannot hold. Students are no longer given educational opportunities so much as managed by the burgeoning teams of student service professionals whose mission is to make sure that they have an exceptional student experience, whether they ever graduate or not. Hence the revised title of the Special Adviser to the President to whom I report and for whom the words *John Staffal* can induce an anaphylactic fit.

Whether at good old St. Jude's or touring and lecturing across the country, John decries the ivory tower tactical proliferation of "isms" that confound rather than contribute to education. John argues that the sheep-who-cried-wolf ubiquitous claims of racism, sexism, etcetera, actually cause the conditions they purpose to prevent by the sheer power of projection. Basically, the "he who smelt it, dealt it" logic draws murderous intent within the university while appealing to the nonacademic world John most commonly engages.

"Just how," he often winds up, "are young people to learn when the supposed purveyors of knowledge and wisdom are nothing more than ideologues with anarchistic social justice agendas?" It is a rhetorical question. "And why," John follows, "are faculty hirings today invariably clones of the very intellectually bankrupt academics who are responsible for the narrowing of learning in the first place?" Ditto for rhetorical redundancy.

While John regards the university as the root cause of dysfunctional utopian ideas, his bombastic honesty probes far and wide. John praises high-quality theater, but his reviews are savage for anything less. He reviews painting and sculpture as well as the newest and most popular of the visual arts: installations. John is not a fan of modern art. He writes long and passionate pieces, conceding the need for art to change and renew before adding that change must have objective artistic merit and not, as does obsession with all things modern, subjective dissonance. In short, he considers much modern artistic expression to be self-indulgent, speaking not to the audience it is purportedly addressing but to the narcissistic need of the artist to be validated. He believes artists must be adjudicated on the basis of merit—with the ability to create beauty in the mix—and although he has been attacked for articulating such a simple and nonacademic standard, he has held firm, arguing persuasively, and has many adoring fans among the great unwashed public. Without intending, John has become a populist phenomenon, even as consensus grows within the university that he is a misogynist, racist, ableist, anything-*ist* turd.

And while the modern arts community demonizes his critiques, he continuously surprises people with his impassioned support for underfunded arts programs. He works tirelessly and is a true patron of the arts—often performing in plays of merit without remuneration, though he could have made a living just as easily as a professional actor as he now does professing English. He is a fierce advocate for the preservation of heritage buildings and even managed to get a beautiful, condemned stone building funded and renovated; it gained renowned for its rendition of, among other dead white playwrights, Shakespeare. John is a highly regarded patron of the arts who consistently offends artists. It is his way.

He has many exes, three of whom are ex-wives. John claims to be able to love—and equally so—more than one woman at the same time, which is the central reason why he is a man of many exes who is perpetually single. Despite his propensity for loving many, he manages to maintain a decent relationship with his exes until something—a ribald comment, views on art—derails the remnants of what was, for the state of what is. Still, he is a charmer and can never stay mad at anyone he once madly made love to. The most salient point about John Staffal and relationships is this: there is no more desirable woman on earth than the one he doesn't have, could never get, and will always be denied.

John disparages frivolous human rights cases; that is, anybody or any body that claims it is a human right to have entitlements beyond equal treatment, access to food and shelter, and freedom from torture. He decries the nonsensical logic that gender, sexual orientation, race, or any of the complex and varied features that make up a human being can be targeted for special status or explains why individual attainment cannot be met. He has passionately argued that far from elevating people for their various identity parts, the sense of grievance that identity engenders holds people back and creates divisions between those who might otherwise see beyond what for who. His simple human rights mantra is equal opportunity does not guarantee equality of outcome. And because of saying the unthinkable to some, and exactly what needs to be said to others, he has become a media darlin', which has resulted, last count, in six human rights cases against him personally, as well as several others that implicate the university.

Most people live in fear of a single human rights case, for which the normal innocence until proven guilty premise enshrined in law does not apply. But John welcomes the opportunity to argue his case regardless of outcome in front the courts, or in the case of universities, committees, and tribunals looking for systemic wrongdoing that requires a reordering of everything. Same argumentative impulse for jurors, judges, audiences, radio and television hosts, student groups, protesters, politicians, strikers, deans, university vice presidents, and most of all, janitors, waiters, taxi drivers, and pretty bartenders.

Which made me once ask, "But don't you worry about the possibility of a guilty verdict, a huge monetary judgment, loss of income, or jail time?"

John, who begins most answers with a "life is as funny as it is absurd" belly laugh, just looked at me as if the thought had never occurred to him. After a pull at his greatly diminished pint, he snorted and said, "These things take ridiculous amounts of time, so by the time my time comes, my time will have long passed. So no, I don't worry, am as light as a feather and free as a bird." Followed by an explosion of laughter.

Let's see, who else? John is as unpopular with his colleagues within the English department as he is popular with his students. Sure, some ideological students despise him for his political views, but to most he is the most passionate, entertaining, funny, and knowledgeable professor of English literature in the department. Students who don't hate him love him. The fact is, until John was confronted with woke-ness, cultural cancellation, and ditto for cultural appropriation—in other words, instructed how to teach and what to think—he was completely apolitical. In the early years, we never talked about politics; we just didn't pay attention. If pressed, we might have described ourselves as liberal, in the classical sense. Then as now, we didn't and don't belong to any political movement or party. On occasions when we allowed real conversation to stray into the political arena, as often as not we didn't agree and yet remained friends. Imagine that! We hadn't woken up to the woke imperative that one must murder those one disagrees with. We were so naive we thought enlightenment had to do with the eighteenth-century Age of Reason, not the elevated state of our uber enlightened and much-esteemed SAP.

Another reason why faculty colleagues as well as most in the media hate John is because of his strong views on freedom of speech. In the maelstrom ubiquity of cancel culture that defines what universities have become, John takes on all challengers. He works to book speakers on a diverse range of subjects, some of whom he does not agree with or else has no interest in, and then fights like hell to prevent pressure-induced cancellations. Having gained a reputation as a defender of free speech, John has recently scored a big booking. The controversial Dr. Jordan Peterson is scheduled to speak and debate at our institution of higher learning in several weeks. Demonstrations from cancel culture proponents will be fierce, and John will take his stance in the eye of the hurricane.

John also challenges ideological embryos that pervade university life. In his theatrical best and loudest voice, supplemented by his equally loud belly laugh, John regularly patrols university corridors where eager students set up tables to convince other students of their cause. John leans forward to discuss, argue, mock, laugh, listen, disparage, or sympathize with the smorgasbord of propaganda against Israel, transphobia awareness, protests against the legalization of men's groups, same for Christian and pro-life student groups, systemic everything, basically anything that seduces young people into following ideological causes, rather than allowing them to work through social issues, search for objective truth, and arrive at an informed view on their own.

John has managed to aggravate and create enemies among members of PETA (People for the Ethical Treatment of Animals) as well as vegetarians. He loves to eat, loves to eat meat most of all, even as it too is being subjected to cancel culture. Despite the cultural drift toward a meatless society, John never misses an opportunity to disparage meatlessness in general, and any lacking of meat on his plate in particular. He hates cats, is not a dog guy like me—he had to have one minor flaw—and attacks the modern penchant to elevate animals to the status of humans and beyond. He thinks men—used in the generic sense to include women—are the superior species on earth, once a self-evident truth, today an unpopular and controversial claim.

As mentioned, John loves women, to excess, which has caused problems, possibly most of his problems. He disparages modern feminism, arguing, only somewhat facetiously, that equality is too low an aspiration for women, who are clearly superior to men. To the waitresses, the actresses, the mechanic who maintains his Fiat, his lovers, and the many more women he has loved but who have not agreed to be loved, he is sincere in his contention of women's superiority. But for those promoted to high office because they are women—saving most of his scathing ire for university leaders—he is merciless, arguing that gender advancement is particularly offensive when senior women emulate the worst of male traits even as they are upheld as role models for younger women.

John has made politicians on both sides of the widening divide nervous, with many despising his penchant for holding them accountable. Politicians tend to resent people who not only remember what they promised but doggedly question why said promise was not fulfilled within a generous timeframe. Recently, John cornered a local politician at a public meeting who promised to increasingly allocate arts grant funding according to prescribed ideological parameters.

For example, John questioned why 20 percent of municipal creative writing grants are reserved for Native American women, who comprise just 1 percent of the population. Last year, there were no Native American women applicants, so the arts council approached an unpublished native painter and asked if she wanted the grant. When she responded that she is a painter and not a writer, she was told she could write something about her painting process. She is a very good painter, but was a bit confused by the writing assignment until she hit upon a plan. In accepting the money, she insisted that she be free to write in her native tongue (Abenaki, an endangered Algonquian language of Quebec and northern New England), which the arts council thought inspiring. Unknown to the council, said artist was a friend and lover of Smokey, St. Jude's Indigenous American Center elder and my recent friend at SAP meetings.

Once I introduced John and Smokey, the conversation was combustible. John howled as Smokey said his friend and lover wrote all of three pages for arts council members who could not read her language, wherein she described the stupidity and condescension of white do-gooders insisting she take money for conjuring garbage in any language. As far as her mysterious painting process, she wrote that she's never really thought about it. But since she is being paid to think and write about it, she'd say the following: "I get up in the morning and have two cups of strong coffee. Sometimes I feel like painting, and sometimes I don't. When I don't feel like painting, I don't paint; when I do feel like painting, I paint. When I do paint, sometimes it is good and sometimes it is crap. When it is good, I keep the painting; when it is bad, I sell it to white people."

Apparently, this last statement wasn't true, but she reasoned that since no one will ever be able to understand any of her three-pager, she can take creative license with impunity. It was a creative writing grant, after all. John did not report this insightful story to the funding body, but he did criticize its decision-making process, which no longer considers that old-school redundant thing called merit to be of merit. He was, of course, branded a white colonialist, guilty of cultural genocide by arts council members.

For all his efforts to expose left wing political excesses, John refuses to be a poster boy for the right. He is genuinely surprised when someone accuses him of having any political affiliations and insists his various protests and pursuits are absolutely apolitical. He often says he is an equal opportunity despiser of all politicians. He has called out lawyers—law being the most common swamp out of which politicians crawl—as particularly deserving of his ire. He quotes Shakespeare—Henry VI's common refrain, "The first thing we do, let's kill all the lawyers."

So, at the risk of spreading himself too thin—a condition he has never actually experienced—John is, of necessity, forever battling university leaders—an oxymoron if ever there was one. He and they are magnets who cannot resist the laws of attraction. John regularly rails against administrators who have passively allowed degree degradation with the inclusion of frivolous woke disciplines. Academic standards have dropped so low that young people are being duped into thinking their cursory, heavily ideological degree amounts to an education that equips them to take on and change the world. Several times in Senate, to great consternation, John gave the performance of a lifetime, citing studies, using sophisticated graphics and statistics that prove a person graduating with a postsecondary degree today is less educated than a matriculating grade eight student a hundred years ago. Basic literacy, computational math, and reasoning skills are the efficacy against which John contrasts the ubiquity of contemporary virtue-signaling, crayon coloring, and protesting. The president, VPs, our SAP, deans, and faculty are outraged at each performance, but to folks who hear about these ivory tower sessions, John is a local hero. And to the horror of ivory tower custodians, John's local hero status has extended across the country.

While John's notoriety and growing fame have been unintentional, he is not exactly a reluctant player. Good attention or bad, he loves it all, which is to say there is no bad attention. All of life is a performance, in which he holds center stage. John has a large following of former students who have taken his Shakespeare course, and he has acted in many Shakespearean plays. He is convincing, tearfully moving from *Lear* to *Othello*, and can deftly switch between Hamlet and Polonius in a class reading, but his Shakespearean role extraordinaire off and on the stage is King Henry's Falstaff. John is the clever clown, the wise fool, the last man standing after a night of ribaldry, drinking, and carousing. But for all his love of and fidelity to Shakespeare, John is best known for his non-Shakespearean role of Cyrano de Bergerac. "How can you not love to play a character that allows you to wear an engorged penis on your face in public?" John regularly ponders aloud in stentorian tones. John is the worst of examples and the best of men.

Leaning in, and with complete disregard for post-coronavirus protocol regarding saliva spray, John whispers, "I've got it."

As always, I play. "Got what?"

"Why, the smoking gun, man!"

Heads crank looking for the source, which is always John when John is in the room.

Rubbing his hands with exuberance: "Neither force of argument nor my considerable charm has quite won the day with the great unwashed public. Know why?"

"Chances are you'll tell me."

"Because, my dear fellow, they need bread and beer, that's why. Ha!"

Then, turning to gaping others, though to none in particular, "Am I right?"

"You know, John, you're an interesting mix of needing validation and yet never actually checking to see if it's there."

John, not checking to see if I am dissing or validating him, continues. "I have that which will convince, entice, win the day, suffice as beer and bread."

He is in his coy mood. "Okay, so you have what for whom, and while you're at it, throw in why?"

"Why? Why? Why?" Each of John's *whys* increases in volume. "*Why*, because of the corruption of this place." And to onlookers, "Anyone want to disagree with that?"

Back to me. "*Who,* include most faculty, and especially the people who run this place, and *what,* well that is *the* revelation of the century, to which only you, dear fellow, will be privy."

"If you just put aside your astonishing ability to project your voice for one minute, I'll be privy to anything you say, and the various onlookers will not hear a thing."

John snorts, looking around, "They cannot hear, must not know, until all will be known, as it must come out."

"Well, I reckon about fifty people here are either trying to be among or hoping not to be among those who get to hear what must come out."

"But not now, Phelim, not now. It'll have to wait until our regular date tomorrow eve." At which point, I direct John's attention to Melissa, who has been waiting—she knows John well—to take our orders. More correctly,

Melissa has been waiting to take my order since John has a standing order for double burger and double fries that is known by all Faculty Club serving staff.

"Chicken and rice, and—"

"Don't worry, I'll make sure the chef slices up the chicken," Melissa discreetly cuts in—knowing I can't easily use a knife—and disappears.

John leans forward on his elbows, his chair hiked up on two legs, groaning under his weight. "I gotta tell you about the most asinine play I've ever seen. Now get this, a version of *Lear* wherein the good king is played by a nondescript, non-Learlike, self-described symbol of all identities, who rages not against scheming daughters or the onslaught of age but against the oppressive lack of celebration for intersectionality among castle occupants. Never mind the play is set in 800 BC, with even Shakespeare's sixteenth-century Jacobean twist not being a time when one could expect tolerance let alone celebration. Now mind, I can be open, encouraging even, to anything done well. But by Jove, my only objection is that the actors couldn't act. Not a whit!" Uproarious laughter, people looking up and commenting from their lunch perch at the outrageous, if occasionally entertaining, Professor John Staffal.

John continues, pounds the table, and howls at his assessment of the play in anticipation of his upcoming theater review. I listen, amused as always, but worried, which I'm mostly not. John is just too easy a target and has provoked too many people for too long. Maybe he has a smoking gun that will be revealed, maybe not; probably not, but whether or not, however right he might be, the cards are just too spectacularly stacked against him, and I fear that there are those, legends actually, who want him to be universally shamed and taken down. It won't do to show fear or to tell John to be careful. He doesn't care what people think about him; he just wants everyone to love him. He is deadly serious about everything he does; everything he does just has to have a joke in it. John is a bit of a contradiction.

CHAPTER NINE

All Souls' Day, at which juncture Paddy's Pub makes an appearance

Back at the Center, I deliberately focus on considering the fact that most days I ignore most of what comes my way. It is my way of setting priorities. While it is true I upset some folks, ignoring non-student types gives me a reputation for being busy, far too busy to return your petty inquiry. Only in a university.

As I glide down the corridor, long before I can hear any noise from the many students crowding our Center, I hear Edie's surround-sound, outrageously amplified infectious laugh. As I round the corner to the reception, Edie springs forward, but not before telling Barry to shut his gob. There is no reason for this. Soft-spoken Barry was not even talking. It is just Edie's endearing way. Barry, who has the patience and demeanor of Mother Teresa and never speaks out of turn, smiles and complies.

David steps forward to inform me that he has reorganized our website according to earlier discussion. No fuss, no reminding, just getting the job done, every time. I hired David ten years ago, for which he expresses eternal gratitude. I am often humbled by the fact that gratitude should be flowing in the opposite direction. He was terribly shy and self-conscious, but belonging here has helped. Apparently, inclusion among our crew has real heft. I make a mental note to find a way to acknowledge David for his quiet, self-effacing good work and loyalty. Yeah, he has many good qualities, but most of all he is loyal, and in the viper's nest in which we work, loyalty is both rare and never to be taken for granted. I also like him.

Edie hands me a printed copy of her correspondence with Human Resources outlining details of the contracts for Aunt Isobell and Sister Sandrine to meet with anxious students, listen to heartfelt difficulties, and find solutions. Neither are qualified counselors, which is flagged as a problem, so with only slight sleight-of-hand, I call them *advisers*, thereby satisfying the professional problem seekers. Offering nonpermanent contracts of no more than six months, I deftly avoid university constraints—which include dictating who we can hire—avoid potential land mines, and escape undue attention from both HR and the union. Except for the few permanent positions held by long-standing peeps, constantly renewing six-month contracts is our strategy for getting and keeping the people we want.

"Excellent," I say. "Can't wait to tell the girls."

"Works out well," Edie howls, "'cause they're both in your office." Then, leaning forward, in a conspiratorial whisper, "It really helped that we didn't have to tell the old gal's age. Helped avoid dumb questions."

"Good," I grin. "We wouldn't want any dumb questions about our disturbing nepotistic tendencies." Then changing gears, "Oh, do we have their offices worked out yet?"

"Yup, you got it, boss. We are putting the four interns into the two bigger offices to free up the two at the end of the hall. Interns are fine with that, so good to go."

"In case I haven't mentioned it before, you are the best!"

Edie bats her eyes in exaggerated manner and says, "Aw, shucks, little ol' me?" She laughs again, then follows with a slight cough. Makes me think we'll have to pay attention to that.

Luna rolls up beside me fast, speeding to an abrupt halt. "Interesting choice for new counselors."

"Advisers, not counselors. Are you suggesting it's a problem?"

"No, not a problem, just interesting. I have a list for each new *adviser* of anxious students looking for someone to talk to yesterday."

"Well, that works out well, 'cause I plan to have the gals start tomorrow. Are you okay with that?"

Luna can be thorny about things like ethics, integrity, and finances. "Well, I thought it was a bit crazy, but then I remembered overhearing your aunt talking to students in our lobby, and it is true that she is very good with them. Sister Sandrine seems very calm, so she will probably be good too." Luna does one of her quick turns by way of exit before saying, "Most of all, since they can start tomorrow, I think it's brilliant."

I laugh but do not respond for fear of jinxing a rare, major Luna concession.

Iggy waits, but knowing me and seeing that I am in a hurry, he gives up and hurries away.

I like the fact that my brother can take a hint.

I rocket across the hall and into my office, with my two newbie employees waiting to be assigned.

"Ladies," I begin.

Aunt Isobell giggles. "Are you still allowed to use that term?"

Sister Sandrine points out, "No one has ever accused me of being a lady."

I pause and change what I was going to say, "You two are *so* going to fit into this office."

"Does that mean we passed?" Aunt Isobell asks.

"Yes, it's a done deal, and if you can manage it, you can start tomorrow."

Aunt Isobell becomes serious. "Strange how life seems to be accelerating."

"How so?"

"Well, I asked to meet with Mother Superior this morning to talk about your generous offer of temporary housing."

"With the temporary offer extending as permanently as you both would like."

"I thought she might not think it quite appropriate, though I knew she'd not tell me I couldn't go. But from the moment we met, I knew she was preoccupied. She didn't object, she didn't think it a bad or even unusual offer; rather she seemed—well, eager for us to go."

"But she really likes and respects you."

"True, and she also said in a heartfelt manner that she will miss me, us, since she likes Sister Sandrine, too. For me, she is relieved that I have some place to go that is not a convent for retired nuns, even if my age says that is where I belong."

"If you don't mind me saying," Sister Sandrine begins, "you belong with people our age."

I feel warm and fuzzy when she looks in my direction, thus equating our respective ages, even if at least twenty years apart. My warmth and fuzziness are not diminished by the realization that Iggy will be disappointed in not having been here at this moment.

Aunt Isobell gives a slight smile by way of acknowledgment and continues, "It turns out that Mother Superior is particularly relieved because she would like us to move out as soon as possible, and she has accelerated the plan to move all the elderly nuns to nursing convents."

"Why?"

"Because something has happened and that above-value offer for the convent now has gone up but is contingent on the buyer taking possession even earlier, by February first. Apparently, the buyer is anxious to begin renovations as soon as the last of our Sisters vacate the premises."

"What? That's just three months from now. Doesn't seem reasonable."

"Nothing about this sale is reasonable. When discussion began last year about selling, the fear was that it might take a year. The convent was never listed, and Mother Superior was approached by a lawyer representing the buyer. All of which was especially surprising because the building is in terrible need of repair, and as a heritage designation with charter restrictions and its location beside the university, it cannot be used commercially or torn down for condo buildings. I'm glad in a way, and so is Mother Superior, and the order really does need the money, but something doesn't seem quite right."

"So when can you move in with us?" I ask with enthusiasm, temporarily ignoring Auntie's other concern.

"Well, I don't know," Aunt Isobell begins. "We don't want to inconvenience you, and there are arrangements to make."

"Wait," I say, holding up a hand and speed-dialing my cell.

It takes Iggy less than thirty seconds to appear. Luna waits directly behind, just in case I want her as well. They usually come as a package deal, so I wave her in.

"Okay, decision time." I have this thing about cutting through uncertainty and throwing caution to the wind in the interests of moving life along.

"Brother Iggy, with your truck and ability to move like a rabbit and lift like a teamster, despite being pint-size, can you move the good Sisters Saturday?"

Iggy, recognizing when I'm in a mood to move both life and nuns' stuff in a hurry, answers without hesitation, "Yes, absolutely."

"Excellent, done. Now, esteemed advisers, can you meet with Luna and Iggy this afternoon to go over your 'advising' role with students and to review the cases Luna has put together?"

Aunt Isobell, who also recognizes my decisive moods and knows the game, answers without hesitation, "Yes to both," before turning to Sister Sandrine for her input.

Sister Sandrine uncoils the slowest, brightest, and most beautiful smile ever recorded in human history. "I would not have it any other way."

I don't see the good Sisters much the next day, their first foray into advising students at our Center. The fact that I don't get in until close to noon may have contributed to our paths not crossing. The additional fact that Luna managed to fill their dance card with students from nine a.m. until after closing sealed the deal. I would have liked to plan something for after their first day, but I have my regular, inviolable appointment, Thursday at six p.m. with Professor John Staffal at Patty's Pub. And yes, I'm well aware of, and am often teased for keeping not one but two steady dates with the fun-loving, trouble-seeking Professor John Staffal each week.

Besides, we can have a dinner with the gals after their Saturday move and get caught up. I catch myself humming while motoring down the corridor and realize that I am really looking forward to having Aunt Isobell and Sister Sandrine at the Center and in our house. The whole affair is so spectacularly unlikely, and yet here it is. Aunt Isobell has always represented a version of home for me, and she is coming home. Sister Sandrine—well, I could get used to her being home, homely as she is. It is also clear, despite her silence, that she has real depth and a world of intrigue that she holds tightly close. I'm intrigued ... for Iggy, you understand.

I can choose to kid myself that hiring my elderly aunt and Sister Sandrine—whose beauty is set ablaze by the presence of brown skin—is a strategic move in the interests of achieving the SAP, Exceptional Student Experience's workplace equity plan. Useful as their particular identity features may be, that is not why I hired them. I just know they will fulfill their need to be useful. And, fringe benefit aside, their immediate impact on both students and staff is palatable. How do I know, not having witnessed said impact? Staff have made a point of dropping in and letting me know, and students have emailed me with the same, as never before. On this, their first day.

The fact that both are Christian would be a problem, if known, which is ironic because strictly speaking, good old St. Jude's has been a Christian—yikes, even Catholic—institution for over 150 years. And though there is some impressive history in the mix, intellectuals have wrung the neck from any objective interpretation, producing a selective history more suited to these enlightened times. A revisionist theme has prevailed wherein heroes have been expunged to allow villains to follow in the wake of wokeness. Despite the revisionist reputation of St. Jude's as colonial oppressor, history records that the good nuns educated any and all people without cost, decades before the school was elevated to university status. In its day and in its way, it was a beacon of progressive action, revisionists be damned.

Fast-forward to a decade ago, when the university chaplain and Catholic priest were quietly thrown out so as not to offend non-Christians. A policy was unanimously passed in Senate as well as the Board of Governors ending the discriminatory religious heritage of St Jude's, making Christianity a "lost cause" worthy of the university's patron saint. The Protestant chaplain's and Father Peterkin's space were designated as interfaith prayer rooms. People agreed that this was the enlightened thing to do. It went unnoticed that no Christian or Jew or Buddhist ever set foot in the newly instated prayer rooms. Someone eventually mentioned the unspeakable, acknowledging that only Muslim students used the interfaith prayer rooms. A single session Wiccan ceremony or event, not likely a prayer session, was held in the prayer rooms, so the issue of interfaith fairness was addressed. The appearance of fairness is accorded high currency in a university.

At the same time, an earnest employee from the Reimagined Branding and Advancement Department at St Jude's, whose purpose is to raise money and "awareness" of all things progressive, came up with the university's new slogan. Again, with unanimous Senate passage—even if under protest from nonmember John Staffal—the new us was packaged: *St. Jude's, the University of Found Causes.* Their strategy was predictable. Fundraisers and student recruitment officers marched forward selling the university to leaders and activists as *the* place to obtain a degree high in ideology and empty of content, appealing to the vacuous and vain from coast to coast.

Also worth mentioning, the Reimagined Branding and Advancement Department developed a byline for their big fundraising campaign, as follows: *History Begins Tomorrow.* Makes you wonder if the history department is going to change their focus toward studying events in the future. My thought is they could bolster the History Begins Tomorrow campaign by adding the byline: *Those who do not learn from the future are doomed to repeat their mistakes in the past!*

So as long as we don't use the title Sister in our dealings with HR, we might just get away with our little scheme. Aunt Isobell is my mother's sister, so no easy connection to Iggy or me was revealed when we gave her name as Isobell Kelly. One could argue that her age is an additional plus for equity in this identity-obsessed world, but no, in the hierarchy of equity concerns, age does not hold the currency of oppression. The term *ageism* is sometimes heard, but no one really cares about old people. After all, they might have the audacity to remember a past that does not jive with modern revisionism. Oldies don't much exist in the university, so problem solved. There are bigger equity fish to fry. Those relatively few older staff and faculty still kicking invariably refuse to see themselves as getting older, as is the modern way, so they don't acknowledge the existence of ageism even as it stares them in their wrinkled faces. Old people also have this terrible inability to see themselves as victims.

I want to ask the newbies about their first day before I leave for Paddy's Pub, but almost ninety minutes after the Center has closed, they are both still in meetings with students.

"Good call, boss," Edie pipes up from across the hall, where she and Barry are still at work. "The students love those gals."

"Hum." I ponder. "Guess they've gotta be good if they're still in demand this late on their first day. So what's your excuse?"

"Barry and I are working on the exam schedule, and Luna and Iggy are checking it against student accommodations, space, and equipment to make sure it all fits together, just like how Barry and I fit together." And with a howl, Edie hops back onto Barry's lap where she has not been for an astonishing stretch of almost two hours. Barry manages to convincingly play the straight man and look uncomfortable at the same time. I laugh, thinking he is a good guy, both dreading the next Edie indignity and loving everything she says and does. Life has these contradictions and searing moments of fun and decency.

Iggy and Luna have a few questions, comments, and suggestions for office improvement as I pass by but know that I am not about to linger. They know more about office procedures and rules than I do, by far. In fact, everyone who works at the Center knows more than I do, but they still ask, God love 'em. I love my peeps, and especially from the depths of my ignorance, I am determined to save them.

I have these thoughts sitting and waiting for John at Paddy's Pub as Jeannie serves my regular Kilkenny in a one-pint glass mug, the first of several to be consumed this evening. It's true I've missed out on some things in life, but no one should miss being a regular at a fine pub where staff see you, know you, and appreciate the same back.

Jeannie and I exchange more of life and more about our lives in the serving of a single beer than most married couples manage in a month. She was once a great beauty, was much sought after, was one for whom the world was her ambiguous oyster. She'd loved and was asked to marry when she was young but had said no for reasons that are not clear, perhaps even to herself. Like many young, beautiful women, she'd been overwhelmed by male attention, and she simply reverted to a defensive posture, habitually saying no regardless of what she felt. She'd had other chances, proposals, relationships, but had never loved again, and time passed. Her great love had moved on and had a pretty wife, three adorable kids, a big career, and a bigger house, whereas she, who had said no, merely persevered without kids, house, or love, working long hours at this pub, long ago sensing that her moment had passed. Without understanding when or how she'd passed the self-imposed demarcation, she had imperceptibly shifted her gaze to the rearview mirror. She didn't miss the male attention that had once stopped cars, but she missed being seen by anyone.

I know what she means, and she isn't talking about being noticed for her physical beauty. The first time I appeared in public after my accident, I went to a shopping mall of all places. Though people then and now gawk at the wheelchair, they no longer saw me, and that perception of how I am regarded has never changed. In fact, with age I have gone from mostly unnoticed to quite invisible. We, Jeannie and I, have faded into obscurity together. While not a tragedy, it is a sad fact of life passage. Hence, the exchange of profundities over the exchange of beer. Our relationship is transactionally heartfelt, and beer and tip are the least of it.

John's entrance is always punctuated by the sound of applause. Regulars know his theatrical antics, his bombastic presence, his need to both create and receive homage to his presence on earth. His unspoken need, evident in every word and action, is a hunger to be larger than, not just life, but every life. Even occasional visitors clap and approve of his theatrics, instantly sensing that John Staffal moments give life to the pub. All of his moments are blatant appeals to his ever-present audience. One wonders how John copes when alone.

On this evening, the clapping acknowledges that John has graced our presence in full theatrical costume, feet planted in the middle of the room, arms widespread, before taking off his ridiculous seventeenth-century French plumed hat and dramatically bowing. He is also sporting a leather doublet, silk breeches, high ostentatious leather boots and a ripe, misshapen sloping nose no less than twelve inches long. John smiles widely, accentuating his full thick moustache that gives his olfactory adornment a run for its money with its ostentatious claim that size matters. John is in his element as Cyrano de Bergerac, the character he is most suited to play, with only minor competition from Shakespeare's Falstaff. His entrance and appearance are John's way of letting us know that he has just come from a dress rehearsal.

"Nice," I say, a flaccid attempt to minimize the obvious impact on his audience, knowing full well that there is no minimizing John.

Jeannie places a Kilkenny on the table without saying a word.

John holds up his hand and booms, "Ah, wench you've got that right, but after such a performance, it will have to suffice as a chaser for a triple Irish whisky. On the rocks, naturally."

Whereupon Jeannie places a second glass of said beverage from her tray on the table, turns and exits with the words, "Do I know you, or what?"

"By God," John shouts, "I'd marry a gal like you for that insight alone. What a woman!"

Over her departing shoulder Jeannie retorts, "And I'd marry you just for the way you look in your silk breeches."

Which as a three-hundred-pound pear-shaped man of seventy who has never exercised a day in his life, is rather pathetic. Still, compared to the twelve-inch olfactory prophylactic hanging over his mouth, his silk breeches are the least of his problems. John never suffers from Jeannie's and my affliction. He is always noticed, never invisible, even to those without sight.

John bows to onlookers and gawkers around the pub before sweeping his plumed hat off his head, again, and sitting down with the dexterity and grace of a hippopotamus. "By God, except for a weak link or two, I think we've got it. The reassembled play, that is." With dramatic flair he then pulls an envelope out of his leather doublet and slides it across the table. "Tickets to the re-opener, accessible seating naturally, a week Friday for you and some of your friends, old and, I hear, recently acquired."

"So you know about the nun caper."

"Bloody genius. I assume you won't have them greet students as receptionists."

"No, they are officially student advisers, and based on a sample of one day, they are hugely in demand."

"Any problems getting by the nun look?"

"Again, based on a sample of one, no. Human Resources didn't see them, our esteemed VP has never set foot in our office, and if today is any indication, they won't get out enough to be noticed by others. You'll have to meet them after opening night."

"I love the thought of two nuns working at the university, since I'm seriously into diversity, and I'm mightily intrigued. You being of a certain age that is not polite to speak of in polite company, I assume that your esteemed aunt is of a certain age, times two or, er, three."

"She's ageless."

"And is her convent companion of equal vintage?"

"Ah, no, guess you haven't heard much about her, have you?"

"No, why?"

"Let's just say that you, who are immune to surprise, may be upended."

"Ha! Interesting my boy, but not nearly as interesting as the little morsel I have that I alluded to yesterday."

"Yes, you did allude, didn't you."

"And my allusion very likely has relevance to your dear old, or not so old, aunt."

John has my attention. "Pray tell."

"Well, as mentioned, it reeks of corruption and, alas, may negatively impact on your recent employment solution."

"Because?"

"The convent is closing."

"Sure, but we've known that for a while."

"Yes, but what was unknown is that it's closing in a very few months."

"How'd you know it is closing so soon? My aunt only found out yesterday, and she is close to the source, that is, Mother Superior, who only found out yesterday."

"It only became known to anyone yesterday, except for the corrupt ones."

"Corporate corrupt?"

"Ha? First instinct no, but now that you ask the question corporate might well describe the perpetrators."

"Well, they have to have deep pockets since Aunt Isobell said they're paying more than twice what anyone else would."

"Ah, key on that. What body or person—even if not a person who's anybody you'd want—has to have that space?"

I blow out air in exasperation, oddly reminding myself of my young exasperation idol, Pearl. "So you're going to milk this, are you?"

"As I always do, my boy, but also because you will kick yourself for not seeing the obvious, once it is revealed."

"Well, let's see. The place is a Wreck of the Hesperus so needs major reno funding unless the new owners like small, numerous cramped nun cells. On the upside, the place has not only good bones, but is frickin' beautiful in consideration of wood, windows, stained glass, and early nineteenth-century religious opulence. It would suit an arts outfit, but they wouldn't have the purchase price, wouldn't pay twice the purchase price, wouldn't have reno cash, and wouldn't demand that the good nuns exit in a few months to our cold, cruel winter. Lawyers often buy the nicest properties 'cause they can, but apparently there are some long-standing conditions for purchase of the convent that they could never meet. Also, it's too big and likely not located where they want to be."

"Now you're onto something. It's about location times three, me boy, and it's right before your eyes."

"Well, based on location, St. Jude's would want the property, but they've always wanted the property, and the convent always refused to sell it, and that is especially true in recent years knowing that the university would use it to help declutter its Christian heritage."

John pounds the table and shouts, "By God, he's got it!" Noting the reaction he has evoked from pub onlookers, he continues. "What changed quite possibly is the allure of the almighty dollar. That and the fact that the nun business and its aging members are a dying breed in need of some TLC as they exit this mortal coil. And now for the fifty-four-dollar question: whomever among the many esteemed officers of our illustrious institution might have the means, wherewithal, and, let's face it, cash to pull it off."

"Oh my god!" I blurt, causing John to cough a mouthful of beer across the table and into my face. Without a post-Covid care in the world and none for my wet face, John continues, "Yes, yes, yes!"

"It's our SAP, Exceptional Student Experience, isn't it?"

"An exceptional answer, and yet and yet, even this revelation pales in comparison to where she is getting the funds to finance said venture."

I wait, dials churning, but without answers forthcoming. "You're going to be coy, aren't you?"

John is experiencing too much joy in the coy with the boy to be any other way. "Bear with me, laddie, and you'll be both astonished and impressed by the logic of it all."

"Okay, Prince of Darkness, coy on."

Cyrano squints, leans forward, and pulls on the end of his substantial fake moustache. "I'm not sure about the renovation money, but I happen to have been given some under-the-sheets intel on where our guillotine gal is getting the purchase price, and then some."

"Okay," I say, playing along and not wanting to tempt more coy from the boy. "So, by under the sheets, I suspect you are saying that your intel comes from sleeping with the SAP herself."

"Ha!" John thunders and yells, followed by spasms of coughing and laughing that not only entertains the entire pub, but has medically trained members in attendance preparing to administer CPR.

Leaning forward in a conspiratorial manner, back chair legs suspended, all weight upon the stressed front two. "I may not have mentioned, as is the prerogative of a gentleman for a lady, but as you can see I, Cyrano de Bergerac, have a reputation to uphold, and well, you cannot expect me to keep you up to date regarding all my many conquests."

"Sure, so what gives?"

If the wooden legs of a chair could groan, they just did. "Do you know of a certain Grace who works as an administrator in the Senate Office?"

"That would be the same office from which you are banned."

"You know about that?" he asks, squinting one large roving eye.

"Everyone knows that. John what does Grace have to do with the sale of the convent?"

"Ah, now we come to the moment of truth, the punchline, that—"

"John," I remonstrate.

"Do you want the good news or the very bad news first?"

I wait, my calculation being that not answering might be the least arduous route to ferreting out John's news.

"So you attempt to out coy me. Very well, let's start with the good news. Do you remember that sixty-six-million-dollar grant you applied for?"

I had a creeping sensation that John had something very bad to impart. "Of course, based on a proposal to develop a new unifying accessibility standard for the post-sec sector, and to apply it to St. Jude's. And we've been told we are likely to get it."

John slaps me on the back before turning to the crowd around the room. "My friend and colleague here is a genius, a rarity in a university." Voice rising: "Someone who actually does something for some manys and not just for some somes, some of the time." People invariably smile and laugh without having a clue as to what John is talking about. Once he captures an audience, John rarely feels the need to enlighten. Entertainment is enough.

John strokes his long prophylactic gland in an indecent manner. "The good news is you got the grant, but, my dear boy, bad news follows hard on the heels of good, for which I am sure you will share in using the word *corruption*."

There are a few times in my life when chaos and uncertainty crystallize into certainty and insight. When that happens, I know, and do not need to check if my instincts or insights are correct. I just know. "She's going to take it, all of it isn't she, and pay for the convent, isn't she?"

John puts his pudgy hand on my unfeeling arm and says with real affection. "Yes, my boy, that is exactly what she is going to do. And as to your next question, Grace thinks that she can."

"On what basis could this be legal or even advisable?"

"Well, first of all, even though you wrote the proposal, and it is based on your credibility for the past thirty years or so, it is the university's grant application. You are the expert, you correctly cite the need and offer your services for its proper application, if successful, but only at the behest of the Department of Progressive Advancement. And in that most helpful department, they may have put in a proviso, unknown to you, that allows for creative accounting regarding how the money is allocated."

"You've got to be kidding," I say, knowing otherwise.

"Quite apart from kidding, I've made Grace promise that she will search around and get us some more intel. Grace will come through, and we'll know more soon. Whatever happens with this travesty, I've got your back."

Which I appreciate, truly and sincerely. Still, the question remains, is there any advantage in fighting to reverse a university decision with the infamous John Staffal having your back? Events of the past decade or so strongly indicate no, so I choose to ignore the past decade or so and start thinking about what to do in the very near future. Besides, political liability that he may be, John is my loyal friend.

"And by the time we next meet," John says, squinting one knowing eye, "I'll have graciously divined from Grace enough food for thought to remain in your good graces."

"And if your food for thought is a mouthful, we'll say Grace."

CHAPTER TEN

Dinner at home, and the retelling of a tale
about a train between Milan and Rome decades earlier

I need to find out about what happened to our $66 million, but as you may have noticed, I'm lazy. Also, I'm hopelessly out of fashion, don't compete for caring, and so I don't see the point of worrying unless or until it serves a purpose. Waking up Saturday at the crack of noon, I decide to wait and think and worry on Monday. I also decide that I will not tell my peeps about the theft, at least for now. Telling Luna or Iggy might kill either one, worrywarts that they are.

My last questioning thought until Monday is whether this theft will be concealed or celebrated. But of course, my last questioning thought is easily dispensed with. The big lie always wins and is celebrated as virtue. From Machiavelli to Stalin, schemers and tyrants have practiced the noble and strategic lie, demonstrating that size matters. As Mark Twain opined, truth has a serious disadvantage in the war of words: "A lie will fly around the whole world while the truth is getting its boots on." I'm pretty sure a victory cry celebrating the scam will soon be shouted from the highest hilltops.

Our move-in celebratory Saturday evening dinner was everything we grew up aching for family to be, but often wasn't, couldn't be, or fell short. I was oldest and Iggy youngest of an Irish Catholic family of seven kids, which is fondly remembered for rare, poignant moments of togetherness punctuated by an epoch of separateness. We were tough by today's standards because we knew that we had to make it on our own, and that imperative led to savage competitiveness and estrangement. Two of our sibs went AWOL long ago, another participates only reluctantly in anything family, and the rest of us are functional but are not and seemingly not capable of much warmth toward each other. Iggy and I admit as much in recent years, and in our meek way try to reach out, if not often, at least with some regularity. It is what we do to keep from doing nothing.

Looking back, I was the worst offender, the most competitive, feigning superiority whenever a brother or sister entered the room, in a way I rarely was with my friends. Wait, what friends? I was too busy chasing skirts to ever cultivate actual friendship. I was also probably an alcoholic by grade 10 because in our large extended family of mostly Irish Catholics, alcohol consumption was simply what one graduated to after drinking milk. No one drank wine in those days, and beer was simply an introduction to hard stuff, the real stuff, the stuff you drank to become real.

Which helps explain why I only had a glimmer of who I was after I quit drinking, after I became a quadriplegic, after I lost everything. Loss does not mitigate desire, and after it became almost impossible, my strongest desire was to have a family, a home.

Iggy, fully twelve years younger—which is not that many years between the first and seventh born—was someone I simply didn't know for the six years we lived together in the same house. But when you lose everything, you gain, if nothing else, insight. Some of my siblings couldn't bear what had happened to me. One brother felt I got what I deserved, one sister quietly slipped away, saying she just wanted to remember me the way I was, same thing I was trying to forget. Dad died before my accident, and my mother— well, she suffered for my suffering, for which I will never forgive myself. She died relatively young, just sixty-six, from Parkinson's disease. God love her, 'cause I sure did.

Iggy was a caregiver, still is, and he just showed up one day while still a teenager, and stayed. That is, until I threw him out. He'd been too devoted, too self-sacrificing, wasn't going to go anywhere tethered to my expanding and unfeeling carcass, so I forced the issue and sent him packing. He didn't take it well, didn't talk to me for a couple months, but is not a creature of resentment and came to see the heave-ho for what it was, heavy-handed as it might have seemed.

He did get a life, picked up a degree and a girlfriend who became a wife, but for all his newly placed devotion, got dropped and abandoned and became depressed. He is intense, and running does not quite relieve intensity or address loneliness. And then it occurred to me that this quietly intense, caring guy might work well at the Center, so I invited him back. Okay, I also missed him. Now that our support is a two-way street; our situation works well, and even among un-emotive fallen Irish Catholics, it has an element of caring that reframes the sketchy mold that is our family history. Dr. A. has often said— equal parts facetious and truistic—it is never too late to have a happy child-hood. I cling to the remote hope that a resurrected phoenix can be pulled from the ashes of my former life. Hope doesn't require a better than even chance to nourish the hungry heart.

It is why our oversized Victorian monstrosity has always lacked. Sharing everything and living in close quarters must have imprinted and shaped Iggy and me from an early age. Although I would not have thought I'd ever pine for the company of two nuns, a personal attendant, and her-know-it-all daughter, that is exactly what I passionately ache for as we prepare for our festive dinner. I like the echo of activity pervading our old drafty house. I want the empty upstairs rooms, that I've never actually seen, occupied. I want empty filled. Emotional scarcity will do that.

Brenda comes out of the kitchen and sighs. "They won't let me do a thing. When your aunt saw me pour your beer, she instructed me to come and sit with you and relax." Brenda carefully places my favorite glass mug on the table so that I can wrap my fingers around the handle. "I know they wanted to make dinner tonight, but shouldn't the old gal be tired after moving?"

I think about this. "She should be, but come to think of it, I don't think I've ever heard her say she's tired. And it's not as if she's had an easy week."

Iggy sets a cardboard box on the table where Brenda and I sit and announces that he is done.

"That's all?" Brenda asks, as our eyes survey the few scant boxes and two suitcases that comprise the totality of Aunt Isobell's and Sister Sandrine's worldly possessions.

"Clearly Aunt Isobell isn't married to Rodney Dangerfield," I quip.

"Huh?" times two.

"One of his most famous lines." Puzzled looks so I continue. "A thief stole my wife's wallet, but I haven't reported it because so far he's spending less than she was."

"Is that joke sexist?" Pearl has inched into the room, quietly as she always does, until announcing her presence with either an intelligent comment or a disarming question.

"Yes," I respond, exposed and disarmed, "but my defense for articulating one stereotype is that I am defeating another as pertains to Aunt Isobell."

Pearl thinks about this; the extent to which she puts thought into what she thinks is reflected in how long she reflects. "If that is your defense, then maybe you should not become a lawyer."

Brenda and I look at each other without speaking, sharing a mutual expression of awe at what this kid comes up with.

"I guess I'm going to have to be careful what I say from now on" is all I can manage.

"As if," Pearl answers.

After a momentary silence, Iggy says, "As far as reasons for being tired, Aunt Isobell and Sister Sandrine easily put in twelve hours each of the days they worked with our students this week. And yeah, Phelim's right, Aunt Isobell has always been indefatigable, and as for Sister Sandrine, she always looks …."

"Yes?" I ask, as Iggy's voice trails off without finishing his thought in consideration of Pearl's penetrating gaze.

"Energetic" is all Iggy can come with.

Which isn't quite true. She is capable, intelligent, and hardworking, but she is also self-assured and calm. Iggy's energy is frantic, anxious, and needing relief, which is channeled by running twenty miles each day. Unrequited libido and deep repression will do that. Iggy can't bring himself to say anything more about Sister Sandrine's energy without thinking sexual thoughts, which he's ashamed of. Oh yeah, and Iggy is wisely being careful around Pearl.

Aunt Isobell comes out of the kitchen wiping her hands on her apron. "Oh good, all done," she says, looking at the boxes and luggage Iggy has brought in. Then to me, "How do you like that beer?"

"Excellent. I just noticed it's not from my supply."

"It's German," Aunt Isobell says, pleased with herself.

"Auntie, you didn't have to—"

"Yes, we did, and it's the first time I ever bought beer." Aunt Isobell giggles. "Ignatius, will you have one yet?"

"I'm a step ahead of you, Sister," Sister Sandrine says, carrying a beer on a tray and giving it to a pleasantly bewildered younger brother, before asking, "May I get you some more white wine, Brenda?"

"Hum." I hesitate. "I feel like we should have a toast, but not everyone has a drink yet."

Aunt Isobell holds up a finger and hurries back to the kitchen. "I'm on it." Sister Sandrine follows, having refilled Brenda's empty wine glass.

Moments later they return with their own glasses of wine. I know drinking wine is a rarity for Aunt Isobell, and I wonder about Sister Sandrine.

"Well, that takes care of everyone, except for Pearl. Iggy, hand me that bottle of Irish whisky, would ya?"

Pearl gives a look of disgust before raising her face into an expression of superiority. "I've noticed that adults get very silly when they drink alcohol, so I think I'll stick with ginger ale."

"Smart," Iggy says.

"I'll drink to that," I intone, "and to my good friends here, who we are thrilled to welcome into our humble house of horrors. May you fill this empty abode with your energetic presence, good company, and an occasional indulgence of good cheer."

"I know that means drinking alcohol," Pearl says, hand on hip.

"But only occasionally," I offer.

Pearl gives one of her knowing smiles. "I can drink ginger ale every day."

"Don't count on it," Brenda says.

Aunt Isobell hears the oven buzzer and waves us to the table.

"She's very excited," Sister Sandrine says with a smile.

I'll have to remember the melting capacity of that smile once the snow comes, I think.

Sister Sandrine and Iggy help Aunt Isobell place the much-anticipated feast on the table.

"I love lasagna," Pearl whispers, in a voice just shy of a shout.

"Another dish! And what is it?" I ask.

"Just a little recipe from home," Sister Sandrine says, almost with embarrassment. "I hope you like it."

"We'll love it," Iggy responds.

"We have very low standards here, so I'm sure it'll be a treat," I say.

"I'm not sure that is good or bad." Sister Sandrine laughs. "Can I serve you?"

"What is it?" Brenda asks.

"A family curry recipe."

"How did you get the ingredients?" Brenda asks, "Because I'm sure we didn't have any."

"We got the ingredients when we bought German beer," Aunt Isobell says. "Two birds with one stone, and close by, too. Which helps 'cause we'll be going back."

"Where did you get the time?" Brenda asks.

"Iggy did all the moving work, which left plenty of time for Sister Isobell and me to shop," Sister Sandrine says, smiling at Iggy. Between the hot curry and warm words, I wonder if Iggy might melt in front of us.

"Have you seen your rooms yet?" Brenda asks.

"Yes, they are perfect," Aunt Isobell answers. "I almost feel guilty."

"Well, you shouldn't," Brenda admonishes.

"I said almost," Aunt Isobell says with a giggle.

"I hear you and Sister Sandrine did well at work this week," Brenda says.

"I hope so," Aunt Isobell answers. "That reminds me. Phelim, I need to tell you something one of my students told me. I think I can do that without breaking confidentiality."

"Sure," I answer. "Anything serious?"

"I don't think so, though I have some concern. Young people can be very troubled. I suppose it is a very difficult time to be young." Then she changes the subject. "Though I suspect that young Pearl will do very well at university."

"I haven't decided if I'm going to go to university yet," Pearl states flatly. "The people I have met who work at university make me think I should seriously think about my other options."

Aunt Isobell's watery blue eyes sparkle with enthusiasm and joy. "Maybe your new friends who just started to work in a university can change your mind."

Pearl allows a weak smile. "Yeah, maybe."

After which, with some prompting, Aunt Isobell tells a stream of family stories, some going back to when she was a young girl. It never matters whether she is recalling what she had for breakfast today or what she was wearing for Christmas dinner when she was ten—she seems to have perfect recall. Or at least that is what we who hunger for family stories of old like to tell ourselves.

Now, recalling an evening forty-five years ago, Aunt Isobell laughs and says, "I remember talking to your dad at ten after eight on a Saturday evening. He called to let me know that Irene had just had her seventh and, he emphasized, last baby. I guessed a boy and then asked if he was going to honor Saint Ignatius—it being July thirty-first, for which he is patron saint, and give his name to the new baby. 'Not sure I like that name,' your dad responded, and really it must be said, I didn't think he'd take me seriously. Well, I said back to him, 'You can always shorten it to Iggy!' Your dad groaned, and yet here we are."

"So I have you to blame?" Iggy says, with a smile.

"I love your name," Sister Sandrine responds, wrinkling up her nose.

If Iggy ever had serious misgivings about his name, he lost them at that moment.

"How long have people called you Iggy?" Brenda asks.

"For always."

"Did anyone ever call you Ignatius?"

"Mostly just my dad, and only when I was in trouble."

"Which wasn't was very often," I pipe in. "Unlike me, whose nickname was and remains mud."

"You weren't so bad," Aunt Isobell says, "Though you had your moments."

Pearl discreetly pulls on her mom's sleeve.

"I think Professor Pearl would like to be excused from this boring adult talk," I say.

Big breath of air. "I'm not a professor—"

"Yet."

Bigger breath of air. "But it is kinda boring here."

"All right," Brenda says, "You are excused to continue reading, no doubt."

Pearl retrieves a ragged and ancient thesaurus from beside her empty plate. Whenever she comes over with Brenda, she picks a different book from my abandoned book collection and studies it as if graduation depends on mastery of its content. She rises from her chair and turns to leave but then turns back and says, "Thank you for the excellent food, Sisters."

Which makes us giggle with admiration which makes Pearl leave extra quickly.

"She is so smart and self-assured," Sister Sandrine says.

"Yes," Brenda begins, "and occasionally a bit too self-assured."

"Better too much than too little," Sister Sandrine counters, before faintly adding, "I should know."

The immediate, silent response from all quarters is perhaps a tad too enthusiastic. We don't know anything about her, about whom we hunger to know everything, and it shows.

Once Iggy and I recline back into our seats, Brenda asks what she means.

Sister Sandrine gives the sweetest and saddest smile ever recorded. And waits. And without a smidgin of impatience, so do we.

Sister Sandrine is calm, serene even, but slight unease comes into her eyes.

Aunt Isobell purses her lips. "Only if you want to."

Sister Sandrine hesitates but only for another moment. "Well, it seems we will be living under the same roof, and it appears we are both an odd family and, oddly too, work colleagues in the business of counseling others, so I do feel I should tell you something about myself. Your wonderful aunt graciously said I do not have to say anything, and I doubt it would come to light if I didn't say anything. Still, if possible, I would rather it come from me than from another source."

The assemblage of the table is, to say the least, all ears.

Sister Sandrine draws in her breath, which expands her formidable breasts, and begins. "I murdered a man. I was tried for murder."

I wish someone would drop a pin so I could hear it scream. Still, the silent scream is enough.

"It is why I became a nun."

I'm impressed. She understands that comprehension is achieved less by the number of words spoken than the clarity and pacing of a well-placed few.

"It was an unusual story in Mauritius, where turning a blind eye is normal. I am the oldest of five, you know, the responsible one."

Mechanically, I say, "I should know but am the exception."

Sister Sandrine smiles, either grateful for very minor comic relief or else thinking me a dolt.

"If that wasn't sensational enough, the man I killed was my uncle."

Out of the corner of my eye I see but barely feel Brenda place her hand on mine.

Sister Sandrine only hesitates for a moment. "I saw the light fade from my younger sister's eyes. Though I no longer was living at home, I came to know that my uncle was regularly sexually assaulting her. He preyed upon her vulnerability and trust, and she believed that she was alone. My parents were weak and dependent on my uncle to make a living. They did not see what was happening before their eyes. Worse, perhaps they didn't want to know."

I lean back to stretch the entropic decrepitude of my spine. Sister Sandrine politely waits as if the ritual might distract me from her spine-tingling narrative.

"So I confronted my uncle—who then raped me. And he wasn't done yet. He decided he could continue to assault my sister with impunity. One evening, I caught him in the act, grabbed a heavy object and hit him on the head. After lying in a coma for three months, he died, and I was charged with murder. In the interests of accuracy, it must be said that I hit him several times. It is an important distinction, because the fact that I hit him more than once became the basis of the case against me. The prosecution argued that it was not a proportional response, was not defensive, and therefore could not be used as a defense for murder. Throughout the time leading up to the trial, and during the trial itself, some six months in total, it was never a foregone conclusion that I would be freed."

We then witness the strangest and most complete change of expression from serious to serene as she finishes her next sentence. "It was a difficult time, but as you can see, I managed to go from convict to convent."

Brenda punctuates the silence that follows with a hollow and yet heartfelt, "If there's anything we can do ...."

Sister Sandrine raises her elegant hand and gives a mischievous and weary smile. "I have shocked you, for which I am deeply sorry. In truth, you have all been most kind, and I am grateful. Still, there is one thing you can all do for me."

"Name it," Iggy says, as if he's ready to win the Olympic marathon for her right now.

"Please don't treat me any differently. That is what you can do for me, and I can assure you I am fine."

"Of course," Brenda responds.

Then with an expansive smile as if to prove that she is fine: "And perhaps one more thing. Maybe our boss can change the mood with one of his amusing stories about human foibles."

"Ha!" I say. "Sister Sandrine, for all your seriousness, you fit in here very well with your rather dry humor. We are at your eternal disposal and will keep our infernal gobs shut unless otherwise instructed."

Sister Sandrine nods, obviously relieved to relinquish the center of attention to the resident ham. I'm still in the throes of her mind-numbing revelation but need to do something that does indeed change the mood. "You asked earlier about Professor John Staffal, who I meet with twice a week for all these years. To most, he's a loose-cannon conundrum, and if you were to ask ten people, you would get ten conflicting versions of the man. Am I still allowed to call him a man?" A rhetorical question, as Aunt Isobell refreshes our wine glasses and people settle into a listening posture.

"John Staffal is both a chameleon, and someone who really knows who he is. I know that doesn't sound like much to pull off, but in my view the true individual is becoming an endangered species. John was something of an individualist phenom from an early age. He came from a prestigious New York family, which used to signify both wealth and social standing. But the standing he wanted, has always wanted, has to do with integrity and notoriety rather than privilege. I know if you listen to people talk about him today you won't hear that, but his record of putting himself on the line is quite astounding. He was never a protester—believing protest too weak a response for what you really believe in. He effectively criticized both the weakness and ambiguity of the Carter administration for failing to uphold America's leadership in deterring Cold War bullies, as well as some of Reagan's excesses combating communism in Latin America, particularly El Salvador."

"How was he able to be effective?" Sister Sandrine asks.

"Well, even as a young guy and even though he wasn't a political pundit, he managed to get several witty and pointed pieces into key publications at pivotal moments. I don't know the details, just that he made a huge splash."

"His size would help with that," Iggy pipes in.

"Well, he wasn't always as big as he is now. But his motives then as now are always interesting. He often takes on a fight, requiring great integrity and costing loss of income and reputation, even for people he doesn't like. So, impeccable reasons, with just a smidgen of personal interest—for example, he had an El Salvador friend, a pretty bartender, I think."

Iggy grins. "There had to be a drinking angle."

"And a woman," Sister Sandrine adds, thereby expanding Iggy's grin.

"The other issue John criticized both presidents for was resumption of peacetime draft registration, which many people thought was precursor for reinstating conscription. People forget just how controversial the draft was on the heels of Vietnam."

"Just a point of clarification." Aunt Isobell asks mischievously, "Does draft refer to conscription or beer the bartender was serving?"

There are a couple seconds delay until we comprehend this most corny joke from this most unlikely source. And then the room erupts.

"Auntie, you've descended to Phelim's level!" Iggy proclaims.

"Sister, I'd say you were hanging around these guys too much if you hadn't just arrived today," Brenda adds.

"It's true," Aunt Isobell concedes, her watery blue gray eyes infused with life in the corny, holy moment.

Then we all turn to her younger companion. "Poor Sister Sandrine!"

"Phelim, we've just got to up the quality of our jokes or else our new housemates might leave," Iggy says, more talkative and animated than usual.

"Or worse." All eyes turn to Aunt Isobell. "Become like them!"

Through the laughter, Brenda cries, "Oh, Sisters, you really don't want to become one of their brothers!"

"So, with his name in print and soon after on television and radio, John becomes a bit of a celebrity until something happens, not sure what, and either he has to or else is highly advised to leave the country for some time. He goes to Ireland and does his master's degree in literature at Trinity in Dublin, before moving to Italy."

"Why Italy?" Brenda asks.

"Ah, well he loves Italian literature for sure, but that is not his main reason. More than literature, he loves Italian food and culture, and more than those paltry items, he loves Italian women."

"There were Italian women in New York. Was he not allowed to come back?"

"Oh no, that blew over, and yes, he was aware that Italian women live in New York, but John always had this need to take things to their, what you might call extremity, and he would claim, their logical and passionate conclusion. He loved Italian women and wanted to love them in Italy. A stickler for authenticity, I guess."

"And did Italian women want John to love them in their home country?" Sister Sandrine asks.

"Ah, good question. Then and now, John throws everything into the seductive dance—his charm, many passions, formidable knowledge, especially knowledge of women, even with his chances of success being very low. He never pushes anyone who does not want his all-consuming attention, but he is persistent with that small remaining percentage of possibility, with some surprising results."

"How do you mean?" Sister Sandrine asks, as Iggy rapturously watches her speak. She then turns slightly, sees Iggy's stare, and smiles while my brother's normally pale complexion turns fifty shades of red.

"I've witnessed a few surprising contemporary examples, but I want to tell you about a legendary example of persistence and personality over the frivolity of good looks and sculptured body. He once had this autobiographical story, which I am about to tell, published in the *New Yorker* as a feature piece. The article was amusing but really left more questions than answers. Like for example how did he get where he was in such short order? Even as John tells it, it's not clear, and yet, while still in his mid-twenties, he establishes himself in Milan, speaks fluent Italian, and teaches literature, mostly Italian literature, at university.

"As an instructor, John was an immediate success, and became very popular with his students. John has always wowed students with his theatrical, literary flair in a way his teaching colleagues could never do and were often quite jealous of. One of the reasons he never got tenure.

"Anyway, with oversized classes, which he not only allowed but encouraged, with the novelty of being the non-Italian expert in all things Italian, and with the notoriety of being John, he experiences an unanticipated aspect of contemporary Italian culture. John is drawn into the quiz show world as host at the end of its popularity peak in Italy. In our splintered entertainment world, it is hard for people to understand how bloody popular these television shows were then. There were only a select few shows, the content was mediocre, and yet quiz shows were the new Italian renaissance. Half the fun of game shows was the way colorful hosts engaged the audience."

"Weren't quiz shows a bit lowbrow for Professor Staffal?" Aunt Isobell asks.

"Well, I've always referred to him in terms of cultural this or that, but there is one thing he's always needed more than cultural stimulation, and that is to be loved. And while he was loved by his many students, nothing compares to the love of a live audience for a show that is broadcast throughout Italy. John quickly became the most popular game show host in Italy.

"And yet that love was not enough. Though John has always been able to love more than one woman at a time—he has three ex-wives among others who can support this contention—he developed an itch, an obsession, what he called love.

"One of the reasons John chose to live in Milan was because he loved opera. And loving opera, he chose an apartment close to the famous La Scala. And of all women, he loved opera divas most, and none more so than the renowned Renata Tebaldi.

"This is getting interesting," Sister Sandrine says with enthusiasm as Iggy looks on with enthusiasm.

"Now Renata Tebaldi was quite a bit older even then, more than twenty years, but that only made her more prefect, more Beatrice-like, in John's mind."

"Beatrice-like?" Brenda asks.

"Um, Beatrice is the perfect woman, from Dante's *Divine Comedy*, one of John's Italian lit specialties. The thing about love and obsession is that it is less what it is than what we conjure up in our minds. Anyway, John had his Renata shrine in his mind, whereas for her he didn't exist. Still, John has never wanted for attention from women. A couple years pass, and John takes a train from Milan to Rome for a special quiz show extravaganza. Though trains were often crowded, and John did not have an assigned seat, he always prowled the length of the car just to make sure he didn't miss meeting personified beauty. Mostly, he focused on general seating, since one couldn't simply take an assigned seat in first class if one sighted a beautiful woman. On this day, there was nothing exciting, so nothing left to do but find a seat and settle in. He had papers to mark, his least favorite occupation."

"But then, the first miracle. In his cursory casing of the first-class car, he stops, gasps, and feels lightheaded, and John is not easy to shake. Sitting at the window, in a first-class compartment that is otherwise completely empty, is none other than—'

"Renata Tebaldi!" Sister Sandrine cries, with delight.

"None other than. Top marks for paying attention, Sister. Maybe together we can work out a sit-down comic routine."

"Brenda, I think you are right, I need to be careful that I not become afflicted with that humor," Aunt Isobell giggles.

"John carefully sits beside his idol and love interest, who gives a passing side glance, with what can only be described as extreme annoyance. And as their train begins moving, John realizes that the most he can aspire to is her indifference. She isn't interested in being his lover, exchanging idle chatter, or being fawned over by an adorning fan. She just isn't. But I did mention that John was persistent?"

"Wait, I have a question," Sister says, with her hand raised. "Even if the first-class seat he has taken does not have a competing passenger on this occasion, wouldn't the conductor ask John for his ticket?"

"Okay, Sister, any more uber paying attention observations and you'll leave me no choice but to get you a Nobel Peace Prize."

"Thank you, but if it's not too much trouble, I'd like the literary version," the good Sister says, with a glowing expression. It occurs to me that she is enjoying an amusing story that distracts from her sad story. It also occurs to me that Iggy could never keep up with her verbal sparring, once she lets loose.

I continue. "Sister Sandrine anticipates the second miracle of this tale. Sure enough, the conductor comes by to check tickets, but after sliding open the door to their compartment, he looks at John and the famous opera diva, smiles, nods, and politely leaves. John had aspired to a few moments in the diva's presence, followed by a humiliating extraction from first class—which he had calculated was well worth it. So, John, opportunist extraordinaire, or fox in the henhouse, has free rein, at which precise moment the third miracle descends upon a newly anointed St. John."

"Oh my," Aunt Isobell says. "At three miracles, one wonders how this little tale has not been added to the Bible."

"Yet," I add, before continuing. "Soon into the train journey on that cold dull December afternoon, the train stops. Not a train-stop stop, but there is mechanical trouble, and it is announced that the train is going to be delayed. The engineer promises they will investigate the problem and report back soon.

"Now, as mentioned, good looks have never been part of John's seduction arsenal, but he does have charm and what better opportunity to exercise charm than to a bored beauty who has just been sentenced to more boredom. John tries again, comes up with something that is amusing; she laughs, he racks his brain and scores another amusement point, and this time she turns in her seat, is relaxed even and definitely open to further amusement. Which sensing, John plays the hand he has been dealt. He ventures that since it looks like nothing is moving, perhaps she would do him the honor of allowing him to take her to the dining car for drinks and dinner.

"Now while John has made himself indispensable to the bored diva, dining together in public is at a whole other level. She considers John's invitation without replying as the train starts and stops several more times. But just as John is about to reissue a more seductive invitation, the engineer comes over the speakers, announcing that technical problems will require several hours' delay.

"Which makes Renata pout in the cutest way, before turning to John and saying, 'Why not?'

"If being in the company of the woman of his dreams is his most fulfilling achievement in life, being seen with the woman of his dreams by the adoring masses is a close second. John drinks in the looks from other passengers as they walk the length of the train, and as they open the door to the dining car, people fall silent in awe of the diva and her companion. Though the dining car is full when they arrive, the best table immediately becomes available. Could be miracle number four, but that might be pressing my storytelling luck. Even as conversation and noise resume, people's attention remains riveted to the great diva Renata Tebaldi and her lowly dining companion.

"The service is slow; they had not planned for so many people. But at the table where Italy's premier diva sits, waiters fight to ensure the couple receives the best of service. Renata has stopped pouting and seems relaxed, and though she makes fun of the several courses and many glasses of wine they consume, she eats and drinks with great appetite. *We have something in common*, John decides.

"Though Renata barely acknowledges the existence of the staring dining car crowd, she obviously is used to and enjoys public adoration. And equally, she seems to bask in John's uber adoration. She laughs at all his jokes, is amused at how many obscure facts he knows about art and literature, and yes, opera. As the night wears on and with several or many glasses of wine consumed, he even ventures to probe if, if, if perhaps, no pressure, but might it be possible to see her again? Might he be so lucky, one day? She looks at John through a thick fog of cigarette smoke of her own making. She is comfortable in the midst of a *character*, and with the effects of wine at its peak, she slowly purrs, 'Perhaps. You do amuse me.'

"Which is more than he could have ever hoped for and says as much. Still, time does not stand still. Perfect moments never hold, time does not slow even for the incarnation of love. As they consume, laugh, and talk, people finish their drinks and dinner and saunter off, but not before paying deference to the great diva and by association to her common companion. None is so bold as to interrupt the dining diva, none dares attempt to talk to the celebrity couple, that is, celebrity extraordinaire and the other, lesser one. Diners are intimidated and respectful in their exit, until there is only one elderly couple left to observe the diva and her amusing nonentity.

"Finally, even this elderly couple get up and vacate their table, respectfully nod as they approach, and it appears as if they too will pass by without speaking. None of the other diners have dared to speak, so why should they?

"But emboldened by wine or old age, who knows why, the gentleman slows to a stop, clutches his hat, lowers his eyes, and dares speak while his wife looks as if she might have a stroke for what her husband is about to say.

"Renata does not bother to acknowledge the couple even as she blows great clouds of smoke in their direction. Ignoring the smoke, the old man shifts from one aching foot to another before beginning: 'I apologize for this momentary interruption. It is just that my wife and I'—at which moment he half turns towards his awestruck wife who shuffles further out of view—'have heard that it is permissible to talk to you. We will only take a moment, and it gives us great delight to tell you that we are devoted fans.' Renata has heard this all before and, noticing that her wine glass is almost empty, wonders where the waiter is who has promised their best bottle of Port.

"'We would not have dared to speak, even now, if we had not heard that you welcome people telling you how much they enjoy your work.'

"Renata's impatience for port is momentarily shaken. She is not known as approachable; she has never let it be known that she likes people telling her how much they enjoy her work.

"'You are the best host, yours is the best entertainment, the best quiz show in Italy. We never miss it on television!'

"John sits upright stupefied, but Renata is immobilized by a smoldering anger as she begins to comprehend. Which makes the old man turn towards her, bend down low and half whisper in her ear, 'It must be quite an honor to dine with such a celebrity.'

"At which point, the volcano erupts. She glares at the old man, for the first and final time, with hatred. But the old man's eyes are now locked on John, and he never notices or else doesn't care, because who is she, after all?

"Though smoke may have billowed out of her ears, Renata Tebaldi never says a word as she exits the dining car. Unfortunately, in her haste to exit dramatically—being both very drunk and quite upset—she falls dramatically, with an effect not quite what she expected, though possibly worthy of an opera. Drowsy waiters spring to life and try to help her to her feet as she screams for them to leave her alone, which causes her to fall again—with perhaps a second opera in the offing. Knowing John, even in a state of faux-love defeated, I'll bet he completed the transition from romance to farce before Renata made it out of the dining car and wrote the *New Yorker* piece that night."

"He might have needed to just to pass the time beside her in their seats before the train arrived at its destination," Sister Sandrine offered.

"I hadn't thought of that—how did they pass the time together after that? Ha! I'll have to ask John."

Aunt Isobell wipes tears of laughter from her eyes. "Well, I don't want to transition from farce to tragedy, but as mentioned I heard something about

John today from one of my students. I won't identify who, but it does seem like something I should tell you. Doesn't need to be now."

"Sure," I say. "But first a toast." On this signal, Brenda brings in a tray with four thin-stemmed glasses, one glass mug, and a bottle of champagne. She begins to fuss over glasses and champagne, and then inexplicably looks up into my eyes and we understand. Having two nuns move in on this festive day should have won a gold metal on the inexplicable front. But no, the prospect of my love and her know-it-all lovely kid Pearl moving in stands higher on the relational Olympic podium. It's not a done deal, it remains a possibility we are getting used to, but I will pursue this inexplicable love in the frustratingly determined way for which Luna claims I have become infamous. With champagne poured and my fingers securely around the handle of my mug, I say, "To family, the one you inexplicably discover as much as the one you are born into."

And after discreet consumption, indiscreet storytelling, and heartfelt good will, the pleasant evening regrettably comes to an end.

CHAPTER ELEVEN

From the beginning of December at St. Jude's University
(attending a very important university meeting)
to decades earlier at Harvard University

The dreaded meeting. No, not the dreaded biweekly meeting of all student service group managers and their groupies. I mean the more dreaded monthly meeting of a much smaller number of directors who report directly to the SAP, Exceptional Student Experience. At the expensive of devaluing the word *dread*, they are all dreaded for their astonishing, breathtaking and gray-matter-numbing tedium. And unreality. And infusion of ego into all issues. And lack of intellectual discourse. And complete smothering of free speech. And lack of humor. And least humorous of all, these meetings are held at the godless, middle-of-the-night hour of nine a.m. And for this one most important meeting, I can't excuse my way into finessing a later time. No, for this one solitary meeting I have suffer the indignity of rearranging my entire routine to give the impression that I arrive at this early hour with some regularity. Or earlier.

As the meeting is only for pedestal inhabiting directors, Luna and Iggy cannot attend, pay attention, and worry for me. Nope, just me and my canine pal, who will sleep for the duration—so apart from moral support, no help at all. These meetings, which I still manage to miss on a regular basis, are mandatory, but I must admit to my avoidant self this one might be important*ish*. There are just too many strange happenings afoot, and as usual, my little band of misfits are left out of happenings headquarters. We are never in the know, but we do pride ourselves on being in the don't know. Luna pleads with me to go to this meeting, with a look on her face that I cannot resist. And of course, she is right. We need to watch our assassins.

As Zigo and I exit my office, at 9:02 a.m. no less, my half-awake state is jarred by an innocuous display of Angel strength. Angel is our cleaner. He was assigned to our floor because he has Asperger's syndrome, the thinking being, I guess, that we might be able to help him out some. Which we are always willing to do, but he is not a student, so what we can do is limited. Still, he had two previous work situations at the university that did not work out, and we are determined that there will not be a third.

Angel is an interesting study in contrast. He is big, not overweight or unusually tall or wide big, but of brutish strength big. And yet, attached to rippling muscles is a riveting high-pitched, voice that we seldom hear, but when words are spoken, they have a counter-soprano high-pitched singsong aspect that takes getting used to. Despite protruding muscles and a thick dark beard that gives Angel the look of an assassin, his high voice and penchant for dramatic utterances when excited undermine this tough-guy image. He was often teased as a child, and we have some evidence that he still is occasionally. Clever people with graduate degrees just can't resist poking the bear as long as they assume he will remain in the cage. He seems to have no idea of his own strength and apparently spends his time after work playing video games. We like and look out for Angel, though none of us know him very well.

As I roll past, he is holding our reception desk upside down over his head as another cleaner buffs our newly waxed floor. Standing watching on the other side of the reception area is Edie, who says, "How do you like them muscles?" to no one in particular. She looks tired and seems to have a slight, persistent cough. But she is an unabashed admirer of male muscles and lets Angel know it.

Angel grins at her and says, "That's what you say to all the boys." He momentarily transfers a ton of metal and wood from two tree trunk arms to just one, in order to play along with Edie's flirting. As I vaguely wonder how long he can hold that monster desk over his head, he turns and gives a high-pitched, effortless, "Good morning, Mr. O'Neill."

As he is possibly the only human being who has ever called me that, I respond, as I always do, "Morning, Angel, and it's just regular ol' Phelim, remember?"

Hitting a high note best suited to the crescendo of an operatic aria, Angel answers, "Oh, yeah, I always forget." As I continue on, I repeatedly hear, "Good morning Phelim," until I round the corner to the elevator. As he singsongs my name, his voice never betrays a hint of strain or fatigue.

Coasting through the concrete tunnel between buildings, I think about what Aunt Isobell recently felt compelled to tell me. She'd been pained to say it but felt it necessary to pass on a comment one of her students had made. A female student said that something was being planned that could harm Professor John Staffal. The student was not specific and said she was not personally involved, but was insistent that something was in the works. I tried to assure Aunt Isobell that John was always in trouble, and something was always in the works to take him down. Auntie had bit her lip with consternation at this information, correctly believing that the world would be better off if people were nicer to each other. She asked her student if what she had heard might in any way be construed as the possibility of physical harm, and the student thought not, so nothing out of the ordinary. Still, something is in the air, even if the university is a place where everything and nothing are always in the air. If I was capable of being worried, now would be the time. Good thing I'm not capable.

Try as I might, my almost-on-time arrival is always greeted by a closed door. Maxi, our esteemed SAP's EA is supposed to book these meetings in a room with an automatic door opener, which many of the meeting rooms in our university are equipped with. If ever I remind her that promised accessibility didn't happen, she feigns surprise. In the university, intention—even if never intended—is enough. On the bright side, Zigo doesn't get to strut his stuff often enough, so when confronted with locked doors he gets to bark to high heaven. And speaking of strutting, once the door is opened and we are confronted by upset people not understanding what a big sacrifice it is for me to arrive by 9:10 a.m., Zigo gets to walk in, wagging his tail like a whirling dervish. His pride in such moments makes me think he's part peacock.

I stupidly smile at people by way of greeting before reverting to a habitual static grin, otherwise known as my meeting mask. Some people smile—at least those not still wearing a mask years after Covid—but do not look me in the eye even as I pass close by at eye level. That is, until I meet Smokey, who lights up and loudly says, "Hey, bro, gimme one." At this I hold up my limp hand and smack his, our sporting-inspired, post-Covid, guy-centric, most inappropriate substitute for a gimme five. Smokey then gives Zigo a hardy petting, congratulating his piercing bark that announced to the world that we were trapped outside. Smokey's petting locates a deep itch, and Zigo enjoys the boisterous scratch with wagging tail beating on the ancient metal heating unit like a big drum. The room waits for toxic masculinity to cease and desist. Smokey mumbles and becomes quiet, Zigo lies down anticipating slumber with one colossal snort, and I resurrect fanciful images as refuge from boredom. The meeting begins.

The Special Adviser to the President, Student Exceptional Experience presides, minions wait with bated breath, and my grin widens to the harmonious lull of Zigo's and Smokey's endearing snore.

Silence almost established, the Special Adviser to the President's voice rises. "First a few announcements."

Smokey snorts, half awake, half listening, but does not speak. He might wake up or just as likely he'll revert to semi-slumber. I say, "Bet ya there's a big announcement about the university buying the convent next door."

"No way, man," Smokey answers. "I like those little nuns you see in their gardens sometimes. Where in the world would they go?"

"I don't think they care."

"When I was a kid, we used to steal vegetables, and they had a nice apple orchard too. We used to call the nuns penguins 'cause of the way they dressed. I remember once I had a bag full of apples, and one of the nuns ran after me.

I couldn't believe anyone could run so fast in one of them penguin outfits, but she was fast. Hey, are your kidding 'bout the convent being sold?"

"No, I think it's coming. If she makes the announcement, do me a favor and ask how much they are paying."

"Sure man. That's a good question, but I doubt ...."

"Our student surveys," the SAP resumes, "once again speak very favorably to our successful student service portfolio. We have achieved a 97 percent approval rating, up from 88 percent last year."

People clap and feign excitement.

The SAP's smarmy Swiss-army knife minion Tim turns and tears off his post-Covid, pre-next-deadly-virus mask for dramatic effect. "No doubt because of your leadership."

Heads nod, and Kendra adds, "And 97 percent satisfaction puts us among the top universities in the country."

More applause. I vaguely wonder how a high percentage student satisfaction survey can place a university among top universities. It seems more likely that an inverse relationship exists between subjective satisfaction and objective achievement. Being satisfied in life doesn't tend to get the job done. Such thoughts are never discussed at these meetings.

The SAP says, "And we improved on several other important metrics. Students gave an 89 percent approval for our safe space network, the only criticism being we do not have more safe spaces available within the academic precinct. As you know, faculty enlightenment tends to lag rather far behind our student service example."

As people giggle at this bold truism, Tim takes the opportunity to add a highly anticipated comment. "I'm sure we all agree that *we* can't share in taking credit for your great leadership."

Our very own SAP allows for a slight curve of the lip by way of acknowledgment. Greatness and humility prevent her from responding with words.

"How many spaces are there now?" the Director of Student Mental Wellness, Mindfulness, and Life Balance, asks.

"Fifty-one, but I'm working with the president on getting the deans to commit funds so that we can create a requisite number of safe spaces within each faculty."

"Will they support you?" asks Zeeander Stevens, Director of the Center for Campus Compassion and Caring.

"The deans are getting resistance from faculty who seem to think office space is more important than safe space."

People giggle at such absurdity, until a simple facial reflex communicates that she wishes to continue.

"The president and I can be very persuasive, and I will remind the deans that a comprehensive network of safe spaces is a central pillar of our mental health strategy. If we fall short of that outcome, they will have to answer to the Board of Governors. One of the outcome measures I take particular pride in is our student self-assessment of personal resiliency up from 78 percent to 81 percent. You'll remember that during the Covid crisis we dropped by 12 percent ...."

Smokey seems to come alive in surges throughout these long meetings, and he has a surge. "Um, there seems to be something missin'." Smokey doesn't attend many of these meetings, and when he does, he usually doesn't speak. Still, when an idea comes into his head, he sometimes speaks without much regard for who he is speaking to, just as he often talks before having fully formed what he intends to say. His unbridled lack of emotional regulation coupled with his compulsive disregard for sucking up is refreshing. "I thought I read that there was some concern about outcomes," he muses. Now Smokey isn't a troublemaker, at least not in my league of making trouble, but he does have this little thing called common sense that he doesn't always rein in. He is the spectacular exception among those for whom commonsensical acuity is about as unlikely as St. Jude's finding its lost cause.

"Graduation rates," I whisper, major troublemaker in action.

"Oh, yeah, um, didn't I read that there is concern over graduation rates dropping?"

She, who does not tolerate amusement, is not amused. "I am focusing on positive outcomes."

Smokey can never see how an icy tone is prelude to fireworks, so he continues. "I just can't help thinking, you know, that maybe after spending all that time and money, it might be more important for a student to graduate than to be satisfied." My own survey of one indicates that nothing is more satisfying than when Smokey blurts out what I'm thinking.

The SAP is self-assured and quick on the draw, usually. When she does not respond quickly, the seconds until she does answer act as gauge to mounting anger. "Do you know what my title is?"

"Sure, Tim must say it about fifty times every meeting," Smokey answers, as my plastered grin widens.

"An exceptional student experience is the lifeblood of existence. An exceptional student experience is what makes our university's reputation, and that is achieved to the extent students self-assess their personal safety and happiness."

"Hum." Smokey listens, considers and strokes his chin, denoting rare male listening skill and deep insight. "So students come to university to be happy?" But before the SAP can answer, Smokey continues, "I didn't think feeling good or satisfied about something was an outcome, I thought it was just a feeling. Reminds me of a funny story my grandmother told me when I was a boy. She used to tell me that we are just about as happy as we make up our minds to be. And anyway, one day—"

"We do not have time for stories," the ice queen admonishes. "We have an agenda."

I'll say you do, I don't say, except to myself for my own amusement.

Smokey stops asking questions and mutters to himself as the meeting agenda progresses. I lean over and whisper, "Hey, Smokey, the Nobel Peace Prize is in the mail."

"Gemme one," he responds, before asking if I know who won the hockey game last night.

At which point, outward mask in place, I go inward. My way of dealing with meetings, bumper-to-bumper traffic, bad news, ideological diatribes, or awakenings at false dawn is to create elaborate scenarios, flights of fancy or escape hatches that are both elaborate and fancy. I was like that as a kid, but between chasing appetite and appeasing ego, it faded. Still, because of Irene, the uber warm, lifesaving hospital cleaner, I resurrected this frivolous, nonsensical, immature way of thinking and became both a day and nighttime dreamer, which saved my life. And then early this morning with the creeping smidgen of light that divides night from day, my false dawn revery became revelation. A plot line and a couple of characters I can really work with were inexplicably born to my imagination. Today, I am a writer, I mused (whether or not I ever commit the fermentation of creative juices to the written word).

For a few seconds the meeting intrudes into my daytime reverie with a report from the Sorority of Safety in their fight against male toxicity. My concentration lapse happens when several directors briefly turn to the back of the room at the mention of male toxicity where Smokey and I sit marinating in our respective toxicity. I'm not convinced we represent toxicity or just profound silliness—granted, a very male version. Still, I do not like work intruding on creativity. I take note, I'll have to watch that.

Okay, back to mentally rehearsing for up my upcoming bestselling novel and hit film. I've alluded to schemes to kill Hitler before he's able to wreak havoc on the world. I now think my allusion might not be illusion. The thought process began at the rehab center the day after Irene saved me with the revelation that I could no longer use anger and bitterness as my reason for being. With ten days of bed-rest boredom to kill, I remembered a short book I'd read years earlier about the many attempts on Hitler's life. As I began to improvise on what I knew, the clock, which had never ticked during previous days and torturous nights, slowly began to move. I don't know why I pondered this particular problem; I just knew that whenever I started thinking about the logistical details of the ridiculous preventative Hitler narrative, I exited self for a better place. More than anything else, I needed to exit self. Any place was better than being me.

I must have mentioned something to Irene, not sure, but the next night, Peter, an older, career orderly came into my room with a copy of a book called *Those Who Tried to Kill Hitler*. He began reading out loud, like he enjoyed it, all night long—all 262 pages, all digested in one colossal gulp, and I frickin' loved every page. I've reread it and other related books many times after that night, and the over thirty documented attempts on Hitler's life combined with my fertile imagination have given me infinite capacity for escape. Escape from insomnia (doesn't happen often, I admit), escape from the arrival of late attendants (happens far too often when Brenda is not working), escape from meetings, and most of all, escape from this frickin' meeting at this moment. I'm an avoidance junky.

So why this particular obsession? Because Hitler's megalomaniac ways could have been stopped, and the fact is, most of the attempts on his life could have been successful. Which leads to the further fact that Hitler had staggering luck throughout his entire reign of terror. We're talking about a storytelling opportunity or obsession of infinite possibilities. So what was his destructive legacy? In directly causing the Second World War, his body count was an impossible-to-contemplate sixty-five million people, of which six million or two thirds of Europe's Jewish population was murdered in the most horrific crime against humanity in world history.

Killing Hitler would have been a serious preventative measure against needless death, but I need something more. Or less. The brutality and astonishing numbers of Hitler's evils are monumental, but my assassination rumination is not only about killing a mass murderer. I want, I hunger, to do something worthwhile—no doubt related to my first two decades of being useless. I need a narrative, a story, something personal. So my early morning revelation has given me a few factual bricks, and together with some fictitious mortar, I've got a storyline to massage for the next one hundred meetings.

"…a new comprehensive digital system within Human Resources to provide DEI training, with enhanced modules on critical race, gender, and the emerging multiplicity of intersectionalization theory, will follow up and monitor faculty and staff until we have 100 percent compliance…"

Or DIE trying, I think. But it is the thought of having to write down ruminations rather than simply ruminate that causes my momentary lapse in concentration. How I deal with landing back into the unreality of reality is to expand my outward grin and go further inward where this meeting, all meetings, don't exist.

The following are my escapist musings from the continually residing mind, easily accessed and perpetually stored on iCloud 9, rendering the act of writing conveniently redundant:

By Phelim O'Neill

> *"The hottest place in hell is reserved for those who, in a moment of moral crisis, opt for their own neutrality."*
> —Dante Alighieri, Italian poet, The Divine Comedy, 1320

Swiss neutrality is overrated. No, worse: is grotesquely misleading. The task we are required to fulfill is not to dispassionately sit on the sidelines while being lauded for restraint and wisdom, but to investigate, weigh, inform ourselves, and then in the absence of ego we are required to not only take a side but pursuit it to the ends of the earth.

Early in 1939, I was a twenty-two-year-old Ivy League bored brat, watching life from the sidelines—that is, from books, innate discussions, and endless Harvard lectures disconnected from the havoc of the emerging conflict in Europe. I'd become convinced that something unprecedented was happening the previous November, when the Nazis burned Jewish businesses and synagogues and then killed and imprisoned Jewish citizens of Germany in a night of infamy called Kristallnacht.

My dad, who was German-born, had been a successful American industrialist, single-handedly creating Amberg Aluminum, later called ALCOA. His name was Frederick Amberg, and I inherited both his goofy name as well as his Aryan features. Before he died, when I was fifteen, he had been insistent that we maintain our German heritage, even as we embraced the American way of life. I was fluent in German and spoke passable French and Italian, all of which made me an American anomaly. I was completing a degree in history and linguistics, was being encouraged to go to graduate school with a promising academic career to follow. But I was hollow; I wanted to live; I'd never even been to Europe. I was looking for some sort of fulfillment that my present life could never fulfill.

And then I met Roma.

She would have been a standout among Harvard blond, blue-eyed beauties, except for her cultivated dowdiness. To the Harvard frivolous and fashion-conscious, her attempts to cover and obscure was somewhat successful, but to my well-honed eyes, she had muted beauty that her self-conscious cloak could never hide. She had impenetrable tangles of blond hair, large, impossibly large inquiring brown eyes, and curvaceous perfection that even deliberate and modest attempts to cover and hide, could only accentuate. Whether it was conceit or discernment of her singular beauty, I was particularly smitten for the exclusivity of my impression. I was never interested in the girl everyone else wanted, whose attempt at fashioning self was to ensure being wanted by all who saw. I wasn't interested in sharing. Besides, a relationship of any depth is ultimately based on recognition and not seduction.

There in the middle of Harvard Square, she paused, intent on something, her attention far removed from me as I admired her, examined her, fell for her. I considered a ruse, an excuse, some credible reason why I could talk to her, but there was none. Still, eventually I came across her reading a Thomas Hardy novel in Harvard Square, and I fumbled with superficial words to mask deep desire. I shouldn't have worried, for our conversations were instantly deep and combustible and, to my everlasting gratitude, soon became intimate. In talking English, German, and soon even some Polish, her native tongue, we were honest, truthful, naked to each other, always. We were each to the other a revelation, a surprise, and least expected, we became what was valued most.

Since freshman year, I'd been sculling on the Charles, seven a.m. every morning, and I'd made the Harvard rowing team. In this, my final undergraduate year, I also took on acting, and I'd made a Harvard theater troupe with a major play in the works later in the term. But once I met Roma, I barely even made it to class and only did that because she insisted we keep up with coursework. She felt an obligation to her brother and her family to be successful and complete her degree.

Her story was complicated even before it became tragic. Her brother had been *the* Harvard designate but had been killed in an auto accident shortly after arriving in the States. Her father, with some American contacts, managed to get Roma into her brother's spot the following year. The need for this arrangement had to do with Harvard's Jewish quota and not Roma's academic qualifications, which were stellar. Being a woman was also a disadvantage.

Roma had always wanted to come to the States for school, but with anti-Semitism in full flight and tensions between Poland and Germany growing, she had been reluctant to leave Warsaw. What she didn't know was that these were the same reasons why her father was determined for her to leave. When Germany invaded Poland on September 1, 1939, Roma frantically tried to call home but could not get through for another two days. Once connected, Roma told her father that she was coming home, but her father insisted that she not come. When Roma resisted, her father told her that there were thirty-five relatives living in their Warsaw apartment at that very moment, with more threatening to arrive soon. Her father had conveyed, and she then understood that the life she had left, the life of her childhood, was over. I was her only consolation, she later told me, and the irony was not lost on either of us that her sole consolation came from knowing a blond, blue eyed, Aryan poster boy of German ethnicity.

Though I would have followed her to the ends of the earth—which is pretty well what happened—I have to admit that part of my motivation was to show her how much I despised the German stereotype, perversely emulated by the Nazis, which I would never be.

For a year, we languished in the purgatory of inertia, asking ourselves what we could do, knowing that the answer was nothing. The news out of Poland was bad. Germany had overrun and conquered Poland in a matter of weeks. Roma had only sparse news of her family, with nothing that could give hope. They lived in a state of deprivation and never knew what new indignity might next descend upon them. And, worse, they had no idea if they would survive these multiple indignities for any possibility of a future life. The greatest deprivation is always to be deprived of hope.

Roma had been despondent for months, and although she tried not to show it for my sake, I knew she was not sure if she wanted to live. Also, there were stories beginning to emerge from Europe about German atrocities, particularly against Poles and Jews, of which Roma's family were both. We became very close, but our love could not answer the question that haunts: if you lose everyone you have ever known, who has ever been family and provided context, who are you? Such thoughts were painful, but in the few times she could be convinced to speak, she intimated that such bleak talk was the torture she sometimes needed to endure.

Still, one day, Roma facetiously floated—this being the closest she had come to making a joke since the invasion of Poland—that being two blond Aryan-looking types, maybe we should go to Germany.

Which I realized was what we needed to do, which is what we did—in time, though neither together nor even in the same year. Still, the imperative to do something drove us toward what can only be described as inspired insanity. In doing nothing, Roma had nothing to live for, and in not doing anything for Roma, I was the same. Besides, after a life of privilege and comfort, I liked the long and unlikely shot. I, in my foolish and idealistic way, welcomed deprivation and hardship without fully understanding the reality of life's essentials denied. Whether to save or vindicate her family, we were going to kill Hitler. The reasons to kill the Führer totaled in the many millions of lives lost, but Roma's direct family was our motivation. This was personal.

I'd always operated on instinct, but now I—that is, we—needed a plan.

At which point, Smokey snorts awake, blinks, and looks around as if he has just descended from Mars. A voice unseen from the front of the room drones into our serenity with persnickety persistent monotones from the pages of a new and important report.

"…positivity best describing the initial findings of our three-year DEI employment initiative. Since this is the first major research or study of lived experience pertaining to the multiple aspects of intersectionality that chronicles our endeavors to capture both statistical, objective data, as well as the far more encompassing personal and subjective actual daily concerns of people struggling against historic as well as newly imposed societal challenges, barriers and negatively entrenched attitudes from the dominant groups of oppression for whom the realities of DEI existence does not penetrate the exteriors of privilege …"

"Are they talkin' 'bout work?" Smokey asks.

"I think the title had the word *employment* in it, but not sure about the content." We had all received this report by email attachment days ago, and while I was never going to read it, I did note that this masterful narrative of nothingness was 168 pages long.

"…for which over a year of intense discussion and consultation with all the representative groups as well as unique individuals, however they chose to define themselves—which as we all know in our academic as well as deeply entrenched personal lived experience often manifests itself as justifiable opposition to limiting boxes and arbitrary categories imposed by the unenlightened, whose unlived poverty privilege is witnessed and captured and catalogued by the knowing and self-aware creative work of equity constituents—in order that we understand, analyze and expose barriers and limitations, and what our initiative along with creative co-contributors wish to receive from their valued participation, offered insight, and experiential narrative. We, who are privileged to study and record for posterity, refuse to impose our expectations of outcome onto those for whom the creativity of contribution in work as well as life are not marred by the necessity to gather income…"

"Huh?" Smokey says rather loudly, which in this assembled group is rather a no-no. "Isn't studying employment supposed to be 'bout getting a job?"

There is no answer. Smokey does not rebut the silence, the moment passes, and the monotone resumes.

I decide I really need to fly to Sweden and pick up and hand-deliver that Nobel Prize to Smokey by day's end.

My dad's brother, Uncle Leon, has always been the family black sheep. Though he lived in California, and sometimes a year would pass without contact, we'd somehow become close. He always encouraged me to be my own man, be a rebel, take life by the horns. He had not been keen on my choice of going to Harvard and had suggested I gain some life experience before inhaling a life of theory without consequence. In the first five minutes of our first conversation Uncle Leon understood that in taking his long-standing advice, I was going to go to Germany with or without his support. And after convincing him that we were serious about killing Hitler, even if it was a suicide mission, his help was needed more than ever. Besides, once he met Roma and predictably fell in love as had I, he was putty in our hands. As for Roma and me, we shared feelings of gratitude to black sheep in general and to Uncle Leon in particular.

Uncle Leon admonished us not to make an attempt unless it was feasible—which in his definition included some chance for us to escape—before agreeing to bank us and help get us contacts with people who would be essential to the operation. After Dad died, even as the family black sheep, Uncle Leon had become involved in Amberg Aluminum, and the company continued to be very profitable. Money was never going to be a problem.

He said we wouldn't get State Department support, but he just happened to know an official who could get us a couple of fake German passports. That person in turn had a contact in the American embassy in Berlin to whom we would never make full disclosure about why we were in Germany, but who could help us in a country we had never visited, among people we did not know, pursuing a task that was impossible to complete. Our American embassy contact knew a closet anti-Nazi of high rank, with ties to the American embassy who might be able to help us, though if Germany and the United States went to war, we were warned that we would be on our own.

Still, we had a credible ruse. The United States passively supported Britain and France in the phony war that had been declared and, except for the invasion of Poland, had not begun. The United States was determined to stay out of this war, had many ties and some sympathy for Germany, and fully intended to maintain an isolationist policy, despite Churchill's many enticements. Besides, Hitler had been on the cover of *Time* magazine in 1938 as the Man of the Year, proving he was no tyrant. For most of 1941, it wasn't an American war.

And there was business to consider. With some help from neutral countries such as Switzerland and Sweden, and with the United States as yet a passive enemy, companies such as GM, Ford, Dupont, Standard Oil, ALCOA, and IBM continued business with Germany. (Historical note: IBM provided Hitler with the technical expertise to catalogue the Jewish population for the enactment of the Final Solution and resultant Holocaust. ALCOA was so generous in its supply of aluminum to Germany for its Luftwaffe's aerial expansion that the US did not have enough aluminum to build airplanes in response to the attack on Pearl Harbor.)

Ironically, we were able to use our actual connection with ALCOA, as bait for making false connections in Germany.

"One more thing," the Special Adviser to the President says, with an uncharacteristic smile on her face. "Our students are not the only people whose satisfaction rate is high and rising."

Her minions respond to this kitschy bit of intrigue with appropriate enthusiasm and curiosity.

Tim responds with "It sounds like Christmas!"

The Director of Self-Awareness and Leadership holds up her hand before speaking as she does in recent years, even in a conversation of two. It is her signature, a stylistic imperative, an individual expression of unconventional convention signaling the intention of speaking before speaking so that she can painstakingly remove her mask to all assembled. People—the pain-stake recipients—patiently wait, their placid faces masking a desire to grab her neck and scream *hurry up* into her masked-up face. "Oh, can we please reference an occasion that is not fraught with oppression and exclusion?"

"And refrain from any allusion to Christianity?" the Director of Campus Compassion adds.

"What about the summer solstice?" The Director of Equitable Social Justice Outcomes offers.

"Are Wiccans religious?" the Director of Self-Awareness and Individual Respect asks.

"I can't imagine after the way they have been persecuted," the Director of Student Leadership and Engagement reflects.

"Actually, they believe in a goddess, a triple goddess, I'm fairly certain, representing the moon, the earth, and childbirth, or more relevant to feminists, their treeing archetypal significance represents the maiden, the mother, and the crone, so they are definitely not misogynistic. And with a pagan goddess as the spiritual symbol, they were very progressive, back even, um, then," the Director of Environmental Solidarity ventures to add.

"The question is, when was then?" the Director of Student Mental Wellness, Mindfulness, and Life Balance posits.

At which point Smokey's interest piques, again, and he stirs. "Eh? Goddess, you say?"

Smokey always interprets nonanswer as agreement and continues, "Bet you didn't know that those crafty Wiccan pagans had two gods, a goddess for sure, but they also had the Horned God. Ha! Bet you didn't know that. Of course, the horn could mean many things, but I'm sure it meant one thing for sure. Know what I mean? Reminds me when I was in college—"

The Special Adviser to the President, Exceptional Student Experience's smile is gone. "I was about to make an announcement."

The living Swiss Army knife shushes us all long and loudly and, with a sad look on his face, feels duty bound to apologize to our morally supine SAP on behalf of the group.

Our SAP continues without acknowledging the apology or Smokey's deep knowledge of Wiccan folklore. "I am very pleased to announce," which is a curious choice of words for someone with a deeply scornful expression, "that subject to the formality of approval from the Board of Governors, we will be purchasing the old adjoining convent building and grounds—and fully thirty acres of prime land in our downtown that has been underutilized for growing carrots, of all things, for our new DEI Center!"

The room erupts in applause.

I lean toward Smokey, stretching my wretched spine in the mix, and whisper, "Told you so."

"Well, I'll be," Smokey says, without taking his eyes from the front of the room. Then with curious indiscretion in full flight, he loudly asks, "How much did it cost, and where did you get the money?"

In the midst of enthusiastic applause, our esteemed SAP either misses or chooses not to respond to Smokey's unanswered questions, nor to the same, asked again.

And in deference to she-who-chooses-not-to-respond, the entire group pretends they have not heard Smokey's questions, asked twice. And yet these are *the* questions that need answers. I'm tempted to erase my silly, compliant grin for straight-faced, penetrating questions. A louder repeat of Smokey's questions, that is. But knowing the answers, I hold my tongue, hold my grin, and hold off asking questions, for now.

CHAPTER TWELVE

Next day, still early December, at the Center

Next day is a rarity—I don't have any scheduled meetings. Of course, there is that one little detail about me not really going to most of my scheduled meetings, making scheduled or not a moot point. Still, it is nice to settle in with my peeps at 11 a.m. sharp and deal with our whirlwind of details, lamentations, demands, acts of kindness, and disasters. Whichever from the proceeding list will take precedence for the day usually greets me first upon my rather conspicuous arrival.

First Luna, who is usually first. "You still haven't responded to the SAP about the DEI employment plan. If we have to cancel any contracts, we should give them as much time as possible to look for something else."

"So, we are talking about…?"

"David and Arthur," she replies. "White hetero males, so no status, target on their back, and no sympathy, except from us, which does not pay the bills. That won't be enough, but it's a start."

"And of course," Iggy adds, "we're screwed without Dr. A. doing assessments and David's e-learning and web work."

Luna turns back to me with a nod. "Yeah, so any ideas?"

"A couple," I answer coyly, which Luna always hates.

"You are so frustrating," she says, with love, as she wheels from my office to her next waiting student.

With Luna tied up, I hope to be able to check emails before the next interruption. But I should know by now such hope is hopeless. Perry, who I really need to talk to, appears from nowhere, as he tends to do. "Hey, glad you're here," I say. "I wanted to tell you that I emailed your manager a foolproof plan to keep you here at least until the end of next term. We're backlogged with testing that needs to get done, and hell, we've got funding, so we'll relieve them of their cost-sharing obligation so they can't say no. Dr. A. is going to write a support letter today to back me up, 'cause he can't possibly move the assessment backlog without you to tag-team with, so should get agreement back soon."

Perry is impassive. No, not quite true. He is unresponsive but looks almost serene. "It's done, last day. Carol said I can celebrate my last day by leaving, and when I didn't immediately vacate, she asked me to leave so they could repurpose my office. Just dropped by to say bye. You made me promise to do that.

"It's okay," he says, in response to the look on my face, and again, that frustrating look of serenity.

"The hell it's okay," I fume. "Dr. A. says he's got more than thirty people waiting for you, and I have no idea what else you were doing for Career Services, but …."

No response is worse than *it's okay*, so I blunder on, "I'm still going to talk to her. It doesn't make sense."

"More time to write," Perry says blankly, looking at the storm of students gathering in front of our reception area. Then, smiling, "And hey, I might even use that as a title."

"What?"

"It Doesn't Make Sense. Suits the novel I'm doing just now."

"I'll look into this and get back to you."

"Sure."

"Promise me you'll stay in touch."

"Sure," Perry answers in retreat and is gone.

You really do fill me with foreboding, I think, turning to face my number-one office wife.

"Boss?" Edie says, before coughing, with more gusto than last week. "Got time for Kevin? He's been waiting for over an hour. Says it's important."

"Sure. Um, Edie," I begin, noticing that her ribald and indefatigable self seems somewhat deflated, "you okay?"

She looks down the hallway, then eases into my office and closes the door. "I don't want you to worry, boss," she starts, and pauses.

"Okay, how 'bout I don't worry if you tell me you are okay and mean it."

"Well, thing is, I need to tell you something, but I don't want a lot of fuss. In fact, after I tell you, I want you to shut your gob and let me get back to work, or at least jump onto Barry's lap."

Our habitual ribald repartee is flat. I wait.

"Test results came back, and I've got lung cancer."

It's been fifteen years since Edie threw a wet blanket over her two-pack-a-day habit. Though she hated exercise—except for jumping men's bones, she always clarified—she'd gone to the gym for an exercise class twice a week for years because that is what people who intend to live forever do. If that wasn't enough, she spent all her waking hours being funny, being positive, and in short, doing everything possible to insulate her life against misfortune, disease, and cancer. And yet here she was.

It takes me a while to process, and even as the word "speechless" comes into my foggy consciousness, pathetic words fall from my gob. "Edie, I'm so sorry—"

She holds up both hands and smiles, that face-altering, beyond-expressive expression of happiness and good intention. "None of that. I'm starting treatment, going to need the odd morning or afternoon off, which I'll make up, of course, but it's all good, and I do not want your sorry mug showing anything else. And I expect you'll make sure to keep everything the same with our peeps out there."

"Don't worry about being here when you have treatment. Chemo can be—"

"I never said I was going to get chemo."

My face goes blank. She waits, enjoying my confusion. "I'm getting both chemo *and* radiation." And she laughs, her loud and loopy, fulsome belly laugh, the DNA of our CSD.

I open my mouth, but she beats me, as she always does, to the punch line. "Now shut your gob! If I need anything I'll let you know, and what you need to know right now is I need my peeps. And one of them is outside and has been waiting for an hour and ten minutes, so you'd better get to Kevin."

Our eyes meet for a moment before she leaves. Neither humor nor the seriousness of life, neither avoidance nor denial. We look at each other and understand. We are family, and this thing that has invaded her, us, will never change that. Beyond mutual recognition, it is hard to know what she is thinking, but easy to figure what I am thinking. I'm worried.

I turn toward my computer but realize I will not have time to check emails before Kevin wheels in. I look at my meeting table nearby where I do most of my work. That is, where I mix it up with my extended peeps called students, which is my life's work and not to be confused with all the debris and noise otherwise endured in this institution of lower learning.

Before Kevin deconstructs my walls, I notice a notepad on the table with a sheet ripped off and a note for me. The note is precise, and most notably, scripted with perfect cursive writing. So I look at it, admiring, wondering, and I look again. Apparently, one of my long-standing regular students had been waiting for me—poor things frequently do have to wait—and the phone must have rung. The message is confirmation of the auditorium booking I made for an upcoming campus debate intended to wake St. Jude's up from its narrow-minded wokeness—leaving it wide awoke. A phone number and contact name are included. But what is uncommon about this passing of common information is the source, the notetaker, my unofficial secretary on this occasion.

The note is signed by Rafi, which is redundant because I recognize his— I'll say handwriting—though it is anything but. I've known Rafi for thirty years, as he has come and gone, progressing through three degrees. He is finishing a PhD, which he is never going to apply to the work world, but which he must finish for reasons that are astonishingly simple and hard to fathom. He was born a full thalidomide, that is, without arms or legs, due to a drug developed in the late 1950s to help pregnant women deal with morning sickness. The drug worked and women were relieved of morning sickness, though the price paid for that relief continues to send concentric waves through time. For reasons never fully understood, thalidomide remained on the market for years as thousands of babies were affected, until someone made the connection to the phenomenon of "flipper limbs," and the drug was withdrawn.

Rafi's case was particularly unfortunate because the drug had been off the market for years when his mother reached into her bedroom drawer, pulled out an old vial of pills, and took the drug. So how did Rafi write a phone message and leave it as a perfect, seemingly common record of the miraculous? On his left side he had maybe six inches of a stump that, combined with his adept mouth, dexterous shoulder, and a simple expandable watch band at the end of his very short almost limb, made him a message-taking marvel. Still, for all that, perhaps most remarkable, and becoming less common, is Rafi's considerable consideration.

Looking up, I see Kevin's wheelchair forewarning of deconstructive intent. In truth, he remains innocent despite scarred wall carnage along the entire length of corridor to the elevator. When someone recently admonished Kevin for his idiosyncratic driving habits, to everyone's surprise he was completely unaware. So we decided that his handiwork is a kitschy installation extraordinaire. In middle age, Kevin is not about to relearn how to drive, so we are relearning how to interpret scarred walls.

"Is-is-is it okay to t-t-t-t-talk?"

"Hi, Kevin, come on in."

Kevin bounces between the doorframe, which makes him frustrated, causing him to lurch forward and, being frustrated, he overshoots and repositions my table a foot or so from where it was. We pretend not to notice.

"How was your weekend?" I ask. This question elicits silence. I know something is up when his habitual introductory Papal bastard insult is neglected. "Okay, so what's on your mind? You've got the look of a man with something to say and the temperament to say it."

Kevin's lips quiver. It's not easy for him to talk at the best of times, and this is clearly not the best of times. My impulse to talk, especially when Kevin slurs or pauses for long periods as he tends to do, is something I've learned with deliberate effort to temper.

"I-I-I … had a t-t-t-terrible weekend."

"Oh?" I say, by way of encouragement, without trying to say too much.

"I-i-it's not G-G-George's fault."

"Our George?" George is one of our campus attendants who does some shifts at Kevin's apartment. As far as I know, Kevin and George have become friends, and I think George feels some obligation to continue with Kevin out of friendship. Friendship between clients and attendants is not exactly encouraged, but nor do we discourage it. If it happens, it happens, and we don't impose artificial boundaries on the limited contact some people have in their lives. Kevin is lonely and has difficulty making friends, even among those who are paid to hang about. George is a good guy, has movie-star looks, and is built like a brick house, and while we could have given him all the shifts he needed in our program on campus, he travels to Kevin's apartment because he is a good guy. Still, for all Kevin's difficulty connecting with people, for some few he can develop a hero-worshipping relationship which has caused concern in the past.

Kevin nods his head as his eyes well with tears. He is not a fan of vulnerability, least of all his own, and spasms with frustration before continuing. "I-I-I-I-I ...."

I reason this is going to take a while, which can be an accurate gauge of Kevin's level of upset. Whenever he finds it particularly difficult to enunciate a word or phrase, he tries to compensate by spitting out the offending verbal detritus. "...didn't, didn't, didn't m-m-m-mean anything."

"I believe you. So what's the problem?"

"D-d-did George talk to you?"

"Nope. Should he?"

"N-n-n-n-n-no! I d-d-d-didn't mean anything, so p-p-p-p-please tell him th-th-th-that, if he does t-t-t-t-t-talk to you."

"Okay. Care to explain?"

"N-n-n-n-no."

"Okay, so are we done?" Kevin knows I won't kick him out, and we both know that he wants to divest but needs a metaphoric kick in the pants.

"I'm n-n-n-n-not gay."

"Not sure that makes any difference to me. I'll love you whether or no."

Kevin's tears start down along deep tracks in his face. "I-I-I-I-I did a s-s-s-stupid thing, but I'm not g-g-g-gay."

"What did you do?"

Kevin swipes without effect at the unaccustomed tears blurring his vision. His self-disgust is palpable. "W-we watched a m-m-m-movie together. I was on the c-c-c-c-couch. W-w-w-when it was over, I d-d-d-didn't want him to leave." Long pause. "W-w-w-w-when he helped me t-t-t-t- transfer to my chair, it j-j-j-j-just c-c-c-came out." And now the crescendo of repressed emotion and the floodgate of tears. "I-I-I asked him if, if, if he w-w-w-w-would hold me."

Neither of us speak. I know if I speak too soon, I'll scare Kevin off before he's finished. Almost in a whisper Kevin finishes, "I just d-d-d-didn't want him to l-l-l-leave. S-s-s-sorry."

I stretch my ever-warping spine before leaning forward and almost out of my chair. I buy about thirty seconds time before straightening up again. "Listen, Kevin."

I wait for him to lift his head and look at me, which eventually he does. "You didn't do anything wrong. I get it, and whether or not you are gay doesn't matter. It just doesn't. Do you understand? You're just human, that's all. Being lonely is a fact of life, not a fault of character."

"B-b-b-but he doesn't w-w-w-want to work with me anymore."

I love my job, but not always, and there are times, many actually, when I really don't know what to say, end up saying something, anything because I really don't know what to say. "Well, he probably doesn't understand. But I do. And it's okay."

A glimmer. "Y-y-y-you do?"

"Yes, I do. I really do."

Edie opens my door ever so slightly. "Boss?" Her intonation connotation asks, *Are you finished yet?*

"Kevin, we'll talk about this again in a few days. Okay?"

Kevin almost smiles, "Okay, Papist bastard."

As his wheelchair pounds against first my wall and then my extra-wide door frame, I know he hurts but that he'll get through this. Eventually. And I have this vague thought: *if all you have ever known in life is loneliness, is it loneliness or something else?*

On a crowded planet of eight billion, the theme continues.

My next drop-in student arrives and drops his bag heavily onto my meeting table. I am used to and impervious to attitude.

I glance at his in-take file, but he beats me to it. "Doesn't matter what my name is there, I'm probably changing it. I'm most likely trans and I heard you may not be okay with that."

"Not true." I smile. "Mind if I call you Steve for now?"

"Guess so."

"Well, Steve-for-now, if trans is the best version of yourself, I am fine with that."

Agreement can be disarming. Still, he is not satisfied. "How do I know that's true?"

"Because I just told you, and for all my many faults, I am good for what I say. Is this why you came to see me today, or is there something else I can do for you?"

"I'm ADHD, so might need some accommodations, but I wanted to make sure you're not transphobic first."

"Sure, I understand. When you came in, you said you are most likely trans. Does that mean you are not sure?"

Steve-for-now did not expect this question. He drops his head and clasps his hands, thinking before responding. Moments pass; not moments to interrupt. Then, with irritation, "Of course I'm sure, or at least I was."

"What happened?"

"I posted that I'm trans on social media."

"And?"

"And everyone, and I mean everyone said I was courageous and that it is important that I do it."

"Any dissenting trolls?"

Raising his head, "No, that's the thing, none. Only one person asked, 'Are you sure?' Since then I realize I'm not completely sure, but now that I've put it out there, it's not as if I can just tell people I don't know what I'm talking about."

"Why tell people anything? Why not just take your time and figure it out for yourself?"

Steve-for-now slowly lifts his head again and more slowly speaks, enunciating each painful word. "You don't understand. I need to find who I am. I need to choose. I need to belong."

For all her indiscretions, Edie's soft knock on the door is always indicative of pressing need. But occasionally I can use an interruption for my own devious ends.

"Edie, unless it's life and death, can you check with Iggy to see if the bus leaving at four p.m. today is full?"

As Edie exits, I say, "Let me explain. A while back a staff member made a connection with a seniors home nearby—some checkers, euchre, music, a few laughs, and a free meal—that has become a thing for our Center. So, from the inspiration of a solitary staff member, a group of about thirty staff and students go each week. It's perfect because the seniors are lonely, and the gang from our island of the misfits needs people to accept them. It is a home away from home for some, and the only place to call home for others; in short, and if only for a few hours once a week, a place to belong."

Edie leans in and says, "Thirty-four people, so all full."

"Good. Now can you ask my skinny brother if he can give up his seat and run to the seniors home so that we can assist him training for his next marathon?"

Steve-for-now and Edie chorus "Huh?" as I press on, "That is, if you are in."

As Steve-for-now hesitates, I add, "Since I have other waiting students, why don't we meet again soon, and in the meantime, Edie can more fully explain what our version of belonging is all about."

With the timing and finesse of a ballroom dancer, Edie takes Steve-for-now's arm and escorts him towards the door with the words, "You'll love it! And once you become one of my peeps, your life will never be the same ...."

Yes, I know it is not that simple; our little inclusion will not erase a lifetime of exclusion, and belonging to our group of misfits will not mitigate longing for whatever pervades his nightmares and dreams. Still, and for now.

As Edie's inclusion pep talk fades, Mary's head bends into my office opening. "Have a minute?"

"Sure," I answer, as we both react to a loud crash from the reception area.

Mary's head swings around to take a look before coming back to me. "Kevin hit Angel's bucket and knocked it over. Water everywhere, students sitting with their feet high in the air, and Angel is not pleased."

I sigh as Mary closes my door. Though now alone, Mary lowers her voice and asks, "Do you know when you're going to talk to Diesel? She is working all week, and the guys seem to be the same as ever, so I guess you haven't laid down the law."

I sigh again, before twisting into my regular back-stretching maneuver. People know I need a moment whenever I stretch, which, being true, also gives me avoidance time when I need it. "I talked to the guys briefly, but I haven't talked to Diesel."

I fail to finish the sentence with the word *yet*, which hangs unsaid between us. Mary waits, and I resist the urge to contort myself into another stretch which would definitely have been one of obvious avoidance. "It's been ...." I search for a word, any word other than *busy*.

Edie pops her head back into my office after a single knock, "Boss, you told me to let you know when David is between student appointments, and that would be now, for two minutes."

Saved by the knock, I think, and I even think of another word for busy. "It's been complicated. I'll talk to her, and to the guys too, when I can."

"Okay," Mary says, in a voice that conveys things are not okay, and they probably aren't. Still, I'm not sure where okay is in the Diesel/guys drama. "As long as you don't think we need to do anything immediately, I'll leave it for you to deal with."

If only she knew that *immediately* is not in my vocabulary. David hangs at the door Edie left semi open. Mary takes David's presence as her cue to exit, for which I am grateful.

"Herr Director, you summoned me?"

During the preceding decade David performed miracles for our Center as a contract employee, for which he has always been grateful. I've been frustrated that we have not been able to get him a permanent position in all that time. Still, he is not a creature of resentment and remains grateful because this is the only real job he's ever had after arriving in the U.S. He is fastidious and formal by nature, and it took ten years and Edie's tutelage to train him to occasionally forgo formal for funny. His jokes are rare, but when he does make one, it tends to have biting dryness that we appreciate. He also speaks six languages.

"I've had a thought."

"Even mountains become plains with enough time," he responds.

Like I said, biting, which some of us appreciate. "Yes, so let me plainly tell you that we need to get you some more profile."

"Oh, why so?"

"Let's just say I know you're invaluable, and I want to make sure others know that too so that when decisions about employment come, your case will be stronger."

"Okay, so who am I auditioning my folk dancing to?"

"None other than the SAP, Exceptional Student Experience."

"Wow and how?"

"Good expression and same for question. It won't be enough to make a case for your value to us at the Center. We've got to show that you are indispensable to her, and I think the perfect opportunity has just presented itself.

"Sounds good, almost too good, but I'm listening, and my student isn't here yet."

"Next week, our Dear Leader chairs a new student service committee designed to create communication linkages between all forty-one of her reporting units. Never mind that we both know the stated purpose of communication is really about surveillance and control. The fact is, they have no idea how to do it properly, and after the way you redesigned our scheduling program, newsletter, and interactive website here, I'm sure you can impress the hell out of them. There have also been several positions eliminated in Tech services, and they are having a tough time finding the proper candidates with the proper political identity attributes, so hiring has been slow as molasses. While you don't have a winning political identity, if you take this on, I'll bet they will condescend to let you do a fine and effective job for them. And this isn't just technical; it requires extensive knowledge of student services to do properly."

"Sure."

"Believe it or not, as of now I'm supposed to represent our office, and you probably don't know this about me, but I don't love committee work."

"Ha. No problem."

"Good. I'll make the call to Maxi, and our SAP will be relieved that I will not be on the committee even before she understands that you will solve all her technology and organizational problems. Oh, and David, can you see if either or both of our resident nuns are available?"

"Sure, and great, thanks! You know without you ...."

I cut him off as I always do at this point. "Be gone, wicked wizard." He's expressed enough, more than enough gratitude, and given how much he has contributed over the years, it's misplaced even if heartfelt.

As David leaves, I watch Angel mopping the residue from Kevin's erratic driving. He looks up as his powerful arms sweep his mop across the floor. He is suddenly alert as Aunt Isobell threatens to walk across his floor while it is still wet. Despite his general lack of expression, he can become quite animated and protective. He drops his mop to lend Aunt Isobell a hand for fear she might slip on the wet floor. The ever-gracious Auntie allows this gesture of gallantry, though she doesn't need it, and is delivered safely to my door. Luna wheels in behind her, and Iggy follows. Iggy, worried about something—he is always worried about something—slips on the wet floor despite his nonslip running shoes. He catches himself awkwardly with a quick outstretched hand to his backside.

Aunt Isobell giggles. "I could have taken your arm," she observes.

"How many miles do you run a week?" I ask.

"About a hundred and twenty," Iggy says, without hesitation.

"And over ice and snow, trail and mountain pass?"

Iggy waits for the next question.

"So how often do you slip and fall?"

Iggy has to think about that. "About two years ago, I slipped on a sidewalk with new snow-covered hard ice."

"Guess slipping has more to do with paying attention that what the conditions are like, huh?"

"Is it all right if I'm here for this?" Aunt Isobell asks.

"Of course, you're in our lost cause family now."

"Guess we kind of barged in on you guys," Luna says.

"That's fine," I say. "I was just going to see how our new gals are doing. I also want Auntie participating in our little case conference and hearing how things can go off the rails here."

Luna looks at Iggy. "A tough case. Iggy has a student with mental health issues who wants an accommodation that we said no to, and now she says she's going over his head."

"So is going over Iggy's head going to me or to someone who matters?"

"She's dropping by in a few minutes to see if after consultation I've changed my mind," Iggy says. "I said we always have case conferences for controversial issues. If we don't give her what she wants she says she'll go to the SAP."

"Who with a title that ends with Exceptional Student Experience, will give her whatever she wants," Luna concludes.

"Ah, and there's more," Iggy says. "She also implied that not giving her what she wants could cause her to self-harm, which we would then be responsible for."

"Overlooking the blackmail threat for the moment, what is she asking for?"

"The freedom to hand in all assignments whenever she wants according to how she feels about her mental health at the time," Iggy says.

Edie is at my door. "Iggy, a student is here for you."

Iggy is like a dog in the headlights. He wants to do the right thing, is a genuinely nice guy suspended between hating confrontation and being determined to remain principled.

"Auntie, take a seat, and Edie, ask if she'll step in to see me for a few minutes."

Iggy and Luna look at me, clearly relieved but uncertain what to do. "Begone, young peepsters," I say.

Edie directs a young woman into my office and introduces Aunt Isobell and me to Desdemona. I say that Aunt Isobell is a young new intern, needing experience, and ask if she can join us.

Desdemona does not react to my request, nor to referring to a woman in her mid-eighties as a young intern, so we proceed to the reason for the meeting.

"It's no use trying to convince me not go to the Special Adviser to the President's office. When I started here, we met at orientation, and she told me that if you ever refuse to give me what I want, I can come to her."

She seems slightly disarmed by my big smile. "You know, it's interesting that you should be asking for complete flexibility for handing in assignments."

"Why?" she asks, suspiciously.

"Because Intern Kelly and I were just discussing the findings of a new study on the issue. Now it isn't published yet, but its finding is quite startling."

"I don't need a study to tell me what I want," Desdemona states, with resolve.

And then Auntie, God love her, rises to the occasion. "No, of course not, and yet the study shows that getting what you want doesn't necessarily translate into getting the marks that you want.

"Especially if you're dealing with mental health stressors."

She wavers ever so slightly. "How can getting what I want not help me get the marks that I want?" she asks.

"Because when you extend assignment dates for several courses later into the term, they pile up. Next thing you know, you are dealing with finishing assignments and trying to write exams at the same time. Very stressful."

"Well, I could just extend the assignments again until after exams," Desdemona says, without conviction.

Neither Aunt Isobell not I speak, having set the stage for logic to set in.

"Of course, you have the option to defer exams," Aunt Isobell offers.

"But then I'd have to do assignments and exams for both terms in the same term."

Our work is done here, I think.

"As you think about this," Aunt Isobell offers, "you might consider a couple other options.'

"Like what?"

"Learning strategies would help you deal with getting assignments done."

Desdemona has some fight in her yet. "You're just trying to get me give up handing assignments in when I want to."

"You know you can get that," I answer, "either here or through the Special Adviser to the President's office. It's really just a question of self-interest. Not so much what you want as what you really want."

"And what do I really want?"

"To graduate," I answer.

She wasn't expecting this answer. She turns to Aunt Isobell. "What else?"

"Counseling. We can refer you to a university psychiatrist."

"I don't like doctors. Why can't I come here?"

"Because as soon as you mention the possibility of self-harm, we are obliged to send you to Health Services."

Desdemona's eyes flash, suspended between anger and honesty. "I ... I wasn't serious."

"That's good," Aunt Isobell responds.

"Do you do counseling?" Desdemona asks. "You remind me of my grandmother when she was alive. Even if you don't have much experience ...." Her voice trails off.

"What was the advice you most remember from your grandmother?" I ask.

Desdemona seems to soften for the first time and immediately says, "She used to say don't make excuses." A look comes over her face, like maybe she's given away too much information.

Aunt Isobell saves the day. "Your grandmother was very wise, and I am honored to remind you, old as that might make me, of her. And I would be honored to work with you as long as you show up."

"No excuses," Desdemona answers, with an actual smile.

After that, I don't need to ask Aunt Isobell how she is doing. She is doing fantastic. I need to get to my emails and phone calls because many contentious cases are not going as well as Desdemona's. And Desdemona-like progress does not always happen. I have to talk to the chair of Social Work about a student who claims to have verbal support from the Office of Lost Causes (what some faculty call us) to physically threaten faculty when upset. I decide that I will tell the chair that we also give out lucrative contracts to kill faculty when they don't behave. The dean of Civil Engineering wants to know why we would ever approve an accommodation that requires an exam to be held on a day other than formally scheduled. It is something we rarely ask for, and there is good reason when we do. I will tell him that, and he will tell me it is too much work for faculty to have to write a separate exam for one student. We won't agree, but the discussion will be civil, which is why they call it civil engineering, I guess. Good thing because we have the same discussion every term.

Maxi, the executive assistant to the Special Adviser to the President, Exceptional Student Experience, wants to know where we are with our pending strategic plan to fulfill Diversity, Equity, and Inclusion employment objectives. (So, SAP, ESE's EA for DEI BS, for those taking shorthand). I will say three things. One, we went out of our way to hire students from diverse racial, religious, and sexual orientations decades before it became a thing. Two, in serving students with learning and psychiatric disabilities, as well as those with autism, Asperger's syndrome, head injury, and sensory and physical disabilities, we have the greatest neurodiversity of any office on campus, and since a university is where we work, surely diversity of the mind is more important than the externals of identity. Three, I will ask her, who has all the answers, to answer this—what else should we be doing?—not aspirational concepts, not using words such as inclusion and diversity to answer how to be more diverse and inclusive, but real concrete ways we can do more to start the discussion about whether we should do anything other than what we are doing and what we have always done. I'll probably have to be careful with this conversation. Good thing I'm a quad.

I think (I am a quad), therefore I am (still here).

For now.

CHAPTER THIRTEEN

Next evening, at Paddy's Pub

T he manager of Career Services answered flat-out no—not her decision, she added, but was unwilling to add whose it was, though we both knew we both knew. I called Perry, who was supposed to be at home writing, because as far as we knew, that was all he did when he wasn't here doing what he used to do. No answer, no voicemail to take a message, so I called again, and again, and then I forgot. Forgot.

I had places to see, people to go. For example, for the past six months, John Staffal and I—as well as a few other miscreants and misfits—have worked through various committees and bureaucratic layers designed to discourage people from doing anything useful in life. We responded to a challenge the university made in response to its new policy on freedom of speech, which was clearly intended to restrict free speech. To get the votes needed in Senate to pass the policy, the new Freedom of Speech Chair challenged skeptics that any speaker could come to our mediocre institution of occasional learning and be heard without being censored or canceled.

And yet the policy restricts all speakers to an approval process by a committee of people whose ideological bias is to approve only those of appropriate ideological worthiness—to prevent hate speech, of course, whose definition of hate is as fluid as a pint of Guinness. Even those of worthiness can only freely express their views within a narrow band of progressive orthodoxy, but the thought of people without worthiness polluting the minds of young impressionable students, is, well, unworthy of consideration. Still, the committee chair, in an insincere moment, did say *anyone* can speak, and we pounced with an anyone who is anything but an unknown anyone.

Dr. Jordan Peterson came to world infamy for his audacious stand on freedom of speech—against a university no less—and has been reviled ever since. Mention his name on a university campus, and watch the sparks fly. Defend his views, and witness spontaneous combustible histrionics. But he has followers too. Millions. A decade ago, he wrote a couple of books that were not particularly political—advising people to take personal responsibility as their cohesive theme—with subsequent book tours to over 150 cities. Still, protests and cancel culture raged. All of which was tempered by the Covid phenomenon, which tempered much of life as we knew it.

After Covid, Dr. Peterson emerged just as popular and controversial as ever before, storming the Bastille with a fifty-thousand-word diatribe against former President Donald Trump's criminal conviction and lengthy (145-year) prison sentence, entitled *In Defense of the Megalomanic who Damaged Civility and Saved Civilization*. Then a new no-holds-barred book entitled *The Three Rs: Reason, Responsibility, and Becoming Real*. The book takes direct aim at corrosive change within universities that narrows critical thought and restricts freedom of expression.

A widely quoted passage has become freedom seekers' rallying cry and provides a fitting synopsis: "The issue is there is no distinction between free speech and free thought. And there's no thought without free thought. Thought by its nature is either free or it doesn't exist. This isn't a battle for some right right. This is a battle for the heart of universities." To this end, Dr. Peterson challenged ivory tower holders of high office around the world to debate. There were few takers, but among the few was John Staffal's invitation from St. Jude's, which Dr. Peterson accepted unconditionally. Because there were so few universities willing to take the bait and feel the heat, the accepted invitation from St. Jude's became a sensational national story. Naturally, recruiting a formidable debate opponent against Dr. Peterson has become an essential battle strategy. It isn't clear if St. Jude's has too many or too few professorial types willing to take on Dr. Peterson, but a defender of university progressive conformity has yet to be named even as the debate date looms.

There have been protests, candle vigils, and group and individual trauma counseling sessions, with campus sentiment overwhelmingly in favor of demanding that the event be canceled. It is both the right and the only thing to do. But prevalent as this view is, the Board of Governors has quietly issued a statement that the university must comply with its public declaration of free speech and hold the event. Though intending to appear neutral, the statement expresses regret for having to make the decision as well as concern over personal safety.

St. Jude's is in a quandary. Universities do not like controversy, least of all in front of a national audience. They want their practices of closed-mindedness to be known and celebrated as shining examples of civil, open and cordial debate about any and all subjects. They want theory to remain unapplied to outside practicalities. They do not welcome scrutiny. So, when some states introduced legislation that universities would have to achieve measurable outcomes tied to future funding, panic set in. Further, when the directive for outcome-based funding was actually defined, an index for measuring freedom of speech was included. It was a low bar by any comparison except as measured against current practices at almost any university in the Western world. Faculty, and particularly the plethora of DEI officers, uniformly view the low bar as existing in the stratosphere. Regardless of one's view, there now exists a requirement to formulate a policy and, worse, the expectation to actually live up to it. The Jordan Peterson debate is on.

Our Senate decision received much media interest, with its canary-in-the-mine-shaft implications for other universities. Media consider it a big deal, but the deal became rather too one-sided in interview after interview, so to keep the deal alive they determined to find an un-woke view opposing cancel culture. Dissenting views existed, some few even on campus, but most dissenters were unwilling to be interviewed.

There was a math prof, a couple of engineering students, that quad in disability services with that weird grin, but nothing to match the passion of those many salivating free speech champions wanting to cancel the event. Which is why all media outlets eventually came running to that ever-popular interview sensation Professor John Staffal for his erudite and passionate response. After all, a controversial story requires controversy which with the inclusion of Professor Staffal guarantees its fulfillment. It was John, more than the issue itself, that made our sleepy little Senate free speech debate into a national story.

With the latest interview filmed just hours before, John and I are to meet at our regular Thursday evening at Paddy's Pub. Apparently someone called the pub and let them know about the national interview, which miraculously comes on the screen just as John and I arrive, to universal applause. John takes a deep bow and with a dramatic flourish pretends to wave his imaginary plumed Cyrano de Bergerac hat.

"I wonder who gave the heads up to the pub about the interview?" I ask, not expecting an answer for which none is given. In addition to not wanting to answer, John is busy hailing a waitress to our table. He is quite accomplished at getting attention, particularly with his controversial views, and people watching us at Paddy's or the Faculty Club might be forgiven for thinking that controversial and political subjects are what we talk about exclusively. They might be surprised that we Renaissance men are deeply engaged and practiced in the art of conversation. For example, Hitler.

John stands up and bows again as Jeanine delivers two pints of Guinness and one choice Irish whisky. She bats her eyes as she departs, her faux romantic routine with John. As John swills and inspects his tumbler, he asks, "How is your novel coming along?"

He means the novel I frequently think about, talk about, but will never write about. I point to my head and say, "It's all up here. Will practically write itself once I start writing."

But he isn't paying attention, and as often happens with the great John Staffal, his question is prelude to where he wants to take the conversation.

John leans across the table, still swilling and not drinking the sacred contents of his tumbler. "I've had a thought, leading to revelation and finally to communication with you, my dear friend."

"Ah huh," I answer, by way of nonanswer to another of John's many precursors to the anticipated profundity of thought.

"Let me ask you this?" he asks, even as he waves and acknowledges newly arrived patrons who have either just seen the televised interview or are John Staffal pub groupies. Probably both. "What would you say are *the* two ingredients that rule history?"

"If I don't answer, will I get *the* answer faster?"

John does not answer my nonanswer, finally interrupts his swill with a swig, smacks his lips, and settles back in his chair to impart expected wisdom. Satisfied for the moment, he holds up two fingers. "Just two ingredients rule all, though neither makes it into the history books." Then pounding his table as patrons point, "Think about it, my boy. Why, it's as obvious as Cyrano's nose, or failing that, Jimmy Durante's schnoz."

Dramatic pause, during which, if I ever knew what he was going to say next, I would not say for fear of deflating a dramatic pause. Enunciating carefully, which from John amplifies into shouting, "Shit and love."

I do not react, knowing this is just the teaser.

"Hitler, who is your obsession and my preoccupation, proves my point. The question is, what was he compensating for?"

"I'm thinking you have both the question *and* the answer."

"I think, therefore I ham!" John thunders, and patrons clap without quite knowing why. "Yes, of course I have the answer, such is the power of revelation to us few. First shit."

"Oh goodie," I respond. "I was starting to think you were going to forget about how shit shaped history into a giant turd."

"Hitler came from nowhere. A pathetic little army corporal, a failed artist, an Austrian nobody saved by the First World War, which Germany initiated and then felt profound grievance in defeat under the weight of the Treaty of Versailles, which became a rallying point, which Hitler later capitalized on even though the pathetic little turd wasn't even a German citizen."

"Ah, and then the little turd becomes a big one," I venture.

"In a manner of speaking, yes." John leans into our table, his chair legs screaming with protest under the weight of something weightier than the Treaty of Versailles. "Hitler was a bitter failure who came to rule the world, and had this weird persona—well, his image was carefully sculpted by his pal Joseph Goebbels, who was the grand wizard of propaganda. Goebbels had only one discernible skill, but its repercussions are still being felt today. He was a master liar. The Fascists got away with the big lie by boldly, extravagantly, indeed forever saying up is down and down is up, intuitively knowing, as François-Marie Arouet de Voltaire was quoted as saying, 'Those who can make you believe absurdities, can make you commit atrocities.'"

"Yes, Dr. A. and I often quote this to each other in the maelstrom of our absurd little workplace," I respond.

"Goebbels cultivated Hitler's image as caring father, patriarch of Germany's children—this being a time before patriarchy had its pejorative meaning—a man who could never marry, being married to Germany—which is weird, since Germany was a Fatherland and not a Motherland like Russia. Still, women loved this guy, despite him being about as sexy as King Charles."

I nod as patrons strain to catch fragments of our passionate repartee, headlined by John's theatrical erudition.

"So he played the role of father betrothed to country, and yet he had a number of secret relationships that were profoundly, pathetically, and disturbingly dysfunctional."

"Okay, so the guy was a pervert. The question is, did this affect the way he operated politically?" This was familiar territory, and I wanted to nudge John, the storyteller, towards his epiphany moment.

"I'm getting there, as you know, I always do. Without doubt, the most disturbing relationship was with his niece Geli. She, of only fifteen years, in confinement both physically within Hitler's apartment and mentally under his narcissistic control. She is desperate to get away but he won't let her. And then she finds a normal boy, decides to visit him against Hitler's wishes, and when he predictably overreacts, she shoots herself with Hitler's gun. Publicly inexplicable, privately predictable. Still, it is ruled a suicide. Not bloody likely! She was frustrated, depressed maybe at Hitler's control, but she was excited about her new relationship and was never going to end her own life. But a boyfriend was a betrayal to Hitler, so she had to go. Now why was she willing to risk Hitler's wrath, anger so deep and pernicious that it got her killed? For the boyfriend? No, boy-toy was a means of temporary escape, nothing more.

"But since then, I, of great insight, have done some sleuthing and have concluded—with help from a couple American psychiatrists who did an assessment just after the war that supports my thesis—that in addition to having only one testicle and a micro penis, Hitler was a practitioner of coprophilia; that is, he got off by shitting and getting shit on by his sexual partners, including and especially his young niece. Can you image? That secret could never become known, so the piece of shit had to murder her. But not only. In his paranoia Hitler was desperate to eliminate anyone, no matter how unlikely to know or tell of his perversity. So young Geli's priest was murdered, just in case she had said anything incriminating in the confessional. Ha!

"And then there was that actress who also committed suicide after becoming involved with Hitler. What was her name?"

"Renata Muller," I answer.

Jeanine lays out another Irish whisky for John, this one a double or possibly a triple.

"Yes, of course. How could I forget Renata, namesake for the love of my life? Though niece, priest, and actress were murdered, none were ever investigated. And this shitty shitter proceeds to murder and war against the entire world!"

"No shit."

"Sure, twenty-five million for the Soviets alone. But the thing is, and of greater import than the horrific numbers, is the question about how history gets made. Was the Second World War inevitable? I don't think so. Hitler drove the world into war, a war so detested that Neville Chamberland committed political suicide trying to avoid it. The political issues were solvable, all of them, but nothing could address Hitler's personal pathologies once in power, none so lethal as his sexual perversions. The world reeled, convulsed in murderous pain, because a perverse piece of shit had to shit. Hitler literally shits on the world!"

"All very interesting, and yet methinks you have an end-thought epiphany to this little rejoinder."

"Isn't it obvious? The very thing loved in one generation for a historical heartbeat, is the most hated and despised in another. How do we confuse greatness with ruin? Even Hitler's generals, even understanding that all was lost, did not have it in them to substantially criticize the little military genius! So, pray tell, why?"

"Easy. Most people, even or especially those who fancy themselves leaders, are actually followers of the snake oil salesman of the day."

Smiling, John raises and tilts his whisky tumbler into my mug of beer. "Just so."

The room is electric with happening as patrons strain to hear John's invective-laden theorem, just as his image comes back on the television.

"Turn it up," someone shouts, as Bobbie the barman does just that.

"Why is it important to allow Jordan Peterson to speak at St. Jude's?" the interviewer asks. John squints one great eye denoting supreme concentration, or else as prelude to profound insight. Or maybe he's just constipated. "Freedom of speech is the foundation upon which democracy is upheld. As we learned throughout the twentieth century, she who controls the telling of the story determines truth. We need true diversity, including uncomfortable aspects of truth, to make informed choices. Unless we are informed, unless we are able to tolerate differing points of view, we do not reform and the lessons of the twentieth century are lost."

Patrons clap, John makes another great sweeping bow before motioning to Jeanine with his empty tumbler for yet another. John's chair is again besieged by weight as he continues his weighty diatribe in the flesh.

"Let me give you another example of the unanticipated and singularly quirky nature of history as it happens, compared to what is recorded in the history books. There have been many instances of persecution, pogroms against the Jews throughout history, but nothing, nothing, my dear boy, compares to Hitler's enactment of murder to the tune of six million individual lives lost. The greatest crime, the most pernicious human taboo in history and Hitler manages to make it an accepted social practice. And where did permission come from? Oh sure, there was some historical precedence, grievance was building, et cetera. But people who had lived together in perfect harmony all their lives were suddenly filled with glee at the prospect of turning their neighbors in for slaughter before raiding their premises and stealing all their processions, down to family photos, mementos of life that record their lives existed at all. From where, what source was this pernicious bile unleashed?"

"Well, I'd say, as recorded in the history books at least, that the Nazis' most pernicious iteration of antisemitism began in earnest with the Kristallnacht. That night was probably the most tangible example of state permission."

"Exactly!"

"You're really laying into it tonight," Jeanine comments, as she lays John's new whisky on the table.

"It is my only means of coping with your profound beauty," John answers, with one of his usual sweeping gestures.

Jeanine bats her eyes again and is gone.

"She who knows us doth observe the same as I," I mention, which John ignores.

"Kristallnacht is exactly right. As many as a thousand people killed and eventually fourteen hundred synagogues destroyed, but the real achievement was the perpetuation of the narrative of Jew as enemy or 'the other.' These are the necessary seeds sown as precursor to genocide. Again, Goebbels was the exemplar, delving deeply into the perversity of human nature. Jews were an easy target, and anti-Semitism has a long un-illustrious history. Still, ratcheting up antipathy towards Jews wasn't enough. Germany had bigger plans. Germany needed more than a convenient foil; Germany needed a reimaged enemy of gargantuan proportions. Do you know what the Jewish population of Germany was when Hitler came to power?"

"You forget I read this stuff. It was less than one percent, compared to say Hungry with over 5 percent and Poland, with the European high of 10 percent. So, yes, I see your point, how did one percent of the population become such a threat and scapegoat?"

"Exactly, and we're not talking about vagrants, or an impoverished strain upon the public purse. We're talking about the professional elite, cultural leaders, the best of doctors, scientists, lawyers."

"Lawyers?"

"Good point my boy, as in Shakespearean lore we'll have to turn a blind eye to the fate of lawyers. I mention lawyers because it is not as if Jews were politically uninformed or did not understand the law as it degenerated into lawlessness."

"Legal and political power are not the same thing."

"No, but the exercising of power as it evolves into absolute power requires a context, a reason to believe, and again I say, it required the brutalizing of an enemy everyone can agree to hate so as to identify a leader everyone agrees to love."

"Well, I'm thinking of the Nuremberg Laws as the other big piece of permission, but that is the consequence and not the thing, I'm thinking you're thinking."

"There is a reason you're my conversationalist of choice; allowing me to do most of the talking is not the only one. Yes, I've given you the shit revelation, and now we arrive at love."

"Oh?"

"Goebbels didn't just want an excuse to act, he lusted for a powder keg to blow the Jewish question into the Jewish solution. Germany needed an enemy to sustain its quest for world hegemony and Hitler had proclaimed the necessity of killing all the Jews with the publication of *Mein Kampf* in 1925. People make their murderous intentions known all the time and we don't believe them, we think that they didn't mean it, they are too nice, they're just blowing steam. Oldest story in history."

"Are you still talking about Nazi Germany, or have you switched to something closer to home?"

Curiously, John ignores the question, looks wistfully away for a moment before continuing. "The revelation, again on the theme of unforeseen determinants of history, is stupefyingly simple, and though it requires a man of depth and intellectual fervor to discover it, it is obvious. We agree that the beginning of the end was Kristallnacht, but what actually started Kristallnacht?"

"Well, there was the young Jewish guy who killed a Nazi functionary in Paris after his parents were sent to a concentration camp. The malevolent weasel Goebbels used the incident as pretext for launching Kristallnacht. What was his name?"

"Seventeen-year-old Herschel Grynszpan," John enunciates carefully, before continuing, "and the accepted reason for the killing of a Nazi was the deportation of his parents, and that reason is credible and was easily believed by the German public. But alas, it was not the reason for the killing, even if it was the political excuse for what followed. The murder may not have been politically motivated at all, and was probably a crime of passion."

"How so?" I ask.

"Why else would our passionately perturbed Herschel pick that particular Nazi functionary? His name was Ernst vom Rath, and this functionary was a nobody, was not even in Germany, where political protest would most register, was perhaps the least likely person to assassinate as a political target. If you're determined and willing to fall on the sword as you do the deed, history shows that you can get to and kill just about anyone. So why not kill Goebbels, Göring, Himmler, or Heydrich? Why not kill Hitler the architect, the source, the one about to inflict evil on Jews and on the world?"

"Well, Herschel was in Paris when his parents were taken away and so it may have been a spontaneous act of anguish and revenge. Besides, the character in my book, the one I'm going to write one day, is going to kill Hitler, remember?"

"Oh sure, maybe Herschel didn't want to waste Hitler by killing him early on. Better to keep him alive for your hero. So what do you think about my astute observations and world-shattering theory?"

"Well, you raise a good point, crimes of passion tend to defy logic, don't involve much planning, so I think the accepted theory that our friend Herschel just headed to the first office with a Nazi flag over its door is still credible."

"Ah, yes, yes, you zero in on the act as a crime of passion but miss the actual passion. What if I were to tell you that the crime of passion was not so much about Herschel's parents as it was about another and forbidden passion?"

He has my attention, which is the point of all John Staffal diatribes and discourses. He continues with glee. "It turns out, even if history does not generally acknowledge, that young Jewish Herschel and Nazi functionary vom Rath knew each other. It was not an arbitrary, unplanned shooting, and more to the point, they—victims and victimized both—were lovers, I tell you, wherein passion reigns supreme. Ha!"

"If this is true, I'm seriously impressed."

"It is most possibly true, far more credible than the political motivation that historical orthodoxy ascribes to young Herschel's motives. And to his everlasting condemnation, that evil genius Goebbels saw and understood all. He turned a potential scandal—a Jewish, German homosexual sexual liaison would have fit that bill—into the opportunity of a lifetime, using the shooting as the spark that gave license to the outrage needed to inspire a whole population to become Hitler's willing executioners."

"You make another interesting point. We often speculate about the world if Hitler had been taken out early. We forget Goebbels made Hitler, including the propaganda that Hitler was a self-made man, so taking Goebbels out early might have spared much of Europe too."

"Without Herschel's shooting, without Kristallnacht at that exact moment, who knows, maybe Hitler's final solution might have been perceived as too final for German sensibilities." Finished, John scowls at his empty tumbler. He looks up bleary-eyed, scanning the room once again for Jeanine.

"John, you've had a lot of wacky theories. This one may be in that category, but it is definitely possible and fascinating to think about. It's also a portal into a whole world of possibility about how history is determined, the extent to which human emotion—and often the worst of that gambit—may rule far more than political conviction. Maybe politics is just a ruse for what's bred in the bone…"

"… will out in the flesh," John finishes, looking uncharacteristically serious. Then, likely remembering what he promised, John raises his head and says, "You've waited patiently for my inside advanced intel about your stolen pot of money."

"Only because listening makes me the conversationalist of choice," I wistfully add, feigning nonchalance as a cover for my hunger to know.

"As we've agreed on many occasions, there are endless subjects in the world of greater importance than petty university politics for conversationalists such as us. But your SAP's theft requires measures beyond conversation, for we will have to formulate a plan to deal with it."

I wait, appreciating his support, but am murky about details and what he can do about the whole debacle.

"I believe Grace's under-the-covers version of events to be correct. The SAP's plan to take your sixty-six million was hatched the moment she discovered that it was likely to be funded. Dear Grace was able to find a Department of Progressive Advancement memo formally requesting funding be reallocated, allowing St. Jude's to expand 'equity' to include all oppressed groups, thereby nullifying your proposal to address accessibility solely for your constituency. The request made your pointed use of funds for disability accessibility seem limited, narrow, exclusive. The memo, signed by the president, was sent the week after you completed your submission."

"Son of a beeswax," is all I can manage.

"This heist must be passed by the Board of Governors, but I expect the plan is for the board and president to provide passive passage without really understanding the nature of the crime. Fraser, one of the few sane people on Senate, at last meeting asked the president where the funding came from, especially with the added expense of creating a monolithic DIE Center. The prez seemed genuinely clueless and deferred to our enchanting SAP, but she was not in attendance, being at an 'emergency' meeting about campus security. So the issue has been passed on to a committee of your SAP's colleagues to handle with predictable results soon to follow."

"The board, being led by the nose, will be on board. This sorry tale stinks to high heaven," I declare. "Only in a place where the stakes are so small can catastrophe seep out of indifference and irrelevancy on any so-called issue." But John's mind is elsewhere. "John?"

"I heard you, my boy. I just wish life had the same luxurious ending without consequence that universities indulge in."

"Oh?"

"I have to admit after a lifetime of 'no regrets,' of not looking back, of saying the past is past, I find myself strangely feeling some regret, while thinking that maybe the past is not past. Maybe things I've done are, well, coming back to haunt me."

I've known John for over twenty years, and never heard him say anything like this, even drunk, as he obviously now is. John is not a saint, has done many things good and bad, but something about the way he is reflecting scares me.

"How do you mean, John?" To reinforce concern, I place a placid hand of concern on his pudgy wrist.

He is staring across the pub at nothing in particular and uncharacteristically does not banter with or even acknowledge Jeanine as she delivers his latest whisky tumbler. His eyes are bloodshot, unclear, and I am perturbed by his eyes not crinkling into mirth. "I've cheated on every woman I've ever been with, not always successfully, but that is a moot point. Half my kids don't talk to me; the other half talk to me about how I screwed up their lives by screwing up the lives of their mothers."

"For some of us, passion rules," I offer, a flaccid excuse for behavioral irregulation.

"Yes, I've always lived by the dictates of passion, but now I think maybe I used passion as cover for just doing whatever the hell I wanted, damn the consequences. I'm having a hard time living with my own unforeseen consequences."

"John, you've done a lot of good. Would you like me to recite a list, starting with a personal example of how you are the most inspiring teacher at good ol' St. Jude's these decades on?" But he is gone. We talk for a while longer; that is, mostly I talk while John stares across the room, unfocused, un-present, except I suspect, for his presence in another hostile place. I can't read him—concerning enough—and vaguely wonder if at this moment he is recognizable even to himself.

CHAPTER FOURTEEN

Same evening at our warm, cozy home,
formally a cold, cruel house

As I exit my van, Aunt Isobell lets me know that Edie dropped by the house earlier. Edie never dropped by the house. Auntie discreetly adds that Edie seemed upset and didn't look so good. Unfortunately, I know that Aunt Isobell's observations are not exaggerated. My auntie does not do histrionics. I'm worried. Still, Edie has just started treatment, might respond well, might beat this version of Russian roulette called life.

"She asked if you were likely to be home at nine p.m., and I told her I thought so. Glad you're back now," Aunt Isobell says, grimacing and looking out of place standing in our laneway in her housecoat. My spring-chicken aunt understands; she seems to always understand. It is 8:53 p.m.

Watching my metal ramp fold back into the van after I exit, she says, "I still marvel at that thing." Then, more seriously, "I know you're worried. Can I get you anything? Lots of leftover lasagna from dinner."

"No, thanks, Auntie, ate at Paddy's. And yes, I'm worried."

Once I'm inside, Iggy and Sister Sandrine hover, they too offering lasagna by way of masking concern.

The four of us sit at the dining room table, and the doorbell rings. Before even fast-moving Iggy can react, the front door opens, and Edie arrives in dramatic fashion. Edie's rather assertive entrance crashes the door into the wall, which makes her laugh and declare, "What's wrong with youse guys, you look like you're at a funeral."

I expect no less.

After exchanging pleasantries, Aunt Isobell, Iggy, and Sister Sandrine rise together and excuse themselves, to which Edie chortles, saying, "You don't have to leave, really. I've got cancer, not leprosy!"

"Are you sure?" is the only minor objection from Sister Sandrine.

"Hell, the more friends the merrier," Edie answers.

Everyone sits down except for Edie, who stands with one leg high on the seat of a chair and declares, "Now since you're all my peeps, I want you to shut your gobs and listen up." Edie laughs loudly, as she always does—the tears of a clown. "I've got lung cancer. I'm getting chemo and radiation and some other such things, and I'm going to do it because I'm a fighter, but the fact is, it's stage four cancer, it's inoperable, and my chances are slim, but what the hell do they know?" She slaps her raised thigh and laughs again.

We, about as useless as a screen door on a submarine, an uncle used to say, sit shocked and unable to join in the laughter. Finally, to break both the silence and the tension, I manage a weak, "If there's anything we can do ...," joined by three other heartfelt nodding heads.

To which Edie responds, "Thought you'd never ask."

Four blank expressions and a collective, "Huh?"

"'Course there's something you can do. You're my peeps after all, and I'll be damned—sorry, Sisters—if what I want you to do is sit around, mope, and feel sorry for me."

Among the many things I like about Edie is that she knows who she is and what she wants in life. "Proceed," I encourage, which she doesn't need, being someone who knows what she wants in life.

"Doctors, who don't know anything, say I don't have much time, so I'm going to double what they told me. I know I'm right, and you all know I like to piss people off—sorry, Sisters." Aunt Isobell has told Edie several times that she doesn't need to apologize, but Edie says she can't seem to break the habit for those in the habit. She has stooped to my level, since nuns have been out of the habit of wearing the habit since before Sister Sandrine was born.

"I've thought about this, and I know you'll be a pain in the ass—sorry, Sisters—if I don't put you to work."

"To work?" I ask.

"Yup, if I don't give you guys a project for me, you'll waste all my limited time offering useless sympathy and make me feel like a sick person." Edie doesn't hear a question or objection, which she seems to like, so she rests her elbows on her raised leg and continues. "You all know my main squeeze, Joey. Well, we've been together twenty-three years, but we never got married. It wasn't the right time, there wasn't enough money, and early on we weren't sure if my two kids by my previous squeeze were ready for another dad. Well, the timing is never going to be more right than now, money be dammed—we can always make peanut butter sandwiches. Besides, my kids are grown now, and they love Joey. So whaddya say?"

There are several moments of silence. I am processing the shock of Edie's stage four news against the juxtaposition of her energetic wedding pitch.

"You want us to plan and put on your wedding?" Iggy asks.

"Phelim, your brother's a genius. Yes, damn it—sorry, Sisters—I want you to be wedding planners and not funeral dwellers!"

Which is what we do from that moment on, with energy and a sense of purpose unprecedented in human history. And every day we tell ourselves, until it becomes our motto, our brand, words to live by: *we're wedding planners, not funeral dwellers!*

Still, we don't have much time. Doctors have given Edie about three months, and even though we believe that she could hang on for six months because she said so, we want to make sure she's alive and feeling herself for the wedding. We want Edie, whom we know and love, to show up for her own wedding, the one she's never had and might never have if not for cancer. We want that one good thing to emanate from her bad news. We want to resurrect something of life from the inevitability of her imminent death.

What happens the next and following days is quite remarkable. First, we have to find a date. Edie said don't rush it too much, "I'll be fine," but we rush it much because much as we want to, we don't really believe her. Two of our office peeps who have put on several successful events for our office are tapped on the shoulder. Diane and Melanie do the complex, labor-intensive student service work for our thousands of students. They work hard at a lowly designation on the university hierarchy.

"Um, it's not in your job description," I start hesitantly, but as they have heard about the possibility of an Edie wedding, I am not allowed to finish my sentence. They want in, are thrilled to get the tap, pleased to be in charge of our entire crew from their lowly hierarchical perch. I tell them to assign our entire staff to do whatever they need us to do, and they do so with the energy and resolve of a drill sergeant.

We drew up a list of what needs to get done at that first meeting, and it is a daunting list. It isn't just the work that needs doing in short order. We also have to find a way for the wedding, all of it, to be cost-free to Edie and Joey. All of this, coming into exams of a busy term, with people committed to peak-time work responsibilities. Melanie and Diane roar out of my office determined to take on the world, obstacles be dammed.

And now the miracle. Everywhere the girls have asked about the remotest possibility of a person or department willing to help, the answer is an immediate and enthusiastic yes. The first coup is securing the Great Hall with views and vistas, plant walls, grand piano, and room for several hundred people to gather. This is the only facility on campus that would work, but it tends to be heavily booked many months in advance. And it was, most of winter into spring, except for one surprising and insanely pressing Saturday afternoon just before Christmas; that is, on the same day as the Jordan Peterson debate, exactly sixteen days from now.

Constructed in the groundswell of optimism and prosperity after the Second World War, the Great Hall was christened St. Anthony's of Padua, patron saint of lost love, which was a nice parallel to St. Jude, our patron saint of lost causes. And without other people, without exception, we are all recovering lost love. It is a perfectly named place for people to stand and declare their recovered love in the form of matrimony. Though some people still refer to it as lost love hall, last year it was formally renamed the House of Diversity, Equity, and Inclusion. As far as we know, people do not want to get married in the hall in order to DIE there. Conventional happenings such as weddings are no longer encouraged, maybe not even allowed. But we're not going to ask for permission, and we call it the Great Hall.

The looming date is far closer than we wanted or anticipated, even as we agreed that we wanted the date to be soon for Edie's sake. The manager of Conference Services says it is available for free—she is one of many who love Edie—but beginning in the New Year, she will be required to charge a full and substantial fee—cost recovery and not recovery of love being the new currency at St. Jude's. And if the impossibly short timeframe and on the same date as the Peterson debate were not enough, to complete the trifecta of complexity, the entire lead-up period coincides with Christmas exams. (Please note: The word "Christmas" is one of several thousand terms and words that have been officially banned for use at St. Jude's. Consequently, we repeatedly make use of the word Christmas and thousands of others whenever we can, just to be subversive as hell. Hell, too is on the no-no list, which is why I snuck it into this paragraph. And yes, likely just one more reason why I'm going to hell, probably on Christmas.)

I ask Melanie and Diane if we can pull the wedding together in sixteen days. Clutching the infamous list of tasks and with quivering lip, Melanie answers yes. I must say I delight watching Luna's and Iggy's expression as I mention that we are going to hold the wedding on the same day, and close to same actual hour, as the Peterson event. "Absolutely not," Luna declares.

"That would be suicide," Iggy echoes.

To which I casually deadpan, "Yeah, but we'll be at the university anyway, so we'll all save on gas." The date is confirmed.

In the next few days, there are details such as tables and chairs, music, flowers, catering, drinks, alcoholic and non, a photographer, etc. And, as in a fairy tale, each request asked, however seemingly wacky, garners a resounding yes. There is something about this improbable event, something about the way foul-mouthed Edie pulls you in and makes you her best, most important peep, that has everyone wanting to contribute, and by week's end that includes people who don't even know her, as we learn when a photographer calls and says, "You don't know me but …." Everyone just knows you have to be there. By the end of the first week, our plans are substantially made, with over a week to spare. Which makes you wonder why people take a year to plan a wedding. Seems about fifty-one weeks too long.

Edie is in and out of the office during these weeks, mostly in. Not to visit but to work, and oh yeah, to socialize. She will not take her doctors' advice and use sick leave; she will not allow anyone else to take over her job responsibilities. Edie is going to face cancer her way, and her way does not include making it easy for herself. She is not wired for easy, insisting instead that she is wired for sleazy. Which gives me an idea.

Among the various and substantial wedding arrangements in play, something is missing. Something important, something none of us can put our finger on, until we remember Joey. Edie has what you might call a strong personality. We know and love Joey, but he does tend to take a back seat to her aforementioned strong personality. Sometimes we wondered if in taking his habitual back seat, he might end up in the trunk.

We have the Edie element covered, but since a wedding is generally about two people, it occurs to us that maybe we should include something particular to Joey. And then it hits me. I make a call and am given the name of a guy who knows someone. Eventually, I get the someone I need to do something. At the top of the list of Edie's many fetishes is her lust for hunky firemen. She loves their rough-and-tumble uniforms, their trucks, the fact that they use a hose and slide down a pole, and not a day goes by without her making jibes, often at Joey's expense, about her lust for firemen. Let's call this a theme.

I've heard about a volunteer group of firemen who, when they aren't sliding down a pole, slide into important events for other people. Four strapping lads will turn up in formal uniform in a fire truck with flowers to garnish weddings, funerals, and anniversaries. I am able to get confirmation that they will show up at Edie's wedding, but I have an unusual request. So I call the volunteer coordinator, and we have the following awkward conversation.

"Thanks for agreeing to show up at our event. It'll be a surprise for the bride and the thrill of a lifetime."

"Yes sir. I understand that the special lady tragically has cancer. I hope we can help ease her pain and the suffering of her family."

"Ah, well, there's a lot of life in her yet," I begin, thinking, *You have no idea what that* lady *would do with the four live firemen if they let her*. "Um, yeah, this lady really is special, and for that reason I have a special request."

"Whatever we can do, sir."

I wonder if that willingness will dissipate the moment I make the request. "The thing is, she has a kind of attraction—well, I'd call it a more of a fetish—for firemen, and so she'll really, and I mean *really* appreciate it when four tall young firemen show up at her wedding in their formal attire."

"Yes sir," the volunteer responds, perhaps with a creeping sensation that this call is going wonky.

"And the guy she's marrying has heard about and put up with her, um, lust for firemen, that is, in their regular casual informal firefighting outfits, for all twenty-three years they've been together."

I take a breath, and the volunteer does not interject, likely not wanting to encourage me.

"So on this their wedding day, with Edie the center of attention—well, the truth is, she always is the center of attention with everyone—and given her history with firemen … well, not history so much as history of fantasy, if you know the difference …."

"Sir?"

I sense the need to get to the point and quickly. "Anyway, we thought, much as we all want to do something for Edie, maybe, just maybe we should also do something for Joey."

"Joey, sir?"

"The groom. I doubt you have ever been asked this before, but when the guys show up in formal uniform, is there any way they could bring, that is, without letting the bride see, an old grubby firefighting outfit for one short, plumpish, middle-added guy?"

The line is not dead so much as sizzling while this weird request is processed.

I begin again so as not to be "sir"ed to again. "That way, we all thought, the wedding day might include Joey too—again the butt of firefighter jokes forever—who might get Edie's attention, might surprise her, and she might then see her new husband the way she has seen you guys for decades. Make sense?"

The pause is painful at both ends of the line. After torturous seconds of nonresponse, the volunteer finally and without expression simply says, "Yes sir."

"Yes sir, yes?" I clarify, "or yes sir, no?"

"Yes sir, yes."

"Great?" I am both truly pleased and being a bit facetious. "That will really make a difference. And we'll get it all on camera in case you guys ever want to expand your service." Okay, so now mostly facetious, even if genuinely grateful.

The volunteer's last words are a predictable, stuck-for-any-others, and final "Yes sir."

CHAPTER FIFTEEN

Continuing along the week,
at yet another important meeting

Iggy strongly suggests that I attend, and Luna informs me that I have no choice. Our esteemed SAP, Exceptional Student Experience announced an hour ago that there will be an emergency meeting of her direct reports this afternoon. So directors only, and no measly managers. Which begs the question, why are some consigned to the measly designation, while others sit among the directorial elite? Good question, for which I have no answer except to observe that there is an inverse relationship between high level and hard work. My directorship (makes me sound like the bossy captain of a ship) was determined years ago, long before the SAP's arrival and ascendency, and apparently had something to do with what our office achieved. Makes you wonder why I accepted a promotion based on merit rather than holding out for consideration of my most oppressed identity parts. Makes me feel cheated somehow.

The SAP's call to arms means that we are to break all previous appointments and get our butts to the emergency meeting even if the expectation is never explicitly made. Most of the SAP's wants and desires are surreptitiously communicated; that is, from the ether we are to infer actual from implied meaning, ignoring words said for what progressive awareness compels us to do, in spite of job description, established means of doing things, personal ethics, or common sense.

Strictly speaking, I was once privileged, had opportunity to be the recipient of SAP largesse, to pork on various entitlements from the university trough if only I would have served the unspoken agenda, of which I always feign ignorance. When she began her appointment, I incorrectly read the tea leaves of swirling university politics and was so naive as to think that serving students still had some gravitas. But alas, in the name of serving students, that is no longer true. I now serve at the SAP's pleasure, and she is not pleased. With me, that is. I am solidly, pervasively and permanently classified as the un-woke dummy of the class, and to say I'm not taken seriously by meeting attendees would be to admit that I even exist in the minds of the inner sanctum of the exceptional SAP's exceptional world. Still, occasionally there is information at these meetings that even the class dummy cannot ignore. Clues to imminent murder come to mind.

I agree with Iggy and concede to Luna that I should go, and yet I'm not sure I'm going to go. The SAP crisis du jour doesn't impress or depress me; the articulation of crisis is fodder for inducing panic, which is the precursor for exercising control, which is the requisite condition for our wholesale ingestion and digestion of absurdity with logical consequence close on its heels. In short, I'll find out soon enough. Besides, I haven't quite gotten over my habitual laziness, just in case that wasn't clear. It should be equally clear by now that I don't want to get over, am deeply attached to, my habitual laziness. It is one of the important attributes from which I derive an identity of indolence.

True, there are some things I might have to do, and quickly, as a result of today's meeting, but I must admit that my decision to attend is for lack of any reason not to attend. Unable to come up with a reason that has a shred of believably, at 2:05 p.m. sharp, Zigo and I wait at the closed door outside the meeting room. The SAP has repeatedly said that once the door closes, the meeting room is sealed, and no one else gets in, but to her everlasting annoyance, she can't exactly bar a quad with a baying hound.

But I'm not going to utilize the Zigo card today. Smokey and I have another plan. No use being predictable, and I don't want to draw too much attention to Zigo's lack of credentials on the therapy and companion dog front. They can scheme all they want on how to get rid of me, but Zigo is a whole other matter that matters. Instead—just so we can demonstrate how cruel they are—I text Smokey to set the histrionics in motion.

At these times, Smokey can be as troublesome as moi. He and I share this terrible affliction best described as having filterless indiscretion. During rare times when the SAP is interrupted, there is heavy—though never actually articulated—group expectation that we cower in silence until the reason for interruption has passed. One can hear the collective exhaling of breath when these threatening moments pass. One can sense danger when these threatening moments are in progress. That is, except for Smokey and I.

"Hey man, right on time." This in Smokey's non-quiet quiet voice as he opens the door. "Join me at the back of the bus." He works the door back and forth on squeaky hinges as he talks, and in order to compensate for the increasing volume of squeakiness due to increasing motion, Smokey has to raise his non-quiet quiet voice further still. "Sounds like two cats in heat on a summer's night."

I enter the meeting room as if returning home after a hostage taking, with Zigo proudly prancing beside me, tail held high in the air. Then, as I clear out chairs blocking my path with my electric plow, Smokey places a hand to the side of his mouth. "See that fight during the Rangers game last night?"

I love it when Smokey uses his hands to accentuate a conspiratorial whisper several decibels louder than his normal talking voice.

Faces contort into the likeness of having recently sucked on a lemon at the mention of sporting events, which epitomize male toxicity. Zigo takes his habitual spot beside an old heating panel, which his enthusiastic tail wags and bangs like a drum as I swing around to face both the music and our exceptionally impatient SAP. Smokey, realizing that others, all others, have heard his whisper, grins sheepishly and says to the room, "It was a great fight. Old style hockey."

As always, I am both grateful and amused by Smokey, never quite sure if he is completely aware or totally unaware. I vaguely hope it is both.

Meanwhile, at the important gathering of Exceptional Student Experience minions, updates and "good news" items are read to us by Maxi; that is, BS by the SAP's EA.

At which point I, silly grin in place, check in with Roma and Fred in their quest to kill Hitler. I've decided to reconsider that part about Roma and Fred going to Europe together in 1940.

Much more dramatic and likely, Roma insists on going back to Warsaw against her father's advice in August of 1939. And she insists on going alone, promising to return to the United States within a month. But she does not. Germany invades Poland on the first of September, and Fred loses contact with her and cannot forgive himself for letting her go by herself.

She of independent mind convinced Fred that it was safer for her to go alone, and Hank, of the American embassy, foolishly agreed with her. Fred decides he has to find Roma, but there are difficulties organizing a trip to Europe in the middle of a war. For almost two years, Fred is told either not to go or that the obstacles are too formidable at this time. Fred comes to understand that a time without formidable obstacles is never going to happen. Finally, at the beginning of June 1941, without knowing that the embassy will be severely limited with the beginning of Operation Barbarossa in three weeks, and it will be closed with Hitler's declaration of war on the United States in December, Fred leaves for Europe, for Roma, for war.

Hank Perkins has tried to keep track of Roma from the American embassy in Berlin, with limited success. Hank has not heard from her in several weeks, and communication has become increasingly difficult since the formation of the Warsaw ghetto. Keeping track of Roma is not Hank's main priority, and he is less than candid about the danger she is in. He just assumes that with the passage of time, and especially after the defeat of Poland, Fred will reconcile himself to the fact that Roma can never return. Besides, she is Jewish and Polish, and thus not an American concern.

With an American and German passport at his disposal, and with papers indicating he is an American industrialist doing business with the Nazis, Fred arrives in Berlin and meets with Hank to refine his cover. Hank arranges for Fred to meet with senior Nazi party and businesspeople to establish his credibility for being in Europe. Introductions, meetings, inevitable social gatherings are estimated to take a minimum of two weeks. Fred never wanted to stay in Berlin for two weeks; he doesn't want to stay for one second, but as an American businessman he needs a credible narrative, with credible people to back it up. Due to restrictions on trading with France and Britain by this date, Germany has a shortage of gas, oil, iron ore, textiles, and especially aluminum, which Fred's family business just happens to have enormous quantities of. Business discussions about Fred's family commodity have gone extremely well, and the amount of aluminum that his new Nazi friends are anxious to secure will make an important contribution to their war effort.

Hank has prepared official-looking letters of introduction, and Uncle Leon also prepared letters designed to thrill Fred's new Nazi friends with the amount of aluminum their company could supply. They will have to be very impressed, because he needs to curry enough favor to be allowed to go and find Roma in Warsaw. Warsaw is completely under German rule, and worse, all Jews have been confined to a ghetto since 1940. It is the conditions of their encirclement that are most disturbing. Over 350,000 Jews, or 30 percent of the Warsaw population, are cramped into 2.4 percent of the city's area, which results in severe overcrowding, deprivation, and poor sanitary conditions. Most apartments hold multiple families. Why would a visiting American, or German for that matter, want to go there?

Fred will not be allowed into the ghetto and has no idea how to find Roma. Still, he courts senior Nazi party members with generous terms for trade and acquires friends in high places. In social circles, he gleefully agrees with all Nazi declarations and anti-Semitic slurs, and he greases a few palms for the privilege of doing business. Fred is a likable American who is about to deliver to Germany the capacity to make several thousand more airplanes, and even though he has only been in the country a few weeks, he is now in a position to call in a favor. With the launch of Operation Barbarossa against Russia (the largest battle in military history) just days away, the Luftwaffe appetite will remain insatiable for the duration of the war.

Fred has established easy rapport with one Colonel Carl Haase, who served under Hermann Göring, commander-in-chief of the Luftwaffe. Most notably, Göring is the person chiefly responsible for the procurement of materials to meet Germany's inexhaustible need for airplanes.

Colonel Carl Haase spent part of a year in the United States when he was a teenager, speaks some English, and is delighted by all things American.

Fred places a call to Carl, and they talk in jocular fashion about a certain sexy woman Fred has had relations with in Boston. She has returned to Warsaw, and he would like to meet up with her again, since he is in the neighborhood. And yes, yes, she is Jewish, and he should avoid her, but she is that good. The liaison Fred craves is only frivolous pleasure, and after all, he is not a German citizen. Could Carl discreetly help?

Carl enjoys the banter with his new American friend. It is an unusual request, but understandable from a brash American. Colonel Haase calls a Warsaw functionary with instructions to locate one Roma Rachel Grossynger and to escort the esteemed businessman Fred Amberg into the ghetto to see her. As soon as the functionary can verify where Roma is, Fred will leave for Warsaw.

Though the Germans surely have up-to-date lists of all Jewish occupants in the ghetto, it takes three full days to discover that she is missing. Gone, and no one knows where she is. Fred demands to know how that is possible; the Warsaw functionary responds that he has no idea. Fred then asks if he can go into the ghetto and talk to her family. The Warsaw functionary doesn't think so but agrees to call Carl back and discuss the situation. After a sleepless night, Fred again calls the functionary's office when it opens at nine a.m. With an impertinent attitude, the functionary says that there is no point going into the ghetto, and Fred should call Carl for the real story.

Fred frantically calls Carl all day but cannot reach him. He leaves a message at his hotel desk that he is expecting an important call and proceeds to plant himself near the phone, first in his room and later in the hotel lobby.

Fred is sick with fatigue but dares not sleep until Carl calls. Once the great clock in the hotel lobby strikes midnight, Fred decides to inform the solitary front desk employee that he is retreating to his room. Before he can speak, the phone rings, but the employee is disinclined to answer it in deference to Fred's approach to the desk. Fred impatiently indicates that the employee should answer the phone, which, with confusion, he does. With a blank look on his face, the clerk hands the phone over to Fred, who anxiously asks Carl if he has heard anything.

Carl laughs and says, "Hi, Yankee Doodle, how is life in the slums?" Fred feigns laughter in unconvincing fashion. After some more torturous banter Fred learns that Roma is indeed gone—taken, actually—and no longer in Warsaw. Apparently, one Colonel Friedrich who had been in the Warsaw office when Roma arrived had taken a likening to her, and well, when he was reassigned to a highly secret base in eastern Poland, he had taken his chattel with him.

"Sorry, Yankee, but apparently you have the same taste as the colonel, which is funny since Friedrich and Fred are the same name. You should meet since you have much in common—that is, an unnatural fetish for the same woman. Ha!"

At that moment, Fred wants to kill Carl more than Hitler. Same for Colonel Friedrich, whoever the hell he is. "Where, where, where is that base?" Fred demands.

Carl, though still in jocular fashion, backs up and says, "Wow, you can't go there, and you can't know where it is. I could get into serious trouble for what I have already told you. You really need to let it go and find yourself another plaything."

Yes, Fred wants to kill Carl most of all and immediately. Hitler can wait.

He contacts Hank, at the American embassy, who responds that there are reports of massive troop buildups in the east, and while he has some ideas where Colonel Friedrich might have been assigned, there is so much activity, it would be very difficult to narrow it down. Still, he has his own resources, and he will look into it.

In his hotel that evening, Fred realizes that beyond his desperate desire to find Roma, he has no plan. The next day, he enters the American embassy just as it opens. In his office, Hank encourages Fred to go home, to forget Roma, to be realistic. Fred's heart sinks, thinking that Hank has been unable to come up with Colonel Friedrich's location. But he is wrong. Hank has surprised himself and easily located Colonel Friedrich. "The good colonel is a favorite of Hitler's and is at the eastern war headquarters, the Wolf's Lair, so easy to locate but impossible to penetrate. Fred, go home."

But Fred cannot go home. Come hell or high water, Roma is his only possibility of home now. And, unknown to both Fred and Roma at that moment— only confirmed at the end of the war—Fred is her only family. All fifty-seven members of Roma's extended family have already been mercilessly exterminated by the Nazis.

The incessant drone of announcements for the many accomplishments of the Enhanced Student Experience portfolio finally ends. The air is electric with foreboding, alive with anticipation. Meeting attendees whisper as Smokey snores. Tim, in an attempt to placate the boss as well as steer the assemblage back to the source, hushes the already silent group and says, "Quiet, everyone, our Special Adviser to the President has an important announcement."

Our exceptional SAP looks uber pleased with herself, even eclipsing ever-eager minion Tim, so I know it must be bad.

"Well, there are two announcements actually, both important, with one decidedly negative though extremely necessary, and the other astonishingly positive and destined to put you, me, my, that is, our portfolio uniquely on the map as never before."

There are murmurs of excitement before the SAP holds up her hand. "Now, now, we'll get to the excitement, but don't forget we also have to deal with some unpleasantness."

There is shifting in seats and exhalations of air as SAP disciples wait for the word to come down from on high. I can't shift in my seat, and my exhalations are too shallow to be heard. As usual, I am the grateful outlier.

"In the early years after Covid, and with the prospect of free tuition, our enrollment hit record high levels. This year, we are three percent below our previous five-year average, and that fact coupled with the government's fascist determination to control debt, means the university has a deficit problem."

"On the backs of marginalized people," some astutely original personage pipes up.

"Be that as it may," the SAP continues, "the president has ordered budget cuts, some deep."

"What does 'some deep' mean?" the director of Mental Wellness, Mindfulness, and Life Balance asks in a panicked tone.

The SAP touches up her perfectly manicured blond hair with her right hand and quells the crowd with her left. "You don't think I'd abandon you, do you? Thankfully, the president in his wisdom has not instituted regressive cuts across the board in equal measure. He has listened to my appeal for a progressive application of the concept of equity. He has issued an order for a three percent overall institutional cut but has left the decision where and to what degree cuts are made, up to the discretion of myself and the vice presidents."

Which is interesting, because lazy sod that I am, I am also a bit of an information junky. I like to know what motivates people, why they do what they do, why character assassination or its moniker—bodiless, bloodless murder—has become ubiquitous in university functioning. The claim of financial hardship is disingenuous at best. Even with a minor decrease in enrollment of about 3 percent, that fact has to be coupled with an ass-kicking endowment increase of close to 40 percent in the years since Covid was declawed and rolled into our annual cold and flu season. If there is one thing that can compete with the ideological wokeness that universities obsess about in these enlightened days, it is money, money, money. Harvard's endowment total topped $100 billion last year, up from a paltry $68 billion in recent years, with no end in sight. St. Jude's is not in Harvard's league, or even among the second-tier universities such as Yale, Stanford, or Princeton. But as a third-tier fundraising powerhouse, St. Jude's still has a whopping war chest of close to $16 billion. Universities are bleeding money as the country heads towards bankruptcy, which raises two questions: Why the pretense of poverty, and what are they going to do with all that money? And just for fun, let's add, why steal more?

"As your leader I can tell you, in the interests of fairness and equity, that cuts will be unevenly appropriated. I have worked out a preliminary plan that differentiates cuts to be as much as fifteen percent, or conversely budgets increased as much as nine percent to Dean Perkins's shop, based on the necessity for achieving DEI goals."

Dean Perkins, once holding the unglamorous title of Director of Equity Services effectively elevated to Dean of Everything, smiles widely, revealing glistening gums and listening goodwill. The title change was absolutely necessary, both to elevate the concept of equity, and to fend off awkward questions about services that didn't exist.

Looking up and in my direction, though never making eye contact, the SAP continues, "I won't say where the fifteen percent cuts are coming, but please rest assured, they will only be enacted where there are adequate resources for that unit to perform its mandated functions. In other words, in all my difficult decisions, fairness rules."

So for me and my crew it is death, or DIE, by the simple dictate of fairness. The SAP is an equal-opportunity assassin. Other departments in the Exceptional Student Experience portfolio might not know it, but our Center is the only department that has successfully raised significant funds every year since its creation thirty years ago. Successful fundraising has always related to added value rather than just more money to do the same old thing. For example, with new funding we take on a new project, expand a service or an outcome beyond what our actual mandate demands of us, so penalizing us for successfully raising funds has always been both unfair and a formula for killing innovation and hard work. I can hear Luna's scream in my mind's ear, and it is shrill.

"Enough unpleasantness. Let's switch to what is decidedly good news."

"It's very exciting …," Dean Perkins says, just to be sure we all know that she knew before we get to know. Which is fine by me, being the last to know all things, at all times. "… and brings to fruition a shared vision of many months."

The SAP smiles indulgently, willing for once to briefly share credit for this piece of news with her coconspirator. We on the outside wait with bated breath—except that I wait with unbated breath, just grateful to keep breathing.

Still, there is need for a minor correction of her coconspirator and ally, just in case there is any question as to who is in charge and where ultimate credit must go. "Thanks, Susan, you have been great to work with, but of course, the actual beginning of what I am about to announce precedes our strategic planning by several years. In fact, the first conversation I remember having was with our former president, who said my plan was laudable but impossible. He was not quite the leader our present president has become."

On cue the assemblage giggles, acknowledging group solidarity for our present president, whose hiring our present SAP facilitated, at the expense of our former president whose firing our present SAP facilitated. Our present

SAP, it is universally acknowledged, is all-powerful, universally feared, and in the parlance of cheerleader Tim, "awesome."

I enjoy my absence of universality. I fear many things in life: loneliness, losing the people I care about, losing the beef I care about, but not the Special Adviser to the President. Most of all, I don't fear our SAP because there is no moral ambiguity about anything she says or does, which leaves moral certainty about anything I do to resist anything she says or does. At least that is my story.

Our former president was a well-meaning, woke-inclined liberal who vainly tried to keep up with the requisite change of a progressive president in the great reset times in which we live. He seemed particularly flummoxed in the great progressive reset acceleration after Covid. Being progressively compliant just didn't work, was never going to work for someone of the improper identity components. So he allowed himself to be compromised, and then with pressure from our SAP and in a futile attempt to show he was worthy of the ever-escalating demand to change what was for the nirvana of what will be, he allowed compromise to become criminal, and it was over. She who had advised him in his conversion to criminality was merely staying ahead of the demand for change, saw her opportunity, and turned him in. I believe malfeasance was the charge, though an accusation of harassment was in the wings, in case his push needed a convincing pull.

"My vision, later to be shared with Susan, came to me when it became clear that the world, thankfully, is changing. The rising awareness of group identity of oppressed peoples has paralleled the demise of imperialism, capitalism, and, most grievous cult of all, organized religion.

"And it can now be said, most grievous of the most grievous, with particular emphasis on us here at this university, we have been liberated by the demise of the Catholic church. And, again with emphasis on our situation at our university, addressing historical grievance has afforded an opportunity for progressive redress. Now what have we discussed, agonized over, and generally competed for in recent years to fulfill our progressive agendas?"

A collective smile infects the room, whereas my ever-present grin registers protest to group subservience, unnoticed as my silent protest may be. Tim's enthusiasm, with raised enthusiastic hand for permission to speak, bubbles over first. "Space, space, space!" At which point, smiles widen into giggles.

"Yes, yes, yes!" our universally esteemed SAP echoes back, to riotous laughter. Most remarkable is the immediate hush that follows riotous laughter with the simple lifting of her regal hand.

"As you may know, I was on the presidential hiring committee, and I managed to get a question included for the interview that required each candidate to reveal their commitment to space for our diversity, inclusion, and equity work. I can now reveal that Brad"—known as President Carson to us minions—"promised that he would take my lead in any initiatives in this regard. Needless to say, he won me over with that answer alone."

More laughter, but not so much that a single word might be lost. "Suffice to say, when we heard that the number of nuns left in the convent next door was very low, we pounced. Not only were we able to purchase the adjacent land and grounds for our campus, but in our enlightened way, we can accelerate our vision for an inclusive, nontoxic and non-misogynist secular society. And between us, to sweeten the deal and make sure that nothing will interfere with our noble goals, we have moved the closing date up so that the future begins now."

Dean Perkins wants back into the credit-seeking arena with a clever thought. "Would it be accurate to say that the nun's death gives us life? Perhaps we can use the jingle, they DIE so that we may LIVE."

The effect is immediate, and more than the dean could have hoped for. More important than spontaneous group laughter is the SAP's acknowledgment of her catty cleverness.

"Precisely," the SAP continues, "and why not? They believe they will go to heaven, so death can't be much of a downer." The SAP's peeps squeal at her rather rash and brash colloquialism, even as she continues, "They have a sort of insurance policy which they might be wise to cash in before convents go under for good and the guarantee of heaven is rescinded."

"We did them a favor!" Tim intones at a volume close to Smokey's conspiratorial whisper. To the extent people of this select group can be described as animated, they currently are. Still, the SAP wants to reclaim silence and to reinstall bated breath among group listeners. "But does anyone want to hear the big news?"

Tim's head swings around, in cartoonish bobblehead fashion. "Shush. Everyone be quiet!"

The SAP waits, no doubt listening for a pin to drop. Group control assured, she continues, "I now have complete agreement with the president and my vice-presidential colleagues. There had been earlier discussion about substantial academic use of the convent space that, let's just say, I've managed to put to rest."

"None of the VPs are even close to you," Tim squeals, then, as he turns from his front row seat, "Well, it's true, and I don't care what anyone thinks!" For someone whose every word and thought is motivated by what everyone thinks, it is an audacious utterance. Still, teacher's pet status sometimes requires such boldness.

Though our SAP does not acknowledge the remark, a slight curl of her lip shows she is pleased. Seeing the lip and noting the SAP's pleasure, Tim's head swings around once again in a nonverbal *told you so* gesture.

Our SAP continues. "First news, we will not be required to share."

"The whole building!" Tim cries, and he actually puts his hands on his cheeks, making it difficult to differentiate between Kevin's expression splashing on aftershave in *Home Alone* or Edvard Munch's *The Scream*.

She pauses to allow for anticipated squeals, which predictably rise, crest, subside, and revert to silence, all in three seconds. There is no need to raise a warning hand. "The entire building is to be ours, and further, because of our mandate to conduct all compulsory training programs, another eleven trainer positions will be created, to ensure that all our constituents, and yes, we include lost faculty in that group, are fully enlightened and committed to all vestiges of diversity training." And now for her magnum opus: "Then we intend for our unique training program to sweep across the nation!"

A collective intake of breath, as the SAP waits for another requisite three seconds. "And I can further report I've received approval for a substantial budget to shape our abundant space according to all our needs. I have been entrusted to put together a committee to work with architects, designers, and marginalized artists to create perhaps the most important enlightened space installation of this or any century."

It should be noted in the post-Covid world in which we now reside, the need for space, space, space has been tempered by the use of teleconference, teleconference, teleconference. And yet the vision, the plan, the hunger for living space dominance persists. DEI initiatives require substantial budgets and special space for reasons the unenlightened public cannot understand. A partial list of space priorities for committee deliberation is as follows: uniquely differentiated, aesthetically inspiring, and fully equipped safe spaces; mental health rejuvenation massaging lazy-person chairs; gender-neutral changing rooms and washrooms; male exclusion inclusive hot tubs and saunas; outside-of-the-lines paint throwing studios; essential-me journal entry booths; mud-slinging emotional articulation dungeons; role-playing and full-emoting display areas; padded rage rooms; properly ventilated incense and sweetgrass burning chambers, with hot-rock sauna; oppressor-awareness shame holding cells; race relations meeting rooms; neutral-colored, scent-free, nondescript, non-upsetting, nonjudgmental zen meditation spots; nondenominational, non-Christian, inclusive prayer rooms; Gestalt therapy wall-pounding mannequin (person-equin) punching cells; play-room acting theatres; active discussion/shouting articulation forum space; town hall auditorium; and of course, state-of-the-art offices for the large and ever expanding DEI officers and trainers of the university to hang out and admire their work. All space needs are essential, and all *must* be created according to exacting specifications after extensive input from marginal communities and approval by the SAP's office. Suffice it to say, insatiable DEI hunger can only be *temporarily* sated by convent acquisition.

The silence that follows is deafening. And I don't mean the deafening condition our Center attempts to mitigate with interpreters and equipment for our students who are deaf and hard of hearing. There is no service intervention for the deafening effect that our enlightened SAP has created.

Then ejaculations of praiseworthiness: "Amazing," "Awesome," "Synergetic synthesis," "Transformational," "You are great!" "Our savior," followed by inevitable pettiness.

"Where is my office going to be?" source unknown asks.

"How much is all this going to cost?" Thistle, chair of the Social Justice and anti-Privilege Committee, asks.

"It must be expensive. I would imagine the nuns' spartan cells require extensive renovations to serve our needs?" Sunflower, associate director of Student Mental Wellness, Mindfulness, and Life Balance, inquires with turned-up and wrinkled nose. Then again, she could be Luwanda, director of the Future Resilient and Enlightened Person-Kind Initiative. Hard to tell. They look alike, each resembling a kind kind of person-kind.

The SAP's half-lifted hand quells further questions, and she simply answers, "There is funding enough for all things, and all things come to good people who don't wait."

Oh, she is on fire today, I think, through supersonic clouds of laughter. Her mood and expression change, and we never do get that dollar figure. "Now we must talk about one other, less pleasant issue. We have that public speaking event to deal with."

Our SAP then outlines the existential threat that Dr. Jordan Peterson represents, and the glorious history of postsecondary resistance to his detested message. (Interesting sidenote: in all discussions with university types in opposition to Jordan Peterson's existence, I have never met anyone who has actually read anything he has ever written.)

There are numerous comments about the end of the world as we know it if he is allowed to speak, and the Board of Governors' grave mistake ruling he be allowed to infect our young people with his alt-right message. Our great leader listens to her compliant crowd, a slight smile creasing her curled lip, before half-lifting her right hand, once again, to elicit passivity.

As always, group response resembles a practiced orchestra following their maestro. "We have a plan," she teases.

The excitement is palpable.

The SAP waits, anticipation always an effective tool for engendering full effect. "It's true, it isn't strategically smart to publicly cancel him, but it is also true that Jordan Peterson represents a security challenge, a severe danger to members of our community."

Pause, wait, and then with as much emotion as she can muster: "We didn't ask for this event, and so we should not have to pay to ensure their safety. And in order to ensure actual safety for such a controversial speaker, whose message is so fraught with potential violence, the cost would be formidable—

punitive, if not fatal. Regardless, we can only do our jobs, and job number one is safety, always." At this point, our SAP turns and, by way of introduction, simply says, "Kale."

Kale Paterson is our top security officer. We can no longer use the word "chief" to denote one who is in charge, so "top" is our default word. They (their stated personal pronoun preference) apparently have another official title to replace chief, but no one seems to know what it is. Kale stands five-foot zero in their police boots and adjusts various paraphernalia hanging from their uniform. Their hand lingers on their newly acquired leather holster—security officers were recently authorized to carry guns. Ironically, now that our security officers are non-male, police work is no longer deemed inherently violent. (The decision for officers to carry guns was reinforced by the design of a new uniform featuring sleeveless shirts, less a fashion statement than opportunity for the public to understand the constitutional efficacy of said decision, to wit, the Second Amendment right to bear arms.)

The last male security officers were put on ice three years ago after a series of debates and successful referenda ratified in Senate and the Board of Governors. At the time, justification for exclusively hiring women—later extended to non-binary officers—was that women and non-binary folk can function as well as men, later adjusted to far superior to men. That accepted wisdom evolved into a 50 percent hiring quota ruling for women and 50 percent for non-binary folk. The reasoning of accepted wisdom was extended to the "fact" that women and non-binary people have superior communication skills and are more empathetic than men. Since then, there has been discussion about having an all non-binary police force, which has been tabled for consideration in a few months' time. The issue of exclusive recruitment and staffing has yet to be solved.

One of the displaced male officers of the previous regime has recently applied to be reinstated as a trans officer. As the legitimacy of the application is considered, debate rages between those opposed to allowing back a toxic piece of oppressive history versus those in favor due to inspiration for people wishing to follow their true nature.

The Board of Governors either knowingly approved or else passed without scrutiny the proposed bold move intended to lead the country into a new category of inclusion. Interestingly, as a further point of non-scrutiny, there were no comments on the irony of excluding males in the name of inclusion. The final piece in the security department transformation was occasioned by a significant spike in campus crime once the last of the male security officers was given the heave-ho. Increased crime experienced by students, staff, and faculty was not of concern. Rather, concern was raised about safety for the new security officer composition. To be clear, there has not been an increase in crimes against officers, but universities never miss an opportunity to raise panic from the contrived possibility of what *could* happen.

And who can argue something that has never happened, won't happen? So in a precedent-setting move St Jude's first allowed and then required security officers to carry guns to protect themselves. Even with guns in full view, crime has risen, but hey, no one is going to intimidate our security officers. Last year, a video game was marketed about the St. Jude's male-less security force and ranks as one of the most popular in gaming history, which means it is making billions (over 200 million sales in China alone). The university legal team tried to get a cut of the action, but alas, for reasons too complicated for my small brain, St. Jude's wasn't deemed to have a case. *The New York Times* wrote a feature article on the St. Jude's inclusion-of-oppressed-people's phenomenon, calling our singular university achievement one of the most significant since the founding of the University of Bologna (world's first and continuously functioning) in 1088. A framed copy of the article is on display in the rotunda of the Equitable Admissions and Academic Inclusion building, where the great unwashed public first encounters the many wonders of our place of equitable learning.

I wish Kale and company well, with a cautionary note. Beware those who elevate, bestow pedestal status, and specialness. Your specialness is a bestower projection of expectations that can never be met, and the full circle of their special designation will take you down. Always. It is the yin and yang of university politics, and methinks Kale may be a well-meaning, naive pawn to the scourge of cleverness, or in university parlance, the synergistic confluence that has infected the post-history, postsecondary mindset, with concentric waves across this country and the Western world. Elitism has had a makeover.

Kale shifts their ballast from foot to foot. If much of admired beauty is symmetrical, Kale fits the bill being equally wide as they are tall. In short, and being short, their best geometrical approximation is square. So, while their symmetry is easily observed, they are perhaps not generally considered conventionally beautiful. Except in my quirky mind's eye. I admire all those excluded from conventional beauty for inclusion into my refined version of the same. It is my exclusive club of the excluded. My island of the misfits pageant peeps are beautiful to me for their uniqueness and determination to persist in and among the deep weeds and relentless vicissitudes of life. They and others may not know they belong among my beauty club imaginings, and it might be a tad awkward to explain, so I don't. My gain, their loss.

They have more piss and vinegar, testosterone and Napoleon syndrome attitude than an pit bull, which gives them a commanding presence from their lowly perch. As a formerly six-foot-three-inch guy with the sensitivity of a pit bull in heat, I have come to appreciate those who are vertically challenged from my equally lowly perch. In my few dealings with Kale since their appointment, they have been impressive, a rarity in the university as one who actually follows up on what they say they are going to do. Most distinguishing feature of Kale is the way they cling to, caress, and love their ever present holster and gun as they talk. "Well, it's not a pretty picture. Security costs, and we're talkin' overtime, lots of it, so lots of security people to manage lots of people in the crowd. The auditorium holds twelve hundred, I'm told it's sold out, and demonstrations are anticipated, so could be a couple thousand more people. And who knows, could be another demonstration of those protesting against the demonstrators. Main thing is, we'll have to be prepared, and that'll cost 'em."

"Who will pay?"

"How much?"

Kale doesn't look as though they like getting two questions from two sources at the same time. But caressing their holster, they soldier on. "They will, the organizers. You want it, you pay for it. As for cost, well, I did the math, and if it ends on time, that would be by 9:30 p.m., I estimate the bill at sixty thousand or more. Oh, and our SAP is going to demand that they pay up front, or else they can't hold the event."

People smile and agree with the reasonableness of it all. I vaguely wonder if our SAP knows I am one of the organizers. I tend to hang back, John being more of a limelight kind of guy, so it is possible she doesn't know. I doubt she'd want to give away her plan to the enemy. But then I think, *Who am I kidding? I'm the enemy, whether or not involved.* More likely, she knows I'm involved and is triumphantly letting me know, who will let others know, that our little event with big ambitions, is in real trouble.

After Kale finishes, the SAP has additional items about the multiplicity of accomplishments within her portfolio—most notably, a workshop on deprogramming notions of gender out of students beginning in kindergarten—greeted by supporting comments from her enthralled peeps. Which Smokey takes as his cue, leans over and whispers, "I know how much."

"You know how much Jordan Peterson is despised?" I ask.

"No, not about him. What's the guy done anyway, murder a few million babies?"

"Something like that.

"Anyway, I know how much moola they got," Smokey says, flatly. "I overheard them talkin' 'bout it in the elevator on the way up here. Guess."

"Sixty-six million."

"Hey, how'd you know that?"

"Lucky guess. I should have been an actuary."

"What's that?"

"An accountant with a crystal ball."

"If you've got a crystal ball, maybe you can lend it to my stockbroker. Lately his crystal ball seems covered with mud."

After which I hear only fragments of the plan of action to defeat Jordan Peterson and the evil defenders of free speech. I think about my previous successful grant from the Walkington Foundation for $500,000 to conduct an audit and develop a plan for full accessibility. They were definitely intrigued by the prospect of assisting St. Jude's to become the only fully accessible campus in the world. That initial audit work was done; the plan was complete; the dream of thirty years, which would give St. Jude's very positive media coverage, was on the precipice of happening. I sit back perplexed and wonder, is she really going to do this? But of course, I know the answer.

"…with the student groups being the most vocal as well as the most visual protesters every day until the event, and with faculty presentations as well as the faculty union posting consistent messages of protest, our function in our student services portfolio, strong as it will be, puts us in a supporting role as far as the public knows, and as always, where we are most comfortable. Even though we conceived, crafted, and have implemented this plan of protest, we will, alas, neither take nor seek recognition for our leadership and determination, allowing others to step forward and bask in the glory. Ours is a leadership style with finesse."

An odor of self-satisfaction fills the room as I plan the fastest way to plow out without finesse. Not willing to endure another second, I make a much-practiced clucking sound, and Zigo responds with a single high-pitched yelp that momentarily silences the room. I immediately fill the sound vacuum with a colossal screech of my wheelchair against two chairs that were pushed across my path soon after entering the room. Before people can recover either speech or a willingness to get up and move barriers, I am at the front door, waiting. Tim, usually Johnny-on-the-spot, stares at me like a Pekingese in the headlights, until I grin and say, "Well?" As Tim scrambles to open the door—which we'd planned to automate as well as every door on campus with the stolen $66 mill—I decline to look at, receive or acknowledge the SAP's withering, murderous, death-ray glare. I exit without a glare in the world.

CHAPTER SIXTEEN

A mid-December night's dream and dinner at home

The question is, what to do? I asked David to dig out our long, torturously long, $66 million proposal we submitted 10 months earlier. David, Luna, Iggy, and I then flipped through the three-part 1,124-page document without knowing what we were looking for. The application process had had a labyrinth of complexity, most of which I had mercifully forgotten. Even more problematic was the new requirement that we, who had independently raised $40 million over the past thirty years—half of which went to other postsecondary institutions needing help with their accessibility—were now required to seek permission for fundraising from our own internal mega-Equity Committee. Permission to enrich the university coffers and enhance its reputation. Permission. The thrust of the proposal was straightforward, simple even. We wanted to become the first fully accessible university in the world, and being closest to that possibility after thirty years of working toward it, the additional $66 million was actually cost-effective compared to any other sizable university.

The bulk of the weighty submission was a detailed technical audit of all 121 buildings on campus, with real-world cost estimates for how to meet or exceed all existing accessibility standards. Even the Equity Committee—who always look for an ideological edge—had to conclude that our proposal was big, it was bold, but it really didn't have much to do with them. Equity, in their worldview, has to do with oppressed peoples and utopian solutions, not with our motley crew's determination to actually do something. Over a thousand pages of sinks, toilets, curb cuts, and automatic door openers didn't interest them much. They have people to blame, statues to take down, and no time for real while there is ideal to aspire to.

Still, there's something, something. I vaguely remember something being a wee bit off just as Luna screws up her nose and asks, "Why wasn't this proposal submitted to the National Infrastructure Agency? Isn't that where you got funding in the past? Who or what is the National Institute for Equitable Solutions that it ended up going to?"

I'm still trying to recall. "We were told to submit to them because of rule changes as well as the large amount of our request. Not sure where that came from, because the Equity Committee didn't give it much consideration."

I take too much time being unsure, which makes Luna apoplectic. "You've got to remember who."

And before Luna can tell me how frustrating I am again, I do. "It was Maxi."

"Maxi?"

"Oh my goodness," Iggy groans.

"Yes."

"This can't be good," Luna says.

And it isn't. I immediately call the university lawyer whose mastery of bland has been refined into an art form. He is not emotional, does not have an opinion, but says he'll get back to me. Which he does within the hour, directing my attention to the terms and conditions section of the Equitable Solutions Agency funding manual, evident on their website in case I doubt his dispassionate recitation. In jarringly legalistic jargon, that section allows successful applicants to modify their spending plans based on "new equity imperatives that alleviate the suffering of oppressed peoples." In consideration of this signpost pointing to corruption, St. Jude's wrote an opportunistic proposal amendment echoing the funding body's sentiments for their "emerging hierarchy of equity needs." The senior officers of the university successfully repurposed the $66 million dollar proposal of 1,124 pages with a single paragraph written by the SAP and signed by the president. Without telling me. As the saying somewhat goes, this was not fiction, just stranger, less believable, and more corrupt than fiction.

The question of what to do is not answered by my beagle-in-the-headlights group at the Center, which is why it is asked again to our shocked assemblage over dinner that evening. What, indeed, to do?

I lay bare the scenario in the middle of Sister Sandrine's painstakingly prepared and exquisite selection of Thai dishes to an audience apparently too shocked to respond. Except, that is, for Pearl. She appears from the woodwork, as she often does—like a moth attracted to light—by the sound of words articulating an adult dilemma which she finds has too much *adult* and too little *dilemma* for her likening.

"Why don't you tell what happened to people who report news?"

This ridiculously naive response is, of course, exactly what I should do. So, how to explain to a kid why I can't do just that? "That is a good answer, Pearl," I start slowly, as Aunt Isobell's head nods and lip quivers. Sensing his cue, brother Iggy attempts to explain adult subtleties, "This situation is very complicated and sometimes it's hard to just tell what has happened, to just tell …"

"… the truth," Pearl finishes.

"Yes," Iggy answers. He opens his mouth to refine his stark answer and then just gives up.

Brenda attempts the refinement exercise. "Pearl, sometimes people take advantage of the truth to do things that are not honest or can hurt other people."

Pearl carefully considers these adult words, as she always does. "So when adults tell kids to always tell the truth, they mean only sometimes, to some people?"

"Not exactly, honey."

Sister Sandrine giggles. "I'm sorry. This is of course serious, but it is funny too. I remember being about Pearl's age and realizing the complexity or hypocrisy of the adult world regarding truth and honesty, and I remember blaming myself for not understanding the rules around why and when to tell the truth. To be honest, I still find it confusing."

"I don't think I want to learn when I shouldn't tell the truth or who I should lie to," Pearl says.

"Good for you," I say. "And you're right. Thanks to Pearl, I know what we've got to do and when."

Pearl who has finished her dinner and is beginning to find our company a tad boring, says, "I've decided I am going to remain a mature child rather than become an immature adult."

We all laugh at this rather profound thought and I think, *I'm liking this kid more and more.*

"Are you going to demand a meeting with your SAP?" Aunt Isobell asks, the course of action I had proposed in my earlier diatribe.

"No," I answer with conviction. "That would only give advance warning for what needs to be done, which is, as Pearl correctly asserts, to tell the truth."

"And to whom are you going to tell the truth?" Sister Sandrine asks.

"Everyone in the news, as Pearl suggests. In less than two weeks, we have both Edie's wedding and the Jordan Peterson event on the same day."

"I thought the Peterson event was likely to be canceled because of those ridiculous security costs," Iggy half asks, half says.

"I've been thinking we would have to cancel until just this minute because of that sixty-k security bogus cost. But I just remembered we have at least that much left over in an account that was supposed to pay the accessibility auditors. The deal that they proposed when they started was that we would hold back 25 percent of the total fee, and we would only pay that portion if their work resulted in us getting the $66 million to create the first fully accessible university in the world."

"But how can you use that account to pay for security?" Iggy asked.

"Already have a couple times. It's a contingency account, not well defined, and we've paid relatively small amounts for security in the past for events we've had on weekends, like that employment fair last March."

In a rare moment, Iggy looks, if not relaxed, at least not overly stressed. "Why did the physical campus auditors offer for us to withhold their final 25 percent?"

"So we'd choose them over the other guys, which is what happened. They were second until that offer."

"How will you explain where the money came from if the SAP wants to know?" Iggy asks, unable to sustain pleasant feelings in the face of what could go wrong.

"I'm way beyond what I would normally ever plan, so that, dear brother, will just have to sort itself out."

"I was afraid you were going to say that," Iggy responds, reviving dread with a sidelong, longing glance at Sister Sandrine.

"And since I have both said it and mean it, I think it's time for a toast."

"That is just what adults do when they want an excuse to drink alcohol," Pearl says, with a feigned yawn meant to convey boredom.

"It's meant to celebrate something or someone, Pearl," Brenda admonishes her daughter. "People often just raise a glass and don't drink during a toast."

"And yet young Pearl does have a point because adults really aren't very honest," I answer. "I think we should change that. I for one always take a big swig when there is a toast, and I make toasts to people and things all the time. In fact, let's have a toast to kitchen toasters to start things off."

Pearl straightens her glasses and rolls her eyes. "You are getting less funny, even if you are becoming more honest."

"Well, one out of two ain't bad."

"I would prefer two out of two," Pearl answers.

"So would we all," Sister Sandrine says, in a conspiratorial whisper.

Aunt Isobell joins in. "I've been waiting his whole life."

"His jokes are so bad, I used to think he wasn't my brother," Iggy adds.

"Maybe he was adopted," Pearl reasons, which causes an eruption of laughter from everyone else.

"Oh, Pearl, that hurts," I say.

"You're not being honest again," Pearl deadpans.

"Okay, you got me, but I'm going to put this question to the entire group. How do we let people know about the $66 million dollar swindle—through news outlets as Pearl suggests—once we have their attention in two weeks?"

"Especially with all the media focused on the Jordan Peterson event," Iggy adds.

"Yes, but not only. Word has gotten out about Edie's wedding. It is unique after all, and I've been contacted by several media outlets who want to cover it."

"What does Edie think?" Aunt Isobell asks.

"That was my first thought. The media love the 'woman dying of cancer finally gets married' angle, which can be good or bad depending on your interpretation. I asked Edie if she wants publicity, and she said bring it on. I then gently asked if she'd be okay if the way they cover it becomes a pity party and she said—we're talking Edie here—'Great, 'cause I love pity, and I love to party!'"

"The sad fact is, she's serious," Iggy adds.

"You mean honest," Pearl says.

"True," I add. "Edie is always honest, which makes you wonder how in the world she's been able to survive in the university all these years."

"I think it is because, outrageous as she can be," Sister Sandrine says, "she doesn't have an enemy in the world. Despite her constant use of four-letter words, she really is a lovely, loving person."

"So, we've got two events at the university," Aunt Isobell begins thoughtfully, "one a celebration, and the other a controversy. The first could use distraction from pity, and the second could use some distraction from protests."

"Yes, some media interest would be healthy without news of the $66 million taking over either event. The balance would be to enhance each event with a timely announcement, communication, something about the great theft. The problem is, these events and our sixty-six mil are not particularly related."

The table is silent as we think about this.

"But they are related," Sister Sandrine insists. "Just yesterday Edie me told how grateful she is for the wedding you are all putting on, and then she added how much she will miss work when she gets too sick, and how much she has loved belonging to a group of trailblazers determined to create the most accessible university in the world."

"She said that?" Iggy asks.

"That is a direct quote," Sister answers, "You seem doubtful."

"I believe Sister Sandrine," Pearl says. "And Aunt Isobell too, of course, whenever they say something."

Aunt Isobell smiles, as pleased with Pearl's honest endorsement as she is at hearing Pearl calling her Aunt Isobell.

"No, I don't doubt it at all," Iggy says, horrified that he has expressed doubt to Sister Sandrine. "It's just that I'm not used to hearing her express herself with such—"

"Eloquence," Sister Sandrine finishes.

"Exactly," Iggy says, with relief.

"What Edie said is not really surprising," Aunt Isobell muses. "It does seem she uses humor to mask deeper emotions."

"We all wear masks," Sister Sandrine says, to my delight and to Iggy's everlasting bewilderment. "And I don't mean Covid masks, but a deep personal means of hiding the naked truth of who we are from many, most people, and possibly even from ourselves."

Iggy is destined to spend most of his angst-ridden night pondering what naked truth might lie behind Sister Sandrine's well-fashioned mask. Even the word naked will guarantee night demon visitations.

"There's more pad thai and tom kha gai." Sister Sandrine says to a stupefied-looking Iggy, whose silent stupefaction is taken as her cue to ladle another serving onto his plate.

Aunt Isobell is amused by this but decides to give Iggy some relief and change the subject. "Phelim, are you satisfied with wedding plans for Edie?"

"Yeah, I think we're in good shape. It only took Diane and Melanie about a week to get the basics done. Especially after Edie did that interview with CNCK and said that she was dying *and* getting married, the community response was rather fantastic. Doors opened, wallets opened, and everything got donated quickly. We got the St. Jude's Great Hall booked; caterers, flowers, and live music are nailed down. Even the university custodians have volunteered to set up and take down furniture, chairs, the works. And since the Great Hall only holds five hundred people, there is fierce competition to get invited to what is being billed as the social event of the century.

"The amazing thing is, no one who has been invited so far has let anything come in the way of committing to being there. People are changing business and conference commitments, personal bucket list items, and family functions, hell, there is even an engaged couple who work in the library who have changed their wedding date, which was supposed to be the same weekend as Edie's, just so that they can be there. No one wants to compete with the wedding of the century."

"That is lovely," Sister Sandrine says, clapping her lovely hands together like a child, in contrast to the stoic-seeming nun we met just weeks earlier.

"I have a question," Aunt Isobell asks in her serious, pondering way. "There has been a lot of goodwill, no great will, toward giving Edie the wedding of her lifetime, and that is commendable. But I do wonder what about the groom. I don't even know his name."

"Joey," Iggy says, prying his eyes from Sister Sandrine and directing his attention toward me. "Auntie does have a point. Joey is buried in Edie's formidable personality."

"Yeah," I say, stretching my wretched back. "He's always been kind of subservient to the giant shadow Edie casts."

"Is there any way he can be made to feel an equal partner at his own wedding?" Sister Sandrine asks.

Iggy and I grin at the perplexity of the problem. "Joey is a great guy," I start, "and is normally content to let Edie bask in the limelight. But we need to shake that up a bit, to show another version of Joey to Edie, and to make her really see him."

"How are you going to do that?" Aunt Isobell asks.

"The best example can be summed up in the little wedding surprise I've been planning for the past few days."

"Oh, do tell," Aunt Isobell intones.

"Well," I begin, not quite sure how to proceed, "as you may know, Edie likes men, and you may further know or not that Edie has a special interest in men of a certain profession …."

"That would be Edie's fetish for firemen," Aunt Isobell says matter-of-fact-ly. "Go on."

"Ah, so she made that known to you so soon after arriving?"

"She makes that known to everyone in the first half hour of arriving. Phelim, really, get to the point." Aunt Isobell has a refreshing, no-nonsense aspect to her.

We are all grateful Pearl has wandered off, no doubt in search of another obscure book to read and possibly borrow. The last few books that have caught her attention include the aforementioned *Great Big Book of Auto Mechanics*, *War and Peace* by Leo Tolstoy, *The Diagnostic and Statistical Manual of Mental Disorders* (DSM6), *Rand McNally's World Atlas*, and *The Friars Club Encyclopedia of Jokes*. The latter book she still has and has warned me that she is going to start telling very funny jokes.

"Okay, then. Well, knowing this, in fact everyone knowing this, I remembered that one of our peeps has an uncle who is an area fire chief, so I called him. He told me to use his name and call a guy who coordinators firemen for volunteer events, which I did, and we now have a fire truck with four firemen in formal uniform arriving at the end of Edie's wedding replete with champagne and flowers for the bride."

"She'll love that," Aunt Isobell giggles.

"But poor Joey," Brenda adds.

"My thoughts exactly," Iggy echoes.

"Right. It is lopsided," I admit.

"And what might Joey's fetishes be?" Sister Sandrine asks.

I think Iggy might faint, and I feel a little lightheaded myself. "The thing is, Joey always seems to like whatever Edie likes, so we don't really know what his, er, interests might be."

"So perhaps," Sister Sandrine begins slowly, "you could do something to make Joey more important according to what Edie's, as you say, fetishes are."

Many, many complex thoughts crowd my brain, in contrast to my feeble response. "Yes, I think that is what we intend to play with."

"It is always scary when Phelim has a great idea, often begging for a redefinition of the word *great*," Iggy says.

I ignore the slander. "Even though the four firemen in uniform are absolutely fitting for a formal wedding, when I heard about formal, I had this nagging sense that something was missing."

"Or maybe Edie would prefer that the firemen were missing their formal suits and wearing their birthday suits," Brenda offers.

"Ah, well, you're on to something," I say. "So I called the organizer of the firemen with a request."

"To ask if he can round up four birthday suits?" Iggy asks with a grin.

"No, but tending in that direction. Everyone knows that Edie's particular attraction is not to formal wear, but to the grubby, pole-sliding, everyday fire-fighting work clothes."

"That is true," Sister Sandrine concurs. "I've seen the calendar on her office wall. She seems particularly impressed by the big boots they wear."

"Yes, yes, yes, so when I called the volunteer coordinator, I asked if in addition to the four formal fireman, can he lend us one grubby firefighting uniform that might fit a short, plumpish, middle-aged man about to be trans-formed into the object of his bride's desire. While Edie is fawning over the formal firemen, Joey can slip away and put on the grubby stuff before making a grand entrance."

Aunt Isobell claps her hands as the group responds. "Bravo."

"He will be *the* fetish on his wedding day!" Sister Sandrine enthuses.

"Phelim, you could play Springsteen's 'Fire' over the sound system as he makes his way toward Edie," Brenda suggests.

"Perfect."

"But there is one problem," says my little brother, who lives to find prob-lems that others would never dream of.

Four pairs of eyes wait for him to articulate the problem that could derail an otherwise perfect plan. "Well, when Edie sees the four firemen, and is clutching champagne and flowers, what if she makes them take her away in their fire truck, and she forgets who in the world Joey is?"

To which we toast our fetishes, creative plans, and the pleasure of camara-derie celebrated with the rituals of dinner, the finest of wine, and the corniest of jokes.

CHAPTER SEVENTEEN

Wednesday during our regular Faculty Club date

John and I have much to talk about at our Faculty Club lunch next day. It's funny; the name Faculty Club once denoting exclusive membership, still adorns our regular eatery since in an effort to be inclusive, the Faculty Club sign now includes the caveat: *all are welcome*. And, inclusively not fully sated, in fine print the Faculty Club sign ends with an invitation to include *all who cannot pay*. That's right: if you want to eat lunch and can't pay, just say so or get up and leave after eating. The original thinking was that few people would claim poverty, and the Faculty Club would seem a shining example of virtue in action. According to John, the thinking was wrong, and the Faculty Club is going bankrupt. Once bankrupt, I ponder, they might qualify for a free lunch; this is, a few morsels of the post-pandemic "temporary" infrastructure trillions government continues doling out in the name of the great suicidal reset.

I win, getting to our usual table at exactly noon on this day, but in usual fashion, win or lose, John greets his many detractors and occasional admirers as if he has just won an Olympic medal.

The waiting staff, in recognition of the wear John exacts upon their chairs, have replaced an injured one with a fresh set of legs. Still, as John sits and leans forward, straining his chair's fresh stems, I swear I can hear a mighty groan over the rancorous dining room hubbub that occurs in the wake of his entrance.

But today his boisterous entrance is short-lived and his demeanor subdued.

"Hey, you okay?" I ask, as John turns toward the waitress and holds up three fingers indicating a triple Irish whisky as his choice du jour.

"Is that still code for a pint of Kilkenny? Hard stuff seems a bit much for lunchtime beverage, doesn't it?" A rhetorical question if ever there was one. Still, in asking the next question, a repeat, I want an answer. "John, something up?"

John sits thoughtfully, without responding, without playing the crowd, without being himself.

"I'm fine," he says, looking downward in uncharacteristic fashion, and then lifting his head, he either feigns or comes to a miraculous transformation. "In fact, never better."

I'm not convinced, but John takes the conversation out of probing range.

"So we are in the clear with arrangements for Jordan Peterson. A couple days ago it was confirmed that Professor White from our university's newly created Critical Race Theory Program is going to take on Jordan. And that's not all."

Daryl White is a brash St. Jude's rising star. He'd been a graduate student at St. Jude's in an interdisciplinary program, that is, courses taken on a range of topics with grievance as the common theme, who not being content to graduate within a nondescript interdisciplinary whatever, ramped up his critical race profile and then convinced a number of faculty, his dean, and ultimately the Senate to allow his in-progress thesis opus to qualify as completing a PhD in Critical Race Theory, even though no such program existed, from which a program was declared with Daryl as its first graduate, first faculty member, and more recently first chair, with twelve faculty hired and in place in less than eighteen months.

Daryl was determined to make a name for himself, and having jostled his schtick into both a PhD and North American program first, who could blame him? He often refers to his surname as ironic. He likens it to his mark of Cain, arguing that even he, who is not white, cannot escape the original sin of whiteness. Professor White receives accolades for his courageous fashioning of self. Never has the word *courageous* been mistaken for the word *opportunistic*.

Without intruding, Estel lays plates with burgers and fries in front of John and me. It is John's standing order, unchanged for these many years, though soon to be unavailable in restaurants as the ban on beef and red meats comes fully into place. Mine is nicely cut into pieces I can manage, and we eat like condemned prisoners consuming a last meal on the day of execution. Stuffing delectable morsels into my gob, I resolve to seek a governor's reprieve for the unfair imminent execution of meat as a culinary option.

"Jordan will slaughter him," John declares.

"Maybe."

"Certainly."

"But only if anyone is listening. Daryl will have the crowd and does present as a sympathetic voice for the oppressed."

"Lack of equality of outcome is not oppression."

"And yet that is the narrative the sympathetic audience will eat up."

"Ah, yes." John becomes animated. "And yet, paltry, pale audience sympathies will pale in comparison."

"In comparison to what?"

"To the millions who will watch as a result of the coverage the event will get."

"Oh?"

"CNN, MSNBC, FOX, and others are lining up, and will send people to cover the debate live."

"Why?"

"Because Congress is about to pass a new bill that will require the post-secondary sector to teach critical race and gender theories or else face funding cuts. And, as mentioned, that's not all. As of today, St. Jude's is offering to have three professors duke it out with the good Dr. Peterson."

"Do tell."

"It makes sense, and their superior numbers will only enhance the need for free speech. The debate with Daryl will talk about reparations and race, but then Professor Marshall of Equity whatever will argue that words are violence, and then that other one, I can never remember her name, says she'll set him right about the wisdom of pay equity and new affirmative action initiatives coming to college campuses, public and private sector institutions everywhere and soon, to hell with Supreme Court rulings."

"Are you talking about the new movement toward oppression pay as the natural outcome of the reparation act passed last year?" I ask. "'Cause, if so, there's a related motion before our Senate next meeting. Apparently, pay will not be the only oppression payoff for designated groups. Soon exterior features will be the main criteria for determining faculty tenure."

"I'm not surprised," John says. "You only get into Ivy League schools if you fit into a designated group; same for faculty hirings. And then because you are in that designated group, you qualify for tenure due to oppression. Makes enlightened sense. Anyway, they figure that if that horrible free speech–loving Peterson has to come, then beat him at his own game. Though their blitzkrieg threesome assault does seem a tad beyond the theme of free speech, it will make for some fireworks, and hence the media interest."

I watch John. He has lost the outward gaze, his ever-present monitoring of how much people watch and are fascinated by him. It is his barometer of success, self-esteem, and amusement. And he did not explode, as was his wont, at the possibility of pay and tenure being determined by external parts. Something is off. His words and expressions are John Staffal, but his eyes, only briefly meeting mine before dropping toward his knife and fork, are not. He will talk when he is ready, and more likely than not, if it is about personal matters, he will only talk years after events have occurred and when discourse can be presented as riotously funny or a ribald tale. John doesn't do vulnerable.

"Speaking of blitzkrieg, how's your novel coming?" This is a familiar thing between us, and apart from our mutual fascination with the subject, it is the thing that allows us to not talk about things that matter. Though he knows I haven't written a word, he asks by way of opening up our continuous dialogue about all things Hitler. He knows my killing Hitler fantasy gig saved my life all those decades ago when Irene hugged me back from the brink, just as it is going to save a few others, like Roma and Fred, like six million Jews, and many more millions of Europeans and Russians. Usually in playing along, I claim I'm making progress which will soon result in actual writing, but today we don't bother with the pretense, and he continues.

"Came across a few tidbits that fit our present situation." He squints one great eye as he leans forward on squeaking wooden legs to deliver his intelligence. "For all the emphasis on the thuggish Brownshirts who beat people up on the streets, which accounts for much of Hitler's early rise to prominence, where do you think most of his much-needed support came from?"

"The universities," I answer. We are never much impressed with the other knowing the right answer about Hitler. But we do marvel at the outrageous nature of the fact re-presented to our audience of two.

"And these ivory tower adherents were not just students but faculty, learned men, experts who know best."

"Goebbels had a PhD in literature," I add.

"And then this—eight out of the fifteen men who created and approved of the final solution at the Wannsee Conference had PhDs. The worst crime in human history is conceived by a majority of learned, credentialed men. Isn't that special!"

I'm impressed, but John is not finished. "And even more a perversion of education and profession, if that is possible, is the weirdness of Dr. Mengele."

"He must have skipped taking the Hippocratic oath, seeing how he personally greeted and directed to their death over 400,000 people in only twenty-two months at Auschwitz."

"Yes, and wasn't it his twin pillar of evil, Joseph Stalin, who said, *One death is a tragedy, one million deaths is a statistic*? Rhetorical question, my boy; I know you know the answer. But I've tried this on people, and I can tell you with certainty that Joe public will always react with more emotion and disgust to what I am about to recite about a single solitary case than any large number, even though the 400,000 statistic represents 400,000 equally chilling individual and deeply personal narratives." John coughs for effect, having achieved the setup he desires.

"Mengele once delivered a baby from a very difficult pregnancy—he was apparently highly skilled and exacting. The delivery took some time and attention to detail, for the mother and child were fragile, and it was a complicated case. Still, Mengele stuck to it with precision and care for many hours without compromise. He was unwilling to be defeated. He was a talented and educated doctor. Then, once the danger had passed for both mother and child; that is, one mere hour after he saved the life of infant and mother, he had them killed and incinerated."

We have an unrehearsed moment of silence. For all our boyish fascination with Hitler, war, tanks, airplanes, and history, we have these somber moments, because acts of both good and evil live in perpetuity. It is what we know, though we don't know why.

"Of course, the modern view is *that* was then, and we, being so clever, no longer experience any of the *that* of back then."

"An interesting sentence," I comment.

"But of course, minus the evil of Mengele, the illogic of woke thinking astounds with comparable contradiction."

"Sorry, but we've moved on from the term *woke*."

"Oh?" John's bushy brow rises with inquiry.

"Yes, the term is now *enlightened*, and I might add, its origin is attributed to our very own Professor St. Stephen of Sociology. And further, Sociology is petitioning Senate to change their department name to Enlightened Human Social Studies."

"The Age of Enlightenment has long passed, and to *enlightened* moderns, it never happened," John says dryly. "Okay, so in deference to the wisdom of enlightened moderns, just how do these geniuses square the following circle?"

"You got me; proceed."

"Two operating rooms with a common wall have two procedures in progress. In each is a woman with a fetus of the exact same number of days, in late second or early third trimester. On one side of the wall, is a woman whose baby has a risky congenital life-threatening problem necessitating delicate and experimental surgery requiring the best specialists from the most advanced hospitals in the world. Assembling this specialist team is like moving mountains, with time of the essence, but difficult as it might be, they come together on this same day and perform a medical miracle that saves the baby boy and his mother. So a happy ending, with unanimous agreement that the millions spent to achieve this end are well worth it. A person's life is priceless, and what has been learned for application to future fetal surgical situations is of incalculable benefit to an incalculable number of people and their families."

I nod at John's summary, knowing the preceding to be merely prelude for the ultimate setup.

"In the adjoining operating room at the same time on the same day, another surgical procedure is being performed on another fetus, again the exact age, performed by just one doctor. However, this fetus does not have a congenital defect, does not require fetal surgery, is completely healthy without need for intervention of any kind. In fact, she is so healthy that her birth, mere weeks away, will happen without assistance or incident, once the happy day arrives. *But*, but, but quite apart from what happened in the adjoining operating room, the she of this room is being aborted. Notice I have correctly identified the baby as 'she' and resisted the expectation to use the impersonal 'it' for a baby that is to be aborted."

I almost speak but decide to allow John to continue.

"Though the fetal surgery next door requires a staggering amount of dedication, resources, and innovation to achieve success, the surgical innovation for the abortion in progress only requires the use of instruments for cutting and severing limbs in order that a late-term, large fetus can be efficiently cut, suctioned, pulled out, and disposed of. The fact of gender and a thousand other details are noticed even as her aborted body is disposed of. One cannot unsee even if one denies its significance. The mind that represses the fact still stores the image. It is how our brain works."

John once again leans forward on his screaming chair and squints with sage wisdom. "And now this: even as late term abortions have become much more common and are increasingly performed, medical technology has advanced such that the successful delivery of babies in distress has become possible to do ever earlier in pregnancy and with a higher expectation of success. How's that for contradiction? Babies weighing no more than this," John says, pointing to the remaining meat on my plate. "Imagine that a barely surviving, solitary pound of flesh can be resurrected to thrive and develop into a full human being."

Estel approaches, looks concerned, and is about to ask if there is a problem when I say, "Don't ask."

"So," John continues, yet again, "within the same hospital at the same time, one baby saved, to grow into that lovable child a couple has always wanted, will always love, and that society greets, celebrates, nurtures, and participates in raising, as a proper village does, forever celebrating his unique personhood and fulsome human rights as an individual."

"Enough with the histrionics already; I get your point," I say to John to no effect.

"Next door, the aborted fetus is deemed nothing more than cells that lived and are no more; no personhood here, can't apply human rights to a nonhuman, with any mention of humanity being the most disingenuous of arguments to a logical mind. Their logic is literally that the cells extracted on this day cannot be protected because it, not she, is simply an unwanted growth on a woman's body. Think of it: at the very second this fully formed fetus could be lifted from that woman's body healthy and intact, it is destroyed as an extraneous part of a woman's body to which it is no longer attached. And even if separate and living for a brief time, we do not accord rights of a human being to this human being. Though nurtured into existence as part of a whole, this child exits with severe attachment issues. What do you think of that?"

I'm not sure what to think. John and I have much to talk about, as in what to do about the stolen $66 million among many other pressing topics, but I know they will not make today's agenda. "You're going to get this little scenario into the Peterson debate, aren't you?"

I've hit the nail on the head, and John smashes the table with his fist, sending french fries across our table and inducing silence from among the many onlookers in the vicinity.

John is back, I conclude. "And how will you be able to get this scenario into the debate?"

"I, dear boy, am moderating, oxymoron as that may be. And, as moderator, I intend to introduce the notion of healthy, constructive debate into robust discussion as foundational to democracy as best exemplified by the grand tradition of university free-flowing discourse throughout the ages. As such, the moment the pace of debate flags, I will introduce my little ethics scenario, with the proviso that it is less hypothetical than a real question that must be solved."

"And what if the debate doesn't flag?"

"I will cut off debate and promise our viewers something of even greater interest and controversy, and they will love it!"

"Hate it, you mean."

"Same thing. The point is, it will excite, it will make blood flow and people think."

"Hum. And I'm thinking you might insert yourself into the solution for said scenario once the bloodbath is in full swing."

John bows deeply as he chews a great mouthful of fries and burger. "Yes, and I think you will agree, it is an obvious solution. Throughout the Western world we are canceling ourselves out. That is, in North America and especially in Europe we do not produce the requisite 2.1 babies per couple to replicate ourselves, let alone expand the population. In some European countries, that number has dropped to as low as 1.3 per couple, from which no country or society in history has ever returned."

I open my mouth to speak, but even though his mouth is full again, John speaks first. "And at the same time that fertility is at an all-time low, couples wait, hesitate, decide no, decide yes, then cannot get pregnant, only to want more than anything in the world to adopt a baby, for which there is little supply. People just can't get enough babies to adopt, and yet we kill millions, millions, my boy, and we can't reconcile these two facts. Two seemingly intractable problems, with one easy and practical solution from someone such as moi, who hasn't any antiabortion history in his checkered, unbiased past. Ha!"

Despite the jocular tone and language, I wonder—is that a barely discernible tear in each of John's never cried, never taken life seriously, never admitted to vulnerability, hard penetrating eyes?

Before I can respond to his latest diatribe, he changes the subject. "How is the planning going for Edie's wedding?"

"Good, no, great. That notion of community we thought was on life supports has some life after all."

"Are the timelines still in sync between our two ventures?"

"Yes, but barely. The wedding should end by 5:30 p.m., with people milling, photos taken, and celebratory drinks and snacks served until 6:30 p.m. That is when she wants you and me and a few others to make our uber short speeches. Apparently, no one from her family wants to speak, including or especially Joey, so it should take about a half hour."

"Okay, and I open the Peterson debate at seven p.m., assuming Security can quail the protesters, so that works."

"But there is one minor caveat," I caution. "You know about the surprise appearance of the four formal firemen in their big truck, right?"

"Oh sure, and maybe they'll be willing to drive their fire truck into the auditorium if the protesters are too noisy at the debate."

"Well, not sure I told you about the other wee surprise. They are going to bring firefighting duds for Joey to slip into when Edie's attention is distracted by the four formal guys, and then I'll play 'Fire' by Springsteen on the sound system for Joey to strut his stuff."

"Ha, love it and wouldn't miss it for the world! But it could be very close to seven by the time that happens."

"I know, and I'll do everything possible to keep things on schedule so that the events don't overlap. There's a good-sized group of my peeps who want to make sure they don't miss your opening remarks."

"I promise to make it worth your while, with your $66 million to be given some profile," John says, before biting off fully half of his burger, which is not more than he can chew. He chews strenuously and within seconds is about to speak again.

Just as John is swallowing his colossal mouthful, I speak. "Back to your interesting and unexpected comments on abortion and the question of what is a life."

John waits.

"I'm thinking there's something you're not telling me about your plan for introducing the late-term abortion ethical dilemma. Methinks you have something more by way of solution for said intractable problem."

John truly smiles for the first time since lunch began, surely a world record. "Intractable problems are always about intractable will. And the will to act is rarely about the complexity of the problem. In fact, the solution to this problem is obvious. We agree that most government intervention exacerbates societal problems because of lack of objectivity, because of ideological underpinnings that contravene facts and common sense. But in this case, government could play an important role."

"Never thought I'd hear you say those words."

"Never mind trying to get legislation that either makes abortion illegal or else allows parents to retroactively abort their difficult children—these being the two polarized views on abortion we are heading for in an increasingly polarized world. What we should do is incentivize women to forgo abortion for moola, greenbacks, cash, or for housing, for social assistance, whatever it takes to allow for full-term delivery, and then again government can play a role with a robust and dynamic national registry linking these many un-aborted babies to desperately wanting parents. We're talking the potential for millions of lives saved, and I include the happy parents who never dreamed they would ever become parents!"

"John, I can think of about ten thousand reasons why people, or more specifically cisgender nontoxic types formally known as women, will object to your idea, beginning with that over-the-top Mengele reference leading to its dystopian potential *Handmaid* resemblance."

John is nonplussed. "The Mengele reference is just that and not a comparison. I like to expose illogical thinking, however dramatically, wherever it lies. As for *The Handmaid's Tale*, contemporary fiction is outside my wheelhouse, but I get the gist and say this; there is no coercion, only choice, and if I may be add, most importantly, dialogue. Besides, all plans or chaos in the world needs an ethical trade-off between imperfect outcomes. We are a utopian-free zone. Remember my aim: free-flowing dialogue, always; with the potential for brilliant solutions such as just articulated, freely given birth."

"Point taken. One more thing. What if the birth mom takes the cash and then wants to have contact with the kid later in life? You know how regret and other human emotions float to the surface in our complicated psyche."

"A good question, for which, as you know, I have a great answer. First, what is the regret redress for women who have had abortions?"

"None. Again, point well taken, but—"

"But nothing. Mine might be an innovative plan for regret redress, as well as a value-added potential relationship for the child to know both birth and adoptive mothers consistent with the aforementioned theme of 'it takes a village to raise a kid.' In other words, bring it on, and work it out, imperfect as the results may be. Dealing with, rather than ignoring a societal mess might just lead to some imperfect bliss."

I lean back, stretching my colossus crumbling column, the spinal one, that is. I look at John, who comes to a rare finish of what he has to say without having anything else to say. And there are those barely contained tears in his eyes again. Again, he won't look me in the eye and gazes down at his empty plate. "Hum, you've really thought about this. For a lightning rod issue, it's rather brilliant in its simplicity. I'm not convinced you could ever convince the public, but if you introduce it into the debate, I think it'll be combustible."

"Just as I hoped you'd say." Then, looking around, John asks, "Now where is that second burger and plate of fries?"

CHAPTER EIGHTEEN

Ten days from E-Day (Edie wedding)
and P-Day (Peterson debate), at the Center

Thankfully, Luna and Iggy are at a meeting when I arrive, so no bad news or pressure to alleviate a bad situation in my first work minute. I can hear Edie in conversation with someone who she advises to "shut your infernal gob," followed by her full body signature laugh. Which makes me laugh, the more so for the bittersweet realization of its pending absence, a silence that will ring in my ears and haunt my late nights into false dawn. And she, maybe sensing my seriousness in a world she desperately needs to keep in the humor-filled holy moment, turns to me and says, "And you can shut your gob, too."

"But it is shut," I protest.

"Not tight enough, she answers. "Besides, I know what you're thinking, and I want to make sure you don't say it." She laughs again, as others fall into her wake, those same who will attend her un-woke wake.

David is first to my office door, a first for him. "Hey boss, how was the drive in?"

"Well, let's see, I got in my van, and noticed that the ramp is starting to stick again. It didn't stick long, and it still works, but it's time to get it looked at. I drove the same streets to get to this fine campus that I have traveled on for the past thirty years. I had to slow down abruptly at one point to keep from squishing a squirrel, and when I got to my parking spot, nobody else was in it, which is never guaranteed. So, both exciting and positive, I'd say. What's up?"

David gives me one of his expansive and generous smiles. "I just wanted to let you know how it's going on the SAP's social media committee you put me on."

"Yes, yes, proceed."

"Just as you said, they weren't sure how to do what I can do with my eyes closed, so I volunteered for everything, have exceeded their expectations and now the whole thing is dependent on me."

"So, in the make-yourself-essential game, you have scored the winning goal. Has our SAP taken notice?"

"Absolutely, and she's putty in my hands."

"Good work."

David laughs. "Yup, thanks to you. Oops, got a student." And with a giant thumbs-up, he is gone.

Ha, I think, *I might have to have David or Edie or anyone other than Luna and Iggy greet me from now on.*

Aunt Isobell creeps up behind me with the stealth of an assassin. But her polite cough gives it away. I wheel around as my office door clicks open courtesy of my newfangled proximity reader. "Auntie, I've told you that you've got to get the garrote around my neck before politely announcing you are here."

Equally here is Sister Sandrine. "My goodness, both of you at once at this early hour. I don't think that has happened since you started."

"We barely see each other except at home," Aunt Isobell responds.

"It keeps us from using a garrote on one another," Sister Sandrine adds.

"Very droll," I say, and mean it. "Come on in."

They both sit down around my table. In order to avoid being conspicuous at St. Jude's during its fervent anti-religion inquisition, neither sister wears her modest gray suit denoting membership in a Christian order. They have shopped carefully, unwilling and no doubt unable to pay much for a new wardrobe, and the results are interesting. Most of their acquisitions are purchased at our nearby used clothing store. Not only are they unafraid to buy secondhand; they prefer it. Aunt Isobell has a couple of business suits, and Sister Sandrine tends towards the same with a bit more color. But today here they are, wearing dresses. Aunt Isobell looks smart in a turquoise print, and Sister Sandrine— well, her attempts to hide herself are completely upended by Mother Nature. She wears a navy form-fitting dress that inadvertently shows more curves than a racetrack.

The dress is not revealing, ostentatious, or daring in the least. If anything, it is understated, almost plain, except for how its simplicity shows off her beauty, like the illuminating effect of a single naked light bulb when turned on in darkness. Just as an honest person cannot hide the truth, Sister Sandrine cannot keep concealed that which she has no desire to display. *Poor Iggy,* I think. This will exacerbate torturing his tortured soul. And for the thousandth time I wonder, does she know of her own beauty? I consider how she conducts herself and understand that she knows, but truly doesn't care.

Aunt Isobell is businesslike as she lays out this week's university student newspaper. She bites her lip and slowly shakes her head as she taps the front-page story. "They have officially announced plans; the purchase of the convent, extensive renovations planned and what they call, and I quote, 'the enlightened transformation from religious oppression to diversity, inclusion, and equity.' The kitschy title is 'Live and let DIE,' with reference to a Dean Perkins quote about letting the old nuns die so that DIE can live."

Aunt Isobell slowly shakes her head again as we digest the enlightened world that has displaced everything that gave us purpose and context five minutes ago. Aunt Isobell has always been *with it*; that is, well informed, mostly secular, realistic, and accepting. To the extent she ever inspired people about Christianity or God, she let her deeds do the talking. Even now she will not comment or criticize. Still, today's non-criticism is filled with sadness.

"I'm nostalgic for oppression" is all I can say.

Sister Sandrine acknowledges my witticism with a faint smile before saying, "The article also boasts $66 million the university raised for purchase of the convent and for extensive renovations. Interestingly, the money is only mentioned in the last sentence of the article after several paragraphs about the need for DEI space to deal with oppression."

I stretch my spine and feel my temperature rising.

"Tell Phelim what else is interesting," Aunt Isobell says.

"This morning, I took some books and a laptop over to the Adaptive Technology Center in the library for one of my students," Sister Sandrine begins, as I become focused on the revelation of words beyond physical form. I silently chastise myself for focusing on her plunging neckline rather than what she is saying. (Okay, so the plunging part is made up). Admission of my bad behavior never seems to result in change of my behavior. Confessions are supposed to mitigate that.

"The books were heavy, so I took the elevator to the fifth floor for the first time."

"Highly forgivable. I take elevators all the time," I say casually, feeling anything but.

"Three people got on with me. I recognized the first as your Special Adviser to the President who is leading this renovation of the convent. She was talking to a woman she seemed quite familiar with, a woman with a large mouth and teeth, who I believe was named Susan."

"Yes, Susan Perkins, formally Dean of Students, who for the longest time I thought was Dean of Caring and Compassion but Caring and Compassion, but that title only gets a directorship. No, she is now, I think, Dean of Racialized and Gender-Fluid Communities, which is a subset of DIE. But I could be wrong."

"And there was a third person, distinctive features, indeterminate gender."

"Um, Kuko Parsons, likely, from Gender-Fluid Communities."

"Isn't that the same title as the Dean?"

"No, she is only director, whereas the Dean's yada-yada title has DIE tacked on the end cause nonacademic deans can do that. You really should pay closer attention."

Like all my peeps, Sister Sandrine has learned to ignore most of what I say. "Yes, Kuko, an unusual name, is what I heard. They were talking about their new space, and how wonderful it will be, obviously related to the new

DEI Center. Phelim, I'm afraid their normal ordering of letters excludes your DIE acronym."

I nod, acknowledging that my unoriginal and yet fitting use of DIE has become a tad overused.

"Kuko then made a disparaging remark about the Professor Peterson debate next week, and Dean Perkins became quite animated and asked what they were going to do about the awful John Staffal? My eyes were averted, and I didn't dare look at their faces, but I did see your SAP gently place her hand on the dean's wrist and whisper, 'Remember, the plan.'"

Sister Sandrine pauses to let me take that in, or else to soften the blow for what is to follow. "Then, maintaining the conspiratorial manner of the dean, that Kuko person whispers, 'I hope it includes doing something about that loose cannon O'Neill, who might be even more difficult because of the money.'"

"What did she say back?"

"The elevator door opened, and I stepped out first, so I didn't hear what she said. I'm sorry; I should have asked her to repeat her answer."

I appreciate Sister Sandrine's capacity for humor in bleak situations. It is what Edie, who is not swayed by her beauty, likes about her best. "Maybe you could ask for a meeting to recap the words spoken as well as get the strategic plan for how they intend to dispose of John and me."

Aunt Isobell has that bleak look again. I continue, "Can't say I'm surprised. John and I are a thorn in their many sides. It has always been thus. Still, there does seem to be something more immediate or deliberate about their intentions now."

"That was my thought, Phelim," Aunt Isobell says. "Your SAP deliberately said the word *plan*, and one does sense that it may be more involved than she indicated at your meeting."

None of us speak for a few moments. Then as always happens, the immediate business of the Center intrudes upon idle speculation.

"I did promise Professor Tippet from Engineering that I would get back to him by noon with our decision about that accommodation request," Sister Sandrine reminds me. "And did you want me to go ahead and offer a group session for students with exam anxiety?"

"Yes, I've talked to Luna and Iggy, so our informal committee has met, and we can support the student, but with the conditions we discussed before. And if you can do that group presentation, and even offer it a couple times, I think we can get a number of students through the exam period, as well as lessen their dependence on accommodations."

"You are right," Sister Sandrine answers, without knowing how gratifying those words are to me. Before I can ask her to repeat her words, she continues, "I've talked to the other coordinators, and I already have far too many referrals for a single session. I think I'll offer one in the evening too, just to make sure we don't leave anyone out."

"Now that's inclusion," I add.

"I made the referral to Health Services, Phelim," Aunt Isobell says, "and Judy has been given an appointment with a psychiatrist. Thanks for facilitating that. I also wondered if you object to me offering groups to students who come in and are obviously stressed and overwhelmed, but do not have either diagnosis or any history with mental health practitioners. I will, of course, keep you informed, especially about making referrals to Health Services as appropriate."

I blow out a lungful of air. "Aunt Isobell, emphatically yes, but I have to ask you if you know what you are getting into. You must realize I have been trying to get other full-time people to do just that, right?"

She laughs. "I do know, and I also think there's no time like the present. Besides, your original idea and me putting it in place just shows what geniuses we are."

For some reason her laugh reminds me of when she first came to see me in the rehab hospital days after Irene saved me, and though delivered from dread and suicide, I was scared, vulnerable, and either clinically depressed or the saddest human being who had ever lived. Probably both. She had surprised me with her visit, and I had not offered much by way of greeting. She looked at me with an intense expression in those watery blue eyes of what can only be described as the epitome of empathy. It passed quickly, and her habitual resolve to roll up her sleeves and get on with whatever work needs to get done took over. She laughed then, that same infectious laugh on display today and told me to stop being so lazy and get out of bed. I loved her for that. I loved her for her empathy, too. I just never wanted to see it directed toward me again. Students were our business, and rolling up our sleeves was how we conducted business. My peeps, the un-woke, worked.

A whisper of a knock can only be Edie letting us know about something that can't wait. She steps inside and closes the door behind her, denoting the need for privacy, further denoting seriousness.

Before she speaks, she coughs. Not a loud or raspy flu or cold cough, but a persistent, not-getting-better, not-going-away cough. And still she will not quit work, either permanently or for a short time. Even her looming wedding does not change her resolve to work. After all, she tells us, she's got to think about building her stash for retirement. I know she is exhausted by late morning after serving dozens of students, and that is even before having to deal with the rest of us. She has finally been convinced—exhaustion will do that—to take a nap each afternoon after lunch. Space is always a problem with dozens of student appointments in play at any given time, but an office with a couch has been found, and once found, we insist that she use it.

Our next goal is to convince Edie to take a few days off before the wedding so that she can be fully rested. Edie agrees with the concept but has not yet agreed to the reality. I am tempted to tell her about the four hunky firemen who are coming to her wedding as motivation to get rested. But no, our gang talks about it, and we decide we want the surprise to be complete. For once Joey is going to be in the know, and for once Edie, the whirling dervish center of attention for all things, is going to be knocked over by the audacity and ingenuity of surprise, and the sheer magnitude of surprise will jolt her immune system into remission. Okay, too much, way too much to expect, but the mind does revert to fantasy when not reverting to humor to get from this one tragic moment to the next.

"Sharon just heard something on the radio. I googled it to make sure, and what she heard is true." Edie knows my tolerance for coy at this moment it is low to none. She continues, "I'm afraid John Staffal's been arrested and charged with sexual harassment, and possibly more. He's not in jail, has been released, but he's been suspended from teaching by the university."

"And so the plan begins," I deadpan. This is not my first thought. John lives to teach, has much to offer, and needs to be the center of attention at all times. He and Edie have this limelight addiction in common. Not being able to teach will hurt John more than the charge, serious as it is. He teaches a first-year survey course in European literature, as well as two courses entirely devoted to Shakespeare. He has taught these courses for over thirty years. John's European lit and Shakespeare courses continue to be the most popular ever taught at St. Jude's, though they are no longer required courses for English majors. John's colleagues in the English department hate John's popularity, whereas the rest of faculty merely dislike him.

It occurs to me that John's arrest will help accelerate the departmental transformation from moldy old dead white writer's canon to the Literature of Oppression cannonball that is waiting in the wings. Without John attracting students by force of will, passion, and ego, complete transformation to literary guilt and grievance will be inevitable. It may soon be possible to get a degree in literature without ever having read any. Hiring a few marginalized faculty to teach woke courses was the department's strategy toward maintaining a balance between old and new, but the acquisition of power by those who crave it is never tempered by success. John knew this, created many enemies in his vocal criticism at departmental and Senate meetings—even if a few silent older faculty offered whispered, anonymous, useless support—and kept St. Jude's from complete takeover, for a time. I feel a chill with the revelation that John's singular efforts cannot win the day, or any days in the nightmarish future into which we have inexplicably woken. A great dark cloud has covered the sun and is not going to pass.

CHAPTER NINETEEN

Nine days until E-Day and P-Day, in bed and later at Paddy's Pub

My first instinct is to call John. But he isn't answering. That in itself is not unusual. He was the last holdout in a world devoured by technology not to have a cell phone. He has a landline in his apartment, he uses email infrequently on his computer in his office, and otherwise we've communicated in the flesh. Lunch at the Faculty Club Wednesday, and beer at Paddy's Pub on Thursday is how we relate, and if I do say so, we Luddites are more conversant than most lifelong friends and married couples. Kind of makes us an exemplary communicating couple.

Still, John did frustrate people who could not get hold of him, including me on this day. More accurately, I could not get hold of John on the day that had passed, with this day yet to begin. It is early morning, just before the light of day, sometimes referred to as false dawn, when thoughts of going back to sleep are undermined by barely perceptible first light.

Being a sloth by nature, I fall asleep easily and often and can just as easily nap during the day. But ever since becoming a quadriplegic, I will wake up into false dawn when something is worrying me. Being paralyzed and knowing attendants aren't available until morning, I used to wake up additionally paralyzed with deep, pervasive fear. Time and space became frozen, paralyzed, immobile, and there was just too much of both. Irrationally, I feared no one would ever come. That feeling has never fully gone away. Though I frequently escape from university meetings into my in-progress unwritten novel, escapism was refined in bed during these early years of enforced immobility. The untethered brain cannot tolerate a vacuum. Time slows, hours between seconds, and the mind seeks engagement or distraction. It is why the act of actually writing the written word is unnecessary. Rumination rules.

Note to self: I have a problem. I am writing about a young American, an outsider, without access to Hitler in any way. To think he can kill Hitler is not credible. I know this, but the fact is, for all the credible attempts on his life, the real Hitler defied yielding to bullet or bomb, and consequently millions died. People from his inner circle standing two feet away couldn't or wouldn't do it, so my protagonists' methods will have to do. I'll just have to make it too believable to be unbelievable.

Though Roma's and Fred's chances may seem slim, in my conjured fictional world their insatiable desire makes killing Hitler not only plausible but inevitable. Fred must get to the Wolf's Lair and find Colonel Friedrich, who has Roma, and somehow get her out from under the German command center, and then they have to travel where? Killing Hitler at the Wolf's Lair is an obvious solution, but nothing could be more difficult.

First of all, sneaking a beautiful Jewish nobody out of harm's way is difficult enough, but Hitler tended to have a fair bit of company around him at all times. And it must be said, the Wolf's Lair, Germany's strategic nerve center, was probably the most secure place on earth. Also, as important as the Wolf's Lair was, Hitler was not there unless he had to be. His preferred place, the location I have most fantasized about since Irene inexplicably hugged me into life has been the Berghof in the Obersalzberg of the Bavarian Alps, near Berchtesgaden, Bavarian Germany. There in the vast beauty, majesty, and loneliness of the mountains, I, that is, Fred and Roma will find Hitler and alter the destiny of millions. (Note to self: and some people think I lack ambition.)

Fred has temporary cover with his newly acquired Nazi friends, but that won't hold once he is fleeing across Poland and Germany with his Jewish lover. So Fred has to be a survivalist savant, able to travel the back roads, live in the woods, and build shelters out of the remnants of the forest floor. Early chapters of this book will have to include his boyhood obsession with the beauty of nature, surviving and thriving in the elements. As for Roma who grew up in a sophisticated professional family in a large European city—well, let's just see if it is even possible to get her away from Colonel Friedrich and layers of determined Nazis. Yeah, if that's possible, camping and grousing afterward should be relatively easy.

Fred decides to pressure his friend Colonel Haase and appeal to his vanity and ambition. Haase has given information he should not have. True, he gave it to a harmless noncombatant who is supplying Germany with vital war material, but strictly speaking, it is a treasonable offence. Fred presses for information about when Hermann Göring will be at the Wolf's Lair, and before Haase can object, he further presses him to arrange a meeting with the chief of the Luftwaffe.

After Colonel Haase predictably explodes, Fred says, "Hear me out. With the launch of Operation Barbarossa just months earlier, Germany is going to need aluminum as never before. Operation Barbarossa is the biggest military operation in history, with over three million invading Germans facing an even bigger number of poorly trained Soviet troops. The success of this operation is going to depend on the Luftwaffe, which is equally true for the defeat of Britain. The Luftwaffe is again leading the invasion but has established itself as the face of warfare into the foreseeable future. All of which makes Hermann Göring the most important person in Germany, next to Hitler."

Responding to Colonel Hasse's frantic objections, who realizes he is in too deep, Fred calls for calm and makes him listen to the following: His uncle just telegraphed with instructions to significantly expand the aluminum deal with the Germans, and for a greater number of years. Not only will Germany need a constant supply of aluminum to win the war on both fronts, but Fred's uncle strongly feels that America's best bet for peace is to actively assist German ambitions and to further entangle their respective business interests. That way, neither country can afford to go to war. The United States has its own problems in the South Pacific, and as long as Germany limits its sphere of influence to the European continent and North Africa, their interests will align.

"Together, their respective countries can remain in peace, and you and I, Herr Hasse, as silent business partners, will become richer than we have ever dreamed. How do you think Hermann Göring, vice chancellor of Germany and Reichsminister of Aviation, might reward the person who set up this meeting that leads to this expanded business relationship? Would you mind being remembered as the person who took the initiative that led to German hegemony in its sphere, as well as finding lasting peace with America? I dare ask, might Hitler also be pleased?"

Fred is here, of course, appealing to Hitler's leadership style. Hitler was very clear about his objectives, greatly rewarded success, and did not tolerate failure. But strategically he was ambiguous to indifferent about means to that end. Hitler's cultivated ambiguity and competition about achieving goals within his inner circle was often referred to as "working toward the Führer." The Führer was not loyal to people, but to vassals who were ruthless in the realization of his will. Fred instinctively dangles the illusory bait about setting up this meeting as Colonel Hasse's one chance to be noticed, to impress Hitler, to be a hero. And though not defined, subtly piercing Hasse's consciousness is the hint that Fred might betray him for what he had already done for Fred.

He doesn't want to actually meet Göring. Yes, he would be a great target to assassinate, but nothing less than Hitler is the goal. Meeting Göring would be a mistake. It would soon be discovered that Fred is a fake, cannot deliver what has been promised, let alone a greatly expanded version of the same. But the prospect of a meeting with Göring gets him a solid reason to meet Colonel Friedrich, after which, once secured, he will risk everything to find and free Roma. Colonel Haase makes a few calls and sends a letter of introduction to the Wolf's Lair, and Fred travels by train in comfort, in full view, and freely, for the last time.

Fourteen hours later, I am sitting at Paddy's pub at our prescribed time waiting for John to make his dramatic signature entrance. I don't look around, but I suspect there are other habitual Paddy patrons waiting for John's habitual arrival. I am not doubting he will show, but I am somewhat apprehensive. I know whatever his attitude—and John is the master of cavalier—he is in a tough situation being accused of sexual misconduct in the university setting. The reality is, whatever happened or not between John and his accuser, he will be made an example of. It is the university way. I know it is a useless exercise, but I pass the time trying to fathom what it means if John shows up, and what it means if he doesn't. I can't decide which is worse. When John walks into Paddy's and lands at our usual table, I am relieved.

He lifts his arms and pivots in acknowledgment of his crowd's collective greeting, less dramatic than perfunctory. Perhaps sensing people can sense he is off his game, he strides over to Rose who has raised her pint glass to John, as she often does, and with Cyrano-like flair he bends and kisses her wrinkled old hand. Rose laughs her smoker's laugh and John does a pirouette back towards our table. His gestures say all is well, his face not so much. Still, he is here, and I am glad. Zigo also seems glad, rising to greet and get a scratch from John rather than simply thump his tail on the wooden floor from prone position. A rare expenditure of energy. I can't help wondering how Zigo got so lazy with me as his master.

As John's chair strains with his bulk, he holds up three fingers on one hand and one finger on the other. Jeanine returns his gesture with a thumbs-up denoting her understanding and intention to deliver a triple Irish whisky and pint of Kilkenny.

Our mutual tolerance for small talk in the swirl of big issues is limited to nonexistent.

I begin, "So?"

John huffs out a gallon of air while scanning the bar in search of Jeanine. She does not disappoint, arriving within the minute with John's triple and chaser, his prerequisites for imparting information. "It was what was once called a romantic relationship."

"All but lost today," I offer, encouragingly.

"After forty years of teaching the *Divine Comedy*, it occurred to me today that Dante's elevated expression of love, captured in the most divine language in literature, was perhaps ruse for sexual harassment. And of course, the objection of the Montagues and the Capulets to a romance between Romeo and Juliet was a commonsensical, contemporary anticipation of male toxicity. And as for Sir Thomas Malory and the notion of chivalry—"

"John, what happened, and just as important, what didn't happen?"

"Ah, an appropriate two-pronged question, for what didn't far exceeds what did, but in today's enlightened world, what did or didn't is subverted for what could have, must have happened." Then, realizing he is venting, John exhales and simply says, "All of which you know only too well."

John borrows a pregnant pause as I fail in my search to find something useful to say. "Years ago, you will remember in this pub after copious drinks we agreed we can't win this, this cultural thing that has descended upon us at St. Jude's and all other universities. We can only keep our composure in the swirling tempest of enlightened insanity."

"We, misfits of the University of Lost Causes," I respond.

John reflects on this. "Yes, thank you, my friend. I needed to be reminded that the friendship we found was due to the cause we lost."

This was more than John would normally reveal, especially sober. Still, we needed to move on to the main event. "So tell me."

This time, John reverses air flow direction, taking in a great swallow. "I can tell you the nature of the relationship, but others will only see the power differential, the abuse of position and privilege."

I do not respond, so John knows it is time to fully divulge.

"The irony here is that I have been a rake, a chaser, a seeker of advantage, and I confess, something of a slut, male toxicity in full flight, but in this case, with this relationship—and relationship is the most accurate word—I was pursued. Ha! Which will be the most unbelievable fact of this sorry tale."

"Not so implausible. Rose looks like she's ready to go right now."

"Ah, but Rose has about fifty years on Heather, for that is the accuser's name."

"It's true people don't appreciate experience enough anymore."

"Long story short, she asked me for a coffee, said although she is an English literature graduate student, she missed getting a proper education, since Shakespeare is no longer a required undergraduate course."

This being a well-worn conversation, he raises an eyebrow and continues, "Don't get me started on that. Anyway, she audited my course, we had more coffee, which led to afternoon drinks, which led to dinner, which led to the bedroom, which I might add, included many involved and interesting conversations, about primarily literature but not only, which is uncommon in the death-by-Netflix world in which we live."

"Have you seen the new season of *Trump in Prison*? I hear it ends with a real cliff-hanger."

"No, but I'll make sure to watch it tonight," John wittily responds. We do this, though John doesn't do Netflix, social media, or anything much of modernity. With his beer untouched and whisky finished, John holds up three more fingers to which Jeanine once again thumbs-ups from afar.

"I'm thinking all's not well 'cause it didn't end well."

"But you see, it never really ended. It just sort of floundered about like a fish on the deck of a boat it has been pulled into. The extraordinary thing is, she didn't want it to end, she actually and shockingly wanted us to be an item with the title permanency on it, which despite three wives, was not something women have much wanted from me, even when I was thirty years younger and a lot less ugly."

"Really?" I respond, with perhaps a tad too much faux incredulity.

"Three wives, six kids, and worse, adult kids. I'm forty years her senior, and apart from the surprise and a moment of thinking I still have it—which clearly, I don't—I couldn't quite see myself as her permanent frat mate. And do you know what finally occurs to the aging debauched to convince one to forgo illusion, if only for loneliness?"

"I have a sense."

"For all my misdeeds and out-and-out scandalous behavior over the decades, I couldn't, wouldn't, finally don't want to be totally ridiculous."

"I get it."

"And of course, if I could and did commit to her, she'd soon figure this out and drop me, so my preemptive disinclination was no great sacrifice."

"Did you tell her your reasons for no?"

"Yes, but she didn't believe me, and who could blame her? Who would believe that the theatrical buffoon who lusts for attention and seems willing to do anything to get it—in other words, someone who is the very definition of ridiculous—would sacrifice a relationship with a sweet young woman so as not to be ridiculous? Even I didn't recognize me, though I was powerless to do otherwise."

"But she did eventually believe you."

"Yes, and though she wouldn't talk to me after our break, the rumor is, she switched teams and ended up with Dean Perkins."

"Really? I guess I shouldn't be surprised, Dean Perkins being the perfect rebound, as in most opposite of you on the entire frickin' planet. Were you surprised?"

"Dear boy, I've spent my entire career in the university, so I'm immune to surprise. If you are asking did I suspect her attraction to women, the answer is no. But as for surprise, I'd say people were more surprised to learn she was ever with me than with her."

"Are they still together?"

"Well, that's the thing. I hear there is trouble in paradise and that our dear dean is distraught over the loss."

"If you like, I can organize a distraught person's support group. Will you invite the dean to join us?"

John laughs at this, laughter being the epitome of John, especially the combination of John and drink for these past twenty years. But John is not entirely John on this our regular Paddy's Pub evening, just as he was un-John-like in our last meeting. There is something, something, but I cannot place my flaccid finger on it. For all our ease of conversation, honesty, and familiarity, there is a part of John that has never been revealed. John's over-the-top, heart-on-his-sleeve transparency is, of course, one gigantic theatrical mask. But I am not of the great unwashed public. Here tonight in this place with my singular, decades-long friend, I suspect there is something tangible, something real that John is holding back that he should tell me. But toxic males do not pry from one another what is buried deepest, even if it is the very thing that most needs to be said. For the third time in rapid succession, quite possibly a record, John holds up three fingers for a triple whisky, and I try one last time, "Are you okay, John?"

CHAPTER TWENTY

Next day at an unavoidable meeting
with the Special Adviser to the President

I occasionally admit to having a list, even a long list of items I really need to do that haven't gotten done. People can easily understand the part about things that I haven't got done, but might be surprised that I keep a sometimes record of what I need to do. Though I am an avowed lazy sod, I do admit that there are consequences to laziness. My defense is, it mostly doesn't matter. I work in a university.

What I don't like is to remember items that I am supposed to do that I have no intention of doing. But how do you forget what you are inclined to forget when you have peeps like Luna and Iggy who are incapable of amnesia and are determined to inflict their condition on you? Mary does that too, and I still have not talked to Diesel. The boys are living the dream, and not being a creature of conventional wisdom, I can't quite force myself to interfere with Diesel's expression of altruism, or whatever motivates her. Yet. Or maybe at all. Don't know.

Luna and Iggy, tyrants as they are, are after me for a dozen decisions that have to be made, and for direction on at least four reports they will agonize over and eventually write. But I am so frustrating and have not yet sent misdirection for their redirection. About decisions big and small, I tend to wait until the last minute, then wait some more. Some people call that procrastination. I prefer to call it what it is: the prudent patience to wait until things matter, and if they don't matter, and they usually don't, never decide. Again, I work in a university.

And yet I am told that the SAP's employment equity directive matters and that heads will explode with how much it matters when I go to my monthly individual meeting with the Special Adviser to the President, a full forty-five minutes from now. These unavoidable monthly rendezvous are a tad awkward—for her, that is. I have a novel escape with my fictitious novel and ever-present silly grin, whereas she hasn't the imagination for a conjured world. The need for control will do that. Besides, her smile isn't silly, it's merely fake.

The twins are at my door with the paper for which I did not give direction, but which they emphatically feel could ruin my career if I refuse to submit it.

They don't fully appreciate that my equity status gives me an unholy halo, even if murderous intent hangs over my head like an ominous storm cloud. Still, I will listen to them as I always do, because they work hard and frankly deserve better. I'm thinking of sitting down (as opposed to what?) and having a stern talk with myself about myself. That'll teach me.

"We worked it out," Luna begins, holding up the report.

"And crunched the numbers," Iggy adds.

"And it's not as bad as we thought it could be," Luna says, riffing off Iggy riffing off her.

"She's right, Phelim. Coulda been a lot worse, and the funny thing is, hiring our Aunt Isobell and Sister Sandrine has actually helped, Auntie being of a certain age, old but unspecified in our report, and Sister Sandrine being of minority status."

"And female," I add, stating the obvious often being my only contribution to their comprehensive work. "Oh, and they can only help our cause if we can continue to hide their identity as nuns. And the dastardly rumor is, they are Christian, too."

Luna looks at me as if I've just grown a second head. "Where have you been for the past four years? We're no longer allowed to name a gender, especially in cisgender-limited language. You do know this, right?"

"But since the exercise is to get rid of males, especially those pesky white ones, as per the SAP's expectation and specific orders, how do we present a profile of our unit's political identity makeup?"

Luna whips her chair around to look at me square in the face. "Duh! As per the postsecondary national survey that we are required to complete, where we indicate either gender complaint or gender noncompliant.

"The latter noncompliant, unspecified gender being male."

"Yes."

"And the former?"

"All the others."

"And how many choices are there now?"

"I don't know, maybe seventy, but that is not the point."

"So the point is to get rid of males without naming them as such."

"No, they are noncompliant. You're being frustrating, and we don't have time."

"So frustrating," I meekly offer, before forgoing frustrating for factual. "Okay, whaddya got?"

Luna springs into action. "If we get rid of three pesky males, who are not full-time permanent, that might just do it."

"To get the SAP off your back, at least for now," Iggy adds.

"So?" I begin.

"David, Alan, and Arthur," Luna says, pointing to a spreadsheet of their staff analysis hit list and our recommendation for meeting the SAP's equity directive.

They leave soon after that. Might have had something to do with me barking at them to get out so I can get to a few pressing matters. Their recommendations make sense, and it could have been worse—thank you, Auntie, for being old, and you, Sister Sandrine, for siphoning your beauty from a popular ethnicity rather than, say, Sweden. And yes, the SAP will kill me if I don't offer up a few white male heads. But I really don't want to.

As I flung Iggy and Luna out the door, they argued that Alan our tech guy will be scooped up and quickly, likely to a better and higher-paying job. David is making himself essential to a project near and dear to the SAP's cold, minuscule heart, so if we dump him, she may pick him up.

That leaves Arthur. Luna, being a realist, argued that difficult as it will be for our unit, he is now seventy-one years old and probably could use a break. Also, she reasoned, he lives alone, hasn't any kids, and, as a clinical psychologist, is the highest-paid person-kind in the office, so he likely has enough money.

Luna's realism is real enough, though finding another psychologist will be hard because we don't pay market value for the privilege of working with us. But the unit is not my concern just now. Arthur is my concern. He is at the top of his game—and why not, Aunt Isobell might ask, her being a dozen plus years older, and also at the top of the office productivity heap. Arthur has had a tough and productive life, and for him to not have an even tougher life, I know he has to remain productive. He works miracles for our students with mental health challenges, and they all have challenges. He also does the same for staff, mostly off the clock, and he never says no. Without meaningful occupation, Arthur's reason for being will soon dissipate into lethargy.

He is spectacularly real in an institution renowned for being unreal. Mental health isn't just his interest; he has, as the saying goes, lots of skin in the game. Both his brother and his favorite uncle died young, losing their battle to the insidious Queen of Spades of mental illness, schizophrenia. It is for this reason that he devoted himself to helping others in a way that is not understood in the narcissism of university politics. Still, our island of the misfits doubles as an oasis, far removed from the St. Jude's alternate planet of Self-Absorption, and has sustained Arthur for decades. Of most concern, a couple of years back, Arthur lost the love of his life. He became a widower and planned to take a taxi from his office to his waiting grave, he joked, though we understood the flippancy of his joke had a certain sanity, logic even, to anyone who has loved deeply.

I have these thoughts as I wheel into the SAP's suite of offices and am greeted, by way of being ignored, by Maxi. She must have been a cat in another life, I think to myself, further thinking I'm not just frustrating, I'm really amusing.

I do not have to wait long. I imagine that members of a firing squad who are conflicted will do the act quickly rather than agonize over the possibility of doubt. Which is a funny thought since I doubt our SAP has ever agonized over what to do to the likes of li'l ol' me. This meeting could be mercifully short, since all I really have to do is submit the report about staff cuts for the sake of equity nirvana. I have no intention of identifying the white elephant in the room by mentioning that I know she stole the $66 million from us. She probably knows I know, but, it being a crime too big to address, she likely reasons I will leave it alone. She is partly right.

I make the SAP nervous. She never knows quite what to make of me and seems awkward because she can't greet me as she does her own peeps by inviting them toward a selection of her posh seats. As always, halfway through the gesture, she remembers that I bring my own posh seat, which I always find amusing, which plasters a silly grin on my insolent face.

Which sets the stage for our conversation.

"I hear conflicting reports about your involvement at one event or another next Saturday afternoon at the university."

This is of course a prompt for me to tell her about my level of involvement, thus resolving conflicting reports, but she hasn't asked a question, so I desist. Besides, she said, "the university" and not specifically good ol' St. Jude's University, which is weird. And another besides, whenever she starts in a huff, I simply grin that winning grin without responding, which rattles her, which makes her even more mad, which I like, which makes me a bad person, which I also like. Luna might term it frustrating.

"Well?"

"Guilty on both counts, both very innocent events, that is."

The word *haughty* cannot do justice to the look that follows. "That is your opinion. Have you secured the appropriate level of security required by the university?"

You mean by St. Jude's University, I almost correct, but do not. It would have been wasted. Instead, I listen to the SAP's diatribe about the necessity for security in this increasingly dangerous world, especially with verbal hate, violence, and sexual harassment at peak levels. I resist the temptation to ask if the present diatribe somehow qualifies as a victim. Barely.

Still, her rant is unusual since she doesn't usually bother to lecture me, surely a lost cause, which is probably why I take issue with her referring to good ol' St Jude's, Patron Saint of Lost Causes, as *the* university. She must know we got the required security and is mad because she was counting on that not happening. I was counting on it taking a full week to process our security expenditure through the business office as temporary cover for the source of funding. She will never ask me where it came from, since she could never let herself appear so vulnerable as to not have information over me. So I listen to the need for security until it ends, compliant foolish grin plastered on my compliant foolish face. The jeers of a clown.

She blinks, perhaps mildly disconcerted by my lack of response or perhaps wondering if she can get that hair appointment later this afternoon. I love luxuriating in the muddled ground between what people say and where their meandering minds travel. It is in response to her next question that my mind travels far and wide—and deep too, 'cause I'm that kind of guy.

"Do you have the Workplace Equity and Diversity Report that I asked of you that is due, that all other managers and directors have completed to my satisfaction?"

My mind travels back to Arthur and how much I owe him. Oh sure, he'd say, "Right back at you, bud." Still, if true friendship is recognition, he and I truly see each other for what we are, and—drumroll please—we are not repulsed, flaws and all. We've confessed and confided in high moments and low, having been mutual therapists, priests, and pals. Unlike with John Staffal, longtime pal of another stripe who does not do vulnerable, Arthur and I can wail and gnash our collective teeth with the best of them. The difference being, Arthur and I ultimately believe there is no other state except for vulnerable, so there is no use trying to hide it.

And there is another reason why I owe Arthur. He gave me Roma. My fictionalized Roma has some basis in reality. After divorcing his mother just after the war, Arthur's father, a transplanted German, met and married Roma, a transplanted Warsaw Jewess. One might assume they conspired to ignore history, but no, the story about Roma receiving a call from her father from the Warsaw ghetto in 1939 while at university is true, the only difference from my novel being that the real call was the last contact the real Roma ever had with her family. She did not go back to Europe, to Poland or to what had been the ghetto, until decades after she had expunged from burning memory the burning bodies of those who been her everything. Against all odds, Arthur's father became Roma's everything, assuming both the privilege and the burden.

Arthur had not known Roma well during the years of her marriage to his father. He and his father lived in separate cities, and while focusing on Roma's cataclysmic losses, Arthur's father failed to recognize the extent of his son's need for a father. One day in 1964, Arthur's father goes to work at Permanent Pigments, a paint manufacturer in Ohio; there is a fire, and he is one of seven workers killed. Throughout her long life, Roma never acknowledged to anyone that everyone she had ever loved had abandoned her to flames. Only to Arthur in later life, only once, did she mention that on the day he died, his father had left an uncharacteristic, whimsical note on the fridge. After years of living a heavy, tragic version of life, Arthur's father acknowledged he and

Roma were incrementally allowing themselves the gift of lightheartedness. The note that day simply read: *The fun begins today.*

After his father's death, Arthur didn't see Roma again until he was sixteen. One month after getting his driver's license, he borrowed his mother's car and drove alone south from Minneapolis for five hundred miles to visit Roma. After that, Arthur saw her every year, and they talked easily about events and amusing stories of their limited shared experience. Neither ever raised or wanted to talk about what had happened to those once loved and lost. It was understood. Sometimes the requisite recognition of friendship exists in the recognition of boundaries, limitations, no-go zones. Nothing in this world is complete, and the satisfying incompleteness of their relationship sustained Arthur and Roma for almost fifty years. Roma may not have killed Hitler, but the life she resurrected out of the scattered ashes of her family from Belzec, Treblinka, or Auschwitz-Birkenau is testament to her victory over the sadistic tyrant who almost ruled the world.

I'm back and can see clouds of impatience gathering in the SAP's eyes and in the taut clench of her silent mouth. Even the uncharacteristic whiteness at the roots of her hair, needing that hair appointment, seem to express impatience. Mind you, I am frequently full of it, which has to be considered.

"No, sorry, still working on it."

What follows is not an exceptional experience.

CHAPTER TWENTY-ONE

Friday dinner at home sweet home

"But what happened then?" Sister Sandrine asks, with her head slightly bent to the left, an endearing conveyance of curiosity. I once had a beagle who made the same expression with the same bent head when puzzled. He was cute, but Sister Sandrine is cuter.

"I played dumb, which I'm very good at, turned and left," I begin. At which point I should clarify my many comments about Sister Sandrine's physical appearance. Though guilty and frivolous, I am far less guilty than many. Brenda for example—and our togetherness is getting better by the day, by the way—says something to me about her beauty, both her inner as well as her knock-'em-dead outer beauty, whenever she sees her.

As time goes on, I've got to admit her inner beauty eclipses her outward magnificence even for the low-life likes of me. Though she is absolutely removed, uninterested, and indifferent to her own exteriors, by word and deed Sister Sandrine is always probing for the inner beauty of others. She wears no makeup, does not own jewelry, wears second- or third-hand clothes, pays no attention to her luxurious hair, and passes mirrors as if they have no function. And she is, and has vowed to remain, untouchable. What an aphrodisiac for the body and tonic for the soul! Her students love her for the way she is able to identify what radiates from within, even if—as judged by our beauty-obsessed culture—many have been denied external brilliance. I should know, being of an age and having acquired a radio face that makes me grateful when I'm considered beneath judgment and merely regarded as invisible. Also, less beautiful women—and they all are—are drawn to her without feeling jealous of her.

Meanwhile, Iggy remains awkward and shy, intimidated and tongue-tied, unless in a group setting as we joyfully are at dinner each evening. Dinner has become a happy family ritual, the one that I thought would never happen, that has spontaneously strung into our daily lives. And no, Aunt Isobell is not forgotten, does not suffer from comparison, and has been our own beauty extraordinaire since we discovered, decades earlier, that she is actually human. That happened around the time she received permission to ditch the old-style habit and gave herself permission to tell a joke. That's right, Aunt Isobell dropped the habit that had terrified us kids at the same time she took up the habit of telling jokes with us kids.

I remember it still. In our childhood world of no money and limited distraction, we entertained ourselves with ongoing, perpetually bad obsessive word play, what we called corny jokes. Only years later did we learn that we were engaged in the more sophisticated and highly creative art of making puns. One day I'll regret not writing down those artistic witticisms, just as I really should be writing down my novel.

Anyway, in those days, conversations in the living room or at dinner table tended to be quickly split between the adult and kid worlds, without a stray word crossing between them. I had just said to my brother, "What do you call a twelve-inch nose?" Answer: "A foot," and to my surprise Aunt Isobell laughed—and yes, she was laughing at *my joke*—before turning to me and asking: "What do you call someone with no nose and no body?" Answer: "Nobody knows," after which she frequently crossed between the adult and kid worlds, with a decided twinkle in her eye whenever arriving back in ours.

Though under Sister Sandrine's gaze it is impossible to lie, I remain coy. "The SAP got mad."

"And ...?" Iggy, who has had it with coy, pleads.

With these my peeps, I prefer honesty, but this being an unusual time, I do not want them to worry about me. Naturally, I play for time with a well-timed spinal stretch. Zigo, knowing the routine, comes up and places two paws on the side of my chair. I give my best pooch peep a placid petting, let out some air, and say, "She gave me an ultimatum."

"To do what and when?" Izzy asks. He looks panicked; Aunt Isobell and Sister Sandrine merely look concerned.

I shrug my shoulders, they being both what one shrugs and about the only thing I can fully move on my own. "Either I make the choice about which pesky white males are eliminated, or she does."

I can see the dials moving in Iggy's brain as he tries to calculate how the SAP's exercise of male exclusion might go. "Don't you think it's better if you do it?"

"Yeah, I suppose, but those we eliminate might not agree."

"When do you have to decide by?"

"Yesterday. I've decided to do nothing and can't delay the unexceptional moment I tell her past a week Monday. So, eons and far-flung planets away."

In uber stealth fashion, Pearl has crept back into the dining room. She hangs on the periphery as she usually does, to hear what there is to hear, before deciding if the issue at hand needs her wise and timely commentary. Apparently it does. "You always say you are lazy."

Heads turn towards the source of the obvious. Uncontested, she continues. "I always believe you."

"Pearl," Brenda begins an admonition, but I politely cut her off and say, "Thank you."

"But not this time," Pearl, the fascinating eight-year-old contrarian, says. "Oh?" I ask, for all of us.

"If your boss has decided to do something bad for the workers, you are not going to do it for her. It sort of sounds lazy, but doing it for your boss would be easier, so you can't be lazy. For once." And, in dramatic and yet predictable fashion, she is gone.

A stupefied silence follows. After a sufficient period of Pearl-awe, I say, "Two things: First, I am fine with my decision of civil disobedience toward the SAP's directive. I don't want you to worry, and for reasons I don't fully understand, while there are certainly many things to worry about, I don't think this will be one of them. I just don't. Besides, consequences are a lifetime, or a week even, away."

Iggy groans, but I ignore him and continue. "Second, I really do like that kid."

"So do I," says Aunt Isobell. "Though she's no longer in the room, there's no reason why we can't toast her."

"Hear, hear," we all say, they holding up thin wine glasses and I my heavy glass mug with its sturdy handle. "To Pearl."

"So, now that we've conspired to push Monday far away," Sister Sandrine starts, "are you ready for the swirling activity of not one, but two major events next Saturday?"

"No."

"No?"

"No. As you know because you work for the Center, I am as lazy as sin."

"Bad analogy," Aunt Isobell cautions.

"I sit corrected," I answer. "But I am not as self-effacing as it may seem, because for all my un-sinful laziness, I have a redeeming quality. I hire exceptionally well, present company included." To which the assemblage lift their wine glasses, to which I tilt my wine mug, again. "Diane and Melanie have done an amazing job pulling together the many details of Edie's wedding in short order, and Jasmine has helped out nicely with the complex organizing of the Peterson debate."

"But...?" the ever-anxious Iggy blurts.

"Yeah, it's true for either event there are—excuse me, Sisters—a manure load of things that can go wrong."

"Only the immature say manure," Aunt Isobell says with a giggle.

"That pun is among the worst ever told," I say, judgmentally. "Welcome to the club."

"Thank you. Coming from the worst, my worst is in the best company."

A contented silence descends upon our little band, no doubt a pleasing combination of food, wine, and each other's corny company.

"Thanks for that lovely meal, Brenda," Sister Sandrine says.

"Best scalloped potatoes I've ever had," Aunt Isobell adds.

"Coming from an Irishwoman, that is high praise," Iggy says.

Brenda nods. "Thank you." Then, sighing, "I really should check to make sure Pearl is not getting into trouble."

"Just to be clear, has she ever gotten into trouble?" I ask.

"Now that you ask, no, never," Brenda answers, half serious and half amused.

"Well, that's a problem, I mean you raise a kid to be glued to a screen, partaking of social media frivolity, and what you do get? A third-grade phenom who reads, dispenses wisdom, and articulates critical thinking better than most graduate students. Ever ask yourself what you did wrong?"

"You're right, Phelim. I think I'll just have a couple more glasses of this fine cabernet and hope she graduates from books to social media."

"Good strategy. Know why?" Aunt Isobell asks, before adding, "Serious question."

"You got me," Brenda answers.

"When these ruffians were growing up," Aunt Isobell says proudly, looking right and left to Iggy and me, "I noticed that their best corny jokes, in other words, their most creative inspiration came from an unexpected source."

"You've got my attention," Brenda says, an enormous wine glass hovering at her lips.

"I think I know where you are going with this," Sister Sandrine suggests.

"Having to do with scarcity?" I ask.

"Exactly."

"Okay, so I'm officially confused, though I invoke the right to blame the wine," Brenda concedes.

"Boredom," Aunt Isobell simply says.

"But Pearl is never bored," Brenda answers.

"Because she actively follows her curiosity and works hard not to be bored, wouldn't you say?" I observe and ask.

"Yeah, that she does."

Sister Sandrine offers, "Many of the young people I see, especially once they are older, are very passive about their interests, and expect to be stimulated from sources outside of themselves. Sadly, it seems people increasingly do not differentiate between external stimuli and the necessity to cultivate an inner life. It seems to me this could help explain the disturbing rise in poor mental health."

Iggy adds, "I had a mother of one of my students call and ask if I could teach her child some resilience in a couple sentences or maybe something as long as an hour-long workshop."

"I've had the same experience," Aunt Isobell says, "and I've used your many years of running as an example of how resilience works. I'll say to parents, learning about resilience is easy; becoming resilient, to use a fitting analogy, exists in the callused hands of a carpenter or the callused feet of a long-distance runner."

Iggy is obviously pleased and salutes his favorite and only living aunt.

"Phelim, I've got to ask," Sister Sandrine begins, changing direction, "how concerned are you about the accusation against your friend John Staffal?"

It is an expected question asked for the right reason. Not knowing John, not seeking sensation, her concern is actually for me. "I'm concerned. Apart from what happened or not, I'm afraid that the accusation will take on a life of its own."

Auntie bites her lip, and the thin pale skin on her forehead wrinkles into fine concentric waves. "I'm afraid that has happened already."

"Oh?"

"I've been following social media sites, blogs and the like, and it's bad. There seems to be an assumption of guilt, but worse, there was an immediate consensus that punishment should be severe and include public humiliation."

"Trolls can be vicious," Brenda says.

"But these are many of the most prominent people in the university, with generous support from other prominent people at many other universities," Aunt Isobell says, shaking her head as if she was mistaken to think she'd seen it all.

"When you showed me some of the comments, Sister, I thought that the mob rule reaction was probably organized," Sister Sandrine says, before continuing, "There was complete agreement about some things for which little is known. And many of the comments used very similar phrasing. It seemed less an exchange of opinion than a copy-and-paste exercise in conformity and condemnation."

"And wait until the mob reacts to John's role in the Jordan Peterson debate," Iggy says, echoing my thoughts.

"What is his role?" Brenda asks.

"He is the immoderate moderator," Iggy correctly summarizes.

"Well, then maybe he should give that role to someone else," Brenda suggests.

"I don't know if it would make any difference," I respond, "and more to the point, John has never backed down from anyone in any situation, and I don't see him doing that now. The looming Peterson debate may explain the timing of the accusation, which is reason enough for John to refuse to capitulate to what the mob wants. "

"What if someone else volunteered to be the moderator?" Brenda asks.

"I can think of a few people who could actually moderately moderate, but as Iggy says, John has an immoderate interpretation of this role as one who stirs the proverbial pot. And for all the issues John is involved in, there is no substitute for John. Still, I will talk to him, and hell—sorry, Sisters—I'll even volunteer to be a moderate moderator if that helps. But it won't."

I pause and take a deep breath, choosing my words carefully to articulate feelings of weirdness for what may be coming. "John's life, his downfall, if this is it—and I have an uneasy feeling it is—his exit, whenever that is, has been and likely will be the combination of a singularity, followed by a supernova explosion, with trailing clouds of glory—as witnessed by some of us—or banishment into Dante's lowest level of hell as prescribed by the maddening mob. John has always lived his life as if half measures have to be doubled, and then tripled. Shaking people out of complacency is what he does."

"And he is very good at that," Sister Sandrine adds. "I sat in on a couple of his lectures. His fight against complacency is his central theme. Many but not all of his students react well to his message. Even those who resist his call to live an authentic and passionate life are oddly captivated by his spellbinding performances."

I watch Iggy's eyes grow wide listening to Sister Sandrine talk about the passionate life before I respond, "Yeah, I've attended more than a few myself. He mostly manages to ban the use of electronic devices, which no one can do anymore. And he even gets a bunch of students to swear off endless streaming of shows and social media for the duration of his course, as a kind of challenge for what he calls full appreciation for the icons of literature. Sister, you remind me that his diatribe against complacency is probably best compared to a pilgrimage or retreat more than to teaching."

"Yes, I like that," Sister Sandrine says, displaying a wide smile and perfect white teeth.

"It will be tough for whoever takes over teaching his courses," Brenda muses.

Again, Aunt Isobell shakes her head with real sadness. "There won't be anyone taking over, and his courses will no longer be taught at St. Jude's at all."

"How is that possible?" Iggy asks.

"Phelim, today your SAP posted a communication that Professor Staffal's departure is an opportunity to rid the university of his"—and here poor Auntie pauses to prepare us for an unpleasant verbatim recitation—"toxic, ethno-Eurocentric courses, for a reimagining of literature from an authentic diversity, equity, and inclusionary perspective."

Sister Sandrine retorts, "The whole point of art, of literature, is transcendence, to allow us to shed our identity exteriors for our higher selves. Race and gender are far from the only plot and character determinants when one immerses oneself in great works."

"Well said," I say, in a low tone, tipping my wine mug.

"What happens to his students?" Brenda asks.

"Ah, the communication included a rather boastful pronouncement that all students will be given *A*s in compensation for the inconvenience, and...." Here Aunt Isobell pauses, truly pained to finish her sentence. "... unlimited access to counseling to deal with their trauma."

"What about giving trampolines so that students can deal with their impulse to jump for joy after getting an unearned *A*?" I say, by way of jest, but without jocular tone.

A glum silence descends upon our little band.

From the far reaches of the room comes a familiar inquiring voice, "Mom, if you adults are finished with your silly talk, can we go home? I need to get my science project started."

"Oh, honey, it's too late to start your project," Brenda answers.

"They have science projects in third grade?" Iggy asks.

"I just have to write down a few of my ideas that I thought about while I was trying not to listen to your boring talk."

"Well, Miss Attitude, I guess it is getting late," Brenda reluctantly concedes. Then turning to answer Iggy, "Pearl's teacher was talking to the eighth-grade teacher, and somehow they conspired to ask my darling daughter if she wants to create a science project at that level."

"Pearl," I say, in a pathetic attempt to lift the group, "when are you going to learn that we are fascinating?"

Pearl blows out a gallon of air by way of dismissal. "I don't think I need to answer when I know you are not serious. But I actually have a serious question for you."

"Shoot."

"At university are you told not to read writers just 'cause they are boys or have been dead a long time, or come from a certain place in the world?"

In a rare moment of uncertainty, I truly do not know how to respond, so I simply say, "No, that is a silly idea. You should be able to read what you want, and you don't have to listen to people who tell you otherwise."

Pearl thinks about this and then responds in one of her many moments of certainty, "Good, 'cause if I could only read certain writers, I wouldn't go to university. I still haven't decided if I want to get my PhD or else become a mechanic."

Pearl has an uncanny way of cheering up the group with her thoughtful, commonsensical words. As Pearl absents herself, we make a toast one last time with a congenial chorus of, "We really do like that kid."

CHAPTER TWENTY-TWO

Five days to E-Day, P-Day, and a meeting at the Wolf's Lair

I arrive at work later than usual. Once Covid had mostly abated some years back, implementation of the $47 trillion Green New Deal necessitated imposing severe gas shortages in all blue states, followed by red ones too (where pesky governors fought the inevitable tooth and nail). Many millions of people are unhappy with new climate change directives, especially gas shortages and climate "stressor" food rationing, and yet people seem to have adjusted to the inexplicable with relatively little protest. The operative word is *relatively.* By way of comparison, the race riots of 2020 involved between 15 and 26 million people at approximately five thousand events, whereas protests against the greening and bankrupting of America have involved less than 10 percent of those numbers.

The media narrative conflates present gas and food rationing protests as unlawful riots and downplays 2020 race riot numbers, which were just peaceful protests after all. Same for that little incident in Canada when the ruling party banned gas-consuming cars ahead of schedule (with an election looming) without either the infrastructure or availability of electric cars to replace the internal combustion engine. As a result of this progressive and successful election ploy, the progressives won another majority and were high as a kite until October nirvana turned January into Dante's eighth circle of hell. Over two thousand people froze to death during that progressive winter hiccup, with the Canadian gas moratorium quietly reversed. For now. When confronted with the grim consequences of putting the uncharged cart before the horse without power, Canada's prime minister is reputed to have said "oopsies," before soberly adding that people died for a truly great cause.

The state media agency championed the PM's "great cause" comment as great, and further championed his green-eyed determination to eliminate fossil fuels as equally great, even if a tad too soon. To underscore his continued determination and honor lives lost, the PM stated his willingness to invoke the Emergencies Act, thereby freezing the bank accounts of Mother Nature. Mainstream media on both sides of the border have led the charge in reframing the negative concept of "gas and food rationing" into a more acceptable statement of "moderating human excess." The meaning of life can now be measured, gauged, and judged according to one's consumption. Borrowing from China's progressive advancements, we will soon be able to monitor each individual's swallowing of tofu and expenditure of kilowatt-hours. The mark of Cain is something we will be un-Abel to escape.

There have not been million-person marches to Capitol Hill; no sanctuary cities have sprung up as a result of restricted travel opportunities; few fistfights have occurred for those waiting in long queues for the last gasp of gas; not more than a couple dozen shootings and only one mass murder have occurred as result of fuel and food restrictions of the last eighteen months. Most remarkable, restraint held after the president announced "temporary" measures would stay in effect indefinitely—in other words, permanently. The temporary measure called War Tax Act of 1917, which we know and love today as income tax, comes to mind as a comparison. A dozen or so deaths each month from those protesting climate change or gas restrictions are considered acceptable and manageable. Most notable, human collateral damage is unworthy of noting in the media. Journalism has evolved from primitive reporting to progressive thought-leading. Complacency on campus and beyond is the ubiquitous new normal.

For years, Iggy and I talked about taking real time, say six weeks, and doing an extended road trip south, toward the Gulf of Mexico and west to California before heading north along the coast, with a final, to be explored destination into the Canadian wilderness. Planning for the trip was well advanced in 2020 when Covid hit, and I even had someone lined up to make changes to my van so that we could sleep in it when getting to a motel wasn't possible. That thought, and the concept of road trip died in the years that followed.

I recently read about a thriving Green New Deal cottage industry, a phoenix-like rise from the ashes of the fossil fuel world that was: RV disposal. The future is electric. Never mind that in this everything-electric brave new world there is no infrastructure to sustain the everything that amounts to nothing. We are promised, though few believe, that nothing will one day spring into something without doing anything. In the president's good news speech of restrictions becoming permanent, people were delighted to discover that there will be a ten-cents-on-the-dollar tax credit for owners to dispose of their gas-guzzling traveling dinosaurs. And get this, to exorcise the sin of having owned an RV, people will have the option to dedicate their measly 10 percent to one of several designated green initiatives. The president said his personal favorite is Friends of National Parks, noting that parks will be greener for future generations because, coupled with the directive severely limiting access to gas, a new directive is about to ban people from ever entering the national park of their former choice. Still, for those raised in a virtual world, physically hiking to the top of Yosemite Falls and internet exploration of the same are the same. Hell, virtual is better, because you can get to the top of Yosemite without the effort of even putting your pants on.

Apparently, your kids and their unborn kids will thank you (those would be the kids of our kids that they never have). An additional apparently is that our nature-loving president is not one for irony.

Anyway, the queue took forty-five minutes for the privilege of getting a quarter tank of gas today, and I arrived late to a good news, bad news scenario. The bad news is that I missed an appointment with a student I am concerned about, so I will call right away and rebook. The good news is, I arrived in time for lunch, and it is chili day in the cafeteria. The good news about the good news is that I am assured I will not be limited in my intake or output, for that matter, of gas emanating from eating chili.

Edie comes into my office with me on the phone trying to rebook my troubled student for just after lunch. But hearing my diligence, she begins to wave her arms, mouthing a silent *no, no, no!* With an exclamation point. I ask for forgiveness for the second time, cover the receiver with my hand, and ask my dear, gentle peep why the hell she has gone insane? Edie says the SAP's EA has been calling asking where I am and insisting that I be at an emergency, mandatory meeting at two p.m. today. I glance at the clock, inwardly groaning at only two hours for lunch after working so hard for the last hour. I consider making an appeal to the United Nations about the unfairness of it all. Ha! That makes sense, actually. Why sweat the complexities of the culture wars, all the acrimony of deciding who gets what for whatever their identity makeup and grievance amount to? Why not simply allow people, all people in equal measure—in the name of equity—the ability, the opportunity, the innate human right to protest and be compensated for the unfairness of it all? Call it cosmic compensation.

Before the world woke from its collective naivete, we used to say life is unfair as a self-evident truth requiring little action and much acceptance. It seems to me a fully matured, progressive worldview will acknowledge the unfairness of it all, and then guarantee to do something about it. All of it. And we, citizens of this post-nationalist nation, should not be satisfied with anything less.

Crazy, you say? Well, I admit I am, but that is another matter. Still, the issue of grievance compensation is the tsunami that has reached our shore, and we owe Covid for giving us the impetus to make the leap from capitalist fiscal limitations and democratic intransigence to freeing ourselves to build back better in government, in the environment, and most of all to people, each according to *their* perceived needs regardless of *their* production. And yes, an enlightened inversion of a Milton Friedman maxim is on the precipice of liberating 366 million Americans. Open borders, sixteen Supreme Court members, two additional states, and permission to print money without Treasury Department regard for debt ceiling have freed America to fully satisfy all its citizens' wants and desires.

Most liberating, individual identity makeup and membership in one's narrow tribe have finally done away with any notion of common values. With unassailable majorities in the House and Senate, and supported by a compliant media, the ruling party has achieved hegemony and will submit its newly rewritten Constitution in the coming months, with results that are expected to be both explosive and enlightened. The legality of substituting this new constitution for the old is not clear, but stacking the Supreme Court and adding two new states was clever preparation.

Still Edie waving her arms, still me thinking and not responding, still a student whom I just stood up dangling on the line. My dilemma is always the same. I can withstand the heat of the SAP's ire, and my peeps know that VP meetings, particularly mandatory meetings, are a colossal waste of time. Okay, so a bit disingenuous, since I do find out about new ideas the SAP has come up with to diminish and displace us. Still, whatever I miss in person is only hours away from being received electronically.

My real problem are my peeps who swarm to make me go to these executive ordered meetings because of their needless concern for little ol' me. I fight them constantly on this score, but they are as persistent as a wolverine. (It just occurred to me that I often use this comparison, but to my knowledge no one ever sees wolverines or conducts studies to determine if they are persistent. I am now officially grieving the loss of our aborted road trip to Canada, where we might have spotted and befriended a pair of persistent wolverines. Speaking of Canada, isn't the Canadian exemplar of persistence the bucktoothed beaver? I'm eager to find out.)

It's time to give some answers. First the phone. "Sorry Peter, how about after your class, say four thirty?"

Then to Edie. "All right, already, if you go away now, I'll go to that meeting at two p.m."

Edie gives me a thumbs-up as she exits, coughing that awful, persistent cough as she always does now. I vaguely hope that both wolverines and Edie's cough will lose their persistence.

With only two hours for lunch, I'm five minutes late for the meeting. Naturally, the door that I cannot open is closed. Again. I can, of course, complain that the persistence of doors closed in my face ignores basic accessibility. And consideration. And decency. I would raise hell if a student experienced the same. But I won't give our SAP the satisfaction. She wants to know she can get to me, and I won't let that happen. I just won't. Besides, I've worked it out with Smokey. Again.

I call Smokey and wait, eager to see which of today's disruptions will be greater: the crashing of my wheelchair into chairs that litter my path, or Smokey's unquiet quiet voice, eager to converse with the only person in the meeting he can relate to. I have this kitschy thought that it might be a tie.

"Hey, bud, whaddya doin' out here?" Smokey understands the game and playfully participates in milking it for all its worth.

"I don't understand," I say, in my best intonation of altar boy innocence. "The door was locked and closed."

"You don't say." Smokey slowly ponders. Oh, yeah, in addition to his remarkable qualities of voice and action, Smokey has this brilliant timing angle, wherein no amount of time that has passed will ever affect how much time he intends to take. He turns to the people waiting for the meeting inside. "Hey, you're right, it was locked. Why was the door locked?"

No one answers or dares acknowledge that today's revelation of locked doors is the way it always is.

"That's okay, Smokey. Even if the door was not locked, I can't open this door once it is closed." Said with my best saddest face.

"How 'bout that?" Smokey ponders some more. "Guess that puts you in the penalty box even though you didn't put an elbow into someone's head or knock down the goalie." Smokey's fawning voice changes to serious intent. "Did you see that frickin' penalty the Rangers took in the third period last night? It cost them the damn game!"

A delightful aspect of the SAP's ever uber vigilant self-control is that she never shows distress or anger. And yet, a practitioner of sensitivity such as moi can see barely perceptible eye fluctuations and cheek spasms that mere mortals cannot. I notice that she, who is blatantly robbing our unit, my peeps, and our thousands of students of millions of dollars, and is about to waylay a chunk of my staff just 'cause, is not in complete control. I, that is, we are getting to her.

The SAP gives a barely perceptible intentional glance towards Tim, her multipurpose Swiss knife minion, and he immediately responds in a commanding voice for us to come in and settle down so that this important meeting can continue.

As we enter the room and sweep past the SAP's assemblage, Smokey decides he is not finished. Pausing in front of Tim, Smokey says, "The meeting hasn't started yet, so it can't continue; it has to start first. And you can't blame Phelim for being outside, and you can't blame me for getting up if the door is closed. And locked too."

Tim cannot think of a retort to this commonsensical analysis. Tim has never actually thought for himself. Besides, Smokey has a smidgen of that male toxicity thing and is a bit intimidating. This guy is becoming a real pal, I think.

Zigo decides he too wants to be a player in the disruption game. As we land at the back of the room, he decides he requires attention, and further decides to make his needs known with his banging of tail against the hollow heating panel. Again. The echo is particularly loud because the room has gone silent. Zigo then comes up on two paws so I can pet him around the ears, as is our loving ritual.

I know that Dean Perkins, waiting, but barely containing herself with quivering lip and pained expression, is next to speak.

She does not disappoint. "I want to thank the wonderful and inspiring Special Adviser to the President that we get to call our own for calling this emergency meeting today. We really don't have a second to lose, and it is up to us to eliminate the ever-present danger on our campus."

"Wow, are street gangs roamin' campus that I didn't know about?" Smokey's whisper booms.

The SAP's eyes lift without much expression. Her eyelids shift, and her gaze uncharacteristically slides to where Smokey and I sit, but just for a moment. I could be wrong, but if I'm a betting man, and I am, that is a look of malevolent intent.

"She doesn't like us," Smokey intones.

"You think?"

Dean Perkins continues, "You are all aware of the sexual assault and abuse of privilege between a rogue faculty member and one of our student victims."

Smokey is about to protest the obvious exaggerations and assumption of guilt, but I give a slight turn of my head, indicating best not to disrupt. I want to see the mob in its naked glory.

"This case is disturbing enough if it was an isolated incident. But I'm afraid it is only part of an all too familiar pattern of abuse that has to be stopped. To that end, we are enacting new security measures, including a three-million-dollar increase to Kale's security budget, effective immediately."

In as close to a conspiratorial whisper as he is capable, Smokey says, "I don't get it. What has that case between a student and a prof got to do with the need for millions more in security?"

I turn toward Smokey in his innocence. "You'll never make it in the woke world, my friend."

I turn my attention back to Dean Perkins's important words in progress. "… so please let's thank our generous Special Adviser to the President for this desperately needed funding."

People cheer loudly and enthusiastically, almost drowning out Smokey's conspiratorial whispered retort, "Almost as loud as they clap for that Dear Leader guy in, you know, North of Korea."

When the clapping stops, I am still laughing as never before.

Kale waits at the front of the room for me to be quiet so they can make their presentation. I can't tell if they is standing or sitting from where I sit, the difference being about half an inch. They and I share that vertical problem, heightened by the requirement to speak in a group setting without a raised platform.

"Well, we're going to be increasing security just about everywhere." Kale tends to swagger when they speak, so they must be standing, I think. "It's bit more complicated, and you might say the devil's in the details. So we got a plan, see, and this here's session is about letting you know what that is ...."

My mind drifts as my mind often does. In these situations. One can argue these situations are unprecedented, but a few details right or left, up or down, doesn't change the fact that it is only slight variation on a theme. Whatever else, never waste a good crisis, and as most often happens, never waste an incident of your making from becoming—however twisted the logic—a crisis that is then not wasted. The cycle of university life.

Fred takes a train to the East Prussian town of Rastenburg, and then, as arranged, he travels by car the remaining five miles to the Wolf's Lair. If this sounds suspiciously as if he is about to be ushered into the nerve center board-room to meet Hitler, nothing could be further from the truth.

Fred is no early version of Claus von Stauffenberg, whose most famous attempt on Hitler's life on July 20, 1944, ended badly. The brave and auda-cious General von Stauffenberg had a legitimate reason for meeting with Hitler and the Nazi high command, whereas Fred is a fraudulent goodwill ambassador and businessman from America with nothing more than a letter of introduction. Still, he has some qualities that cannot be seen, but may well be felt if circumstances allow.

Despite the Lair's high level of security, Fred is not completely conspic-uous. His letter from Colonel Hasse is convincing, his appointment with Col-onel Friedrich seemingly legitimate, and there is much activity at the Lair. The compound has more than eighty buildings, with massive concrete bunkers over two meters thick for the Nazi elite.

Fred has few options, which makes his plan uncomplicated, even if aston-ishingly dangerous. He is almost certain that Roma is with Colonel Friedrich at this time and in this place. Fred also knows he has one and only one chance to get her out. His one chance does not include an option to vacillate.

Fred is directed to a building, barely distinguishable from all the others in color and shape. There are two immediate issues. Might there be any other soldiers or officers with Friedrich, and would he and the colonel be meeting in his private quarters or in another location?

Through the haze of fear and anticipation, Fred notices oppressive humidity and the prevalence of mosquitoes. The soldier who leads him to building number 32 does not stay. Fred exits brilliant sunshine and enters claustrophobic hovel with a naked lightbulb illuminating its windowless gray walls. A featureless fan clicks and hums dead, stale air into something breathable. A tall balding officer stands and introduces himself as Colo-nel Friedrich. Fred accepts the proffered cigarette and proceeds to play the extravagant American industrialist and Nazi sympathizer. It is a role he has become comfortable performing. Having to pretend in front of the monster who has Roma is not likely to produce his best effort.

Still, Colonel Friedrich likes what he hears. "I only wish you could extend your stay and deliver the terms of your new business offer directly to Herr Göring. I can assure you that the Luftwaffe wants your aluminum, all of it, and both Herr Göring and the Führer will be very interested in the fact that your uncle has access to President Roosevelt. If Roosevelt is as disinclined towards war as your people are convinced he is, I can assure you that this information will solidify our enduring relationship."

Though a midday snort is the farthest thing from his mind, Fred accepts a glass of schnapps in recognition of Colonel Friedrich's celebratory mood. After they toast, Fred says, "The president is playing a delicate game, pretending to appease warmongers and Jews, but is committing no more than to supply equipment to Britain on the Lend-Lease Act, which we agree will not change the outcome of the war. Once you have defeated both Britain and that stinking cesspool Russia, you will find the United States far more interested in preserving our respective interests."

Fred empties his shot glass, deeply inhales his cigarette, and enunciates his words. "It will be, as we Americans like to say, a win-win situation."

(Note to self: I lay awake last night thinking first about Fred as written, even if I haven't committed a single word to the page. My dispassionate little ol' self, metaphoric pen in hand, has been displaced by the inner workings, fears, and motivations of Fred in the flesh. In order to walk the walk, and I do like the thought of walking, I'll try reverting back from third to first person for in-your-face immediacy).

My words are mechanical and rote, even if sounding casual and unrehearsed, for my mind is decidedly elsewhere. Does the doorway from this dingy little room go to his living quarters, or are they, and Roma, in another building? I search for a nonintrusive way to find out. Looking around at the stark concrete, I summon all the casual I can muster and say, "With victory soon on two fronts, perhaps you will allow yourself the indulgence of time away from these aesthetically challenging accommodations for a suite at the Hotel Kaiserhof."

Colonel Friedrich seems pleased with my comment and raises his refilled glass again. "Yes, victory will most certainly be imminent. Your people can tell President Roosevelt that Germany is doing America a favor by ridding the world of the Bolsheviks. If we don't do it now, America would have to do it in ten years. And the Hotel Kaiserhof is, of course, a favorite of my kind."

"And mine," I respond, adding, "which I suspect means we are of the same kind."

Colonel Friedrich smiles an expansive row of yellow-stained, crooked teeth. He seems to have decided I am an agreeable ally.

I continue. "I am hoping to spend a couple days at the Kaiserhof before I fly back to America. I was given access to some very beautiful and willing ladies last time there." Then, raising my glass, "I would be happy to share with my own kind, Herr Friedrich, if you can take a furlough to Berlin."

The colonel responds with a wicked smirk. "I have enjoyed many of the ladies of the Kaiserhof connection, but in recent months, I have had less need."

"Oh?" I respond, with jocular parlance and boiling blood.

"I have with me, in this place, a concubine of unusual beauty and dexterity."

I look around at the shabby, spartan walls. "What, here? Surely not in this place?"

Colonel Friedrich laughs. "No, not here, though in truth not much better. Still, aesthetics aside, I can assure you what happens in building 43 makes the Führer's suite at the Kaiserhof seem shabby."

"What? Is she here of her own free will? Can someone so beautiful be left alone?" I am very close to the edge, but he doesn't seem suspicious so much as proud.

"She is a beauty, but she is also a Polish Yid. It is understood by others she is not to be touched. And as for leaving, where would she go? Did you notice any place to escape as you traveled to the Lair? Still, I keep her under lock and key," the colonel finishes, patting his left side pocket, at which precise moment, requisite information received, I strike.

With my right hand I cover the colonel's mouth with a rag that has a condensed dose of formaldehyde. With my left hand I plunge a poisonous syringe into his neck obtained from a contact Hank gave me days earlier. After extracting the key from the Colonel's left side pocket, I smooth out my disheveled suit and walk briskly across the compound, feigning that I actually belong in this murderous, bug-infested hellhole.

At number 43, I unlock the door, enter a utilitarian outer room, take a deep breath and use the second key to open the next room. Inside, sitting in a chair beside a small table with a reading lamp, Roma looks up. The book drops from her lap, she gasps at the sight of me, and falls out of her chair onto the concrete floor.

The shock of seeing me negates pain from the fall, she later tells me. I cannot get her to admit to any physical discomfort as she sobs and clutches at me in disbelief. It is a moment we wish would stretch out forever, if not for the fact that we will surely die if we dare stretch it out for mere minutes. I put my hand under her chin and make her look at me. "We can talk and hug and compare notes for a lifetime if we get out of this, but at this minute we have to get out of this. Put on some makeup, your best dress—nothing too fancy—and a coat. Make sure to bring any sturdy, warm clothes you have for walking and for the cold. Dry your eyes, and we will walk to the car and driver waiting for us. Security isn't expecting us to stay long, but if there is trouble it will be at the gate. If they stop us there, it is over, but I won't regret anything because I got to see you. But we must leave now."

Roma does not ask questions, does not speak, and is ready within minutes. She understands and is ready to go. And with one quick last embrace, we open the door and together leave unit 43, in our pathetic attempt to resist the will of the world as written by the tyrant of all time.

My car and driver are parked nearby, within sight of the security guards to reinforce the fact that our hasty exit was anticipated. Rather than hurry to the car, I casually walk past the guardhouse, chatting and joking with Roma. A guard looks at Roma's smiling face, I joke about how unappreciated and important he must be providing security for the Führer at this vital location. The guard seems confused but does not object and we wave over our shoulders as we stroll in carefree fashion to our waiting car. I don't know how Roma is able to smile under these circumstances, but her performance is disarming and convincing.

When the gate is lifted and our driver shifts into first gear, Roma squeezes my hand with a strength I barely think possible. After we've driven no more than 400 meters, a loud siren goes off. Our driver looks into the rearview mirror and says, "Tell me if that is for you."

When I don't immediately answer, he says, "We have a few minutes, this is a fast car, but I need to know. I am no Nazi lover, and I can help if you let me. You can't go back to Rastenburg; they will have it covered before we can even get there. They will call the train station first, and that is the only way out unless you have a private plane."

Still, I hesitate, and he continues. "I assume that the large bags that you placed in the trunk when I picked you up are for an overland escape. I know where to drop you."

"What will happen to you?" I ask.

Our driver looks into the rearview mirror again, and we have a moment of eye contact. "I borrowed the car from someone who owes me money. He is a Nazi collaborator and I've been looking for a way to expose him, so thank you."

I'm speechless. And yet our driver's anticipation of our immediate needs is not finished. "One more thing. I believe you might have need for a gun."

"Yes, and we have money. Please, how much?" I have found my tongue and lean over to pull money from my pocket.

"Sure, leave something," our driver says, making eye contact again. "I have a nice fairly new German Luger, but don't leave too much. You'll need most of what you've got to buy food wherever you are going."

I had predicted our chances of escape from the Wolf's Lair to be about 1 percent. I now feel confident doubling that figure. Roma speaks for both of us, doubling my sentiment. "Thank you. Thank you."

It isn't the only time we will need or receive help. Good thing, because our journey—excruciating under normal circumstances—will take us to the limit. The physical exercise we are about to endure will also become an exercise in gratitude. As fugitives under threat of death, with war and deprivation at every turn, we began our journey to Hitler's Berghof in the Obersalzberg of the Bavarian Alps, almost 800 miles away. That is, 800 miles as the crow flies, so far more for fugitives having to dodge getting caught, to find food, find places to camp, and live. Some things in life are best attempted without overthinking. Planning, innovating, adjusting yes, but not examining feasibility, playing the percentages, succumbing to futility. We have a mission, and we don't expect to get out of this alive. All of Roma's extended family are likely dead, my life is no longer my own, and although we have each other, we cannot think the *we* of the present moment can last. We are determined and have nothing to lose, and pathetic as our chances are, this last attribute makes us dangerous.

As our astute driver has noticed, I prepared basic equipment for our overland journey along the back roads, paths, forests, and fields of Poland, Germany, Czechoslovakia, and Austria. That is the rough plan, though I am reluctant to fully formulate a plan for fear that its stark details will force us to face its stark reality. Stark reality likely murdered Roma's family and is killing Europe, so we will tread in the blur of cautious fantasy until reality fully and forcefully intrudes.

A loud knock on the door derails the meeting and my fanciful fantasizing. No one moves until the SAP decides whether to allow the intrusion. Before she can adjudicate, another loud knock pierces the silence, followed by an audible attempt to open the still locked door.

Smokey's conspiratorial whisper is only slightly less loud than the sound of the rattling door. "Told 'em they shouldn't lock the door."

I widen my silly grin and answer, "Actually, this time you left the door locked, my friend."

"Oh yeah, my bad."

At a barely perceptible SAP glance, Tim leaps up and opens the door. Two diminutive security officers report that an emergency has occurred requiring the need to talk to the head of security.

Kale swaggers over to their waiting minions, which results in animated discussion. The SAP is about to tell them to close the door and continue discussion outside, but Kale beacons the SAP to join the frantic crew. The SAP's demeanor remains calm as she joins the security group. The SAP motions for the three security officers to step outside the meeting room. The group of four disappear from view, and the door is closed, until the SAP hurriedly steps back inside the room and motions to Dean Perkins. The SAP's face does not betray panic, so evident among security personnel; rather her eyes seem fixed into an expression of controlled calm. Dean Perkins's mouth forms into a half smile, perhaps relishing the excitement, or more likely the pleasure that she alone is singled out for inclusion into whatever of importance is happening.

Together they disappear out of sight, and we are left with whispered fragments of hurried conversation. Until the scream. Then wailing of the word, "No, no, no!" More screaming follows an incomprehensible scramble of words.

"Wha'd she say?" Smokey asks.

"Not sure, but I think I heard the words, "She's dead.""

CHAPTER TWENTY-THREE

Murdered, actually. At least that is the rumor that spread throughout campus within minutes. Though unconfirmed, word is graduate student Heather Theodore is dead and, without any details, that she was brutally murdered. Both unconfirmed details are taken as fact, with narrative highlights, as follows: Heather was murdered by John Staffal for daring to tell her truth about their abusive relationship; this was not John Staffal's first murder; many toxic faculty at St. Jude's are murderers, and drastic means are required to prevent more deaths of innocent victims; there are more ways to commit murder than to enact physical murder; the blood—whether or not blood is involved—of murdered victims will be on the hands of St. Jude's administration unless emergency measures are taken to apprehend all perpetrators of violence; violence is whatever a victim perceives it to be.

Which results in rumors about what measures will be taken to address rumors about what was taken as fact for what actually happened, as follows: the security budget into the foreseeable future will be unlimited; providing adequate security will necessitate hiring some staff outside of St. Jude's; because other institutions are not as enlightened as St. Jude's, there *might* be a temporary requirement to hire some well-vetted officers identifying as "male," but only those with proper training and enlightened views; all academic classes will have to be suspended for an indeterminate period; the Eye-watch project —an eye-scan, facial recognition—all-building identification surveillance system able to monitor all students, staff and faculty at all times, in all places— must be immediately funded and implemented; all nonacademic, nonessential events must be suspended, subject to approval by a new security-conscious committee appointed by the SAP, Exceptional Student Experience. I am soon given insider information—that is, an unsubstantiated rumor from someone lusting for their schadenfreude moment—that *both* Edie's wedding and the Dr. Jordan Peterson debate will be canceled. "Well, I can't say I heard your employee's wedding is absolutely canceled," my insider informant gushed, "but certainly the horrid Peterson debacle is canceled for good, and good riddance. Your employee's wedding might only be indefinitely postponed."

"My employee, my ass," I grunted through clenched teeth and a particularly silly, malevolent grin. And would Edie's wedding, vetted through some ridiculous committee six months from now, involve exhuming her body for presentation at the altar?

I was not in a good mood. I had just met with Luna, Iggy, Aunt Isobell, and Sister Sandrine, and relayed the information. That is, if you can call unsubstantiated, scurrilous rumors information. My peeps reacted with predictable stupefaction. Our mood inspired little conversation; there were few questions. Thank God, Edie heeded our suggestions, which is to say my direct order, that she take a few days off from work to prepare for her wedding. Thank God I did not have to face Edie at this moment, though the next crushing thought was, *I cannot let her hear the rumor of her canceled wedding from someone else.*

Through the glumness of it all, I have this vague question, where is Aunt Isobell? For some reason, she left as soon as I told the group, without reaction, without shaking her head sadly or offering comforting words, as has been her lifetime habit. I need some comforting words just now. I am about to ask our glum group when my office door opens, and Auntie quietly enters and sits in her recently vacated chair. She does not emote glum. Her mood is decidedly out of sync with our collective glumness. Not only not glum, in her low-key indemonstrable way, she seems to glow.

"Auntie?"

"I won't keep you in suspense. I've just had a conversation with Benny Tang."

When none of us react, Aunt Isobell continues. "I mentioned to you I'd seen him since I started working here." I don't remember; she doesn't stop. "No matter, he's one of my former students, from my medical records days. Bet you didn't know I taught a couple classes at your rival university, in their library science program."

I knew none of this but don't want to ask anything that might slow Aunt Isobell down from whatever it is she has to say. "He now works for the police department, is head of their records department. When we met a couple months back, he said my classes and the letter of recommendation I wrote helped him find his career. He also said that if I ever needed anything, I shouldn't hesitate to ask."

At this point in Aunt Isobell's discourse, she pauses to catch her breath or to allow us to catch up, not sure which, but the term *bated breath* applies here. "I asked him, just now, and he confirmed that the young women who died is Heather Theodore, so no need for speculation or rumor there. He also said an immediate autopsy is pending, and because of the sensationalism of the case, it may be conducted as early as this evening, and most important, he overheard that the cause of death is very likely not murder but will be confirmed as suicide."

Aunt Isobell lets out her breath after an uncharacteristically long sentence, as do the three of us upon hearing the content of her unusually long sentence.

Finally, Iggy: "Auntie, you're a superhero!"

"It's true," Aunt Isobell replies, with mock hubris.

"I've witnessed her charm and intelligence many times," Sister Sandrine adds.

"Auntie, I hope this won't get you into any trouble over legalities," I say.

"Let's talk about values, common values most of all, rather than legalities, shall we? We share a value for truth, and we cannot allow an innocent person to be falsely accused."

"Hard to believe you work in a university," I say, in a markedly un-glum way. I want to ask a question, but Aunt Isobell reads my mind.

"Benny will let me know the cause of death as soon as it is confirmed. Unofficially, could be soon, tomorrow even."

"That's a relief. Without giving away our source, I will want to let John know right away."

"Will you let him know about the Peterson cancellation rumor?" Iggy asks.

"And will you let Edie know?" Sister Sandrine adds, somberly.

I think about this. "I really don't want to tell either of them events are off until we know for sure, especially Edie."

"And you're quite sure they are to be canceled?" Sister Sandrine asks.

"I don't like being ruled by the rumor mill, but the woke, I mean, enlightened mob does tend to get its way."

"Even if cancellation brings unwanted attention to St. Jude's?" Aunt Isobell asks.

"How do you mean?" Iggy asks.

"Well," Aunt Isobell begins, her thin pale skin wrinkling into an expression of consternation, "your friend John managed to make controversy regarding the Peterson debate into a national story, and the unique circumstances of Edie's wedding have garnered quite a bit of media attention, wouldn't you say?"

"Indeed," I answer, liking where Auntie is going with this.

"Cancellation for any reason after promising that St. Jude's is a beacon for freedom of expression will draw negative press, and as for canceling Edie's wedding, well, that is the feel-good story that distracts from all the other negative stories out there."

"And," I say, encouragingly.

"And both cancellations will also have to be justified, which could result in making this suicide very public. Especially with the connotation of sexual impropriety adding to issues universities are very sensitive to."

"I think you've got something. The problem is, the ideologues say bring it on while the president and the Board of Governors, where the buck theoretically stops, don't like bad or controversial press. The question is, how do we make the university realize what its own self-interest is, without attack from the mob?"

"Start a rumor," Sister Sandrine answers. When the three of us look at her like inquisitive beagles, she laughs and continues, "All of us get questions about Edie's wedding every day, and Phelim, you've been interviewed several times. And your friend John must have many, many media contacts after making the debate a national story. Feed the media rumors, which will soon be fact if nothing is done, and get them to pester the officers of university who care about bad publicity to either confirm or deny whether the two events are going to be canceled."

If not for the formidable facts that a) my hands don't work, b) she is in my employ, c) she is a nun, d) any and all contact today between all people for any reason is highly suspect, and e) especially in the university, f) especially, especially involving toxic male types, I would have grabbed Sister Sandrine at that moment and kissed her on the forehead (notice my astonishing restraint not to have said *the lips*). Okay, so I tempered where I'd have kissed her in order to make the scenario family friendly, but you get the point. And besides, for all the enlightenment that has descended upon us, a fella can still dream—and still call himself, if only to himself, a fella.

So instead of kissing her, I acknowledge her genius—more satisfying for her, but decidedly less so for me—and articulate the beginning of a plan that springs into my sinister mind. "I just realized I have an email from John with a list of his media contacts that he sent me two weeks ago. Since the original story was all about cancel culture, especially at universities, I think they'll be interested if there's any hint of cancellation. There are almost four thousand colleges and universities in the US, so our freedom-of-expression test case has huge repercussions. And while it's not exactly a test case, media people love the story of Edie's wedding; that is, a local story with national interest potential. They see a tearjerker in this story, so what would they think if our gal was to be denied her one wish and desire at this point in her short life?"

"They'll eat it up," Iggy answers.

"There are a lot of contacts on John's media list, across three time zones for both stories, and we haven't got much time. In channeling Pearl's honesty, what would you say if I order a couple pizzas and split up the contact names, and we hunt down any media we can by either phone call or email? Oh, and I'm paying."

The room erupts. "Well, since you're paying." "It's the least you can do." "Only if you include garlic bread."

CHAPTER TWENTY-FOUR

Thursday, just two sleeps before controversial E-Day and P-Day,
on which day meetings are not enough and a town hall is called

For the love of steak or money, I cannot reach John. No surprise for the world's foremost Luddite. Still, I'm worried. The more so because while his brief romance or whatever it was may not have the gravitas of Romeo and Juliet, the enlightened mob will never believe it could have been anything other than oppression and abuse. Still, I suspect in his limited quirky way, John did love Heather. Although he claims to have fallen in love with every woman in his life, his rogue persona was borne of actual feelings of love that were unfamiliar and threatening. And possibly ridiculous. Also, I needed to reach him and inform him that her suicide was unlikely to be about him. She'd moved on and had had at least one relationship with someone else.

Our little band of nuns and brother worked until eleven p.m. last evening, making extensive inquiries with key media people who might be prevailed upon to prevail upon university functionaries who might entertain the notion that cancellation as the path of least resistance might be the path of greatest aggravation. Our media emissaries understood that cancellations made in response to Heather's death would forever entangle, not liberate, the university from culpability because of increased public scrutiny. In today's connected world, guilt by association and guilt by deed are indistinguishable to many of the great unwashed public. I hope this is the closest I ever get to resembling a troll.

Back in the Center at the first light of noon, I have to smile and encourage Melanie and Diane as they enthuse about their plan for decorating the Great Hall for the wedding. I don't like faking anything, especially anything about Edie's likely-to-be-canceled wedding.

I leave yet another message on John's phone, same for writing another email, with yet another reason why he needs to contact me, and now. I have no doubt that the fate of both events will be announced before day's end.

My office phone rings. Though I usually ignore phone calls, I recognize the number and answer it immediately. "Edie, you're supposed to be resting, or making yourself beautiful, or I don't know, admiring your collection of firemen calendars, anything but working."

"Ha!" Edie's familiar and welcome jocular refrain comes through the line. I can feel my impatience dropping away. "Just making one call to you, chief.

Lucy got a call from the SAP's EA, and you gotta go to another emergency meeting today, same time, but get this, it's a town hall in the auditorium. SAP wants all her managers and directors, and you can bring staff, and faculty will be there too. Something big is up, and you've got no choice. Lucy says you ignored her messages, though you made a good joke when you wanted to get rid of her. Poor thing lacks in-your-face assertiveness with the boss, which I just happen to have in spades."

"That you have, me dear. All right already, now get lost, and we'll see you in just two more sleeps."

"Not if I see you first."

I glance upward at the clock. Oh my goodness, I have to suffer the indignity of less than two hours for lunch, again! What next, a vegan cafeteria? Well, I have my standards, and I'll never go to a place where Zigo refuses to eat. He is not a fan of salad.

It's 1:55 p.m., all staff have scheduled appointments except Aunt Isobell, who has a rare cancellation, so she is my escort. Despite her promptings, we are five minutes late. My response to her protest is that I am usually ten minutes late, so in defiance of consistency, I am actually five minutes early.

The auditorium has a capacity of twelve hundred and is full to overflowing. I have never attended an event in the auditorium that was even half full.

"That gentlemen on the far side seems to be trying to get your attention."

I scan the horizon until I spot Smokey waving his arms. He cups his hand around his mouth for a conspiratorial shout, which may have been something like "At least you didn't have to wait behind a locked door."

I give Smokey a wave of acknowledgment, and he sits down.

There are five chairs on stage. Our SAP is center stage, presumably intending to address how a St. Jude's student's experience of death was less than exceptional. Her reasons for exceptional shortcomings are unlikely to be self-incriminating. Not yet sitting is our security person Kale, who looks animated and sways like a kid who has eaten too much candy. A distraught Dean Perkins sits between two women from the Racialized Communities for Equity and Social Justice, and they seem to be trying to provide comfort to her. I do not recognize either woman, which does not mean they are new to St. Jude's. Nor does it mean that they are low-level unionized staff who do not get out of the office much. The progressive model at St. Jude's flourishes because of the plethora of obscure, highly paid managers and directors for whom outcomes are someone else's responsibility, even as grievances are pointed and endless. All chiefs making decisions, no Indians carrying out said decisions. Not my terminology; the banned words are from Smokey.

My theory is that most university initiatives of recent years were inspired by watching Zigo chase his tail. No purpose, no reason, no end in sight, just swirling madness. Zigo takes neither credit nor responsibility.

Still, at the epicenter of university inertia, the auditorium is electric with happening. The mood is not subdued as one might expect; death has not flattened people's conversation and expression. This is less funeral parlor than Roman Colosseum. I wonder if the mood of the speakers will match the mood of the crowd. We do not have long to wait. One of the women whispers something into Dean Perkins's ear before approaching the podium.

I notice, as I always do, the setup is inaccessible. I advise universities from across the country on accessibility issues, only to be ignored at home. Every time. And possibly on the SAP's express orders. I am not a prophet in this place of profit. You may wonder, but what about the exceptional experience of students with disabilities? Good question. For better or worse, my peeps work their asses off to counterbalance the SAP's misdirection. If I am speaking, my peeps will float in just before I go on and take care of whatever inaccessible minutia the SAP's minions have either neglected to correct or have willfully created. I'm not a conspiracy guy, but it's real enough. We, that is she and I, are engaged in a huge chess game that I am likely to lose. But hey, I've got Roma and Fred to comfort me with their nothing-to-lose mantra. While the chess game rages, I'm thinking of starting a grievance.

The woman at the podium stares out into the crowd and waits until silence envelops the auditorium. She knows her audience, I think. Being reluctant to talk to Aunt Isobell as the podium speaker waits for silence, I slip back to Fred and Roma.

We have managed to survive these past ten days, mostly traveling by stealth at night, and sleeping in secluded spots during the day. Trying to determine a discernible route in darkness, along back roads and forest paths that are unfamiliar, has slowed us. The fact that Roma speaks Polish has been invaluable for occasionally asking Polish peasants for discreet ways to circumnavigate German soldiers. Same for buying food. Between Roma's knowledge of Poles and Polish, coupled with her beauty and charm, we are able to get sufficient food, and we even carry some cheese and sausage for more difficult days ahead. Food isn't plentiful, but peasant Poles are approachable mostly, and Roma is beautiful and charming, always.

If ever we make it to a place that does not have a concentration of German soldiers, we will switch, traveling during the day and sleeping at night. If we can blend in, we can travel further, faster, as well as find more opportunities to buy or charm for food.

Our journey is far from easy; there is privation, hardship, cold, and rain, and we are dirty, confused, and occasionally filled with self-doubt. But we do not suffer ambiguity of purpose; we will not suffer regret. There is no part of us that wants to change our goal, impossible as it might be. Either Hitler dies, or we will die trying. That is set, that is unassailable. In the midst of hardship is some tangible good, far beyond my wildest expectations.

Roma is alive, I actually found her, and we are together. With these gifts in mind, privation becomes motivation.

For example, for all the putrid food we eat, and occasionally go without, for all the terrible conditions and fatigue we endure traveling at night, as the first vestiges of false dawn appear on the horizon, we look forward to finding a secluded spot to rest, to lie together, and to feel safe in each other's arms; in our chosen hovel for at least this coming day, we achieve temporary sanctuary against a hostile world. Privation cannot pierce the perfection of bliss we choose to feel. Even Hitler and the most powerful army in the world cannot rob us of each other. We never pray for more food or better conditions, only that our shared existence continue, one step, one embrace, one cold, rotten, blissful sanctuary hovel at a time.

"My name is Clarissa Johnson, and my mission is simple." She has a lovely Caribbean accent that does not match the import and meaning of her words. "A woman of color has been murdered, and justice must be found. I know you will agree that catching the perpetrator will not suffice. We know who the murderer is, and he must be arrested, but I know you will join me so that *me* becomes *we*, and we demand the end of systemic racism and violence against women. In order to both apprehend and punish the murderer as well as address rampant systemic racism and violence against women, gays, lesbians, BIPOC, and trans people, we will need to cancel all events unrelated to the academic mission as a minimum, until we can control the process. Make no mistake: this murder and the systemic violence we are no longer willing to tolerate are directly related."

At which point, the door near the front of the stage slowly opens with a loud and painful screech, as if metal hinges have become unhinged. With great trepidation, a short, innocuous middle-aged man steps through the open door, stops, and blinks as if seeing sunlight for the first time. Clearly, whatever he intended by interrupting this meeting, he hadn't quite thought beyond this moment. The man, later identified as the chairperson of the Board of Governors, beckons, walking towards the stage and managing to utter, "Please, madam Special Adviser to the President."

Our slim and athletic SAP stands and walks towards the chairperson with full composure, in sharp contrast to the demeanor and stature of the one she has condescended to meet. Together, they exit the auditorium, she a full head taller, her eyes fixed on the shiny glisten from his pale, bald skull.

Members of the audience quickly fill the excitement vacuum with impassioned hubbub. I turn to Aunt Isobell. "Will the top dogs of the university know about how she died yet? That guy looks official."

Aunt Isobell leans towards me. "Yes, I talked to Ben first thing this morning. They know, even if it isn't official. By the way, not that it matters, but I saw a photo of Heather, poor thing. She looks Italian or maybe Portuguese or Spanish, black Irish even. But the speaker made a point of saying she is a woman of color. Why?"

"She may or may not have some small percentage. Irrelevant as it seems, my dearest aunt, only time served in this august place will demonstrate to you why it could possibly matter. It has to do with perceived disadvantage inspired by the narrative du jour, which, you may have observed by the reaction of the audience, is real enough."

"I see," Aunt Isobell ponders, willfully not seeing, which is why she is one of my main peeps, though she now understands.

As we wait, I check my phone for messages. Sure enough, there are several from both Luna and Iggy, among others, directing me to a just-released news item confirming that our two events are going ahead as planned. Cancel culture has been temporarily canceled. The president and chairperson of the Board of Governors are both quoted confirming the story.

The auditorium door creaks open with the audience muting its discourse in anticipation. No one comes through the door but obviously someone out of sight is beckoning to someone on stage. Kale nervously points to themself and, presumably receiving an affirmative, hurries out the open door. Kale soon bounds back on stage and walks toward the podium, looking oddly determined and uncertain. It occurs to me that they have never addressed a crowd this size before. I like Kale and feel for them. They are clearly too short to use the microphone at the podium, and worse, they could not be seen by most people when standing behind it. They try to adjust the adjustable microphone, but it refuses to cooperate even as it makes loud squeaky noises as if resisting arrest. A chicken having its neck wrung seems a fitting comparison.

Clarissa stands ready to help take control, whatever the situation requires. But Kale being a go-to person and, not wanting to relinquish the ability to act, which is expected in their role, abandons the neck of the uncooperative chicken-like microphone. They then step around the podium and collects themself by pulling upwards on their belt and swaying in customary fashion. Their voice does not easily project, but knowing this, they shout as best they can. "This here town hall's over. There's been some information received that has to be considered for this here investigation. As for events that had been scheduled for this weekend, well, it seems they're all going ahead as planned."

All of me wants to kiss all of them.

CHAPTER TWENTY-FIVE

One more sleep until the big events,
and I am an early morning spectator at the Great Hall

On this, a Friday, the last day before Edie's wedding, most of my staff did a terrible thing. They booked off. Booked off from taking student appointments so that they could help with arrangements for the wedding. Excitement is in the air, and I share in it by arriving at the office at the obscenely early hour of nine a.m. Well, 9:30 a.m., if you require accuracy.

I immediately go to the Great Hall where staff members—not unlike Santa's elves at the North Pole toy shop—are busy transforming the utilitarian open space into an elegant palace worthy of kings and queens, Santa and reindeers, people and personhoods. There are many more volunteers than my peeps from the Center.

"Who are all these people helping out?" I ask Diane.

Diane slows, being reluctant to stop with things to do and people to see, and gives me a simple answer. "They are all the students who were supposed to meet with coordinators today who decided to help out once they were given the option to reschedule and meet here this morning."

"All of them?" I ask.

Mildly perturbed, Diane turns back toward me and says, "Yes, without exception."

"But they're students, and it's Friday, and morning," I say, or rather protest to an audience of none, since everyone who is anyone is happily occupied.

"So this is what I get for showing up to work early," I mumble, while thinking, *Bloody hell, this Norman Rockwell scene might be the key to resiliency and the magic bullet for good mental health. Throw in gratitude, and you've got a formula for a life well-lived.*

Arthur stands nearby in skeletal silhouette, an ill-fitting suit adorning his bag of bones. His ancient suits seem suited to someone who has lost a hundred pounds or so. When asked, he responds that he weighs the same today as he did when he was twenty. When he asks why I ask, I play dumb, which I am really good at. The phrase *for no reason* provides a heap of plausible deniability in life. Still, as bodies flail and swoosh across our line of vision at the speed of youth, we hang together, he being about my speed without the need to move any faster.

He draws himself up and says, "Sir, just arrived from the Department of Redundancy Department."

I love this guy, and equally so, for his encyclopedic memory of Python skits. But someone, someday, is going to have to tell him that his many Python references to his many students tend to fall flat because they have no idea who the hell his Python peeps ever were.

"Yes, I recognize the redundancy of your oft-repeated joke, my friend," I answer.

"You are here early to witness the pre-festive festivities, no doubt," Arthur offers.

Which I can take two ways. On the one hand I'm impressed he notices. On the other, I could be hurt that my 9:30 a.m. appearance is so noticeable as to be an event.

"Of course, we all want as much of Edie as we can get these days," Arthur muses.

He is right, and I do not want to miss anything associated with Edie, whether or not in the flesh. Still, my reason for appearing at this early hour is a bit disingenuous. John never did answer my many inquiries except to let Paddy of Paddy's Pub—yes, such a person exists—know that he could not make our regular Thursday evening meeting, and would Paddy let me know? Which Paddy did, which kept me from going to Paddy's Pub, which got me to bed early, which meant I woke up early, and with Brenda being my attendant today, I had a rare instance of flexibility to be able to change my time for getting up. I begin thinking I should forsake pub going and carousing to partake of regular early morning delights, when Arthur speaks again and thankfully pulls me from delusion.

"Phelim, I want to let you know two things. The men's mission contacted me, and I can get work there, so if you have to get rid of me, that's okay, especially if it saves someone else's job."

"I see, and since I used to be on the board of the mission, I'd say their ability to pay you would amount to mission impossible."

"Correct, strictly volunteer, which I'm happy with. I'd also be happy to stay here as a volunteer."

"Hum, much as you would do great work at the mission, it won't involve doing assessments, will it?"

"No."

"And I don't have to tell you that there is no one who can do the work you do with students. Your expertise conducting assessments and the forty years' experience you bring cannot be replaced. The problem is not that we can't pay you. The problem is, for all your experience, expertise, and sunny disposition, there is a moratorium, an expiry date, an abolition of your political identity components, and in the name of tolerance for all others, they are no longer willing to tolerate you. And I know what you're thinking, looking at me sitting here—'Damn, that guy's lucky to be a quad.'"

"Well, no comment on the latter, but as to the former, I know the score, what you are up against, and that's why I didn't volunteer here first, and hence my contact with the mission."

"I thought they contacted you?"

"Well, they returned my call."

We chuckle at the silliness of it all. "Arthur, do me a favor, and hold off—don't do anything for a while."

"We both know you're stalling and that eventually, soon eventually, you have to do this."

"Stalling is what I do, but it sometimes makes sense. Besides, why go now?"

"You know why, we've watched the great unraveling of the university over the years, it's not a pendulum that's going to swing back." Arthur says, with sadness, "Besides, people who can be convinced of absurdities—"

"—will commit atrocities," I finish, and we laugh again, less silly, with just a touch of bitter without the sweet. Still, I'm not ready to give up. "How about: people who refuse to believe in absurdities—"

"—will still be subject to atrocities, by absurd rule of the mob," Arthur finishes.

"Yes, but with integrity. You're doing this for me, and I don't need you to fall on the sword. I need you and everyone else to stop worrying about me and give me some time to figure it all out. Final thought: do what you do best and stick with the students, and let's agree to revert to humor whenever politics intrudes too deeply into life. Call it implausible undeniability."

Arthur smiles, then looks pained, takes his sweet time, and finally says, "I'll think about it."

I know Arthur thinking about it means he won't think about it and instead will do what he considers the right thing, which is the only thing he can do. And yet I know that his most heartfelt altruistic instinct in this instance is the wrong thing. I pounce. "Well, think about this. If you want to do something for me, here is your golden opportunity. I, we, all of us are dealing with Edie and a disheartening sense of loss in advance of the fact. I know, I know, stay in the moment, mindfulness BS, enjoy her while she's here and all that, I know, and I do. But in another moment, we will be out of the moment, remembering that she has passed from the moment, and remembering that moment will feel terrible. Thing is, I can't lose anyone else just now. I just can't. That's right, I'm that selfish. If you can't stay for you—and I know you love it here, which should be enough—forget about you and do it entirely for li'l ol' me, myself and I." Pretty darn convincing, I think, metaphorically patting myself on the back.

We laugh, Arthur leaves, and I am left by myself but never alone watching my peeps and their peeps performing the miracle of human communion. All activity and blister, pace and urgency. God, I love these people, even the ones I am seeing for the first time doing something important for the Edie event of the century, which will cement this moment in their lives forever. Six students, all names unknown, setting up five hundred chairs in the middle of the Great Hall. Two guys on ladders washing the eighteen-foot-high windows that frame a spectacular view of the river that flows below. Melanie has two recruits helping to arrange flowers (anonymously donated) along the aisles and at the front of the hall with the main flower arrangements arriving tomorrow (another, unrelated anonymous donation). On another ladder, Stan, the wood sculptor, cleans his sixteen-foot-high curvaceous masterpiece positioned beside the living wall to dramatic effect. Angel helps wherever he is needed, and most of all where he can apply his understated and yet highly useful strength. For example, a couch needs to be pushed to the side to create more room for chairs. When Melanie asks Angel if he can move the couch, she assumes he will find at least one other person to help, but without hesitating, he picks it up in an impossible gesture, swings it over his shoulder and walks away as if strolling in the park. A photographer, name unknown, association with Edie unknown, but here he is taking in angles, photography locations, figuring how to take the best shots so that tomorrow is perfectly captured in perpetuity. Two women scale high ladders to manicure the top of the twenty-four-foot living wall on Denise's orders, so that no dry or dead plant life remains for the big day. Cafeteria people—all volunteers since they were not allowed to do so on company time—bring in stacks of plates for munchies and trays of wine glasses for the series of toasts planned for after the wedding. Someone with an artistic flair is arranging brightly colored handmade paper decorative thingies on raised tables where people can gather who do not get seats among the over-capacity expected wedding guests. Alan, our computer guy, is helping Professor Stephen Wilson, chair of the Music Department, wheel out the antique grand piano beside the living wall where he will play, and our resident opera singer will perform "O mio babbino caro," surely the world's most beautiful aria, to start the walk up the aisle to the front of the hall where Edie and Joey will soon be married.

Much as I love mixing it up with people, there are times when I want to sit and drink in, unobserved, invisible, *the forgiveness life has to offer.* I often cite this line, a quote from a Springsteen song about a guy watching his bride getting ready for their wedding, savoring the intimacy of the holy moment in anticipation of the nuptials the following day.

But it cannot last. It never does. Alan signals me, and I wheel over to the piano where Stephen and Denise are in deep discussion. Stephen has a perplexed look on his face that belies the words he is saying. "Okay, we can do this. A minor glitch, but we can do it."

"Are you sure?" Denise asks.

"Yes, of course, it's her wedding."

Denise turns to me. "We've had a request that means we have to make a change to the music, basically cancel our opera diva's second aria."

I am concerned. "Oh? And who is the troublemaker, and why would we change anything for anybody?"

"Edie. After the first aria finishes, she's asked for her and Joey to walk up the aisle to a recording of Aerosmith's 'Don't Want to Miss a Thing.'"

"Yikes, you're kidding, right?"

"Wish I was, but no."

"Holy moly; sorry, Stephen."

"That's okay, it's okay," Stephen says, trying to put on a happy face with a bit too much resolve.

"How will our diva take it?" I ask.

"Don't worry, I'll take care of her. Performers are used to unforeseen changes to performance schedules."

"I guess," I venture, "but there is that glaring little item that one might call contrast. As in operatic grandeur and grand piano versus recorded whiney voice and rock schlock."

"There is that," Stephen says, exhaling and putting on a brave face. "But it is her wedding. It is Edie's wedding."

Stephen's brave face extends to his entire body. He is a good guy, a much sought-after pianist and composer who came back from another city while on sabbatical because of his regard for Edie. Edie has that effect on people. With anyone, and I mean a host of anyones with whom she has nothing in common she has a bond, a friendship, a communion, a laugh and an understanding that defies logic. And most baffling, and even awesome in the true sense of the word, she doesn't have an enemy in the world. Allow me to repeat, she who is unwoke and has worked in the university for the past fifteen years doesn't have an enemy in the world. Surely, a world's first.

So it is settled, and I go back to my office to perform my many responsibilities, and let's face it, eat lunch. But first, I extract my phone, open an app that downloads any recording ever made in a millisecond—convenient, astonishing, but also a bit scary and not how it is meant to be—and type in "Don't Want to Miss a Thing."

It has been a while since I've heard the Steven Tyler classic, and I cringe as it begins. It is grating, over the top, and absolutely frickin' perfect for Edie on her day, if only for the title of the song. Edie hates being off work, hates being away from her infinite number of peeps, never wants to miss a thing, is not going to miss a thing, is the thing. In the torrent, hurricane, and tsunami of university politics, I can resurrect a moment of perfection in perpetuity whenever I tune into Steven Tyler hitting the high notes and belting it out just for Edie.

CHAPTER TWENTY-SIX

That afternoon, making final arrangements at the Center

Back at the Center, anticipating a full lunch, I make the mistake of answering my phone. Kale, head of security, wants to meet with me as soon as possible. I say I have a rather full day and suggest we talk over the phone. They hesitantly, almost apologetically respond, "No can do. Been ordered by the SAP to meet and make you fully aware of your responsibilities to keep people safe for the events you are involved in this weekend."

"I see," I say. "How about four p.m.?"

"Ditto no can," they respond, "and seeing how it's almost noon, how about 1 p.m.?"

Ouch, I say to myself, wondering how anyone does lunch in one measly hour. "No way, how about three p.m.?"

"Nope," they re-respond, "have to meet and update the SAP about security at three p.m., and have another meeting at two p.m."

"So, one thirty p.m. it is, then," I concede, noting to myself that I am giving up precious lunch time for the third day in a row, a new and disturbing record.

If the compressed ninety-minute lunch isn't enough, there are other obstacles between me and the world of carbohydrates. Lucy, in very un-Edie like manner, is waiting shyly, not talking, just waiting for me to notice, acknowledge her existence, something.

After a few minutes, looking up from my keyboard, sensing rather than seeing a presence, I say, "Word to the wise. I feel bad you are waiting there, especially since you waiting there means there are probably ten students at the front desk waiting for you."

"Yup," she responds, looking back to the front desk from where she stands at my open door.

"If, when trying to get my attention, you act like patient Griselda and resemble a shrinking violet, there is a distinct possibility decades will pass before you are noticed. Take your cue from Edie: speak up and tell me what I need to do, and don't forget to order me to do it now."

Lucy giggles at her telling me what to do and at filling Edie's shoes. "I'll try."

"So, try away."

"There are three people waiting to see you, and one is actually a group of three."

"But it's lunchtime," I protest.

"But they've been waiting for a while 'cause we didn't know you were going to spend time at the Great Hall."

"That's more like it. Tell them they each have one minute and not a second more. And you're welcome, by the way."

Lucy hesitates, torn between asking and fleeing to the front desk. She decides to ask. "Welcome for what?"

"For the assertiveness training for dealing with very difficult, and yet surprisingly fascinating, people."

Lucy giggles again. "You're welcome, too."

"Thanks, Lucy."

Kevin is first up. I don't turn around, keep at my keyboard, but know who it is by the sound of his unstealthy advance through the many obstacles this life has to offer.

"D-d-d-don't hurry, C-c-c-Catholic bastard, I c-c-c-can wait."

"Good, 'cause I've got nothing to do, but it doesn't seem right being available to you right away." Then swinging around, I say, "What's up?"

"I w-w-w-wanted to tell you about G-G-G-George."

"Ah, right, I know he's not working with you anymore. I'm sorry he didn't want to come back. For what it's worth, he let me know it had nothing to do with you. Said taking two shifts in residence is all he can handle with schoolwork." I've been worried about Kevin's reaction and expected him here days ago.

"It's ok-k-kay."

"It is?" I respond, truly not expecting, but happy to hear this answer.

"Yeah. He c-c-c-called me. Told me he's n-n-n-not coming back." Kevin then heaves upward with spasm.

Tempering impatience though knowing the one-minute allotted time is up, I wait, knowing he hasn't said what he has to say.

"George t-t-t-told me the same th-th-th-thing. Said he's t-t-t-too busy, but that w-w-w-we could be f-f-f-f-f-f-f—" Impatience rising both because of lunch and truly wanting to know what in the world Kevin wants to say, my expression is either encouraging or verging on desperate. What is the completion of that word beginning with *f* going to be?

"Friends."

"Friends?"

"Y-y-y-yes. George suggested we get together for pizza and watch a movie once a month."

I can't help noticing that Kevin's last sentence is spoken with less stuttering, and that he seems pleased. "So that's good?"

"Y-y-y-yes, of course. Even if its only once a m-m-m-month, we're friends." And seeing Lucy standing at my door, like a thuggish bouncer, Kevin happily takes his leave. "C-C-C-Catholic bastard."

I like happy endings and not just with Brenda. I'm happy for Kevin and glad that George seems to understand the extent to which a small thing can unearth or elevate someone's world. We shouldn't, or if we do, only reluctantly give people that kind of power. Still, in the zero-sum game of living—unless you believe there is something more after shedding this mortal coil—how do you not? Saying no to all of life's big risks, human connection being the biggest of all, leaves you sitting alone in a room wondering why.

"Is it okay that I stood here to remind him that his minute is up?" Lucy asks.

"Hell yeah, and good for you. You're learning almost as well as Edie could teach you."

Lucy hands me a student file. "Student's name is Omega. She's Luna's but wants to meet with you. Besides, Luna and all the other coordinators are at the Great Hall, so you're it. There's a note inside that explains why she's here."

"Always nice to know I'm it," I say, to an exiting and newly sassy Lucy.

An alternatively dressed student comes into my office and, without offering a word by way of greeting, comments on the shabby nature of my office and sits down. My discreet use of the word *alternatively* dressed is code for body art and piercing to most exposed body parts. And cold as it is here in December, much geography of said body parts are exposed. *Judgmental*, the thought police might accuse me. My answer to this and all my students is that I hope they achieve their heart's desire with whatever external adornments excite their creative juices. My fear is that this student and a host of others will wake up one day and look in the mirror with a crushing sense of self-loathing. Conformity in the guise of originality is not consequence-free.

"I like to think it's eclectic." I smile. "What can I do for you?"

I lower my eyes and scan an email in the file outlining a situation in residence, in the cafeteria, and in classrooms as a consequence of her doctor-approved, legislation-guaranteed therapy ferret. As if on cue, she reaches into a well-worn bag and pulls the snake-like creature out.

"It is my human right to have Satan with me at all times. It is essential to my mental health, and yet there are officers of this university who are constantly challenging us."

Yes, and who doesn't want to be companionable with Satan at all times? It isn't clear to me how we as a society allowed the term *therapy* to be applied to pets who, I am fairly certain, have no idea of their therapeutic prowess. Of course, I have my boy Zigo, who stands up alert when Satan makes his appearance. I reach down and with a placid stroke reassure the boy that Satan is no killer. Destroyer of souls maybe, but nothing to worry about to the body. Zigo puts away his firearm, stretches, yawns, and lies down again. I never got a doctor's note for Zigo since he is not my therapist or emotional support anything, much as he and I derive emotional and guy ritual support from each other. I just started bringing him to work as a puppy, and as I am a quad who everyone assumes has unlimited needs, no one ever questioned if it was allowed. I thought the puppy coming to work with his dad gig would last for a day or two, but five years later we're still pulling the wool over people's eyes.

"It says here that Satan defecates in the cafeteria and in the classroom, with the suggestion of number one in the mix, which is harder to detect."

"We've all gotta go."

"And when he is in the cafeteria, Satan is infamous for raiding people's meals."

"We've all gotta eat. But the real question is, what are you going to do about people questioning my human rights?"

I consider this and ask, "What do you understand human rights to be?"

"I get whatever I need for my mental health."

"And what about other people?"

"What about them?"

"What about their human rights?"

Omega considers what may be a novel concept. "They have to get their own letter from a doctor."

"Sure, but what about when your human right conflicts with someone else's human right?"

"As if."

"We've had a couple complaints from students about your ferret on that basis, one because of religion, and another who is severely allergic and is afraid that Satan will crawl on her and cause a serious anaphylactic reaction."

As this sinks in, I continue, "And while not quite a human right, what about the decency to not subject people to pee and poo?"

"What am I supposed to do about it?"

"Well, I'm not sure, but training, regularly getting outside, and timing when you feed dear Satan in consideration of when you come to class or when you go to the cafeteria all come to mind. Thing is, it's not really a human rights issue."

"It is so, and I could sue St. Jude's."

"Sure, go ahead."

"Really?"

"You could do that, or you could deal with the problem."

"How?"

"Well, Lucy standing at my door, God bless her as my emissary for those whose time is up, is known as a bit of an animal whisperer, and I'm willing to bet she either knows how to train a ferret or else knows someone who can help."

"Oh, can I see him?" Lucy asks to a very receptive and yet stridently suspicious student. And why wouldn't she be? Lucy may be the first person who has ever eagerly longed to hold the wretched creature. I feel both bad and guilty that ferrets are not an endangered species, at least that I know of. Lucy and Omega then move to the reception area of our Center, which because of lunch has mostly been cleared of students, so low to no defecating ferret incident potential.

In fact, the only remaining students are the three guys, who motor in maintaining the same order they always travel in, which tends to determine their order of speaking. It is an ordered road show.

Either out of deference or not quite knowing how to start they also tend to hold off their order of speaking until I begin the proceedings by asking a perfunctory question. "What up, guys?"

I turn towards first up on the speaker's list.

"We've got something to tell you about tomorrow."

I pause and encourage, even if my expression conveys urgency for their remaining half minute. "Okay, shoot."

Next on the list. "We're coming to the wedding tomorrow."

"Yes, I know, Edie asked specifically that you three be invited."

Next up. "We all rented tuxedoes."

"Really? How nice," I say, thinking about my fashion-compromised aging suit and wonder if I should have gotten a new one. "You'll look like a million bucks, and Edie will be pleased."

First speaker answers. "Think she'll notice?

"Of course, why wouldn't she?"

Number two. "C-c-c-cause we're not f-f-f-firemen."

We all have a good laugh over that one, and then number three speaks. "Edie is only part of the reason we rented tuxedoes."

"Oh?"

I swivel back to number one. "Yeah, we also want to impress our date."

"Wow, great, you mean you all got dates?" I am truly impressed.

Tag-team to number two. "Yeah, all of us got dates, and we all have the same date."

I'm confused, possibly because of hunger, and I cannot tell where this is going. "Who?"

And now as a harmonious team, they respond together, "Diesel."

In response to my stupefied look, number three continues the relay. "We want you to know, so that...." He hesitates here, before turning to the other two guys and asking, "Why did we want Phelim to know again?"

Number one steps up. "So that no one is surprised and no one feels awkward."

"Is th-th-that okay?" Number two asks.

I pause, hesitate, both incredulous and in a rare state, I'm speechless. Lucy once again stands at my door, a true and much-appreciated sentient. Without knowing what I'm going to say, I blurt, "Abso-frickin'-lutely okay. See you tomorrow guys."

Kale arrives early. And I'm late. The combination of the two phenomena means they have to wait fifteen minutes. I'm apologetic even as I think, *So sad, too bad*. I also chastise myself, thinking, *Don't be unkind*, as we settle into my office.

"Nice space," Kale begins, "Though a bit crowded."

"True enough," I say, looking around. "Problem is, I can't think of a thing I could do without."

"What's that?" they ask, pointing.

"Ah, that's an authentic Irish shillelagh," I answer, thinking, *They can't think I could do without that?*

"And those?"

"Those are a collection of old Irish whisky bottles from Ireland, a couple dating back to the potato famine. Which makes for a weird collection, since during the potato famine, my ancestors were not likely concerned about Irish whisky when rotten Irish potatoes were the most an Irish peasant could hope for. Makes you wonder why they didn't go for a putrid version of vodka."

"What about those?"

"Those strange little dolls make up my voodoo collection, from Haiti and Louisiana."

"Strange," they muse.

"Not really; I think the purveyors of university politics today channel my wee dolls in a funny kind of way."

"How's that?"

"Well, sticking pins into dolls, as is the voodoo way, is a bit like saying harmful things about a colleague who cannot defend themself because they are unaware of what is being said. Weird, but sort of like how things work around here, don't you think?"

"Huh, hadn't thought of it like that, but maybe you a have a point." Having lingered on the preliminaries, Kale loses their wistful look and gets down to business. "I have to tell you that our SAP is very worried about tomorrow. She thinks there could be trouble."

"For which event?"

"For the debate, of course. No real worries about the wedding, though the SAP seems to think you're up to something there too. But not me. I'll be working tomorrow, and I'm really looking forward to seeing Edie get married."

"Yes, it should be nice," I say wondering if there's anyone who doesn't know and like Edie.

"The SAP wants security to keep an eye on things, but the debate is really the only game in town for us security people."

"Well, we've paid a chunk of money for the debate, and we're glad to have you and your people there, so what do you need to tell me?"

"I'm afraid there is rather long list of things I must go through. Then I can answer questions, and then I need you to sign this here legal document. The SAP got the lawyers involved, and they came up with a three-page list."

"They want me to sign? It's not my event. I support it, but there is a group dedicated to free speech who took this on."

"I know but you paid for security. Besides, we tried to contact Professor Staffal, and we can't reach him, so you're it."

"It? Hum, I seem to be full of it today."

When Kale doesn't laugh, I say, "Okay, shoot."

Kale's eyebrows rise at the word *shoot*, but rather than commenting, they take out three copies of a legal looking document and begin reading. "I agree and all my associates agree, and anyone associated with my associates, including but not limited to disassociating associates …."

I'm sure my eyes glaze over, even as I continue to look at Kale, with my mind slipping back to where Roma and Fred rest in a Polish forest.

I've been able to get maps, but most of our way-finding is conducted by searching for misfits, miscreants, and weirdos—basically, people who do not look like they have anything to hide. We are drawn to people who have nothing left to lose, are hanging on, trying to survive, to make it from this one miserable day to the next. People like us. The only difference being, we intend to kill Hitler, whereas our cast of misfits only fantasize about doing so.

We don't see many people, traveling as we do at night. But when we encounter anyone, my hand always goes to the German Luger I carry. I'm not intending to use it, if possible, but am very willing to do so, if necessary. Most often we pass strangers without a word spoken, but when exchanges are made, it is astonishing what stories people have, why legions of people have to sneak from place to place under the cover of darkness. For all the uniqueness of our situation, half of Europe has been displaced, with the other half on the verge of experiencing the same.

People traveling in ones and twos is common enough, but we've been warned about marauding gangs that rob and kill and are especially dangerous for women. I'm determined to discharge my Luger before I let that happen. Dying seems relatively easy for both of us, and we regularly discuss the realities of our situation. If there comes a time I cannot defend us with the Luger or by throwing a decisive punch, we each carry cyanide and are prepared to take it. The thought of having to use it is not threatening but almost comforting. Come hell, high water, or Hitler, we are unwilling to be taken prisoner, to surrender, to let them, who have taken everything, win.

Sometimes when we come upon remote villages, or farms, we approach with caution, and if it feels right, we continue and barter for food. The farmers we deal with are suspicious and uninterested in talking to us until Roma, subtly, demurely, and quietly, works her charm and lets it be known that we can pay. As we travel into late autumn with the harvest fully accounted for, however compromised by war, we are able to get sufficient food for small amounts of money. Once suspicion is dealt with, peasants tend to be easy to talk to. We occasionally learn something about the war: another victory for Hitler, the first rumors of difficulties for the Nazis in Russia, the prediction of a particularly cold winter to come. We also learn that food is getting scarce in the towns and cities, that buying and storing root vegetables is smart because they last longest, and that getting food will soon become uncertain.

The Nazis are still confident of victory over the Russians, but for the rest of us, uncertainty rules our lives and haunts our nightmares. I develop a habit of checking for my Luger on my left side every hour, just as I feel for our store of small turnips in a bag I carry on my right side. Cyanide, turnips, and the Luger, the essential elements of our existence.

Twelve weeks in, winter settling in, we have an unexpected incident near the Austrian border. Who am I kidding? Every incident of every day is unexpected, and no amount of time receiving and dealing with the unexpected gives us any sense of what to expect next. Much depends, as always, on what we see and what our intuition tells us once we survey what we are up against. We have had good advice and are becoming adept at finding remote locations where soldiers do not patrol.

Though this extreme caution slows us down, we do not have a set timeframe, and we have to survive winter somewhere. Weeks earlier, we bought used clothes and blankets to go with our rudimentary tent, so we are somewhat prepared for winter. Sharing body heat is a big part of our winter survival plan.

Once across the Czech-Austrian border, we decide to travel west, continuing into the area of Salzburg, where we must turn south into Germany. Berchtesgaden is high in the mountains near the Austrian-German border. That part of the journey is going to be physically challenging, especially in winter. It also affords less likelihood of encountering people. Part of the package I threw together in Berlin included a couple of pairs of hiking boots and crampons for steepness and ice. There are roads and pathways leading to where we need to go, so no actual winter mountaineering is required. Still, we need to be able to travel far away from marked pathways deep into the forest to rest and hide during daylight hours. Since snow began falling, we have to give extra consideration to obscuring our footprints where we camp at night. Sometimes we simply use a pine limb to brush the path after our footfall, a technique I picked up watching a Western film once.

Lately, farmers and villagers increasingly warn us about the wandering gangs of desperate men. They are hungry, horny, and ruthless. They have been displaced, or have deserted armies, don't expect to last long, and that expectation is very likely correct. It is a formula for desperation that rages across Europe. We are hypervigilant and avoid potential gang locations as much as we avoid soldiers. Avoidance as a strategy has its limitations.

Gangs are far less careful than us, so generally they are not difficult to avoid. Our caution is specifically reserved for German soldiers who do not wander the forests and fields of Europe in groups of two or three. When soldiers sweep through forests in pursuit of defined targets, they come in large, noisy armed formations.

So, with some experience, we have a sense of how to hide and when it is relatively safe to risk contact with the outside world. Still, we know one mistake can ruin us.

We make our one colossal mistake. Early one morning before first light north of Salzburg near the German border, we start our usual search for a remote place to sleep. Being close to the border is not a concern, since we are in a very secluded area, with many miles of deep forest to hide in. There are no passable roads nearby, and the border is still at least five miles away.

We are mad with fatigue, it is raining, we find a spot that is less than ideal and doesn't quite fit the criteria we have set for where we will settle each morning, but we compromise, decide it is good enough. So no excuse.

Usually, our method is to choose locations that cannot be found even with deliberate, taxing effort. We look for steep inclines, thick underbrush, uninviting forest. On this occasion, our compromised choice is a place that can be found, and so grievous is our colossal mistake that it is found by people who simply stumble upon it. In fairness, our fatigue and hunger are extreme, and we have searched for and chosen a place deep in the forest under the darkened sky of a moonless night. Still, no excuse.

After sleeping like the dead for a couple of hours, we are woken by a group of German men who have surrounded us. They are young, late teens likely, do not wear uniforms, and even with distorted perceptions due to panic, they do not present as threatening. Also, curiously, outside the ring of young men, there are two young women, one of whom has a guitar.

I hold my Luger, under our blanket in its designated spot. I resist my first instinct to use it and ask questions after the fact. Roma, sensing the same, searches with her right hand for where my left hand holds the Luger. Her light touch asks for restraint.

LARRY J. MCCLOSKEY

"What are you doing here?" one of the group asks as the others look at us looking at them from our prone position.

The tone of the question is not of murderous intent, is a bit disarming in its innocent curiosity. I feel my fingers relax on the trigger of the Luger as Roma relaxes her grip on my wrist.

Roma's social wherewithal returns before mine. "Trying to sleep. Who are you?"

"You first," the first speaker's companion answers.

Roma and I have talked about explaining who we are many times before. Generally, we say as little as possible, though saying nothing is not always an option. To Nazis, or Nazi sympathizers, saying who we are would certainly result in either death or a one-way trip to a concentration camp for Roma, and less certain but possibly the same for me as an American citizen. No matter, our lives are one, what happens to one of us happens to the other. To people who are neither Nazis nor sympathizers, we might reveal a little more, but only if necessary. The young people, at least the two who have spoken are German, so we remain suspicious.

"We are two travelers trying to survive," she responds, "and you?"

The group seems to think about this less-than-explicit answer. Another voice says, "Your German is good, but you are not German."

"Nor am I," I say, wanting to deflect from Roma. Turning toward the speaker without yet standing, I continue, "But you are German, right?"

"You seem to want information without giving it," the first speaker responds.

"What is there to say?" Roma begins. "There is a war on, we lost our home, and we are sleeping here at this moment because we must."

A woman's voice comes from behind the five males who have encircled us. "She's right: they're here because of war, same as we are."

"But you are German, and you are winning," I can't help saying.

"You are a Yankee, right?" the youngest-looking one quickly asks.

I don't see any reason to lie. "Yes," but I also don't see any reason to explain. "It's a long story."

"Did you know that we are officially enemies," the young blond man continues, "because that dog Hitler declared war last week on America."

I'm truly surprised and apparently show it.

"You really didn't know?" the young man seems to delight. "But what that actually means is we are not enemies—we are friends."

"I certainly hope that is true," Roma says, encouragingly. "Please explain. We could use a friend or six."

The woman who has just spoken steps forward and speaks. "We are rebels against the Hitler Youth, and we rebelled because we hate Hitler, hate the

242

Nazis. Perhaps you've heard of us. Stories have been written. There is a price on our heads. We are the Edelweiss Pirates."

"This is almost too good to be true," Roma whispers.

"It's true, all right," the second woman says, also stepping forward. "I can prove it," she says, turning her guitar around and slinging it so that she can play. And sure enough, she not only sings a song about protest with insults and clever barbs against the Nazis, but the entire group joins in the chorus, which has Göring, Himmler, and Goebbels pulling their pants down and bending over for Hitler. It is in all respects, music to our ears. We are of course delighted, though we wonder about the wisdom of singing where it might be heard. Still, we are powerless and in truth reluctant to do anything except listen.

I'd read something about the Edelweiss Pirates in the *Boston Globe* before leaving the US. They had been portrayed as brave boys and girls in a heroic struggle they could not win. The story served to inform Americans that not all Germans are crazed Nazi lovers and that even determined young people are able to resist indoctrination. Later in Berlin, I read one short piece about a few spoiled brats in Cologne who resisted the Hitler Youth and had become Communists. The article assured readers that the collapse of Russia would end Communism and ensure a healthy respect of our youth for the Fatherland.

The song ends. I lay the Luger down under the covers and we clap. I then ask, "Please tell us about this declaration of war."

"Ah, yes," says the youngest-looking, and most enthusiastic of the group. "It happened because Japan invaded the United States."

"What?" I'm incredulous, to the delight of the young person telling.

"You did not know about Pearl Harbor?"

"Pearl Harbor! But that's in Hawaii."

"Yes, yes, and the Japanese bombed it to smithereens." I don't know the last word and Roma explains later. "It was a total surprise. The Japanese came across the entire Pacific Ocean and surprised the Americans." Then remembering that I am American, he adds, "Your very own people."

The tall dark-haired teen beside him says, "America declared war on Japan, and, as you must know, Japan is an ally of Germany, so Hitler foolishly declared war on America. I hate the Nazis, but I think Hitler made a stupid mistake taking on the Americans. I think your President Roosevelt means business."

I am astonished. I knew that the Pacific fleet was in Hawaii, but the thought that Japan has attacked America, and from a distance of over six thousand miles, is beyond belief. And yet these young people seem credible. After all, who could doubt a choir that composed and sang a song about Hitler bending over his evil minions?

———————

My silly plastered compliant grin has saved me in many instances. Because my expression doesn't substantially change, it is easy to assign deep concentration to complete vacancy. After Kale asks me for the second or third time, who knows, I am back. I decide that Roma and Fred are at least temporarily safe, so not a bad place to leave them.

"Okay, so how do you do it?" Kale asks again.

I need to find out what they are asking about without betraying my absence. I must admit I shamelessly use the fact that I am a quad in these instances to advantage. People naturally assume a mental lapse, wayward behavior, or even obnoxious comments must be attributable to my terrible affliction. Why correct ignorance when it can serve so well?

"Sorry, I must have had a spell. Do what exactly?"

"Sign this document in triplicate indicating you have heard and agree with all I've said or have read to you today."

I look down to where Kale holds a pen over the designated spot for signature.

"Oh sure," I say, reaching for a custom-made splint hanging on the side of my wheelchair. I need to take a minute to place the splint around my left hand. Same one I just used to eat chili in the cafeteria. Funny how cafeteria staff notice and understand seeing its use once, whereas officers of the university seeing it a thousand times remain perplexed and awkward.

As I struggle and then manage to slip on the splint, as always happens, Kale asks, "Can I help you with that thing? No? Should I put this here pen in there? No. Okay, I'll hold the paper for you to sign. No? Okay, I'll sit down."

"Would you? There, all signed. Now for the second and third copy. I'll let you fill in the date. Thanks."

"My pleasure." Standing at eye level, Kale finishes with, "I hope none of the stuff in this here document happens."

"What stuff?" I ask, with perfect sincerity.

Kale momentarily replicates the same deer-in-the-headlights expression as yesterday, before deciding I'm being funny. "Ha! You had me for a few seconds. Forty-three items you heard three minutes ago and you pretend you can't remember any of them. That's a good one."

Not as good as they think, I think. "Have a good day," I offer to their exiting backside, and I mean it. I like Kale, but for all their elevated status as recently promoted head of security, I have the feeling my departing words are not the good wishes they need. We are cogs in a machine, looking for the power of one. The one who finds a solution, the one who others look up to, the one who saves the day. And most of all, the one who finds another one to meld into one. This weekend promises to be one to remember.

CHAPTER TWENTY-SEVEN

The evening before the big events, at a regular family dinner

I need to know that John is okay before I can enjoy dinner. I also need to know he is going to show up tomorrow for Edie's wedding and the Peterson debate. I am disturbed that he hasn't wanted to talk to me yet, but I understand. Sort of. I want to help; I think he needs help. We used to talk about most things that matter, so my sorry *sort of* is the extent to which I understand. I'd be fine if he had any other intimates, either male or female, he could talk to, but I'm fairly certain he does not. Who am I kidding? He does not. Maybe with a few drinks at the wedding reception after the debate, he'll loosen up, and we can commiserate and talk. Just talk.

On Sister Sandrine's suggestion I've called and left a message inviting him to dinner with us this evening, but he hasn't responded. Finally, just as dinner is being served, I receive a text message—something John only learned how to do weeks ago—with the following curt message: *Will be at wedding and debate tomorrow. No need for you to get me to the church on time. J.*

I feel relieved as well as bewildered. I can't make out what is on John's mind, and I vaguely wonder why it took Sister Sandrine to remind me to ask John to dinner. Why hadn't I asked him before? I think about this, but don't like the answer that begins to form in my brain. John is the best of company, but he is not easy to mix into company. He likes to be the center of attention, the vortex around which everything and everyone swirls. He is the entire company. Listening and making light conversational chatter at a dinner party is not wheelhouse. Being listened to as he holds court is where John is comfortable, where he is at home, where he thrives. Which prompts the question, who would he be if he did not have an audience with whom to feign being at home?

Our daily dinner party increasingly feels like home, and that feels good. We are an odd crew our two nuns, a depressed brother, my resident attendant and lover, her genius daughter, and last and truly least, one crazy-assed quad. Hum, sometimes best to go with what works and not question why. Such as the misfit beauty of our gathering around the dining room table at this moment.

Tonight is a particularly festive dinner in anticipation of Edie's wedding, even if worry for John lurks between courses and will stalk my dreams. There are issues about the stolen $66 million, the sale of the convent, having to lay off staff without the correct identity stripe, the sexual harassment case against

John, whether George will show up for that monthly movie with Kevin, what to do about Diesel, and a multiplicity of more serious student and staff issues, but this is Friday evening and time to put worry away. Time to exit strife for life.

In uncharacteristic fashion, Aunt Isobell makes the first toast. Come to think of it, with almost every assumption I have ever had about Aunt Isobell, from growing up right to and including our recent getting-acquainted habitation, I have been wrong, so why do I think anything about her qualifies as uncharacteristic? I've finally learned that her most enduring quality is to keep us guessing.

Iggy and I are responsible for dinner tonight, and there is pressure on us, since all preceding homemade meals have been extremely impressive. The meal pressure has been ratcheted up by tomorrow's big events, and since Iggy and I are of that toxic gender type, there is skepticism we can pull it off. I admit, but only to myself, that the skepticism is well placed. Iggy and I have talked about possibilities since last week. A couple of years back, we would have had the gourmet meal to beat all competition, all-time, for specialness. Then we would have put out for filet mignon, a delicacy none of us has tasted since groundbreaking legislation to phase out the selling and consumption of beef was passed by both Congress and the Senate two years ago. At first there was opposition to the great meatless reset by various steak-holders, but when the renowned Peter Luger Steakhouse in Brooklyn declared its intention to go vegan, protest dissipated like air from a balloon. To continue the metaphor, the flaccid balloon lying on the floor resembles the vegan steak from a photo of the Peter Luger reset menu.

During the phaseout period it is theoretically possible to buy very limited amounts of beef through a complicated government process. I did look into the current process and the waiting time, only to discover that it was going to be a minimum of two years, or put another way, just one year away from the final phasing out of the cow. Unwilling to be cowed by the cow, I officially protested the unfairness of denying us steakholder status. However, the email I received explaining the timeline did try to entice me to visit their website and marvel at the wonders of vegan meat derivatives. "You won't be able to tell the difference," I was promised. I wrote back promising that "I'll know the difference." To my surprise someone returned my note, or else a computer-generated answer was sent telling me that eating vegan meat derivatives can be embraced as my contribution to combating climate change. I wrote back that vegan meat derivatives won't exactly win us any culinary awards, now will they, mate? Apparently, there is no computer-generated answer for that question.

Depressingly, it did occur to Iggy and me that all the other dinner party meals prepared by Brenda, Aunt Isobell, or Sister Sandrine were casseroles, pastas, and rice dishes, light on meat and heavy on preparation, imagination, and expertise. Obviously, the others are getting with the program, while we are so not. We're screwed.

Finally, upon extensive examination of our severely limited options, we capitulate to our go-to take-out pizzeria. Giovanni's is where Iggy and I have either eaten in or had takeout twice a week for the past ten years, which is reason enough to entice others to regard pizza from Giovanni's as special. Pearl likes our choice, but when she hears me use the word *special* to describe pizza, she asks why we aren't going to have pizza after Edie's wedding tomorrow if it is so special? I don't answer, pretending to be caught up in other conversation around the table. As she leaves the table out of boredom or to explore, as she always does, she says to no one in particular that when people don't answer a question, it means they have something to hide. And naturally, I like that kid more than ever.

"Oh Phelim," Aunt Isobell says, disengaging herself from a discussion about National Hockey League standings with Iggy, "I've been waiting until Pearl left to tell you this. Just as I was leaving work this afternoon, I got a call from Ben. Again, it's not official, but he did pass on some interesting information about that poor dead girl."

"Oh?"

"It's even more tragic than we thought." Aunt Isobell bites her lip and slowly shakes her head. "Not only suicide, but it turns out she was pregnant."

"What?"

"Yes, about sixteen weeks, apparently."

"But…." My mind goes back to the conversation with John about his relationship with Heather, but I can't for the life of me remember when it had ended, or if John had given much indication of timeframe. Was he the father? Did he have any idea? Was there someone else between her relationship with John and her subsequent rebound relationship with Dean Perkins?

Four pairs of eyes wait for me to finish my sentence. Finally, I say, "I have no idea what to make of this, but it does seem I need to talk to John more than ever."

"What does it say and how might it impact on her accusation of sexual harassment against him?" Sister Sandrine asks, which no one presumes to answer.

"Before she accused him, John was distressed by the relationship but was neither determined to end it nor quite regretting that it was over. I know he actually cared for her, but I doubt he knew she was pregnant."

"I thought it was interesting when you said that after a lifetime of debauchery, John may have loved the one he could have had but wouldn't allow himself." Aunt Isobell finishes with a profound summary of this and all relationships. "Love is complicated."

As our faces register incredulity, she continues. "Oh, I see, because I've been a nun for these sixty years, I can't know what love is?"

The four of us, mutter variations of denial, without much conviction, as Aunt Isobell sits upright in her chair and says, "Would you agree it is a mistake to assume we know the inner workings of another person?"

The four of us mutter variations of agreement, without much conviction, though we know she is absolutely right.

"Well, I had a beau once, a very long time ago, mind. Still, the feeling of being in love never fully leaves. And of course I've loved often, still do, present company included, and unromantic, transcendent love is actually more important than the romantic stuff. Actually, in a pure sense, you could argue they are the same."

"How so?" Iggy asks.

"I mean there is no hierarchy of love with romantic on the top of the pile. The difference that matters is lasting authenticity, not fleeting passion."

The old gal is a marvel. Iggy asks what is on everyone's mind. "What happened?"

Aunt Isobell draws in her breath and frowns as recollected thoughts tumble back over sixty years. "He'd traveled the world and then became a distinguished soldier in the Korean War during the time of great optimism that characterized the years after the Second World War." Aunt Isobell's frown deepens, and her expression becomes pained as she adds, "And yet, he died alone, in an accident on his family farm."

"Oh no, how?" Brenda asks in a whisper.

"He got his arm caught in a thrasher he was trying to fix."

A collective and heartfelt cringe envelops the room.

"He was alone, and he would have suffered for many solitary hours, perhaps for days. Imagine that, in close quarters cheek by jowl for over three years with sweaty soldiers where everything you say and do is witnessed by others. And you come home, do something stupid, and die in agony and alone, hours and minutes without end, with only recrimination and pain, thinking what? Maybe that he wished he was back in army barracks playing euchre to pass the time with his chums." Aunt Isobell does not allow for self-pity, self-indulgence, or histrionics, but just this once these many decades later, heart laid bare, she has one great tear in each eye that she will not allow to fall.

"Funny thing is, I thought about it often, of course, though less and less as the years passed. I didn't dwell on what I, we, had lost, what we might have been, and the convent has given me a good life, thank you very much, so no regrets there. Not loss exactly, but I've often thought about him alone and suffering, and I've tried to imagine what he thought about. Isn't that funny? Did he feel he had been abandoned? I just don't know."

The marvels continue. Sister Sandrine seems to sense that Aunt Isobell can use a distraction from her rare state of vulnerability. "I once loved a boy from my village. In fact, we carried a delicious secret of our engagement for many months."

"Why secret?" Brenda asks.

"We were very young, and there were tensions between our families, tensions in the region. That part is a very long story; perhaps we were the Mauritian version of the Capulets and the Montagues. By the way, in answer to the bubbles over your heads asking what happened, the answer is, my uncle happened, and you know the broad stokes of that unhappy story."

"Do you know what happened to the boy you loved?" Brenda asks, with trepidation.

"I only found out years later that he had lots of children," and rather than get teary-eyed as expected, she continues, "and that he lost his hair, put on a great deal of weight, and turned out to be the type of man who thinks the role of a wife is to be kept pregnant and in the kitchen. Seriously. My loss was my gain."

It is the comedic break we need. Brenda, without being asked—a historic first—raises her glass and says, "Well, adding to these stories, you know that Iggy and I were once married. Though don't get any ideas, it was not to each other, and Phelim—well, he has always been a rake, the difference today being he is my rake. I think in the interests of love on this wedding eve, we should raise our glasses to Edie—oh, and Joey too, who we always forget. To love."

Pearl reappears with an expression of displeasure on her face, having listened to the very odd toast we have just celebrated. Sister Sandrine seems to notice first. "Pearl, you disapprove of love, or at least the celebration of love?"

Pearl thinks about the question carefully and exhales as if imparting wisdom to adults is a reluctant chore she feels compelled to perform. She takes another moment and adjusts her glasses before speaking. "The problem is not love; it's how silly adults get when they talk about it."

"That is so true," Sister Sandrine admits, with a broad smile.

Brenda, who had offered the toast thinking Pearl was out of earshot, cautiously asks her daughter a question. "Pearl, since you obviously heard what I said—"

"Obviously."

"—in my toast, um, are you okay that Phelim and I are—"

"Sleeping together?"

"Becoming close?"

Pearl continues in her most exasperated voice. "I know you sneak back to Phelim's room after you settle me, Mom."

"Well, I don't sneak," Brenda says, somewhat defensively. "But I, that is, we are fond of each other."

"You mean you love each other?" Pearl trills with ease, adding one of her unique and yet oddly classic half smiles.

To which Brenda and I, who are supposed to be adults and in love, cannot match Pearl's easy forthcoming eloquence. We look at each other, tepid deer in the headlights, victims of the inarticulate speech of the heart. After an awkward pause we manage to simultaneously articulate a single syllable. "Yes."

"And what about me?" Pearl asks.

Brenda turns to her and responds, "You know I love you, darling. I tell you every day."

At which moment it occurs to me, and possibly to everyone, that Pearl is not asking her mom. Brenda turns towards me, the others already watching, and Pearl won't make eye contact. I use all my requisite time doing an elongated spinal stretch, blow out a gallon of air, just like Pearl does, and say, "My parents never told us they loved us. They did love us, but their generation, especially the Irish Catholic version of their generation, were locked out of making direct declarations about how they felt, about anything and especially love. Iggy and I, and all our distant siblings for that matter, have struggled with the same emotional, or non-emotional baggage. But there is no doubt in my mind that any relationship with Brenda is a package deal, and more important than that prerequisite has been the astonishing revelation that I, Phelim Patrick O'Neill, love you, Pearl Daisy Adams."

Pearl answers, "You don't have to get so mushy," before beginning to exit the dining room.

But Brenda is not finished. "Pearl, is that all right, what Phelim said?"

"He'll do," Pearl answers, in whimsical fashion before stopping and turning back toward us. "Besides, he's got cool books on dinosaurs and auto mechanics, and he works at the university, so if I decide to do a PhD, we'll get free tuition. Bye."

Brenda is about to ask another question, press the issue, seek clarification, admonish, but I place flaccid fingers on her wrist and say in a low voice. "That's fine, more than fine actually. In fact, beyond my wildest expectations, fine."

With the table in harmonious glow, I propose that we refill our wine glasses and have another toast. "To Pearl, and to all configurations and permutations of love."

Pearl is soon back, and we wonder if she needs follow-up, refinement, or clarification of what has been said. But no, she merely wants me to know that my phone had been ringing, three times in the last five minutes. "I know you don't usually answer your phone when you are home, but I thought you should know in case something important is happening."

"Thanks, Pearl." Then looking at the group, "This is odd. I need to check this; could be John."

I wheel back from the table and notice it is not John but Alan, our tech guy, who has never called me outside of office hours. I call back, and he answers immediately. "Yeah, just thought you should know. At the end of the day, I came across something that I've never seen. Your computer's been hacked. Someone's been monitoring your emails and documents."

"Holy moly," I say. "David used to do something to prevent that, but he's been mighty busy recently."

"Yeah, I'm familiar with the software he installed, but it's no longer on your computer. That's the first thing I noticed. I'm installing a new program now that will end the problem, but thought you should know."

"Any idea how long someone's been able to look at my stuff?"

"A couple weeks anyway."

"Can you check to make sure I'm protected from now on?"

"Sure, if David is too busy."

He is too busy. Since being assigned to the SAP's group to help with a strategic communication, David has become indispensable to them, and less available to us. Which is good. It was my plan after all. And just today David dropped in to see me, excited, wide smile, gracious, and filled with gratitude that my plan has worked. He's been offered a more senior and permanent job from the SAP herself, beginning as soon as possible.

I wheel back to the table. "Sorry. It wasn't John, though I did leave him another message."

"Anything important?" Iggy asks.

"Not sure," I answer, both not sure and not wanting to talk about what it could mean just now. I have an allergy—no, call it an anaphylactic reaction—to work intruding into my nonworking hours. And now that I have an adopted family, with the potential for a meaningful relationship—a word alien to my preaccident philandering—and someone I can possibility adopt, I'm more determined than ever. I look at Brenda, who looks back at me, we two stealing a moment of intimacy at a shared table of intimates. And I think about Pearl and all the machinations and wondrous evocations of miracles that came together to create who she is.

Still, looking at Brenda, still holding her gaze, I have this revelatory thought, which may appear as a statement of the obvious from what has just passed: *I'm in love.* Brenda and I, eyes locked still, all previous defenses down, my lifetime practiced reasons for not believing dissipating into the past, and I think, *She actually loves me too.* Anyone who has really loved and been loved will understand, will not take for granted the wonderful singularity of the most readily available and rarest of commodity in the universe. It is the seemingly cosmic oxymoron that is actually the elemental reason for living. And defense against death.

Sister Sandrine, of all people, ends the mood with an anticlimactic, piercing question. "Well, that pizza was good, though I'm not sure it wins the coveted award for culinary dining. I'd say it all hinges on the answer to this question: what's for dessert?"

Iggy doesn't hesitate. "Donuts."

From the far reaches of the front room, Pearl, evidently still listening and not yet gone, issues a curt, decisive response: "We have a winner!"

CHAPTER TWENTY-EIGHT

Early morning of the big day, and traveling to the Berghof

I fall asleep within seconds of lying down, as is my habit. I will wake up between four and five a.m., whenever a proverbial thorn has been placed in my overactive brain. I went to sleep, willing myself to bask in the singular glow of Edie's wedding day. But I know I'm kidding myself. The day will be all about Edie, but what remains unspoken about all things Edie is the bittersweet fact that she will soon die. She's said a couple times leading up to the wedding that it'll be a celebration of life while there's still life in the old gal. She figured she might have to miss that other celebration of life others will put on after she is dead. She then said, "Hey, maybe then Eddie will have the gumption to hold a celebration of *wife*," followed by that laugh, earth-shattering and oddly calming.

Especially lying and lingering in this state of rumination. I've been a lazy, laid-back, "don't fight what you can't control" type of guy since breaking down in the arms of Irene those thirty-five years ago. Even now if I get worked up about anything, I think about that day—it being about the same hour as now—and I remember the profound relief of my letting go, of laying down the burden of anger. Justifiable or not, anger corrodes and diminishes.

I've never gotten fully used to waking up and being unable to move around to distract from rumination. A neurotic thought stalks me that I am the only person left in the world. And I hang suspended, waiting, trying to will myself back to normalcy, back to—not living, for dying doesn't scare me—but back to believing that people still exist outside the room in which I am trapped. Back.

Having Zigo sleeping beside me for these past years has helped. Having Brenda sleeping beside me these past weeks has helped even more, but don't tell Zigo. Fortunately for our relationship, Brenda has not tried to extract from me who is more valuable as a sleeping companion. Come to think of it, neither has Zigo.

My defense against the irrational verging on panic is not complicated, is not very surprising, is easily accessible and far away.

———————————

Roma and I are comforted by the thought that the Americans are now in the war. Without fully realizing it, our desire to kill Hitler has been motivated by the need to take responsibility, even if that responsibility takes our lives. There seems to be nothing that can stop Hitler, so we have a responsibility to stop Hitler. That simple. We aren't shattered by the thought of failure to kill Hitler, for that is a foregone conclusion, but are despondent that no one else will ever succeed, that lives lost, especially Roma's family, will be in vain. Without realizing it, we have been, if only by a slight margin, relieved of the solitary obligation to fix a dying world. We hadn't thought about it like this, but with the Americans now in the picture, we no longer feel completely alone. That is something.

We have trekked over eight hundred miles. It is just past mid-December, and we are twelve miles from the town of Berchtesgaden, the tiny town closest to and just below Hitler's Berghof mountain retreat. Oddly, and perhaps counterintuitively, the closer we get to Hitler's hideaway, the less we see German soldiers. But that can change.

More than fearing soldiers, I've been obsessed with seeing Hitler's mythical and dangerous retreat. I have a file, scattered information, photographs, old drawings of the Berghof—courtesy of Hank from the now defunct American embassy in Berlin—as well as the newly constructed compound near his residence. What I have is far from what we need, but it is all we are going to get.

We suspect that strangers without a state-approved purpose will be arrested if caught wandering around the Berghof grounds. We hope our saving grace might be Hitler's popularity. Although Hitler has bought up all property and buildings on the rolling hills below his newly constructed residence for several miles, adoring legends are allowed to get close to the main residence in an area cordoned off by a wire fence. Crowds gather to catch a glimpse of the great man and to see his splendid Berghof. Hitler, in turn, likes to be of the people and is especially fond of seeing families with young children. He is known to regularly come from behind the fence and mix it up with the adoring public. Most interesting, some select few might be invited into his residence, which means that even with the protection of soldiers, the Führer has some vulnerability.

I have faded photos of Hitler charming his Germanic *Volk*, at least half of whom are happy children ecstatic to be with Uncle Adolf. Roma notices several photos with the name *Bernice Nienau* neatly written in pencil on the back. Apparently, she was a repeat child favorite. In an attached note, we learn that, singular among all other children, Bernice was chosen from the crowd to visit Hitler on April 20, 1933, to share their common birthdate and a bowl of strawberries. Young Bernice subsequently became a favorite visitor until Hitler's aide, Martin Bormann, discovered her grandmother was Jewish and so tried to have her banished. Oddly, Hitler desisted against Bormann's predictable anti-Semitism, and she continued to visit. Given Hitler's perverse relationships with young women, this tolerance for a state-detested Jewess, is possibly scarier than his blatant anti-Semitism.

But we are not cute Aryan children, and for all our obsession to kill Hitler, Roma and I do not have a plan, for that would require more detailed information. Most of all, we do not and cannot know his schedule. But we do resolve to be among the adoring fans when they gather so that we can determine what can be known.

Included in my file is a rudimentary drawing of the property before Hitler bought it. There wasn't much more than a simple cottage and some outbuildings when Hitler began renting the property in 1928. Originally, Hitler had come to the area to visit a friend, Dietrich Eckart, and for reasons unknown—though the notorious nature of early Nazi politics has to be considered—he traveled under the name Herr Wolf. Hitler purchased the property in 1933 after becoming Chancellor, with proceeds from the sale of his antisemitism diatribe, *Mein Kampf*, so the Berghof was the original Wolf's Lair.

The mountain property has a steep slope just below the cottage location, which was situated for maximum exposure to spectacular views of the Bavarian Alps. But there was one interesting notation on an old survey showing that some kind of rudimentary, perhaps wooden constructed tunnel, had existed linking the cottage to something below. The Berghof residence is guarded and supported by a much bigger complex nearby. The Obersalzberg compound has eighty buildings and a vast concrete bunker or underground concrete town that was constructed to support Hitler's last stand, should that unlikely event occur. The bunker world of Obersalzberg is not particularly close to the idyllic Berghof residence, which is far removed from war, weapons, and the need for security. So that questions remain. Is there anything of the old tunnel left, has it rotted, or was it filled in with new construction in the late 1930s?

The last feature of the Führer's compound that merits consideration is the Eagle's Nest, located high about the Berghof. It is a small chalet, on a six-thousand-foot mountain outcrop, which was completed in 1939 for Hitler's fiftieth birthday. Hitler is likely less closely guarded when he is there, but we would be completely exposed up there even if we could climb that high, so a nonstarter assassination site. Besides, there is rumor that although Hitler loves mountain views from the Berghof, he is afraid of heights, and the Eagle's Nest scares him. It seems unlikely Hitler often visits the Eagle's Nest.

While hiking these past months, a monotonous minimum nine hours each day, we have had lots of time to endlessly think about how to kill Hitler. Later in our hovel as Roma sleeps, I've spent many, too many hours going over the file that Hank prepared for us. I've also wondered what happened to Hank since Germany declared war on the United States. I hope he had the good sense to get back to the United States. He, not being me, probably did just that.

As we got closer to Berchtesgaden, the reality of our situation sank in. It isn't as if we could luxuriate in the notion of our goal becoming easy once we reached our destination. And being challenged as we were each step of the way, we did not dwell on practical solutions to future challenges. Images of pulling the trigger, watching the life drain from Hitler's face after pulling the trigger, yes, but not much about seemingly intractable logistics. We lusted to escape the intransigence of the practical for the transcendence of dreams. Nicely put, but no help, I think.

But the practical problem of how to gather information about Hitler that can only come from getting close to Hitler is upon us. And the most immediate problem: where can we safely hide? Most of the rolling hills surrounding the Berghof are out of the question, for they are too open, too likely to be patrolled. We will have to find out how far afield German soldiers guarding the Berghof regularly venture. Do they guard the estate with a stay-at-home garrison mentality, or patrol wide and far in search of would-be assassins?

Tomorrow we will risk exposure by mixing it up with *Volk* from the municipality of Berchtesgaden, a spread-out population of 3,500. There is a scattering of hamlets and farms but no significant-sized towns. If not for the fact that people come from great distances to see Hitler, we might stick out in a remote municipality that size. Depending on who we talk to, we will become either tourists and adoring fans, or else farm laborers. We have worked on our Bavarian accent and have deemed it sufficient. We hope Bavarians agree.

The tricky part about seeking information is that Roma is much better at getting it than I am. I am far more likely to be regarded as an object of suspicion, whereas she seems to elicit trust. A word of greeting, and people are drawn to her, seem to want to talk to her. Beauty and charm will do that, to both men and women. Roma and I argue about exposing her to these situations, but she is determined, convincing, and no shrinking violet. She easily wins all arguments, which reinforces her skill for using words and beauty to get what she wants. How could she lose that argument to me?

As is demonstrated the next day. We talk to a few people, cautiously, mostly about the harvest, cold weather, the warm heart of the Führer. We don't see much opportunity, and we aren't sure what to do next. Then serendipitously, we come across an old man working a vegetable stand.

His face is disfigured, and his right leg has been amputated. He served in the First World War, but Roma miraculously elicits that he never agreed that the root of all Germany's problems was the imposition of the Treaty of Versailles. Then this stunner—the old man comes precariously close to stating that Hitler is not Germany's salvation. With some gentle probing, while buying and praising his vegetables, Roma discovers that German soldiers guarding the Berghof are of the stay-at-home variety and rarely venture into the heavily treed and mountainous northeastern section below the Berghof property, especially in winter.

The old man says the going is rough on that terrain—he used to hike and climb there as a boy when he had two good legs. He adds, you can always find evidence if people go there by markings in the snow. It is of course a simple test we have used often. Incredibly, the obvious question is never asked, and we do not have to explain ourselves. The old man seems starved for an audience who accept his sorted stories as fact. We are unquestioningly accepting and deferential to every utterance. The old man continues with a diatribe against the modern pampered soldier, often drawing comparison to the hardship he endured during the First World War. He concedes he was old even then, lying about his age and enlisting when he was almost fifty.

"Today they're all soft," he says again, as we collect the vegetables we have purchased, "and that's why they're going to lose to the Russians on the Eastern front." He smiles when he says this, a gaping hole, all gums and shrunken lips except for three lonely, teetering teeth. Best part, whether real or made-up, the old man says his name is Wolfgang. The pervasiveness of the word *wolf* is a constant Hitler theme.

After Roma concludes her chatter with Wolfgang, we continue on and are able to buy stale bread and two more blankets. We begin hiking towards the forested section of the mountain below the Berghof during the remaining sunlight. We have a rough idea how to get there without passing too close to the Berghof residence, and once darkness falls, we will enter the forest and stumble and grope our way to a safe place for the night. We have a sinking feeling this hiking plan as executed will be more difficult than as discussed. We are not wrong. Still, difficulties we can handle. It is the thought of getting killed that is mildly off-putting.

One does acclimatize to the prospect of danger every waking hour, even if punctuated by nightmares whose worst outcomes don't necessarily eclipse reality. A noteworthy human attribute is that we can acclimatize—to the point of knowing nothing else—to what we once couldn't imagine having to endure for a single minute.

I remember what it was like to move with ease, to be able to simply get up from the couch and gloriously explore what the world has to offer without an intentional thought in the world. The memory of movement is easy, the concept of movement is natural, but movement as a natural phenomenon is no longer possible. If I am being unclear, consider flying. You can imagine soaring, but enacting the mechanics of flight, not so much.

We luxuriate, sleeping in, with Bill booked to show up around ten a.m. He lives nearby, and I call when I need him. He likes the flexibility in a line of work that tends not to have much. Brenda no longer works weekends for anyone, and she no longer works for me at all. Attendant shifts are now something she does for other people during the week. It isn't healthy for one in a couple to have the obligation to be an attendant for the other. When attendants can't show, being backup is part of the couple deal, so no big deal.

I had a live-in girlfriend years ago for whom backup attendant service was not, was never, going to be part of the deal. She left me stranded a number of times, and though that meant hours unable to move or call anyone and, on a couple of memorable occasions, marinating in my own urine, I always forgave her. The day after she finished her nursing program, which I'd paid for, she left me permanently stranded. I was devastated but always knew it was going to be this way. Foreknowledge is not insulation against stupidity. People who know me can't believe I was that guy. But I was, and still am if I let myself. Still, I've learned a bit. First rule of relationships, don't give away your keys of happiness to someone else. Second rule, if you ignore the first rule, make damn sure you don't give them to someone who will kill you. True, and agreed, I should become a couples therapist.

"What time is it?" Brenda asks, before turning to her bedside table clock and answering her own question, as is her habit. "Almost 8:30 a.m. We've got a lot to do today, so maybe we shouldn't sleep anymore." And with the prospect of having to get up becoming a real threat, Brenda stretches and yawns long and loud before curling around my bulk like a contented cat.

"I've squared with Bill. He'll come anytime."

"Big day," Brenda purrs. "I don't think we've ever had such an action-packed Saturday. It's almost surreal, don't you think?"

"Yeah, sure, but I've come to a point in life where I think everything is surreal, that surreal is just the real that we become aware of, and when we think life is an endless, uneventful repeat of days all the same, we have slipped into a portal of unreality. A heightened appreciation of life, and the reality of its inevitable end called death, will pervade this day of great excitement, but at least we won't ignore reality for complacency, because that's death in advance of the fact."

"Well, aren't we philosophical early in the day. Let me guess, you woke up early this morning and did some thinking?"

"You could say that, but nothing bad."

"I always tell you to wake me up if you need some company, but you never do," Brenda pouts.

"You being here in this bed is all the comfort I need."

"What were you thinking about?"

"You know me, just tinkering with my novel. Can't decide whether to cast Beyoncé or Sophia Loren as the female protagonist."

"Isn't this fictitious fictional character Jewish and young, and Polish for that matter?"

"Cute. She is not a fictitious fictional character because she lives in my head, and she'll jump from the page into your head once I get around to writing it all down one day. And yes, Jewish and young, and Polish."

"Well, I vote for Sophia Loren. We've got to do all we can to defeat ageism, since it seems to be the only ism that no one is doing anything about. By the way, have you decided which suit you're going to wear today? I see you got two dry-cleaned. Not a chance I'm going to leave it to Bill to get you dressed for this wedding."

"I'm thinking the darker one, but I'm not sure you'll be able to stuff my bloated carcass into it, so the other is my backup plan."

"The sands of time do shift."

"Or in my case, gather in huge clumps in the same convenient location around my belly."

"Which is what I find so sexy about you," Brenda whispers in my ear as I steal an indulgent look at her exposed and extraordinary nipples.

"Poor you," I retort.

"Poor you once I move in here with my furniture, my controlling ways, and my daughter. What do you say to that?"

"I say," I say, lifting the sheet ever so slightly more, "That I am ecstatic for you, these nipples, your ways, and dare I say, your daughter, in unrelated, random order."

"Oh my goodness, last night I forgot to say I hope you weren't offended by what Pearl said about getting free tuition now that we're a family. I don't know what got into her. I don't know anything about tuition, so how could she, and she's only eight years old for goodness' sake. It almost gave the impression that she and I, we, see you as our meal ticket, and I really don't like that. I'll talk to her."

"I may have mentioned it to her. She is a planner, you know. Besides, I was really glad that she said what she did."

"Really. Why?"

"Because Pearl can't easily admit to thoughts of a, of our bond, and for good reason. So, when she has feelings, same as creative urges, or in other words, right-brain thought, she always deflects by saying something from the left-brain domain, something utilitarian, unemotional, but when you really get to know her, you can't help but get her drift. I was worried before, but I think maybe she accepts me."

Brenda doesn't respond, and we just lie there for a while. As my eyes survey her wondrous naked beauty, I glance upward and notice that her eyes are moist. I decide there actually is a more beautiful sight than Brenda's Botticelli perfection, which surprises even me. I also realize Pearl and I are alike: difficult for us to admit to what lies deepest and matters most.

I decide to ask the unasked natural question that lies between Brenda and me, the one that has to be asked rather than assumed. "Bren, are you sure you want to take on this lazy carcass, lard ass, somewhat broken, though highly charming husk of a man until death or else until you find a better squeeze, do us part?"

Brenda doesn't always appreciate my humor. "I'm sure about you, but I sure don't like your constant self-effacement. I don't want to hear again any hint that you are broken. You care about me and Pearl, and that does a whole lot of good for what was our broken family."

"Yeah, I care, can't help asking, can't assume, can't hold you to it if at this late hour you have doubts. I kidded myself in a previous relationship, and I know you could get lots of guys. When I look in the mirror the aging clown staring back is a bit frightful, and as for your needs—"

"There you go again. Do I have to tell you, oh philosopher king, that beauty resides in the eye of the beholder? Read my lips: you, my pear-shaped Adonis, are beautiful."

"Poor you. We can treat that, by the way."

"And as for my needs, I'm sure I've told you this but if you missed it, tune in this time. In the last decade I've been with three men besides you; my former husband and two dalliances, none of which resulted in orgasms if we are crudely discussing those needs, rather than, oh I don't know, my financial portfolio. With you and our mutual, let's call it creativity, orgasm is regularly achieved, and therefore those needs are fulfilled. Got it?"

"Yes ma'am."

"Good. I've got to say, I'm excited about our life together."

I feel a glow, a sensation, a sort of heat, calm, contentment, an electricity, a feeling so euphoric that even if it were to end this minute, its echo would continue forever. Oddly, it feels like the entangled inverse of waking up after my car crash with a sensation of lifeblood draining from my body.

"Shouldn't you call Bill?"

"Soon, soon, but not yet," I reply.

I don't want to call Bill yet, and she doesn't want me to. Not yet. Whatever the demands of the day, however rushed we will soon be, we choose to luxuriate, together, in the holy, fleeting moment.

CHAPTER TWENTY-NINE

The Peterson debate in the auditorium;
Edie's wedding day—and it turns out Joey's too—in the Great Hall

Showtime. I arrive early, the idea being that as the guy responsible for the day's proceedings, I should probably check what the arrangements are and plan for all contingencies. The truth is, I'm here early because I want to be, not that I'm needed. I will be, if not needed, at least tolerated later when it comes time to pay tribute to Edie and Joey on their day. But as far as arrangements are concerned, there is a beehive of capable people in the Great Hall hours before the five o'clock wedding to ensure no planning stone is left unturned. Still, I like to pose, captain, O captain, at the front of the vessel surveying the tearful crowd on the shore moments before raising the masts and blowing to foreign shores.

It is three hours until the wedding. Melanie, Diane, and Denise stand in front me at the agreed time and place to go over last-minute details. Behind them people, chairs, tables, flowers, food, and drinks seamlessly move across my line of vision, everything churning toward the outcome desired.

"I've heard rumor that the three of you are here today to give your collective resignations due to being offered obscene amounts of money to become wedding planners for the rich and famous," I say.

"Oh, and where did you hear that rumor?" Diane asks.

"Well, I heard myself telling someone, which has to be considered. Anyway, this hall is transformed and looks terrific. Great job!"

The girls are proud and have every reason to be. But they are not yet willing to rest upon their laurels.

"So I understand the firemen have agreed to arrive at 6:30 p.m., and they understand they need to hang back unseen if they are early," Denise reiterates for the third time.

"Yes," I answer. I talked to the coordinator yesterday. And he also assured me that their guys will bring the grubby firefighting outfit. A guy named Don will be looking for Melanie."

"Good," Melanie begins. "Joey will be looking for my signal, and as soon as I spot Don, I will grab the outfit and grab Joey, and we will go to the room 203 off the Great Hall. Same place we'll all be changing once we finish setting up."

"Do you still think the wedding ceremony will end at six p.m.?" Denise asks.

"Yup, I've talked to Stephen and Dawn, who is presiding, and we added up the time they need, and assuming things start on time, which it is important we do, six p.m. should do it."

"How many pieces will Stephen and the diva singer do?" Melanie asks.

"Just two, the aria to begin, and another to end. They were going to perform another, but when we inserted the Steven Tyler classic for the walk up the aisle, we realized we didn't have enough time for a second aria."

"I hope they are okay about the second aria being bumped," Denise says.

"Stephen is fine; not sure about the opera singer. I think in order for an opera singer to grow into a full-fledged diva, she is required to be unhappy about most things."

These, my gal peeps, are used to my corny jokes, so they don't react much, whether or not they find my latest crack funny. Good thing I don't have corny joke self-esteem issues.

A light lunch is being set up for the ones setting up. Denise calls out the group, and fifteen people gather for vegetarian pastries. The spinach-filled pastry is fine for our midday snack, but the dinner, as per Edie's insistence and unlike my home experience, is going to be all about meat. Once the story about Edie's pending nuptials got out, I shamelessly played the sympathy card to engineer getting Edie a sizable side of contraband beef. Donated, of course. More important, if we'd gone the government climate change approval way, it would have arrived, well, never.

I made a pitch to an outfit that makes dreams come true for people who are dying, sort of the adult equivalent of the Children's Wish Foundation. They were somewhat interested, but not quite sold by the phone call inquiry I made after the online application. So with the job not quite done, I drove to their offices, and me being a quadriplegic, I was able to ramp up the sympathy angle to steroid proportions and win the day. Ramping up was assisted by their absence of having a ramp. Basically, I wheeled and dealed while sitting on my wheels in their parking lot. Shame can be a persuasive force, I'm ashamed to say.

The beef is being carefully prepared in our Faculty Club kitchen, without cost, of course, and this too will be a surprise for the anti-green, meat-loving lovers. Others can pick away at the green rabbit food de jour.

Kale and a couple from their crew will soon drop by from the auditorium to check out our scene. I have no doubt Kale has also been instructed by our SAP to make sure we are behaving and conforming to all rules that can possibly be applied to a wedding. (We are way ahead of them with gender-neutral figures gracing the top of the wedding cake.) Kale will poke and prod, because in addition to being ordered to harass us, they will have to report harassment results back to the SAP. I feel sorry for Kale. Still, it will be fun to watch them tie themselves into a knot trying to contain the wedding, and most importantly, the Peterson debate. I just hope they have enough left in the tank to do what we are being forced to pay them to do: provide security.

Kale swaggers through scattered peeps working the Great Hall with two of their staff. They are all gender-indeterminate so I will make sure to keep saying *they* unless they instruct otherwise. We nod at each other, and Kale gets right to business.

"Any security concerns here?"

"The spinach pastry wasn't hot enough," I say, to blank stares, so I continue. "No security concerns and none anticipated, unless Edie tries to run away with the four firemen when they arrive."

Already a member of the ignore Phelim's corny joke club, Kale says, "I did check with parking, and they know that the fire truck will be parked directly in front of the Applied Abstractions building from approximately 6:25 p.m. until 6:55. Assuming that is correct, are you sure there are no other security concerns?"

"Kale, as you know, security was forced on us by our SAP, no disrespect intended to you and your officers."

"None taken."

"And what could we possibly come up with that would be of concern?"

Kale thinks about this. "There's a reason I'm asking."

"Okay, shoot."

"We prefer not to use that word in the security business.'

"Shoot?"

"Correct."

"Oh, shoot, I won't say that again."

Kale's eyebrows rise high on their left side, before squinting and bearing down. "Fact is, a large crowd is gathering across campus, very large, and well, if you have no concerns about security, I hope you don't mind if I take my detail off your event and reassign them to the auditorium where the debate will be held."

"Absolutely, no problem, good idea, don't give us another thought," I answer, with a tad too much enthusiasm.

Kale seems to think my answer acceptable but has one more issue on their mind. "I hope you don't mind, but before leaving, and now that you will not have an actual security detail for the event, I'm required to go through this list of your responsibilities, based on what you signed for yesterday, plus, er, a few more items the SAP added today."

"So in forgoing security that we paid for but clearly don't need, and because I am willing to allow said security to go to the actual event where security may be needed, which we also paid for, I am now required to hear once again security issues that almost certainly won't apply here."

Kale follows my every word—in sharp contrast to whenever I let fly a corny joke zinger—considering and weighing what I have said before responding, "Correct."

Kale promises to be brief when I mention having to go home and pick up my date and her daughter in time for the wedding. Clearly, Kale and I do not agree on the meaning of the word *brief.* "You agree with, and being responsible, you further take responsibility for ensuring all fire, safety rules and university regulations are strictly adhered to. You agree with, and being responsible, you further take responsibility…"

Very odd, assigning all-encompassing responsibility for all people in all possible life-threatening situations to an irresponsible guy who can't much move or feel below the shoulders. Still, if I'm the superhero able to scale any building and sign any document in the name of security, maybe I should ditch the suit and wear a cape to the wedding. No, I'll wear the suit. I'm not a superhero, just merely a security-savant. And with that penetrating insight, I exit for date, daughter, and daring deeds.

Finding our way to where we do not know, is difficult. Movement in the dark and snow and hilly to steep terrain is difficult and does not feel safe. Then a small solitary distant light pierces the darkness and takes our breath away. For brief few seconds we stand looking at lights coming from inside the house, Hitler's house, from a distance of about half a mile. Oddly, standing, shivering in the cold without any idea of where to sleep or whether this day might be our last, the smallness of that light source from this distance gives us a sense of Hitler's vulnerability, for the second time. From this distance, the illuminated rooms make the Berghof look like a perverse little dollhouse.

We continue, mostly downward, for about three miles, though in present conditions it is hard to tell what distance we have covered. It is also too dark to be able to judge where it might be safe to settle and make our temporary camp. We huddle together for hours and wait. With first light, we can search for a better hiding place. Just as the emerging light gives us the first outline of forest details, we find our spot, densely covered by trees and brush, far from any paths, and hard to impossible to find without knowing where to look. We settle, talk, and take comfort, each in the other, shrouded in cover and darkness once again.

We've spent so much time focusing on getting to Hitler's part of the world that we seem oddly bankrupt of ideas now that we have arrived. Partly, we just assumed we would figure it out, but mostly we didn't think we would ever arrive in Hitler's part of the world. Truly frightening, unless we or someone does something about Hitler, his part of the world will rule and ruin the lives of millions.

After two days of resting, thinking, and eating raw turnips and sausage, we venture out, cautiously, dressed as Bavarian peasants. I cannot convince Roma to let me go by myself, in part because she reasons correctly that if we are to learn anything useful it will only happen if she is there. We would have liked to find work, both to buy food and because we need a concrete reason for being in the area if questioned by German soldiers. But there is no work, the harvest is long past, and we are strangers.

It is a risk, but at midday we go to the cordoned-off area near the Berghof to see if there are any people who can give us any information. Before arriving at the fenced-off area, we can see it is empty so we reason that Hitler must not be at the Berghof. But how do people know when Hitler is in, to know when to wait outside in the condoned-off area? How do they know when greatness has descended? Surely, Hitler's arrival and departure from the Berghof is carefully guarded information.

The answer is strangely yes and no. One cannot ask Martin Bormann, his secretary, or his housekeeper when Hitler will be in or away from the Berghof. But word gets out, which becomes common knowledge in the surroundings farms and hamlets for the simple reason he wants it known. Hitler loves his adoring fans, and when he has guests, he wants them to witness the love of his *Volk* for their Führer. For the third time, I come to understand a point of vulnerability in the armor of the world's greatest tyrant.

And then some luck. We go back to the vegetable stand. We are surprised that Wolfgang is still there. He has supplemented his few vegetables with some simple Bavarian ornaments for Christmas. It is odd to think about Christmas in our current hellhole, and it is not a tradition that Roma celebrates. Roma no longer has traditions to celebrate, so we joke about celebrating each anniversary of killing Hitler in our old age. When I ask Wolfgang the date, I discover Christmas is just over a week away.

"And guess what?" Wolfgang says with a knowing wink. His knowing wink becomes so fixated on Roma that I step forward to give her some relief.

"I can't guess," I confess, "but I promise to be enthralled if you tell us."

Wolfgang turns back to Roma, reasoning that the sensational nature of his disclosure should not be wasted on me with all that beauty right before his eyes. I cannot disagree.

"Hitler's going to be home for Christmas, and guess who his house guests are going to be?"

Roma demurely plays along, while I dig my hands in my pockets to keep from strangling the old man.

"You'll never guess."

"I couldn't possibly have any idea," Roma admits, which is not good enough.

"Oh, come now, Fräulein, you know the players, the actors. Guess who Hitler would want as his most trusted friend and closest confidant for Christmas?"

"I really can't say."

"You, Herr Kesler?" We had told him this was our surname.

"Hermann Göring."

"No, no, no. Göring is a pal from the old days, so some loyalty there, but he has to prove himself with the Luftwaffe in Russia, especially since he failed to do so in Britain. And if he proves that the Luftwaffe is as capable as he says, he is a potential rival for the Führer, so no Christmas exchange there. No, Herr Kessler, not Göring, try again."

"Himmler."

"No, though not a bad guess. But Himmler is a functionary, a senior functionary, but not an intimate of the Führer. I am talking about someone very senior and"—Wolfgang touches his nose—"between you and me and this beauty, like Himmler, he is about to do something important or shameful, depending on your sympathy to the Jews. Mark my words."

I know of several possibilities, in part because I was well briefed by Hank before leaving the American embassy in Berlin. Reinhard Heydrich comes to mind, but this is not a subject I want to discuss in jocular fashion, especially in front of Roma.

Before I can answer, Wolfgang begins again. "I'll give you another clue. Really this will give it away. Who does Hitler love to greet most of all when crowds gather near the Berghof? And if even that clue doesn't make it obvious, who are the people we most want to spend Christmas with?"

I've had it with this game. "Joseph Goebbels, his wife Magda and their six children."

Wolfgang gives me a knowing wink.

"But, Herr Wolfgang, how would you know such a thing?"

Wolfgang loves the opportunity to restart the game. "Ah, that's easy. Housekeepers buy vegetables, and they talk, that is, mostly complain. The one who complains the most gives away the most information. Young and plain Anna Plaim is my best mole."

"And does what she tells you turn out to be true?"

"Of course, she is young, unattractive, and not bright enough to have an imagination for deception."

"Did the young, plain, and unimaginative gossip know when the esteemed guests would arrive?"

"They'll arrive to a fantasy Christmas in the Bavarian Alps on the eve of Christmas Eve. And who do you think will play Christkindl and give presents to the children on this Christmas Eve? Can you imagine Hitler as the blond angel-like Christ child? Ha!"

"Does he really call himself that?" I ask incredulously.

"The children call him Uncle Adolf, and last year he called himself St. Nicholas when he gave the children gifts on Christmas Eve, but even they knew he is mixing up dates."

I'm about to ask Wolfgang how in the world he knows all this, but I refrain. We agree to help the old man move baskets from a farm nearby to his stand in exchange for his gossip before leaving. We have not been careful and have been perhaps too curious about Hitler's schedule and houseguests, although Roma assures me that the old man was desperate for an audience. Still, we have enough sausage and vegetables for several weeks and will not return to the old man's vegetable stand.

CHAPTER THIRTY

Showtime and showdown at both venues

I drive home, and Brenda squeezes me into my dark suit. Barely. The task is difficult, mostly for Brenda, and I decide then and there to organize a benefit concert on behalf of sardines everywhere. Sting, Bono, Taylor Swift, Beyoncé, the usual suspects, and maybe I'll invite Steven Tyler. The suit is particularly tight around the crotch, as reported by Brenda, and I realize there are times that not feeling is an advantage. The three of us arrive back at the Great Hall at 4:30. I have left a few messages for John, both email and phone, but do not get a response. I am concerned but do not doubt he will show up for the wedding and Peterson debate. He is probably busy sorting out how to proceed with the debate, given the gathering crowd of protesters.

Brenda looks beautiful in a long navy blue gown, and Pearl wears an orange and green dress, which she describes as her new favorite colors. She is careful to add that it is not at all princess-like because she is all over the princess thing. I concur. Once we round the corner into the Great Hall, Brenda and Pearl stand astonished. The space is transformed, is beautiful, and is electric with happening. Most of the seats are taken, with the rest filling up quickly. Pearl leads Brenda away to check out the hall from different angles and to grab a couple of seats. Since my role is to start the ceremony, introduce key people, and move the whole thing along, and because I have brought my own seat, I do not join Brenda and her genius non-princess child.

I watch the great unfolding from my usual useless perch until David stops by with a warm greeting. "Hey boss, or former boss, but still the best boss." Then looking around. "This is going to be exciting."

"I think so." I've wanted to have a word with David, something not fully formed has been gnawing at me to ask, and I hoped a question would come into focus next time I saw him. And yet here he is, and I can't quite think my way to the words. I revert to small talk. "How's the prospect of a new job?"

"I think it'll be great. It really does help making yourself indispensable, so thanks for that advice."

And then it hits me. "David, while I'm thinking of it, I've been having problems with my computer lately, and I'm trying to locate a file, but I can't remember what I named it."

"Is Alan not able to help?"

"Yeah, he'll fix the computer problem, but I remember us talking about the file last year when I forgot the name then. You'd think I'd have learned. It was our application for $66 million for accessibility, and I gave it an obscure name."

"Enigma," David responds, with a wide smile.

Then I turn to Diane, who has just come up to us. "Hey, great job. I think it's time to present you with an official wedding planner designation, or if you'll settle for less, an honorary doctorate?"

Diane ignores my comment as expected and says, "There are a bunch of journalists looking for John, but they might settle for you. In fact, there's quite a few and there seem to be more every time I look where I told them to stand. They say they're here for the debate, but there is interest in the wedding as well. I told them we're going to start the wedding soon, so you won't have time for an interview, but that may not keep them from seeking you out."

"I am kind of conspicuous."

But she is gone, having informed me she has things to do, including steering David toward possibly the last empty seat. I want to thank David for reminding me that the file's name is Enigma, but he and Diane are out of range. I have people waiting with questions, to be greeted or directed or both. And I have journalists to talk to and to steer toward John when he arrives. We have agreed that John will handle informing the media about the $66 million dollar debacle. He has something dramatic planned, as he always does. They can then circle back to me for details.

Still, in the scramble of what I need to do, I think about what David has just told me. He seems pleased with himself that he remembered the name of my file, and I wonder if he will realize what he has just revealed. He has given me exactly what I needed to know, even if it is not something I wanted to hear. I'd like to remember that I did tell David the name of the file last year in the fictitious conversation I just alluded to, but my predawn musing has convinced me I never did. I never told anyone.

The Great Hall is full to capacity, every seat taken, standing room only. I take in some of the many rich details of this fast-tracked magnificence. And yes, I try mindfulness, because presence in the present is a very healthy place to be. A few from my staff look very elegant in dresses far removed from how they dress for the daily grind. Arthur wears the same ill-fitting suit that hangs off his skeletal form every day, but he looks happy to be here, happy to be anywhere.

Luna wouldn't say what she was going to wear, considers fashion needless extravagance that does not interest her, being too serious for such frivolity. But she has obviously gone to some trouble and wears a black dress with fashionable boots that make her look quite beautiful. And trendy. I'll find a way to tell her later, and she'll find a way to tell me to sod off immediately.

Still, somewhere, at some time in that tiny crevasse of her protected shell, my deflected comment will seep in. It is our way.

Behind Luna sits Aunt Isobell, and a moment later Sister Sandrine gracefully sweeps across the floor and sits beside her. Auntie is wearing a pale blue suit and looks very dignified and purposeful. Sister Sandrine's graceful sweeping is complimented by a plain, simple black dress whose effect is anything but plain and simple. In deference to the bride everyone should be looking at on her wedding day; I'll end my description there.

Speaking of there, there is Kevin banging his way through the crowd with his erratic wheelchair, only minor injuries to forgiving people. Kevin is not in a suit but is as dressed up as he ever gets in this lifetime in a beige cardigan and pressed white shirt. His pants look of this century, and best of all, he is with a friend. In a tailored suit, looking like a Hollywood A-lister sits George, so not only is he going to be a friend to Kevin, he is not afraid if people think they are a couple. I don't want George any more than he wants Kevin, but I could have kissed him for being such a pal.

And continuing with the Hollywood analogy, like Academy nominees lined up on the red carpet waiting to be interviewed are the three guys, impeccably dressed in black tuxedos and with their collective date, Diesel. Diesel wears a sweeping red gown, with a dramatic, eye-popping—if people's reactions are any indication—revelation of cleavage. Her dress, and the body it cradles, might tempt a few eyes that should also be looking at the bride on her wedding day. The guys look pleased with themselves, and I am pleased for them, and why not? Yes, stay in the moment, guys, enjoy it all you can, because for all the modern emphasis on mindfulness, who can actually hold the moment, not feel nostalgia for what has passed and anxiety for a future when what once was will be no more?

It is time. The clock strikes 5 p.m. Stephen, impeccably dressed in his tuxedo, holds his hands over the piano keyboard. Madeline, our rented opera diva, assumes an impeccable operatic stance, and in a flowing cobalt blue dress, she looks decidedly self-assured and regal. I look out at the fulsome crowd, with a hundred or more people standing behind the chair dwellers. Still, I am unwilling to give up or share my seat. Denise gives me a thumbs-up, I nod to Stephen, he gently begins, and our resident diva sings a powerful rendition of Puccini's "O mio babbino caro." This aria sets a solemn mood for the wedding of the century but has been relegated to merely prelude to the main event. The expectant couple wait at the back and will not walk up the aisle until the second, recorded piece of music begins to play.

The second piece of music sharply contrasts the first. Serving Spam after filet mignon on the same plate might be a fitting comparison, though in our new meatless world, brussels sprouts after french fries is more accurate. But the crowd is here for Edie—and, oh yeah, that guy she is marrying—and not to be music critics. Edie, who is determined not to miss a thing, is walking up the aisle with the man she is going to marry serenaded by Steven Tyler belting out "Don't Want to Miss a Thing." It is a perfect moment, with Steven Tyler's high notes relegating nightmarish perfection into perpetuity.

Edie glows on her walk, on being the center of attention, on having all eyes on her on her day, and Joey, though he looks like he wants to escape, seems happy. Her glow and his petrified look are photographed from every angle by the many media outlets who are vying for the best shot to grace the front page of tomorrow's newspapers.

It is easy to think that the walk up the aisle will be the highlight of this photographic opportunity. But Edie has other ideas. Early during her very aggressive cancer treatment Edie began wearing a wig for obvious reasons. It more or less replicated her hair loss in color and length. Edie had been a brunette, but her hair had turned completely white in recent months.

So, for her wedding she decided that blondes in black wedding dresses really have more fun, and in her case, more flair. And yet she who dares to flair is not done. As Steven Tyler's final whine winds down, and just as she and Joey arrive at the end of the aisle where she is to be married, Edie abruptly turns around to face the crowd, dramatically pulls off her blond wig, and says, "Ta-da!"

The astonished crowd falls silent after initial gasps of air. Even those used to Edie's delightful antics are not expecting this. After maybe five seconds of suspended reaction, Edie lets out one of her signature full-volume chortles and says, "Just thought I'd give you a heads-up on what the bride will look like naked tonight." Her pink and white bald head shows more accurately what she looked like as a baby, but no one challenges her claim. As people begin to laugh and clap, Edie throws her wig back on her head and says, "All right, already, I'll get back to my Marilyn look, and we'll get this thing done."

The laughter is full and sincere, but with a lingering touch of uncertainty. People are relieved when the ceremony continues without further incident or bridal histrionics.

I'm paying close attention to the clock and so far, our timing is perfect. The ceremony ends, a few quick photos are taken, and champagne is served as designated speakers line up to pay tribute. Each of a number of close friends, all Edie's and none of Joey's, takes their requisite two minutes and passes the mic on to the next. I am second last, with John to finish with his signature eloquence before having to dash back to the auditorium for whatever is happening on the Peterson debate battlefield.

The timing is tight, with the fireman soon to arrive, and there is no doubt that audience attention will immediately shift when they arrive. At 6:25 it is my time to speak, and still, John has not arrived. I cannot delay. "I want to begin by giving you a sense of Edie without using words."

I play a looped recording of her laugh taken from a radio interview she did yesterday. Her loud and distinctive laugh fills the great hall, with six hundred people adding to the sound of unsullied glee. I tell the story of how Edie and I once had a bet, witnessed by the entire office, that she could not stay quiet for the length of one full week. For the silence that was beyond golden, it never seemed to occur to her that she was doing exactly what I wanted. In the second hour of that Monday morning, the limits of her willpower were surpassed, there was an eruption of laughter, and the bet was over. I won, but with golden silence relegated to the past, I lost too.

I now gratefully cut my heartfelt congratulations short as John Staffal, rumpled man of mystery, makes his way to the podium. The time is 6:27.

With opening comments, John is funny, dramatic, outrageous, and the perfect speaker to end the perfect ceremony, and yet something is slightly off. In the mix of emotions, John is emotional, almost shaken, which, given the heightened sense of life and death present in the room at this moment, is not surprising. Still, as brilliantly as John can act out and articulate such emotions, he has never displayed vulnerability in the character of himself. Others would not know this, but I do.

John wears his great Cyrano de Bergerac plumed hat, removing it with a flourish as he begins, and then sweeping it back on his head as if its placement represents a unique theatrical performance. After which he makes his way to a cluster of journalists who swarm him with questions about the impending debate. I sense it may be difficult for John to work the $66 million dollar swindle into media swarming.

The firemen have arrived, and I can see Joey shuffling toward the changing room where Melanie is waiting with the newly arrived firefighting gear. I am about to announce the presence of the firemen when Edie steps boldly forward and pries the mic from my cold dead fingers, saying, "Not so fast, boss."

As in all her endeavors, Edie's tactic is intended to get people's attention. "Phelim, I'd say get a grip, but clearly that's not going to happen. I promise I won't take long, and I promise I won't take my wig off again. I've got two things to say, so shut your gobs and listen up. First, I want to thank all of you here today. It means a lot to me, and oh yeah, same for that guy I just got married to. What's his name again?"

An eruption of laughter from the crowd conjoins with Edie's familiar laugh for a Norman Rockwellian equivalent of sound.

"My dumb boss here, the people who threw together this amazing wedding in about fifteen minutes, all my peeps, youse office buddies and students, all of ya, you're frickin' amazing, and I love you. You know what you mean to me, so don't forget it, and don't forget me." A strange emotion, equal parts tears and laughter pervades the hall, until Edie provides relief and changes the subject.

"And there's something else, something for all these journalists to feast on who think a silly wedding just a bit too boring. The place I work, St. Jude's Center for Students with Disabilities, is the best in the country, maybe the world. My dumb boss here who's been around since Cain slugged Abel, has much to do with it, but if you ask him, he'll say it's the elves, so don't ask him." Chortles, followed by heartfelt laughter, before continuing. "St. Jude's has an opportunity to become the most accessible university in the world. Phelim went out and found the money, and together we know how to do it, but there's a problem. There always seems to be a problem when you can do some really good work. We're talking $66 mill here, which ain't chump change. The thing is, no matter how rare the chance is—maybe only once in a lifetime—someone is always, always there to say no, to interfere or be a pain in the sorry ass.

"So, to you journalists here today, if you want to become one of my true peeps, ask Phelim here about our center's accessibility opportunity and why it might never happen—that is, after we all dance our asses off over at the reception." Looking out into the crowd, without seeing firemen, Edie raises her glass and says, "Seeing as I can see that the lot of youse have got your greasy paws on some vino, I want to finish this little talk with a toast. Open your gobs, pour some wino crap down your thirsty throats, and know I'll always love ya."

I hadn't expected this from Edie, though I also hadn't expected Edie to be Edie when we met fifteen years ago. I love people's capacity to surprise those who supposedly know them best. It wasn't clear to me how she knows what she knows and understands what she understands, but John is the likely source. Or, who knows, maybe she just picked it out of the ether. Anyway, what she said is picture perfect. An out-and-out accusation of theft, corruption, or malfeasance would have been too much for this crowd at this wedding on this day, even if totally accurate.

Marrying her love for her work peeps, who created the chance for her to get married, to our work at the Center was brilliant. The opportunity to be the most accessible university in the world was not just shop talk, it drilled down into who we had become as a result of what we had done. Together. Not aspirational, theoretical, an abstract *me, me, me,* but the actual thing the royal we are capable of doing, if only we can rid ourselves of the ever-present naysayers and thieves. And to the many journalists gathered, amused but not seeing an explosive story in the wedding of the century, Edie has dangled the bait that should inspire the bite. All they have to do is follow the money.

Edie never does notice the absence of Joey, which, given his historic placement in the back seat of their relationship, is not surprising. Meanwhile, the crowd begins parting as the four formal firemen walk across the Great Hall with flowers and champagne in search of the bride. When Edie sees the firemen and comes to understand that they have arrived with the express intention of honoring her, she is ecstatic. It would be impossible to describe the look on the young firemen's faces as she whispers suggestive to lewd comments in their ears, one after the other. One can only imagine, and yet the startled firemen don't have to imagine what has just been explicitly laid out.

Then the grand Joey entrance. As Joey begins to strut, I put my phone up to the microphone, play Bruce Springsteen's "Fire," and watch the fireworks. With her attention all over the Fab Four, Edie is probably the last to see him. But once she spots her familiar little guy transformed into a sashaying, testosterone-strutting action hero and fashion sensation extraordinaire—possibly for the first time in her life—all her attention and all her amorous desires become squarely focused on Joey. Even when he finally finishes his sashaying (which is both a marvel to behold and a skill we didn't know he had) and stops in the middle of four strapping firemen, she only has eyes for Joey. It is a very good moment, that serves to banish the specter of death that has stalked the epitome of life that walked up the aisle an hour and a half earlier.

People had been instructed to make their way to the reception hall only two miles away, but no one wants to leave the festivities. Reception festivities have been much anticipated, but nothing can beat the feeling in the Great Hall at this moment. Only when the life of the party packs up to go does the crowd disperse and head to the reception hall for immediate reassembly.

We have a volunteer crew waiting to clear away dishes, wine glasses, and garbage. Some of my staff are also intending to go with me to the beginning of the Peterson debate, at least for John's explosive opening comments. Brenda and Pearl, whom Edie has taken under her wing, go ahead to the reception. Iggy, Arthur, Luna, Aunt Isobell, Sister Sandrine, a couple of our counselors, and I walk to the auditorium together. It is exactly 7 p.m., but we have tickets with assigned seating so we don't think getting seated will be a problem.

We are wrong. In the parking lot before we reach the auditorium, we see vehicles from every news outlet in the country. Then as we round the corner, we see several hundred demonstrators chanting slogans and waving banners. In the planning of this event, it seemed as if Kale and their burgeoning security team might equal the number of protesters. A few security officers are on the sidelines, but clearly nothing is going to equal the size or mentality of the gathering mob. I wheel to the front of the group, turn to Luna, and say, "Let's play the sympathy card and see if we can lead our group through the throng and get inside." Turning in the other direction I say, "Auntie, stay close to Iggy and me."

We manage to get into the auditorium lobby, which is crowded and chaotic. There, Kale and four of their staff are trying to talk down a crowd shouting protest slogans. Kale is in heated discussion with four toxic male protesting types who look menacing and are well over six feet tall. Even in uniform, Kale and some of the other security personnel don't seem particularly authoritative speaking a full foot upwards.

A number of the protesters try to talk the non-binary security staff into solidarity with their protest against the fascist organizers of the debate. Security staff look sorely tempted, or at least unlikely to provide resistance to the protesters.

I want to push on through, and with an electric wheelchair at my command, my pushing power has some heft. But people are now leaving the auditorium, and there is no way to go against the human flow. I'm also worried about Aunt Isobell being jostled, but I reason that once most of the crowd vacates, we will be able to circle back and enter the auditorium. I know John is determined that the show must go on, and Jordan Peterson is used to controversy, so they can weather a few hundred protesters.

Once we turn to go outside again, it seems as if the number of protesters has doubled or tripled. But it isn't just the number of protesters that has changed. The crowd is decidedly angry and determined, swarming, shouting, and randomly pushing people around. Then a half dozen people all wearing black masks and hoodies hurl bricks at the long bank of windows that front the auditorium foyer. These moves are coordinated, orchestrated; they know what they are doing, and there are no debate supporters or security to resist.

A few objects are lit up and thrown in the air, someone shouts "bomb," and the crowd begins to panic. There are no bombs, but by now it doesn't matter. A few people are knocked down, but Iggy has the good sense to move Aunt Isobell between my wheelchair and where our little group stands. Aunt Isobell never loses her composure, but there is no going back into the auditorium after the crowd thins out. The Dr. Jordan Peterson debate, eighteen months in planning, a North American postsecondary test case for free speech, with interest expanding from local to international media coverage, and a personal crusade for Professor John Staffal, is canceled.

Once we move to safer ground, I say to Iggy, "Can you use your jet burners and run around to the back and see if you can locate John? Tell him we'll drink scotch triples and commiserate. Tell him Edie expects him at the reception." I'm still telling Iggy what to tell John long after he's applied the jet burners to the parking lot and beyond.

Being Iggy, he really is fast, and returns in about five minutes. "Nothing. One of the security people thought he and Jordan Peterson maybe went somewhere together. I checked the pub, and they weren't there."

"How'd you get all that done so quickly?" Sister Sandrine asks, to an obviously pleased Iggy.

"He's fast in everything he does," I answer, to a horror-stricken look on my little brother's face.

"Not everything," Iggy corrects. "We'd better get to Edie's reception."

"You know what's weird?" Luna says. "There are no police here yet. And I called 911 as soon as we came out of the foyer."

A little later on, we can hear police sirens, but more than half an hour has passed. I think, *Yeah, that is weird.*

The dinner and reception are boisterous, long, and happy. No pending death threats are stalking any of the wedding guests, and this is especially true of Edie. We had worried about her level of energy, and we hoped the day hadn't taken too much out of her. But we needn't have worried. She is a whirling dervish, does not get tired, is the life of the party, and is the last person to concede it's finally over and agree to leave. We bought Edie and Joey a night in the bridal suite at the best hotel in town, which is the only reason we are finally able to convince Edie to pack it in and leave. I sweeten the deal by telling Edie that four recent young acquaintances are waiting for her under the covers of her bridal suite bed.

As we are packing up and getting ready to go, I ask Edie about her new husband Joey. "Joey who?" Is her instant reply. Joey hears this exchange, but, still basking in the glow of his recent strutting stunt extraordinaire, he doesn't mind. This glow is reinforced by newspaper photos of Joey in his firefighting attire next morning, the first day of their married life. Joey and Edie make declarations of being both forever grateful to their peeps, and the happiest couple in the world. And they are. For the eternity of this moment, we have successfully managed to chase away lurking death for present life.

It is two a.m., we are exhausted, except for Pearl, and there has not been any word from John. He probably went to a bar with Jordan Peterson, but who knows? Maybe frustration about the event and comfort from whisky combined to compromise his memory and sense of obligation. I know this reasoning is nonsense and say as much to Brenda as we drive home.

"Mind if we take a five-minute detour?" I ask. "It's because—"

"We know you want to find your friend, so of course we should go," Pearl answers from the back seat.

We float by John's building. There are no lights in his third-floor apartment. I drive into the back of the building, but his car is not there.

"Should we call the police?" Brenda asks.

"And say what? We saw him at 6:30 p.m., so he's not a missing person."

Brenda doesn't respond but yawns long and loud.

Muted by the sound of Brenda's colossal yawn, I whisper, "Maybe tomorrow."

CHAPTER THIRTY-ONE

Sunday, our Island of the Misfits residence,
formerly known as the O'Neill house

For as long and as well as I've known John, we've hardly ever gotten together on weekends. I'm a homebody, especially with my newly acquired
strange and eclectic family residing at my, our, home. According to his tall
tales, weekends were when John made his many conquests or, more likely,
when many women who he expressed interest in refused to become his lover. So as I think about how to locate John, after trying and not receiving any
response from multiple phone calls and emails, I really don't have any ideas. I
know of but have never met any of his three former wives and many children.
I don't know his other friends, where he hangs out when not hanging with me
at Paddy's Pub. I just don't know. I am confronted with the uncomfortable
fact that John's life is extremely compartmentalized and that our friendship is
just one compartment. We have a great friendship and often say so one to the
other,, but now without any idea how to locate John, I realize that it is limited.
And that surprises me.

I decide to drive by his apartment again. There is no indication John has
been back, so I call the police department. Someone listens, and when I finish,
she asks if that is all before advising me to keep trying to reach my friend, but
it is too soon for the police to become involved. As I thought while feeling
useless, as I surely am.

For the rest of the day, I wait. I decide that whatever else is going on, John
would not simply disappear. He would stand and fight if fighting had a fighting chance, or he might retreat under heavy protest, but with dramatic flair be
determined to live and fight another day. In short, he would do anything other
than what it seems he has done. Obviously, much more is coming. It is not a
comforting thought.

It is an odd, ominous Sunday, and I'm glad when we, motley crew that we
are, assemble at the dinner table so I can escape my many ruminations. Pearl
always sits with us at the beginning of the meal until she eats a decent portion,
before we bury ourselves in boring adult gossip as she rather accurately calls
it. Adult conversation she can take and might well participate in, but she is
always bored when we revert to endless talk about what people say or do to
each other. We honestly aren't aware we do this until Pearl challenges us. For

a few minutes we talk about history, politics, and philosophy, until someone makes a comment about how one of these big subjects relates to someone we like or dislike, at which instant Pearl is gone.

"She has a point," Aunt Isobell giggles.

"Are we really that boring?" I ask.

"It appears so," Sister Sandrine says. "I think Pearl has given us fair warning that we do not read or get out enough."

"Ahem." Pearl's fake and deliberate cough is reserved for when someone talks about her, believing her to be out of the room. She isn't concerned about someone saying something disparaging but rather does not want to be praised while in earshot. Weird kid. "I forgot to tell you," she begins, addressing me. "Yesterday when we came home after the wedding, and it was hard to start your van, you said you thought the problem was the starter motor."

I think about this and concede Pearl has represented the problem and my conjecture about the solution accurately. "Okay."

"I thought what you concluded is the problem didn't seem right, so I checked with this auto mechanics book, and I think the problem is your alternator. If it was the starter motor, it would have made an annoying grinding sound when you tried to start the engine. When you tried to start the van last night, you didn't have enough power for the motor to turn over. You need your alternator to be able to charge the batteries, or else your van soon won't work at all."

We've all witnessed Pearl's eight-year-old genius on big subjects (e.g., her opinion that Carl Jung's version of psychotherapy makes more sense than Sigmund Freud's comes to mind), but this accurate diagnosis and solution to my practical van problem takes the cake. We stiffly respond in stupefied manner, which is to say, not at all. As Pearl begins to exit the room, I manage to say, "Since you're leaving, and you didn't bother to take the cake, please come back and have all the cake that you want a little later."

"Oh my," Aunt Isobell says. "That does take the cake."

"And I can't even find the engine under a car hood," Brenda concedes, "just in case anyone thinks there is an inherited trait."

"Can I offer a toast?" Sister Sandrine asks rhetorically. "And it won't be in praise of Pearl, this time, since that embarrasses her. But I would like to raise a glass to those who tried to hold last night's debate, regardless of the outcome."

"Phelim put in a lot of time and effort," Iggy says, glass in the air.

"Thanks, Sister," I answer. "But the outcome is disturbing. Most of those planted protesters were definitely of an anarchistic bent. It's tough enough to find common ground among people you disagree with, but when you encounter people who just want to take down everything—every structure and everyone—compromise does not exist. It raises the question, where do we go from here?"

Aunt Isobell is shaking her head sadly. "I've never talked much about the decade after the war, but I do have distinct memories, young as I was. There was hardship and deprivation, and our father never made much money as a part-time carpenter. Going to bed still hungry after a scant dinner was not an uncommon occurrence, and we were four to a bedroom. But no complaints, mind. It's not what stands out. Generally, people were still in the glow of having pulled together and won the Second World War. For that conflict, people agreed that it had to be fought, Europe had to be liberated, Hitler had to be defeated, and we all had a part to play. You never met people who complained or disagreed that what needed to get done was wrong. This family gathering for me this evening, the hospitality we have received from Brenda, Pearl, and the O'Neill brothers, is something to feel and express gratitude for and is the closest thing that remains of what seems to get lost on a daily basis. Does any of this make sense?"

It takes some effort to hold back the tears. Sensing I might lose the battle, I make something up and quickly. "Common values and family, however much concocted, made-up, serendipitous, divine inspiration, or luck, these are what matters. Thanks, Auntie, and to this, more than most things, I will enthusiastically drink!"

"I did want to mention something else, now that we have dispensed with the mush," Aunt Isobell begins with a giggle before becoming more matter-of-fact. "I recently exchanged emails with someone I knew years ago. I was somewhat known among Catholic institutions because of my years in medical records, but I also did some work that was recognized, as an amateur historian, particularly of convents associated with hospitals and universities. This woman, one of my early protégés—"

"Of which this country, thankfully, has legions," I take the liberty to insert.

"... Emailed me about the sale and imminent renovation of our convent. She belongs to a Catholic organization that does this sort of research. She said that she uncovered some original documents in the Library of Congress regarding obligations and responsibilities between St. Jude's University and the convent. She said her research is far from complete, but if she can find supporting documents, it may change the legal assumptions the university is working under. In other words, documents might exist that invalidate either the sale or renovation of the convent as planned, or both. She asked if I wanted her to continue her search."

"Holy moly," I say, looking off into space. "Sorry sisters. What did you tell her?"

"I told her don't bother," Aunt Isobell giggles. "Of course, I expressed delight and that we are anxious for results."

Iggy's face registers extreme anxiety until he realizes he has been had, by a nun in her mid-eighties, once again. Even poor Iggy feels the comic relief once he recovers.

"I have something," Sister Sandrine says. "It struck me as strange, but I haven't had a chance to mention it. I got a call from Counseling Services. They have a student who they want to refer to me."

"Sure," I say, "we get lots of students with disabilities from them."

"But that's what's odd. This student doesn't have a disability, well, at least not yet. As explained to me, the student, who is white, identifies as Native American, has asked for a colored or BIPOC counselor, and hence the referral to me, even though I've never considered myself either white or a person of color. Growing up in culture of mixed ethnicity, color was less relevant than class or religion. It was not always so, but with most people being shades on a spectrum, our prejudices and societal pathologies became somewhat color-blind. All of which is to say, since the colored counselors are no longer taking clients, I am considered the answer. Apparently, we of a certain shade are very popular."

"Probably not a good time to play that song by Procol Harum," I deadpan.

"Huh?" from the assemblage.

"Their big 1960s hit, 'A Whiter Shade of Pale.'" When no one responds, I further deadpan, "Maybe you could star in the new film sensation, *Fifty Shades of Beige*."

With a straight face Sister Sandrine refines her non-response. "We are not laughing so as to enjoy our schadenfreude moment."

"Our what?" Brenda asks, wrinkling up her nose in the cutest way.

Sister Sandrine turns to Brenda and places a hand over her mouth in conspiratorial manner, "To secretly delight in another's misfortune, in Phelim's case comic misfortune."

It is my turn to giggle before returning to the issue Sister Sandrine has raised. "I'll bet you are busier than their counselors. What did you say?"

"I said I'd talk to you. But then the person from counseling indicated this student is also very stressed and may claim PTSD on the basis on being a woman of color, so intersectionality, leading to disability."

"Ah, now that is an issue we are trying to sort out. Strange, at a security meeting in response to the accusations against John, the student in question, who is clearly white, was referred to as colored."

"Apparently the student wanting a colored counselor knew Heather, and it is because of her suicide that she needs counseling."

Brenda clears dishes and goes into the kitchen. I ask, "I'm curious, what is the student's name?

"Tofu Marshall."

"Why does that name seem familiar?" I wonder.

"Well, counseling did mention that Tofu is Dean Perkins's daughter."

"Yikes!" Iggy exclaims.

"We don't take a referral because of who a student is related to. We also don't say no for that reason. In fact, we've never said no to a referral. Go ahead, but be careful, and please let me know how it goes."

"It does seem young people are increasingly distressed," Aunt Isobell laments. "In some ways, if I may generalize, they seem to have difficulty coping with everyday demands of life."

"True as never before," I answer.

"And why do you think that is?" Auntie asks.

"The fifty-four-dollar question," I ponder, attempting to rise in my seat and stretch my spine. "I think it's a question of meaning. The discontentment of modern life is often expressed as grievance over past perceived wrongs or failure to fairly redistribute power and wealth which is called inequity. But as your working life shows, common purpose rather than uncommon wealth gives meaning. And as an entitled brat I certainly didn't have any purpose. I didn't get that until after my accident. Still, it wasn't being a quad that miraculously gave me purpose, it was exiting my foxhole of self-absorption that did it. The catalysts being Irene's hug and Aunt Isobell's timely visit. A winning combo, I'd say."

"I suspect there's more to this story," Sister Sandrine reasons.

"I'll tell you some day," Aunt Isobell responds, "and my version of any O'Neill story is always the most accurate."

"You are the family historian," I concede.

"It's the only reason we even know we're brothers," Iggy adds.

"Does that mean, if not for your Aunt Isobell's work as a historian, you might believe you are sisters?" Sister Sandrine says with a straight face until breaking into an uncharacteristic giggle.

We, who know her both well and not at all, are not quite sure how to respond. I smile, but Iggy looks positively shell shocked.

"Sorry; apparently I can surprise people," Sister Sandrine responds, showing that beautiful wide smile, which truly does surprise my awestruck brother.

"Sister Sandrine, you so fit into the pathetic humor around this table," I conclude.

Then a lull in the conversation, as people sit back in their chairs and contentedly sip wine. I change both the subject and the tone.

"You'll remember that Alan told me my computer was hacked some weeks ago. Well, before the wedding yesterday I was talking to David, congratulating him on his new job—which I orchestrated him getting, by the way, so no problem there—but for reasons I don't understand, I just suddenly asked him a question that I've been pondering."

"What? "Iggy asks.

"I asked him if he could remember the name of the file I used for our application for the $66 million accessibility funding."

"So?" Iggy puzzles. "I'm sure you never gave the file name to me."

"No one knew it. I didn't share it, didn't think we had much chance. In retrospect, I think I was looking for plausible deniability for St. Jude's poor support for accessibility over the years—despite our national reputation. Even with the size and scope of becoming a world's first, our submission was low-key. I was inadvertently trying to defend the institution, which I now realize was a mistake. But let me repeat, no one knew the name of the file. Ever."

"So David couldn't know the answer?" Iggy concludes.

"No way. The file is called Enigma. And no one who has not been into my computer could know that."

No one spoke as the repercussions sunk in.

"So are you saying that David hacked your computer?" Aunt Isobell asks.

I exhale. "He certainly knows how to, often helped me with computer issues. I'm not saying he did it, but—"

"How is it possible he didn't?" Iggy finishes, in a rare moment of assertiveness.

"If I may quote Sherlock Holmes," Aunt Isobell begins, "'Once you eliminate the impossible, whatever remains, no matter how improbable, must be the truth.'"

CHAPTER THIRTY-TWO

Early Monday one week before Christmas, at home and at the Berghof

I wake predictably just after four a.m., exiting from discomforting dream to rumination fixation. I vaguely wish to access the dream again, discomforting thought as that may be. It occurs to me that Lenny, who is the superintendent in John's building is my best bet for locating or at least getting information about where John may have been for the last thirty-six hours.

I think about the other business that to my everlasting surprise did not come up at dinner but surely was on everyone's mind. Today is the day I have been ordered to submit a plan to the SAP, Exceptional Student Experience with names of those without the correct political identity to be eliminated from our office. I wonder if the SAP would mind if I gave her a cute nickname like Senator McCarthy.

I don't deal well with indecision, but that has passed, and today will be a day of resolute civil disobedience. I am fine with my decision. I can live with the consequences. I could say I'm centered and calm, but it is just as likely I am simply lazy. I have spared my peers the aggravation of participating in making the decision. Innumerable pots boiling on the back burner, some about to boil over, but everything will be dealt with in the morning, not this morning in which I now live and breathe, but the later morning of today when light appears and business gets taken care of.

Fred and Roma are at a critical point and need my full attention. And let's not pretend that this is only about Fred and Roma. Many, many lives hang in the balance, and we—that is, my precious protagonists—are our only hope. As Brenda snores beside me, more buzz saw than breathing, I disembody, disassociate, and yet remain refreshingly engaged.

I say, "Absolutely not, there is no way I will allow you to keep me company doing the dangerous surveillance work that has got to get done."

Roma responds that she is under the impression she doesn't need my permission to help do what needs to get done. "And as for danger, tell that to all the members of my extended family who have likely been taken and killed by the Nazis."

I have no reply. Roma and I conduct the dangerous surveillance that needs to get done. Together.

Under the cover of darkness, we travel as close to the Berghof as we can inconspicuously get, without being seen and therefore killed. We watch, with little hope or expectation, what there is to see on the grounds outside the house. The house is lit up, there are large windows affording views into the house, but we are too low and not at the proper angle to see people inside. To see inside, we would have to be within fifty meters and on level ground, and that would be very dangerous. For the first two nights we hang back, observing patterns, noting security, watching for patrolling soldiers. To our surprise, there are no regular guards patrolling the grounds, at least at night, the assumption perhaps being that the Berghof is remotely located and therefore safe.

Occasionally, a maid, a soldier, or members of the kitchen staff come outside for some night air or a cigarette, but no one ventures far from the house. The only anomalies are Blondi, a German shepherd given to Hitler the previous Christmas by his aide Martin Bormann, and when she is at the Berghof, Eva Braun with her Scottish terriers, Negus and Stashi. They need to go outside to do their business before going to sleep for the night, and the duty to take out the dogs does not fall to Martin Bormann or Eva Braun. Different people, likely house staff, share dog duty, but they do not linger.

The terriers don't stray too far, but Blondi reacts to a sound, an animal or something, and barks and lunges toward the distraction. It definitely concerns us that Blondi might catch our scent and come for us. German shepherds represent German terror, and for good reason. We are able to determine that Eva's dogs come out for the last time around 9:30 p.m., but Hitler's gangly puppy comes out anytime between eleven and 1:30 a.m., for the four nights we watch. This time anomaly may have to do with Hitler's penchant for watching late night films. We speculate, but do not know. Before morning light, we return to our hideaway for sleep and relief.

If Wolfgang is the oracle of information he fancies himself to be, Goebbels and his family will arrive two days before Christmas, and we, or at least I, will be watching. The question remains, will the observed patterns of the last four nights change? It seems unlikely, but who knows? It would help to somehow find a way to watch the house and its occupants' habits during the day, but that is far more difficult and too dangerous. We could not come nearly as close to the house during the day, and it is likely German soldiers patrol the grounds when it is light. We are uncertain how to proceed.

We proceed with caution, understanding that getting even one shot at Hitler would be monumental before all hell descends upon us. But we are not cautious out of fear—well, at least not fear of being killed by German soldiers while trying to kill Hitler. We are afraid of being caught alive. We have both cyanide and the Luger if it comes to that. I know I might have to shoot and kill Roma and then myself, and she knows she might be called upon to do the same if I am injured. We rehearse scenarios in order to steel resolve. There will be no tolerance for bad nerves. We have been hardened by war beyond what we would have thought possible in our earlier life. We vaguely wonder if our earlier life was a dream.

The next day and night we stay and rest in our hideaway. Being out in the open cold the previous four nights has exhausted us. We need all our blankets and body warmth to revive bodily strength and flagging spirits.

We also talk, for the first time, about how we might escape if we manage to kill Hitler. We assume for good reason that killing Hitler is next to impossible, and escape after killing Hitler is impossible. Still, I need to convince Roma of the distant possibility of the impossible. Though we are happy together, there are times I feel her slipping away, ready to embrace the specter of death.

She agrees we will travel overland through the Alps, in winter, with our store of vegetables and sausage, and not chance going back to towns and villages where German soldiers would swarm. Though discussion of distant possibility does not change or deflect from impossibility, it is tonic for the soul. Talking about a life together even as we face death has a weird and wonderful effect on her, on me, on us.

Roma is not recovered the following late afternoon, on the day the Goebbels family is to arrive at the Berghof. She does not object to me doing surveillance alone. I had hoped as much but from previous experience did not say so. The solitary three-mile trek through darkness, snow, and steep slopes is long and unpleasant. Still, as I get closer to the Berghof, skies clear, revealing a bright white moon that is almost full. The light off the snow is as bright as ever happens on winter nights. Without revealing to Roma what I am going to do, I am determined to move closer to the Berghof than previous nights in order to see better, and possibly hear scant conversation. Also, though I think the exercise is unlikely to yield useful results, I want to explore the steep slope directly below the Berghof where my map indicates a rudimentary tunnel once existed. Boredom inspires fool's errands.

From 6:30 p.m. until almost 9:30 I slowly crawl around the expanse below the Berghof, looking for something that may have once been a tunnel entrance. I cup my hand over my flashlight, which I seldom use, relying mainly on moonlit snow to give me direction. The most I am able to find is a space where concrete was used to cover a hole about one yard square. I then climb up to where Roma and I lay down the previous four nights to wait three torturously long hours without incident. Our spot is under large pine tree limbs where needles rather than snow cover the ground. Pine branches provide cover; pine needles do not leave an impression.

There has been no indication that the Goebbels family has arrived, and in our four previous nights of surveillance we did not glimpse Hitler or anyone recognizable. Lying under swaying pine branches in possibly the loneliest place on the planet, I realize tomorrow is Christmas Eve. It occurs to me that if the six Goebbels children have arrived, the Berghof schedule may have shifted toward earlier bedtimes for the entire household. Everyone may be asleep, though the notion of Hitler going to bed early to be ready to join children for Christmas fun does seem beyond silly. Even as host and Father Christmas to his many young guests, Hitler's night hawk habits seem likely to prevail. I am hungry for information and tired of speculation. I slowly move to a clump of bushes closer to the house.

As time slowly passes, much more silliness flows through my strange brain. The door opens, and I try to guess if it might be Carl the soldier or Marta the maid, names Roma and I made up during our previous long nights. Due to their previous appearances, though far from establishing a pattern, they are expected. But it is not to be. First Blondi bounds outside, followed by two people, one of medium stature, the second diminutive and with a slight limp.

Without thinking, I hold my breath. Can they be—is it possible? I am about fifty yards away, the moonlight is good, and rather than return to the house once Blondi does her business, the two men casually stroll along the path in animated discussion. I begin to hear fragments of Hitler's diatribe against Americans, the Russians, and his generals on the Eastern front. There is also praise for the audacious Japanese. Goebbels's voice is muted, less clear, but clearly, he tries to pacify the other with deference, compliments, and his unwavering faith that the Führer will prevail, as always.

They continue walking along a well-marked path, with intermittent lights, which has been cleared of snow. Blondi playfully bounds back to Hitler, which seems to please the Führer, as evidenced by the change in conversation. After a few disparaging comments about Hollywood corruption for its 1930 making of *All Quiet on the Western Front*, Hitler issues a stern decree: "Let's watch *The Lives of the Bengal Lancer* tomorrow night." But then his mood shifts, and he positively giggles with delight, deciding the Gary Cooper film can wait. Suddenly in a light and expansive mood, he wants to rewatch the twelve Mickey Mouse films that Herr Goebbels, Minister of Propaganda, gave him for Christmas in 1937. "After all," Hitler says, "it's Christmas!" Goebbels agrees, nonplussed by Hitler's metamorphosing mood, and they go back inside the house. Over two million Wehrmacht troops are freezing through a Russian winter, with one million killed or captured in the previous six months, and Hitler wants to watch cartoons because it is Christmas. It is an inexplicable moment. For this moment alone, it has been worth the effort. But it is not enough.

I receive the call at 7:38 a.m. Kale, head of security, as a courtesy they tell me, calls to convey the news before I hear it from the police. John is dead, murdered, and brutally so, over the weekend. Having said what they officially planned to say, Kale goes off in an unofficial, unregulated manner. "I've just never seen anything like it. Blood everywhere, first seeping under the door, then when the door was opened by the cleaning staff, just before six a.m., there was a sight you won't forget in this lifetime. And I don't just mean blood, though that would be enough for me, thank you very much. But no, there he is hanging from these ropes attached to the ceiling, all pink and naked and the size of a Hippopotamus, broken and tied up, and get this, with a giant spike up his ass." And then realizing they are head of security services and not just shaken-up Kale, they quickly compose themself. "But take that on the QT, would ya? I know he was your friend, but we wouldn't want this getting out to the public. They're already scared, and who knows what kind of killer is out there. So what time can you get here?"

Emergencies do not help mitigate the fact that spontaneity is some thirty-five years in the rearview mirror for me. Quadriplegics cannot dress themselves or perform bathroom routines, mundane as these daily functions may be, just because a friend has been brutally murdered. Brenda has most of my routine done by the time Bill shows up to finish. They tag-team to do the bare minimum, which allows me to get to the university at the record early time of 8:48 a.m.

A police officer is waiting and asks a few perfunctory questions, none of which are the right questions, had he allowed for informed conjecture. He doesn't, for example, ask if I have any idea who murdered John. He asks how long we have been friends, how often we got together and where, and when I last saw John. The police have no leads, I am told, and if they continue down the same line of inquiry, none will be forthcoming, I think.

If asked, I wouldn't have named names, because I really don't know who killed John, but I could have given some context for understanding, that is, motive. Come to think of it, on the subject of motive, I could have suggested a couple dozen names, so maybe my conjecture would not have provided much focus. I could have framed his life as politically controversial at a time and in a place that does not much tolerate controversy, and as a result, he had many enemies, with at least one capable of murder. Well, unless seriously invested in conspiracy theory, many had motive, but likely only one person did the deed.

I could have explained what people don't understand about universities. They are places of murderous intent, even if the intent does not usually result in a dead body. Character and reputation for the crime of thinking are taken down every day. In a place of thinking, it is important to follow the thinking. A line has been crossed. A dead body is not theory. University politics are no longer kitschy fun, and oddly the viciousness of this act renders Henry Kissinger's famous quote a colossal fib. The stakes are no longer the least bit small.

CHAPTER THIRTY-THREE

Same day, but not just any day, at the Center

Iggy, Luna, Sister Sandrine, Aunt Isobell, and I sit in my office, door closed, thinking, numb, not talking, as the faint sound of my old mechanical wall clock ticks its way to nowhere with Swiss-like accuracy. Silence is not enforced or expected, but not having anything to say, we don't say anything.

I have something to say, which I have to unburden to the group, but I have not yet worked up enough nerve. Unknown to my audience, I stole a glimpse of the crime scene, which I discovered was not allowed. I seem to have a talent for discovering the obvious.

After the police officer interview, I went over to John's office in the old Tudor-style building where the English department is located. It has recently been renamed, with a name that is very long and which no one can remember. Say Tudor, and people understand. For reasons unknown, John had the largest office in the English department and, if architecture is to be considered, the most appealing at St. Jude's.

A large area outside of his office was cordoned off with yellow tape, which I conveniently chose to ignore. Well, I consciously charged through it, would be more accurate. The moment I got to John's office, the door opened, and a police officer came out. Depending on your perspective it was either perfect or apocalyptic timing. Not knowing how to react for a few seconds, the police officer stood still, with my brain taking in the entire and shocking scene like a great aperture stuck open on a single image that would be forever etched on my brain.

My heart sank. I thought, *No, John, no.* Still, and incredibly, through the maze of confusion and shock, a tiny part of me, which I still have trouble admitting to, thought the horror before my eyes, the body of John as revealed, had some slight logic to it. Not my logic, but John's logic to which I was privy. Ninety-nine percent utter shock; one percent *but of course.* Still, I did not, could not, attribute meaning to the one percent revelation, if that is what it was.

I was scolded and told I shouldn't have crossed through the yellow tape. I was told I was not supposed to be here. I was not arrested but warned to stay away. Who says you can't get away with doing stuff if you are in a wheelchair? But I had seen what I had seen. Hieronymus Bosch images are relatively quaint and innocent, pastoral even, by comparison. Nightmares and terrifying visions abound.

I begin slowly, uncertainly, my peeps sensing their best contribution is silence. I am compelled to tell but cannot describe. "John and I talked about many subjects, history, culture, and politics being at the top of the list. John had a kind of fascination with Roman, early Christian, and medieval methods of torture. Many of the vilest methods, designed to rend the body apart and cause the most pain, were justified as contributing to or upholding religious, royal, or state orthodoxy. It really was true that throughout history, the worst of human pathologies became intertwined with the will and ego of the rulers. He and I often compared and saw parallels between tyrants and their tyrannical ways from antiquity right up to and including the present day. We were nothing if not inclusive.

"And human brutality; that is, the abuse of powerful elites over those without power, is essentially unchanged throughout the ages. Different methods, same effect. Religious doctrine and royal decree have been supplanted by ideology and societal pressure to conform and adapt to the proper causes within a narrow range of possibility. John and I, and Arthur too for that matter, have often bantered and parsed together a well-trodden quote when discussing such parallels as follows: 'If you can convince people of absurdities, they will commit atrocities.' People might think the quote is absurd, at least as applied to the modern world—though it actually is a modern quote—without realizing that torture and even murder come in many forms and do not always leave a body."

Knowing there has been a murder which has resulted in a dead body, my colleagues may be justifiably confused. Still, I need to think this through, even at the expense of confusion leading the confused. "Sometimes, murder simply hollows out and kills the mind or spirit. But unlike the early Christian martyrs, or the young people who attempted the Arab spring uprisings in Iran, or the Ukrainians against the Russians, or the students in Tiananmen Square, or the last of the young rebels in Hong Kong or Taiwan before they lost their lives and independence, in the West today our ability to resist is low to nonexistent. John was constantly amazed at the extent to which we have relinquished real choice, original thought, and critical thinking for borrowed thinking, dependence, and complacency. Anyway, these were our discussions; this was John's constant diatribe of recent years, which informed his need to take decisive action at a time and in a place where inaction and indecision are most often regarded as enough. It is why staging the Peterson debate became his crusade."

My peeps' silence and remarkable listening skills hold firm.

"Sorry for the lecture, but I'm trying to process toward something sane. As I said, John was fascinated by ancient methods of torture, how people could withstand them, how anyone could perversely inflict pain and mutilation in the name of some righteous cause."

I pause at this juncture to collect myself for what is to follow. "There was one particular form of torture that caught his attention, that he often referred to, and he even showed me medieval drawings displaying how it worked. I hate to say it, but it was a bit like the auto mechanics diagrams from the book Pearl showed us last night."

I elicit a few grim grins, but no one dares interrupt. I continue. "It was called the Vigils of Spain. The means of torture, I mean. A couple years back, John found what he said was a very rare book, and he asked if I could photocopy it for him. I did, and I made a copy for myself too, intending to look at it, but not being fascinated with torture, I never got around to it and forgot about the book until today. The book, published in 1813, is called *Torture of the Christian Martyrs*, and I asked Lucy to dig it up from my heap of junk when I got back from seeing John's body just now."

"You saw John's body?" Iggy asks, in a spasm of excitement.

"I'm almost there," I say, with measured calm, holding a lid on the caldron of my emotional state. "The book has a chapter, a diagram, and a couple of paragraphs on the Vigils of Spain, and for reasons unknown, it fascinated John. Just now I looked it up. I'm going to read you a short excerpt because I don't want to try to describe it. It was written by some French cat by the name of Augustin Nicolas in 1684. Here goes: 'A man's wrists and ankles are bound to four chains attached to the ceiling. He is lowered onto a pointed rod which is inserted into his anus. By sheer muscular effort, he must support himself for hours to avoid sitting on the pointed iron, which pierces him with insufferable pain.'

"Damn—sorry, Sisters—I almost gave you the book's page number, like we're in a graduate seminar, all kitschy theory and some such stuff that doesn't apply in the woke world."

Aunt Isobell asks slowly, carefully articulating each measured word: "Phelim, are you actually saying that this was what you saw in John's office?"

The completion of my stall tactic spinal stretch is keenly anticipated. "Yes."

"But how is that possible?" Iggy blurts, which everyone is thinking including myself, whose imprinted image makes denial impossible.

"I don't know. What I saw was not possible if not for the fact that I saw it. I'd had a bit of preparation from what Kale told me when she woke me this morning, but nothing can prepare you for that."

No one spoke for what seemed to be an inordinate time. In a moment of historic rarity, I couldn't think of anything else to say. Someone needed to say something.

"Does Brenda know Kale woke you in your bed this morning?" Sister Sandrine deadpans.

"Oh my goodness, I can't believe you just said that, but it's exactly what I need, and weirdly it's the kind of black humor John would have said and appreciated, or I to him in reverse circumstances."

"It is only because I do know you that I took the liberty," Sister responds, having reverted to her former proper self. "I spent a year at our mission in Honduras and another eighteen months in Brazil, two countries with among the highest murder rates in the world. I've been close to terrible violence, both witnessed and its aftermath. You will need to talk about what you saw when you are ready."

"Kale shouldn't have told me anything, but I'm glad they did. Auntie, do you think your friend at the forensic lab …?"

"Ben is his name. He's not in the actual forensic lab, but close enough. I'm on it," Aunt Isobell answers, getting up and closing my office door behind her.

We don't so much wait for Aunt Isobell to return as sit like lumps on as log without talking for several minutes. I will soon tell my intimates fully what I saw, but I'm not quite ready.

Aunt Isobell is not long. When she returns, she does not immediately confirm that Ben will get us the forensic information about John. She opens the door, and says, "Phelim, this young woman insists she give something directly into your hands. She says it is important and that you will want to see it immediately."

A tall, striking-looking woman with long dark hair smiles at me from behind Aunt Isobell. She has a medium-sized, box-shaped package in her hands.

"Who sent this, and why do I want to see it immediately?"

The woman confidently steps forward and places the package on the table directly in front me. "I don't know. I only know what I was told. I was told it has to go directly to you, if you are Phelim O'Neill."

I nod, and the woman steps back. "Good, because my terms stipulate, I'm not supposed to give it to anyone else even if they promise to deliver it to you. And now, having presented it to you, I have fulfilled my promise and have earned a thousand dollars for thirty minutes' work. Thanks."

"What if I don't want to accept it?" I ask.

"Ah, yes, that. One last point I forgot to mention. If you are resistant, I'm supposed to say one word, and leave. Falstaff."

The tall willowy brunette without realizing the gravity of the situation carefully closes the door after leaving. I don't know why she is willowy, but it seems accurate. We four remaining lumps on a log remain silent. The unspoken consensus seems to be that talk will resume once I have something to say. I remain unspeaking.

An awareness of the ticking of my wall clock is the only intrusion into silence. Foreboding fills the room.

Finally, I half lift my arm, which Iggy understands as permission to open the box.

Inside the box is another box, beautifully wrapped in gold paper with a silver ribbon.

Iggy slides an envelope across the table with my name on it. He pulls an ornate card out of the envelope, and without reading the message, places it before me. In beautifully scripted calligraphy are the words: "To die is to be a counterfeit, for he is but the counterfeit of a man who hath not the life of a man; but to counterfeit dying when a man thereby liveth is to be no counterfeit, but the true and perfect image of life indeed."

"What it that?" Iggy asks.

"Henry IV, Part 1, Shakespeare. Open this box."

Iggy pulls the ribbon off the box with the caress of a longtime admirer gently disrobing the princess who has agreed to share her beauty. I wonder if Sister Sandrine notices.

Iggy picks at the scotch tape as if afraid of offending.

"Rip it," I command.

When Iggy pauses as if unable, Sister Sandrine rips the gold paper like a princess tired of the frivolous prelude. I wonder if Iggy notices.

"The quote is Sir John Falstaff, one of Shakespeare's most enduring, and certainly most unique characters. It is John Staffal's way of saying, *It's me*."

An old ornate and tattered hatbox is revealed under ripped paper.

"John's hatbox," I say.

Sister Sandrine opens the hatbox and pulls out John's old Cyrano de Bergerac plumed hat.

Underneath the hat is the prophylactic nose that John wore when he played Cyrano in Edmond Rostand's 1897 play that created the Cyrano myth, the comic, tragic, great-nosed, eternal lover of Roxanne. The nose got around as did the wearer, Paddy's Pub being its most frequent habitat.

Inside the card is a letter written in John's hand that begins *Dear Boy*.

Placing the letter in front of me, Sister Sandrine's assertiveness has run its course. "Perhaps you would like to read this letter alone."

"Yes, thanks, I think I would."

The door clicks shut as they exit. I am oddly reluctant to discover what the letter will reveal.

Dear Boy,

Do you remember the first time I mentioned the Vigils of Spain, and you said, "I thought Virgil was Italian," do you? Ha! It was how I got you to sit in on my first-year survey course. And when we got to Dante's *Inferno*, I talked about how Virgil, even as an esteemed poet and guide, would have to go to either Hell or Purgatory because he was born before Christ's time. (He never seems to decide which, though Hell does seem a bit severe for Virgil even for Dante.)

Anyway, we talked and you did learn the difference between the Virgil of Italy and the Vigils of Spain. It turns out, I have an appreciation for both.

First, you must know that for all the theatrics of my exit gesture, I did not suffer. Ask your dear aunt with her contacts in the pharmaceutical business about the newest drug—apparently it was a Covid treatment innovation that came too late to deal with that now mostly defunct malady, though it will have other miraculous applications once it becomes FDA approved. As to your question about how I got it, best answer is don't ask. Its name escapes me, but in feeling nothing, I will have felt, finally, something akin to what your unfeeling physical existence has endured all these decades attached to a wide-awake, expansive mind.

To Martha, who cleans the English Department and environs, I do apologize for the mess. I wouldn't have a clue how to clean it up. It does amaze me how many tasks, especially practical ones, I never was able to fathom. I think I half expected all of life's imponderables to come clear in my twilight years. Instead, I have wondered my way through to my final days. Anyway, you'll likely be spared seeing my bare-assed tangled carcass, though I hope you will gain from what follows. I suspect you will be among the first people the authorities will contact.

I'll let you puzzle on this: how did I get myself into a full Spanish Vigil? You can either try to settle the dilemma or else luxuriate as the mystery of murder excites the great unwashed public, none more so than the fearmongers of St. Jude's. I guess that makes this little episode less a whodunit than a how-the-hell-did-he-do-it?

When they finally cancel the English department, it won't just be because of distaste for dead white European male writers with imperialistic instincts, but because they will need to divert most university funds toward security personnel, endless safety measures, and compulsory reeducation seminars designated to make the world one gigantic safe space with floor mats, coloring books, and autonomically indistinguishable gender-neutral play dolls. What fun!

What will I think about as the seconds count down? I'll likely experience hours between seconds, but I'm hoping my additional euphoric cocktail (including some of the finest whisky on the planet) will afford some gentleness and help to relieve boredom, which as you know is my worst fear.

I had a dream last night about my oldest, Constance, when she was about two years old. She wore a yellow sweater that she loved, and pink pants. We had a bond, which I foolishly thought would last forever. I remember us two looking at each other one day, with a vividness beyond memory, and her gaze held, as if we both knew it was a sort of transcendent embrace never to be repeated. Bit much for a two-year-old, I suppose. I'd forgotten, or so I thought until I felt it percolate and then utterly captivate my consciousness in the vapors of dreamlike effervescence. Inexplicable. So why remember now? Not sort of, kind of, but so real as to be the most painful experience of my wretched life when moments later it was gone? Why didn't I seek more of whatever that was, then? Why did I let it go? There are mysteries, my dear boy, far beyond what the police might solve about how and why I got strung up.

What else? I'll think about making love to Renata Tebaldi ... Ha! Maybe, but in one's final letter one isn't allowed to prevaricate, self-delude, or bullshit. Fact is, women liked me, submitted to me, but didn't love me. Still, Renata did once tell me I made her laugh. That was something.

Almost forgot this little piece. The jig is up. I have stage four pancreatic cancer, weeks to months without this, er, exit gesture, so it amounts to the same thing. And being powerless and anticipating boredom, I thought you might enjoy the fireworks of murder and mayhem this little episode will cause. I suppose there is a possibility you'll be a good little Boy Scout and surrender this little package, thereby murdering the murder narrative. More fun if you don't tell all; will create some havoc in the university maelstrom of university politics which certainly needs shaking up. But I'll have to leave that to you. Either way we'll laugh about it one day at the Faculty Club or at Paddy's Pub in the great beyond.

JS

PS: Aside from my little deception here, I have tried and paid the price for allegiance to the truth. The price being that I have more enemies than there are Irish drunks. There is so much I am ashamed of, but for telling the truth, always, I am proud. There is more to this, more intrigue, more deceit, just more, but I couldn't get to it in time, have run out of time ….

I almost forget about lunch. The prospect of murder immediately eclipsed by elaborate suicide tempers appetite, and I barely notice the time. I'm supposed to meet briefly with the SAP today and submit my plan for firing and shafting people I like and whose absence would damage students—not just their exceptional experience—including their ability to pass courses and graduate.

I was never going to go to that meeting. But now that there is a sensational murder raising the institutional temperature, the SAP's EA will not follow up and hound me. Thanks, John.

I call the front desk rather than circle through the reception area and ask Lucy to relay a message to Iggy, Luna, Aunt Isobell, and Sister Sandrine to meet again in my office, but not before someone gets me a sandwich or two. Iggy will likely pound downstairs and get me two. It is 12:30 p.m., so they shouldn't have appointments until 1p.m.

Almost immediately the door opens, and the troops file in, including Iggy with a pizza box. "A career service workshop just finishing, with most of this left over. Okay?"

"More than, thanks, but I thought there was an understanding that Angel gets all the leftover food from workshops since he cleans up the boardroom afterwards."

"He phoned in sick today," Iggy answers, "so we can feast on the carcass."

The no-nonsense side of Aunt Isobell is in full flight. "Ben has confirmed there will be another emergency autopsy, this one on John Staffal, likely this evening. He wonders if my presence at St. Jude's has anything has to do with the two recent deaths, and if this pattern might continue." Auntie looks grim, is not used to dipping her toes into the murky waters of black humor. "He will let us know what he knows when he knows it."

I chew fiercely, wanting to get some carbohydrates down before it is my turn to talk. There really isn't much else for others to say until I have divested the contents of the letter.

I ask Sister Sandrine to read John's letter to the group which she does without emotion or hesitation. The group is thoughtful, the only sound being the smacking and chiseling of my lips and teeth on pizza. I am not fine, but the extent of not being fine does not manifest itself in permanent loss of appetite. Appetite of the present moment will not mitigate wakefulness at false dawn and the thoughts and images that will pervade my dreams.

Aunt Isobell slowly shakes her head and bites her lip, a portrait of consternation. "This is terrible. I'm so sorry, Phelim." Heartfelt sentiment communicated, Aunt Isobell takes a deep breath and proceeds in utilitarian fashion, "I did read about that new drug. Can't remember the name, though I know it was the result of Covid research for pain management. The drug is a breakthrough, a sensation, the best pharmaceutical ever created for canceling pain, but it was withheld from FDA approval because it creates complete paralysis while allowing the mind to remain awake and intact. It is also extremely difficult or impossible to detect in the blood stream after use. Can't imagine where he got the drug."

"So it's true he didn't suffer," Sister Sandrine offers.

"Yes, that seems highly likely." When none of us responds, Auntie continues, "The question is, do you surrender or keep this intel from the police? And yes, I do understand but do not see it as my place to impress upon you that withholding information might be construed as interference with a police investigation. So in asking, I'm not telling you what you should do. I only want to help."

"Thanks, Auntie, I know. Though I don't know what to do, I appreciate how you put it and the supportive position you've taken."

"I feel the same way," Sister Sandrine declares.

Iggy nods his head, and Luna simply says, "You know us."

"Good and thanks. Like I said, I don't know what to do, but I'm not thinking of giving this to the police, at least for now. As John hints and we have lots of evidence, things are rotten in the state of Denmark, which as you know is Danish for St. Jude's. I want to try to answer a few questions, like why Heather made the accusations she did, and whether she acted alone, how in the world the SAP thinks she can take and spend our $66 million, how the debate was so easily sabotaged, and how it is that whenever events just happen around here, they seem to coincide with feathering someone's nest and furthering someone's agenda."

No one speaks, so I continue. "Despite his nonchalance, this had to be very, very difficult for John. And how the hell, who the hell helped him—no, that would be who in the plural helped him get strung up in that impossible, torturous way, which took painstaking planning, logistical preparation, guts, brute strength, and a bit of insanity."

"So sit tight with John's box?" Luna asks.

"Sort of, but John thought what he did would shake things up, so sitting tight might not be an option for long. His endgame seems to be that which is hidden will cause things to be revealed. So call it active ass-sitting as an anthem."

"I think we can all sing to that," Aunt Isobell says without expression, now firmly in the dark humor club.

CHAPTER THIRTY-FOUR

Monday into Tuesday, the week before Christmas, at the Center

With news of gruesome murder, St Jude's is both alive with excitement and dead to business as usual. Universities take an unusual view of the word *unusual*, as a place where conducting business of any kind is secondary to correct thinking of every kind. A university-wide state of emergency is declared, though no one seems to know what that means. Not knowing what it means means that something must be done to keep people excited (officially called being vigilant) and well-informed (reams of information and updates designed to obfuscate and confuse).

By late Monday afternoon, with John's body removed to the morgue, it is declared that nonessential work of the university (so all of it), out of concern for safety, will revert to an online format as practiced during Covid. As such, the frequency and intensity of meetings increases, particularly related to safety. There has never been a murder since St. Jude's humble beginnings in 1864, and yet John's murder proves, to those who choose to believe, that murder can happen at any moment to anyone. And supposition being true, it follows that many murders can happen at any number of moments to any number of ones. One cannot abandon logic in these trying times.

A criminology professor is sought out by a local television station and asked for his expertise on the veracity of imminent threat, and his answer is a decisive "Yes." He continues, "What people don't understand is that women's safety is a feeling and not about statistics and reassurances from people who have never had to feel unsafe." University Communications is so impressed by the television clip that they later discuss using it for their annual Women's Safety campaign.

However, the term "women" is adjudicated to lack inclusiveness and is on the St. Jude's docket to be banned. I hear about, but do not attend, the meeting in which Smokey is reputed to have responded, "How 'bout using the word *people*?" With no answer forthcoming, Smokey is further reputed to have said to no one in particular, "Did anyone notice that the person murdered is a dude?" Smokey's reputation has almost descended to my lowly depths.

The term *essential service* is not defined. One wonders what point of comparison might exist within the institution. Making the distinction is left to each manager's discretion. For this reason, next day most university offices are closed. A small number of offices revert to skeleton staff. I give staff the choice to come into the office or work from home.

I arrive at eleven a.m. Tuesday to a full house. It isn't complicated. We are open because we want to be. We like each other's company, and it is better to meet with students in person, so that's what we do. Some students choose to meet by teleconference to save having to commute long hours, but most show up in person. None declare they are staying away for fear of personal safety. It is a mystery how a manager can declare her service nonessential without branding the office as irrelevant. Same for faculty wanting to only use record-ed lectures. On my way to the Center, to my delight, I notice that the cafeteria is open. So, between our Center remaining open and Winston's genius work-ing the grille for we few who remain, I declare that all essential services are in place. We are saved.

Sister Sandrine is about to escort a student into her office, but once she sees me, she hurries over, bends low, and whispers in my ear that she has to see me as soon as she is finished. She estimates this particular student will require about twenty minutes. Though I haven't slept well, I cannot help but feel the sensual warmth of Sister's breath on my ear. I think, as I usually do when I think about Sister Sandrine, that my time in purgatory will be long. And, again thinking sensual warmth, it will also be hot.

Sister knows her students well and twenty minutes later is in my office. She closes the door. "The student I met with before this last one is Dean Per-kins's daughter Tofu. She told me something that I need to report to you."

"You have my undivided attention."

"She is course very upset about her friend Heather's death. The reasons why she is upset are complicated. She is understandably emotional and highly subjective, so take it with a grain of salt. Still, I assume you want to know anything that pertains to John."

There is a faint knock on my door.

I call out and Lucy opens the door. "Sorry to interrupt, but Angel hasn't shown up for work today, and a student just threw up in the reception area, and other students are complaining, but there's nobody to clean up."

"If ever there was a truly essential service, cleaning up barf would be it. I can think of about 500 university staff working from home, but not actually working, who could use doing a bit of real work. I'll make up a list, and you can start calling."

Lucy is used to my antics and knows she can easily outwait me by not responding.

"Okay, so call Harvey. I saw him down the corridor earlier. It's not his area, but he and Angel cover for each other, and I'm sure he'll help. By the way, what's with Angel? He's never sick, but two days in a row and he doesn't call in?"

298

"No idea. I'll call Harvey."

When the door clicks shut, Sister Sandrine continues, "Tofu said that Heather, though prone to occasionally histrionics, was more or less fine when she learned she was pregnant. Heather first confided in Tofu and then another friend, Melanie Tilson, that she was pregnant. Apparently, Heather confirmed that the father was an old fat white guy who teaches literature. Interestingly, what these three young women have in common is their recent decision to identify as Native American. I know you heard that Heather began to identify as colored, but Tofu refutes that point. They discussed and decided to identify as Native American together and at the same time. And get this, Tofu says when her mother first got her faculty position, she made the claim of having native ancestry and again when she petitioned to become dean.

"And is she?"

Sister Sandrine smiles. "Tofu said she didn't think so, but then got upset with me for asking. Apparently, in the new paradigm, actual lineage is secondary to what she calls identification of ethnic spirit."

"Good thing she doesn't know you're a nun."

"I did have that thought too."

"Luna knows someone who works for Dean Perkins. I'll see what she can find out. The new paradigm, spiritual or not, doesn't allow for cultural appropriate for personal gain," I add.

"Unsurprisingly, it is Dean Perkins who inspired the three girls to claim their new identity, even though Tofu claims to hate her mother. She says she and her mother have always clashed but that something happened recently which has resulted in complete estrangement."

I sense that Sister Sandrine has come to the bottom line.

"Apparently, when Dean Perkins found out that Heather was pregnant, she was upset. But when she further discovered that she was likely pregnant by Professor John Staffal, she had a complete emotional fit. But that's not the reason for their estrangement. When Tofu found out that her mother had been having a sexual relationship with her friend Heather, she had a meltdown too. Heather and Dean Perkins only met because of Tofu, and she now feels betrayed and abandoned by both of them."

I'm about to ask a question, but the good Sister isn't finished. "Tofu thinks her mother was so incensed that she planned harm to John, and although she didn't use the word murder, the Dean definitely hated him and wanted him dead. Just after all this happened, Tofu saw her mother in intense conversation with Melanie Tilson's boyfriend—name is Andy McPherson, I think—on at least two occasions."

"Not sure I follow this last piece of intel."

"Melanie Tilson's boyfriend is not and has never been a student at St. Jude's, but according to Tofu, he is unstable and desperate for money for reasons unknown." Sister stops to let this sink in.

"This is definitely weird, interesting, and in a whodunit kind of way, the boyfriend becomes the number one murder suspect, except that with John's note we know it wasn't murder, so it seems a sinister dead end. But we'll have to think about it some more. Thanks, this helps."

Sister Sandrine gets up to leave. "Open or closed?"

"Leave it open, and if Luna's free, ask her to stop by."

My revolving door changes players. Luna slides around the corner and into my office with speed and an athletic grace that Kevin can only dream of.

"Make it snappy," Luna says. "Got a student."

"You've got a friend, what's his name, works for Dean Perkins."

"Owen."

"Any chance he can find out if his employer used her Native American status to get her tenured faculty position or deanship?"

"She's Native American?"

"No, that's the point. Well, almost certainly not. Anyway, only pursue it if he can be trusted. I don't want this to come back on you."

"He just received his walking papers Friday in the name of equity, so he's done, has no job by end of next week, and he has been after me to go out with him for a couple years. Also, I'm his number-one job reference, since he won't ask Dean Perkins for one, so yeah, I think we can trust him."

"Only three reasons? Well, in that case, maybe he can get a DNA sample from the esteemed Dean while he's at it." I'm not serious about the sample, but Luna doesn't necessarily take it that way. In a second, she tears around my corner and is gone.

Behind her, Lucy steps back quickly to keep from being run over. She looks agitated and uncertain, despite avoiding a collision with an unsuspecting Luna.

"How's the barf situation?" I ask.

"Done, and Harvey's gone. There are two police officers here who need to see you."

I look up from my desk. A male police officer in uniform and a female in civilian clothes appear from around the corner, waiting to be welcomed into my office. I lift an arm and indicate that they can sit at the table and chairs in my office.

The civilian takes charge. "This is Officer Renton, and I am Detective Kritanta."

They do not offer to shake hands. People rarely do when they see the wasted hands of a quadriplegic. Ninety-nine times out of one hundred, people will opt for avoidance over awkward. For the record, I've always felt not being asked is more awkward than avoidance, but my weirdness is legendary. For that one out of one hundred who will actually ask, the answer is shake away, no different. I just can't much shake back.

Detective Kritanta sits down and says, "I hope you don't mind if we ask a few questions."

I don't dislike police, am not among those who fight for the defunding of police in our strife-torn post-Covid world. Murder rates and violent crime have spiked in all cities for all years where significant cuts had been made with pressure to cut further still. Perhaps more significant, police have become so sensitive to accusations of overreach that many no longer are willing to do the most basic work to prevent crimes. Truly regrettable, *cover-your-ass syndrome* has become ubiquitous and acceptable. Still, my wariness about the police, unfair as it might be, is that they tend to be the bearers of bad news. Though not official, I first learned I'd never walk again from overhearing one cop casually shooting the breeze with another as I lay on a gurney waiting to have my head screwed into a metal halo. I knew it was true when I heard it, and it was anticlimactic once the doctor said the same.

"I assume you are here about the death of John Staffal."

Detective Kritanta gives a sympathetic smile and says, "No."

"No?"

"No, others are investigating that, and I'm sure they will want to talk to you about that again soon. I am talking to them too, but for now we have another matter to ask you about and unfortunately tell you about. Did you know Mr. Hercules Angelopoulos who worked at St. Jude's on this floor as a cleaner?"

I go numb, again, not unlike when I felt the lifeblood drain from my body after my spinal cord accident. The detective has just twice referred to Angel in the past tense in a single sentence. "Yes, of course."

"I am very sorry to tell you that he was found dead this morning in his apartment."

"What happened?" I dumbly blurt out.

"We don't know, and that is why we are investigating."

"Was he murdered?" I fully blurt, not aware of any reasons to refrain.

"We don't know. It is what we consider to be a suspicious death, and therefore we need to find out more. Did you know Mr. Angelopoulos well?"

"We only knew him as Angel because of his last name, and weirdly it suited him. He was also the strongest human being any of us ever knew. Are you saying his real first name was actually Hercules?"

"Yes."

"Well, not knowing his first name probably gives you some sense that although we liked him very much, we did not know him very well. Everyone just called him Angel. God love him."

LARRY J. MCCLOSKEY

"Did you know anything about his personal life?"

"Not much. I knew he was Greek, has a sister, but I think his parents are dead, and his sister lives on the West Coast, I seem to remember. I've never met her. I should tell you that he ended up working on our floor because he was having problems working at a couple other locations at the university. We tried to look out for him. Guess we didn't do a very good job."

"What kind of problems?"

"Problems with people. He's on the spectrum."

"Explain please."

"It's called Asperger's syndrome, so bright enough, nice or at least well-intended, but he has had difficulty relating to people, making friends, communicating clearly. Emotional regulation can be a problem too, though we didn't see much of that here."

"Did you know any of his friends?"

I take a deep breath and stretch my spine. "Sad thing is, I'm not sure he had any friends, or if he ever mentioned someone who might qualify as being a friend, it was the last time we would hear his name. I never heard him mention having any girlfriends. Sorry, and I feel terrible about this, but I don't know if he had any friends at all."

Detective Kritanta looks at me for few moments. She has kind eyes, I notice. "Well, he had at least one friend. In the weeks leading up to his death, he had regular communication with your friend Professor John Staffal."

I am unable to comprehend what this could mean.

"Their communications are about arranging times to meet. Do you know why they would want to meet?"

"No idea."

"Do you know how they originally met?"

"They likely met here. John dropped by my office occasionally, and I guess I saw them exchange pleasantries a couple times—that is, John initiating a bit of banter. Angel would respond if someone talked to him, but only if he knew them. He rarely spoke on his own. He was also terribly self-conscious about his voice."

"How so?"

"He was built like a brick shithouse; sorry for the analogy."

"No need, the image is clear."

"And coming out of the mouth of this Herculean body was the voice of, I dare say, Newton."

Detective Kritanta's face goes blank. "Please, who is this Newton?"

"You know Hercules' sidekick Newton, a centaur from the cartoon series when I was a kid called *The Mighty Hercules.*"

Clearly, she doesn't know, and I realize I am flustered, confused, and confusing. I attempt to reframe. "His voice wasn't just high, it was as timid as a mouse. But John could bring anyone out of themselves, and he did it with Angel. But they only met, here at least, a couple times. John was always talking, joking with cleaners, waiters, et cetera. For all his acting chops and academic eloquence, he had instant rapport with blue collar folks, who he liked best. But I just can't believe …."

"I can see you are upset, and I am sorry to bring you this distressing news."

"Sorry for reverting to cliché, but I can't believe they're dead. I can't imagine what their connection could be."

Those kind eyes again. "My name in Hindi means 'one that can rule over death.' Isn't that ironic? I cannot rule over death but am determined to rule over these who cheat others of life. Here is my card. I'm sure to have other questions and will let you know what we discover in our investigation to the extent I am able."

When Officer Renton and Detective Kritanta exit my office door, Luna and Sister Sandrine are waiting to make the exchange.

Luna wheels in with the speed and dexterity of a spinning top. "Owen's on it. He says he doesn't have much else to do since he's about to get laid off. He says he's heard Dean Perkins talk about her native roots, but he doesn't know anything about whether it is true. Like everyone else, people just assumed it must be true. But he called someone he knows, an administrator for the Senate office, and she recently heard a couple of faculty discussing whether or not Dean Perkins's native roots are real, because—get this—her new kitschy equity initiative is for individuals to be free and fully entitled to self-identify or claim one's ethnicity, to hell with biology!"

"Well, isn't that special" is all I can come up with.

Luna continues. "Phelim, if you start identifying as Chinese or Mauritian, Sister Sandrine and I are going to start self-identifying as Irish."

Luna rarely attempts humor, and as judged against my lifetime litany of corny jokes, it is a valiant effort. But I'm not all there and can't immediately return her jest with a stinging rebuke. Still, she waits, and so I say, "Luna, if I self-identify as Chinese, I'll probably get hungry for change an hour later and end up Mauritian, so you're off the hook."

"Poor Sister Sandrine," Luna says. "I don't think she'd like being among the fighting Irish."

Ignoring us both, Sister Sandrine says, "You know it's clever. I recently overheard a couple people from the Special Adviser to the President's office talking—being dark-skinned and unknown does have its privileges—and it's not just talk, but there's an actual plan to hype Dean Perkins's idea for people to be free to fully choose their own racial identity."

"It seems absurd to me," Luna says. "If Phelim seems frustrating now, wait until he's Mauritian, or worse for me, Chinese."

Two for Luna, I think.

"Still, this is consistent with what I overheard. If people are free to fully choose their ethnicity, and we don't sweat the biological efficacy of that claim, and they can identify or choose skin color regardless of their actual color, then the equity inclusion movement can perversely claim to be for the content of character rather than be judged by the birth color of skin, the concept made famous by Martin Luther King. The criticism of recent years that equity is overly concerned with immutable skin color can now be flattened by individual choice. It allows for the rehabilitation of Martin Luther King, since according to this new equity paradigm, you are literally showing character by choosing your ethnicity and skin color."

"By that logic," I say, "there is also a convenient means of mitigating the original sin of being born a pale oppressor. Problem is, the strength of the woke movement has to do with dividing the world into oppressors and the oppressed. So if you can switch sides, what do you do when you run out of oppressors?"

"Ah," Sister Sandrine intones, "history teaches us at every turn that will never happen."

"So let me guess," Luna begins. "This is premised on the assumption that ivory tower folks will universally opt to bail from pale."

"Correct," Sister Sandrine answers, "though the campaign they are creating may not make explicit that assumption."

"Will this campaign take hold?" Luna asks.

"In a related way, it is under way." It occurs to me that this campaign, this subjective hallowing of logic—implausible as it might seem—is exactly where the swirling events of recent years have led to. "Almost all of our students have big needs and we try to fulfill them without necessarily agreeing with what they think they need. But many of our newer students no longer want our experience or formal assessments from psychologists to determine diagnosis. Increasingly students want their claim of compromised mental health to be enough. People want to choose their story, their truth, emphasizing certain circumstances and identity parts, a sort of free flow personal interpretation of intersectionality. Personal interpretation now rules. Since that guy won his case in Holland, there have been a number of rulings to establish that it is a human right to choose one's age. Choice, the illusion of choice, may soon dispel reality, with an individual's subjective interpretation overruling objective measures. The new paradigm seductively dangles the ultimate fixation: to change what was yesterday agreed to be an immutable human feature and to choose otherwise. The fact is, my esteemed colleagues, despite your hard work, in the not-too-distant passage of time, we and our work will all be finished."

"If choice extends to race, my Chinese relatives will be seriously unamused," Luna states. "Come to think of it, won't people of color and Native Americans be offended?"

Sister Sandrine thinks about this. "Maybe, but it might also be perceived as complimentary for people to admire your immutable feature and petition to join your esteemed tribe. Deep down, everyone knows what shade they actually are, so aligning with the oppressed, even if that becomes the overwhelming privileged majority, becomes a kitschy feel-good game."

I'm impressed at Sister Sandrine's grasp of contemporary university life. "And as the demand for immutable choice of formerly immutable features flourishes, there is an overarching political motive. People captivated by the illusion of choice will vote for the party that offers the illusion of endless party favors."

"Okay, philosophers." Luna has had enough. "Back to Owen. He managed to borrow a couple strands of Dean Perkins's hair and will deliver them later today. If Dean Perkins's new equity movement takes hold, it might not matter what anyone's DNA composition is, but for now we've got hers. Your Aunt Isobell apparently has her man in Havana, Ben, who knows how to get DNA tested. So even if choosing ethnicity becomes in vogue, I doubt it was okay to make it up when a faculty position and deanship were on the line."

"Good work," I say distractedly, and I am, though my mind is suspended between confusion and grief. We are bantering and corny joking our way along as we always do to get from one tragic moment to the next. It is what we do to keep from admitting what life adds up to for many, for most of us, I guess. At least these are my dark thoughts in this moment, which I hope will lighten into the next.

"So those cops—what else did they want to know about your friend, John?" Luna asks.

I need a few minutes or an hour to think. I will always share with my peeps of the inner sanctum, Luna among them, but at this moment I cannot. I need the equivalent of a thirty-minute advance avoidance spinal stretch, without having to actually stretch that long. I don't want to cause a spinal injury, after all. Finally, "No, not about John this time. I'll let you know in a few minutes, but just not now."

Luna swings her wheelchair around with blistering speed before heading to the door. Implied, but unspoken, I am so frustrating.

CHAPTER THIRTY-FIVE

Next day, I wake at false dawn covered in sweat. John and Angel have pervaded my half-formed dreams as distorted, misshapen caricatures of themselves. Brenda lies beside me sleeping like Rip Van Winkle. I look at my wall clock. Curiously, 4:34 a.m. is also the exact minute Fred arrives back at base camp. Fred and Roma's situation is dire, and it is where I need to be.

Unlike Brenda, Roma has not slept. She has been exhausted from the previous four nights of surveillance, and though badly needing to sleep, she has lain awake worrying that I would not return. She laughs at herself, at us, for what we have come to. She's always seen herself as independent, especially of men, living in a big city with a career that matters and an income to match. "How pathetic," she says, "to realize that without you I have no life. There are no others. You are it." I say as much back to her, me to her somewhat easier than it is for her to say to me. I reach under the blanket she uses as a pillow and extract a small vial that holds the cyanide she surely would have taken had I not returned.

We talk. She wants to know all the details of my journey, uneventful as it may have been. I tell her about uneventful, all the details, all leading up to the moment of my solitary nighttime sighting of Hitler and Goebbels. She is animated, excited, anxious, but she has doubts. Can we really do this? Can we, who are nothing, do what no one else has done? She sits up, cannot sit still, but there is nowhere to go. I gently take her arms and say, "Look at me," despite the darkness. "This is frickin' Hitler, this is Joseph frickin' Goebbels." We go over what we know about Joseph frickin' Goebbels to remind ourselves why we are here.

Goebbels exists to implement Hitler's will. He does not have his own mind, has always been in search of someone and something to park his faith in. And to the terror of the world, he found Hitler. As the purveyor of Hitler's will, when the Nazis first took power in 1933, Goebbels organized the burning of un-German books at the opera house in Berlin. University professors and their students were the most malleable and enthusiastic participants. Joseph Goebbels has his doctorate in philosophy with particular interest in German literature from the University of Heidelberg. So much for the universality of university.

Though we have never felt that our chances of killing Hitler are grounded in reality, with Goebbels's arrival at the Berghof at the exact time we are there, I cannot help but entertain the fantasy that it is a Christmas gift. I hope to convince Roma of the same. There is very little Roma is willing to believe in anymore, but if this is a gift, we must be determined not to waste it. Roma has difficulty daily with dark thoughts and depression. But gift or not, Roma wants it understood that she is determined to do wherever we need to do to achieve the impossible. We share a moment of dark humor in darkness as she imitates me and says, "We're talking about frickin' Hitler and frickin' Goebbels, after all."

At which point I say, "That's my gal, and that's the spirit." I barely see the lines around her mouth form into a generous smile. I think the moment might be right, so I continue. "Roma, I need you to really listen to me for a minute."

Her smile fades, but she is listening. I search for the right words. "We've had this idea about killing Hitler for months, years actually, and the idea feels good, in part because the action is always in the vague undefined future. But this is different. This is now, and this will be our only shot."

Roma opens her mouth to speak but does not.

"If I was properly prepared instead of foolishly focused on surveillance for a future action, I could have killed Hitler and Goebbels last night. That was my mistake, and it is my responsibility to make sure it doesn't happen again."

"But how do you know, how do we know we'll get that chance again?" Roma centers in on the key question.

"We don't, and that is the problem. Our chances of success and of escape are low to none, even if we get another golden opportunity. So assuming we don't get another chance, I may have to do more."

Roma takes a moment for this to sink in. "Meaning?"

"Meaning I might have to make a decisive move when I—I'm still hoping to convince you to stay here—go back tonight. I'm hoping their guard may be down on Christmas Eve, and we don't know how long the Goebbels family, or Hitler for that matter, will stay after that."

"I'm coming, so you have to get rid of any other idea. Got that?"

"Yes ma'am."

"What are you thinking of doing?"

"Well, first of all, wait. I would love, am salivating at the possibility of another gift, with Hitler and Goebbels strolling under the midnight moon. But that is unlikely to happen."

"Why do you think they came outside last night?"

"Not sure, but Hitler's dog needs to do her business, and that's not likely to change. Makes you wonder why we didn't see Hitler with Blondi during the previous nights. But it really is harder to believe that Hitler sometimes takes her out for her evening pee than that he'll do it again."

"Why not? It is a perversity of evil that the man who can kill millions of humans without a sympathetic thought will care for his animal. Maybe when staff take the dog out, they use a different door, and when Hitler does he uses the door where you saw him."

We both think about this for a while. "So the fate of Europe, perhaps millions of human lives, rests on pee habits of a dog and his owner's decision to attend."

We laugh at the absurdity of what may double as a truism. Still, I know I need to press on and achieve serious understanding. "Roma, whether we are given a gift or I have to steal one, there is no going back. Tonight is it. Understand?"

"Of course. It is a suicide mission. And we are going together. There is no me without you, so don't insult me and try to talk me into anything different. Understand?"

"Yes." And I do, and she does. We do.

She is not finished. "Have you worked out how you will steal a gift if your father Christmas, or Santa as you say in America, does not leave one under our proverbial Christmas tree?"

"For a non-Christian you seem to have an acute understanding of our wacky rituals." It is odd how we humans can use dark humor in the darkest moments. "I haven't quite worked it out yet. I've spent most of the time thinking and blaming myself for the missed opportunity."

"But you have an idea."

"Yes. Really, it's quite simple. Whether or not Hitler comes out again, someone will come out to smoke, or smooch, or let Blondi out. And there is also Hitler's girlfriend's dogs that we know are let outside earlier in the evening, but I probably won't strike then. I want to see the activity that comes out the other door off the kitchen that staff use. There's probably more activity there, which is good and bad."

"How so?"

"Well, more activity, more choice, more chances, and they are not soldiers there, that we know of. Not being soldiers, they will not be armed, capable, and willing to sacrifice and defend. In other words, they are most likely to run for cover if an intruder enters the house."

"So you will storm the house?"

"I think I'll have to. And watching various people go in and out these last nights, we know that doors are not locked during the evening. The difficulty will be getting past whoever is on duty. I think there is only one guard inside the house. Only one, and even that one guard may be off duty by a certain hour. We know there is a barracks outside the house and down the hill, but they seem to be there to prevent a military strike. On the layout of the house from the map Hank gave me, there are three potential spots for groups to gather in the evening, and they are in easy proximity to one another. There is a huge dining room, and the living room is attached. Those open areas are the two most likely places they will be. But if not there, Hitler has a downstairs screening room and apparently loves to watch mostly Hollywood films every evening. By midnight that is where he and his entourage usually gather, and that is my preferred location too."

"Why?"

"They will be distracted, unlikely to hear the sound of my entrance—unless I have to kill a guard on my way—and they will have their backs to me."

"What if the children are there too?"

"I've thought of that. But they are young, and it will be late, so it does seem unlikely. Besides, if I am spotted, they will cower with their mother, which Goebbels and Hitler are unlikely to do, so the group will likely be divided. Besides, I only need two shots, three at the most and I have the element of surprise, maybe. Two or three shots to change history, and I'm not thinking of stopping and watching the end of the movie."

"Even if it's Mickey Mouse cartoons?"

I've already told Roma about Hitler's childish delight in opting for cartoons. I've dreaded admitting to her what we have to do to complete our mission, which will end our time together on this earth. It is nice to hear her respond with humor. For both of us, surface humor helps hide deepest feelings. We are not the types to wear our hearts on our sleeves, especially her. Besides, this is not the time.

"Yes, even if cartoons are on. But I still don't know the plan and hope to learn something useful when we go back tonight that might help formulate what course of action is best."

"Whatever your plan is in the end, you have to promise me you will tell me exactly what it is before you go in."

I don't ask why, but I don't prevaricate either. "Promise." And I mean it.

I can't say I'm happy that Roma has insisted on being present for what will surely be a suicide mission. But I also understand it doesn't matter—suicide is the most likely outcome for both of us. I have to—even if with real difficulty—reconcile myself to the fact that I found Roma against all odds, and we have come this far. That is something, but since I desperately want a life with her, it is not an easy something. I do not tell her explicitly how desperately I want a life with her, because on the threshold of losing all possibility, it is too much. Still, we have much to talk about, a lifetime actually, short as it may be. We talk from darkness until the sun begins to reflect off the snow. As morning breaks, we together admire the revelation of unspoken beauty. The spoken plan, if that word can be used for our naked determination, is to go back to the Berghof in the dark after sleeping this Christmas Eve day and hope against hope that Hitler and Goebbels take a repeat stargazing stroll.

Thirteen hours later, we are back in our familiar spot under pine limbs just below the Berghof, for the last time. The side door opens, and a familiar-looking maid comes out for a cigarette. She is joined by her suspected beau. Neither is dressed for winter, and their rendezvous can be expected to last for the duration of one cigarette. They talk in whispers, their voices rise, a range of heightened emotions crest and fall until the cigarette is stamped out. They are enjoying their clandestine relationship. They agree to meet later. It is unclear where and when. "Maybe we should follow," I joke.

"Maybe I should," Roma says, calling my bluff. It is 9:13 p.m. I try not to check the time too often. Time moves more slowly when one checks too often.

Roma and Fred are in tough. So why am I back here in bed, unable to hold on to their dilemma, feeling envy for their—what, their resolve, clarity? Thoughts and worries have intruded into my tried-and-true means of escape from life, and that is rare. Maybe what I need is to attend a meeting chaired by the Special Adviser to the President, Exceptional Student Experience. Even waltzing the name across my brain induces the need for escape and slumber. I will count SAP-like sheep jumping over an exceptional fence in the hope that sleep by way of escape comes again.

Another rarity, first time in fact. I call Lucy before going into work and ask her to get my main peeps to meet in my office as soon as possible. Lucy says she didn't recognize my voice at the crack of ten a.m. She is becoming more confident. In my office, confidence is defined by being able to tell the boss the way it is, or to not laugh at his jokes, or to try to best him in the corny joke Olympics. I am proud of their maturation and only a little wounded at their audacity. Lucy says they all have appointments with students and can only meet at noon. I say I was afraid of that. I ask if she can order us some sandwiches. She says no and hangs up, which I understand to mean it will be done. The specter of Edie's work style lingers, and Lucy is doing her best to emulate. Though Lucy is coming along fine, I really miss Edie. We hear her honeymoon is going well.

I slow down my breakneck speed morning preparations, knowing the threat of having to arrive by eleven a.m. has passed. Noon will be fine. Funny term that, breakneck. Odd, it just came to mind, and I can't remember using it before. I should use it every time I feel rushed as justification for slowing down. And just who is going to argue?

The tray of sandwiches beats me to my office. Lucy can sass me all she wants—she is Edie's protegee after all—as long as she maintains her uber efficiency. Luna and Iggy are waiting for me as usual, and Aunt Isobell and Sister Sandrine arrive as soon as they finish with their students. They seem to have the impression that students are our priority.

"So," I start, "been thinking, as no doubt you have, and I want to compare notes to try to make sense of this thing. I won't know what to do with John's letter until we confer."

"I talked to Ben," Aunt Isobell responds. "He says early lab results indicate that John died as a result of injuries incurred through torture. No surprise there. He says it will be a long and gruesome report, but what matters to us is that his blood toxicology tests showed a cocktail of, and very high levels of alcohol, but significantly no detection of Covidioid—which is the name of that new wonder drug we were talking about, by the way—and therefore murder will remain foremost in the minds of the police."

"Just as John wanted, and thank God with his devious plan, he didn't suffer," I say. "And you said Covidioid is not detectable, didn't you?"

"That is what I read, but it might depend on the type of test they do in the lab. Still, if they are neither familiar with nor looking for Covidioid, it seems unlikely it will be detected. I have something else," Aunt Isobell says in a conspiratorial manner. "And it was passed on to me at great risk to Ben, but he says he trusts me fully. And by extension I know I have the same trust between the five of us in the room."

"He'd be fired for what he has already given us," Luna says.

"Yes, but what I have is on my phone, so this time there is a record." Aunt Isobell opens an email and shows us photos of the murder scene minus the body of John Staffal.

It is hard to look at the coagulated blood on the floor. Instead, I focus on photos of the torture device that held John. The heavy iron device John's body had hung from was at the intersection of huge old wooden beams attached to the ceiling, creating an overarching cross at the center of the room. I just can't get my head around how in the world he could have been suspended as he was. He weighed three hundred pounds, so his staged suicide would have required the coordinated work of maybe three or four strong people. No, it didn't make sense. Murder was awful but actually made more sense than the staged version of his death evident from his letter.

I imagine four men lifting John into the contraption attached by an iron ring, hook, and metal plate anchored into the beam with long screws.

But the photos fuel other thoughts. He had been hoisted and held up by four, not chains as indicated in the Vigils of Spain description, but ropes. And then I realized that attached to the brackets were pulleys for the ropes to allow for leverage and sliding.

"What is it, Phelim?" Sister Sandrine asks.

"Is it possible?" I murmur.

"Let's see the other photos again, please Auntie."

As I lean in, Aunt Isobell flips through sixteen photos once again.

"Wait, hold that one."

"What is it?" Iggy asks.

"His desk, heavy as crap, sorry Sisters, but it may matter. Okay, now back again. No, one more. Okay, that's it."

"What are you thinking, Phelim?" Aunt Isobell asks.

The oak desk and that ancient couch have two things in common. Both are out of place and are unbelievably heavy."

"And …," Luna says encouragingly, indicative of mere seconds until being really frustrated.

"And I know this is going to sound crazy."

"We are beyond crazy, so please proceed," Sister Sandrine further encourages.

"What if the furniture was slid over and out of place in order to tie off John's ropes, as he was painstakingly lifted, one rope at a time, one inch at a time. Pulleys and rope would allow for that kind of gradual work. Pull one rope, tie it off, then pull the next, four ropes in stages until three hundred pounds is suspended several feet off the ground. From there the metal rod on the stand is inserted into the anus."

No one dares speak as I pause before continuing my half-baked thought. "What if what seems like a feat that only three or four brutes could accomplish, could, using that method, be done by one person of Herculean strength?"

"Oh my goodness," Luna says, as the others catch their breath.

"Sorry, Sisters," I say, apologizing for Luna, "but holy ham sandwich, if this was physically possible for one man to do, our Angel was the one and only, and John knew that."

"It does make sense," Aunt Isobell says, nodding. "But does that indicate Angel was murdered or did he commit suicide?"

"I've thought about that a lot," I answer, "and I think we might have failed Angel. I think he was terribly lonely, and after doing what John very likely convinced him to do, maybe Angel couldn't live with himself."

Aunt Isobell is shaking her head again. "Terrible, terrible." Then reverting to her practical self, "You won't be surprised, but I am expecting the important details about Angel's toxicology tests from Ben as soon as they are available."

"Good," I say. "And if this isn't enough, I think we need to find out about that guy who Dean Perkins was talking to. The fact that she was talking to a male alone qualifies as worthy of intrigue. We know they didn't kill John, but what was the dean up to? What was he who talked to the dean up to?"

"Maybe I can help," Sister Sandrine offers. "Tofu Marshall called after our appointment and said she intends to return. But she also wanted to know if I would be willing to see her friend Melanie Tilson. She then said something that I almost objected to but didn't. It seems that Tofu assumed that I am Native American, and I have let her keep that assumption. She made several references to 'us' and 'them,' which was a bit disconcerting, but I just let her talk. That assumption might help to establish rapport."

"Brilliant, when are you meeting her?"

"Tomorrow morning. If I can discreetly steer the conversation towards her boyfriend, I will do so."

"Who knows, if you're able to maintain the fiction you are Native American tomorrow morning, maybe by noon you'll be dean."

CHAPTER THIRTY-SIX

Thursday, five days before Christmas, at the Center

John's death is instant news since he is well-known and highly controversial, but once the police call a press conference to help find his murderer, media coverage explodes. Exactly how John died has not been made explicit, but the police certainly are consistent in asserting that death is likely murder. And of course at receiving limited details, the public clamors for more and begins endless speculation.

Then the death of Angel, deemed as suspicious, takes public interest and speculation to new heights. The police say they do not know if the deaths are related, but two investigations are ongoing. Our city tabloid comes up with the kitschy headline "Angel of Death," not because they have any information or even a theory relating Angel's death to John's, but they like how it sounds and what it suggests. It occurs to me that they might be closer to the truth than they realize.

Edie's wedding receives plenty of media coverage immediately after the nuptials, but interest in the story that Edie had pleaded for has not. John was not able to speak about the need for public scrutiny regarding our repurposed $66 million as he intended to do at the canceled Peterson debate. After that, he'd been tied up, both literally and tragically. The point is, our story, the need for media to make our story into a story, hasn't happened. While I am still determined to make it happen, it appears the Special Adviser to the President, Exceptional Student Experience, for whom good luck seems to follow her every devious, political move, has dodged a bullet and won, again. While it is possible that John's and Angel's deaths are only temporary distractions, it seems unlikely that media will come back to our $66 million dollar story. More likely, our story, like many of the stories that matter, has either fallen into the category of yesterday's news or else never happened.

Sister Sandrine waits for me at my morning roll-in. I am very interested in Sister Sandrine's session with Melanie Tilson but was hoping to slip down to the cafeteria for one of Winston's superb mushroom omelets beforehand. Zigo has the same thought since the cafeteria always pays big dividends on the discarded food front. But it is not to be.

Sister Sandrine sits down at my table and Aunt Isobell appears in the doorway behind her.

"You don't have to ask, Auntie," I say.

"Good," she responds, "because I have some new intel."

And at the speed of light, without warning or words, Luna and Iggy come around the corner and are at the table.

"Age and beauty first," I say, nodding.

"Thank you," Aunt Isobell begins. "Ben has confirmed Angel had more than enough fentanyl in his blood stream to kill him, I'm afraid."

With heavy hearts we think about this unexpected development and what its implications can possibly be.

"How was he able to find that out so quickly?" Luna finally asks.

"A simple blood test and having some idea what he was looking for. We don't have a toxicology report, just this naked fact, as stated. It doesn't rule out that something could have killed him first, just that the fentanyl in his bloodstream was enough to do the job."

"And what we know about Angel is that he did not smoke or drink at all, and I remember him once telling Edie that he thought legalizing marijuana was crazy. I'm ashamed we didn't know him better than we did, but it seems highly unlikely he took the stuff on his own."

"Angel didn't even eat junk food, except maybe pizza," Iggy adds, "and he often said his body was his temple, so yeah, not too likely."

"My session with Melanie was, let's just say, interesting. She has some disturbing ideas, none more so than about relationships. She both despises men, as per the dean's encouragement, and yet, in a relationship she is totally subservient to what men tell her to do. As she explains, she both loved and hated her boyfriend in the extreme. But hate is in the forefront now, since he suddenly has new money and a new girlfriend."

"Well, if she kills him, that will certainly add a fascinating new dimension for public consumption. Don't suppose she knows where he got the new money? And does former boy toy have a job?"

"She doesn't know about the money. As for work, he is sporadic. He is a bodybuilder and has been a personal trainer, but that work doesn't pay well, and he is, according to Melanie, lazy. He is also a small-time drug dealer. He seems to go from having lots of money to having none."

"The drug-selling pension sucks too," I say, without audience response, which I am used to.

"Does she know if he knows Dean Perkins?" Luna asks.

"She says she doesn't know, and I was afraid to probe further since she became suspicious when I asked that."

"Anything else?"

"Yes, one curious item. She said he expressed interest in coming to our Center."

"Does he have a disability?" I ask.

"I don't know, and Melanie went off the deep end at that point about what she would do to the creep if she saw him on campus."

"What's his name, again?" I ask.

But I remember. It's Andy McPherson. I make note, determined not to forget again. But then I forget. Well, not so much forget as relegate to irrelevant anything unrelated to present preoccupations. Short version, I get busy. I have phone calls and emails to answer, meetings to pretend to be at, and students to reassure, or convince, or listen to, or strong-arm, or let know that they matter. It is exhausting work, and I wouldn't have it any other way. Any student problem or staff concern is good, especially anything to keep me from falling back into the quagmire of university politics. Me and good ol' Henry Kissinger, that is.

I have an unusual practice as Center director. Most often, I allow students to drop by and casually meet. No appointment, no problem, as long as you don't take too much time. It is a good use of time since students want to be listened to, after which they are generally happy to be referred to someone else in our office for follow-up, including the person they came to my office to complain about.

I've had students march in, all piss and vinegar, determined to get something from us, and having vented to patient old moi, have left satisfied without getting the something that occasioned the meeting. Such is the static power of listening. The cliche "less is more" has occasional application and wisdom. I'm tempted to say more but am opting for less.

Students also come to see me who are not registered with our Center. Many want to ask questions, before agreeing to our process and submitting documentation verifying disability.

I am the guy in charge who also happens to allow for informal questions which makes for easy, stress-free discussion. Also, unlike the staff coordinators who do all the work, I am not taking notes to be put into files. I might not even remember their name an hour after meeting unless there is a reason for me to remember and follow up.

This particular Thursday is particularly busy because for many reasons we are in catch-up mode, and students have many issues needing immediate answers. I have given up on reading emails and returning phone calls and hunker down on the assembly lineup of students waiting to see me. Student number thirteen (Lucy keeps count since I'm never going to), or my lucky number thirteen as later referenced, has what we call an attitude.

He mentions his name, which I fail to take in, and then proceeds to complain about how students with disabilities have an unfair advantage. I notice his eyes never stop moving, and even while he is trying to press a point on me, he will not look directly at me. As his constantly shifting gaze covers the room, I notice that his eyes are also dead. Odd combination. As to his contention, I am tempted to ask if he thinks I have an unfair advantage going into a classroom that has furniture blocking my entrance for the hundredth time, or trying to get into my van in snow when I can't get up the ramp, or waiting by myself for the fire department to carry me down the stairs when an elevator breaks down. Or maybe my advantage is trying to hold a pen or eat a meal with a hand that doesn't grip, or trying to respond to that drunk guy who punched me in the face because his girlfriend just dumped him, or just being able to pick up anything without having to ask, the way the "disadvantaged" without disabilities take for granted every day.

I'm tempted to ask but I don't. Not because I'm afraid to or I'd be too embarrassed to ask, but I'd seen him before. Not exactly this guy, but the entitled tough-guy shtick with impunity is not original. Frankly, the guy didn't interest me enough to bother. And I am busy. Even Zigo is tired of his rant; he gets up, stretches, and then gives a low-grade growl, indicative of serious, even if nonthreatening, canine displeasure. I bend down to my left side and give him a pat on the head to acknowledge his legitimate feelings, which have to be tempered in the interests of maintaining his status as office mascot. The guy vents some more, I grin my disconcerting grin some more, and whoever he is gets up and leaves.

Lucy comes in and says there are three more students left who want to see me today. Looking at my untouched cool mug of tea, she asks if I want her to make me a new one. That is an offer I would usually and gratefully take, do so several times a day, but now for some reason I don't. "Nay, send the next victim in to see the mad scientist."

Lucy leaves, and I sip room-temperature tea, vaguely wishing I'd taken her offer.

My next student, Penelope Crenshaw, has a file with the Center. She did not request accommodations for exams in September when requests are normally processed. She thought she could do without accommodations this term, but her exams have not been going well, and she is terrified that she will fall apart without them for her last exam tomorrow. It is weeks after the deadline for making accommodation requests for December exams, and her coordinator said no to her late request just yesterday. She has a note from her mother indicating that not getting accommodations would be detrimental to her daughter's mental health.

I have sympathy for Penelope trying to do her exams without accommodations, but less so for the mother who wrote the note. Penelope talks for a long time without pausing, and I have several questions for her whenever she stops. But when she finally does stop, I can't remember what I meant to ask. I also forget what her name is. I almost laugh wondering if her name might be Nick, or maybe St. Nicholas. I'm confused, but not out of sorts. In fact, as will be revealed to me afterwards, I am happy, feeling no pain, high as a kite. And then I black out.

I wake up slowly. I'm not feeling quite right, I'm not feeling quite wrong. I just don't know, but I know I'm not where I'm supposed to be. Standing around my bed are Luna, Aunt Isobell, Sister Sandrine, and Iggy. It is not my bed in my bedroom, and given the fluorescent lighting and utilitarian furniture, I realize I am in a hospital.

No one speaks, so I do. "I've woke—up, that is. Lucky me."

There is a frenzy of excitement and concern, so I follow this revelation with a question.

"Given that the gang is all here, did you steal my office furniture, or have I recently been given a new job as VP of Waking Up Woke?"

"Thank God, Phelim, we were worried, you know." Aunt Isobell seems to be speaking for the group.

"Yeah, you almost died," Luna says, in the blunt way that we have come to love. "Which would have been really, really frustrating."

"But now that you've pulled through, I guess I don't get your room at the house," Iggy intones.

"Nor I, your spacious office," Sister Sandrine adds.

"So what happened that caused my unwokeness?"

"We think you were poisoned," Aunt Isobell says.

"Holy crap. Sorry, Sisters."

"We'll forgive you because of the poison," Sister Sandrine responds.

Then holding a photo before my blurry eyes, she asks, "Is this the student you saw before your last student, Penelope?"

"Yeah. Weird guy, forget his name, but why?"

"This is Andy MacPherson, Melanie Tilson's former boyfriend. It will soon be determined by a blood test, but it seems most likely that he poisoned you."

"How do you know this?"

"Melanie called to say she saw Andy on campus, and she wanted to warn us about what he might do. It seems she knew more about his conversations with Dean Perkins than she let on."

"Holy crap. I'm still using my swearing pass while I can. Still, not sure how …."

"It seems likely your tea was drugged. The doctors concur that your symptoms are consistent with drug overdose. Good thing you didn't drink too much."

"Holy crap," I say again, for lack of words to say anything else.

"I've always thought that is an odd coupling of words," Aunt Isobell ponders. "Anyway, would you like us to get you a pizza downstairs? You slept through dinner."

"Yeah, I'm actually starved.'

"No wonder," Aunt Isobell laughs. "You had your stomach pumped, as a precaution since they didn't know exactly what the problem might be."

"Huh. Then can you get me some breakfast and lunch while you're at it?"

Aunt Isobell gives me a stern look. "You realize that you probably narrowly escaped being murdered, right?"

"Yeah, guess I should have realized that someone wanting to kill John might want to kill me as well."

"We all should have," Iggy adds.

"Wow," I say, leaning my head back for a moment and looking upward.

"Are you okay?"

"Do you feel faint?"

"Do you need some help?"

"Are you going to croak on us?" My gang instantly responds, the last penetrating and sensitive question coming from Luna.

"Just a creak in my neck, not a big problem." But as I make a futile attempt to relax the calcified discs of my decrepit neck for the millionth time, it hits me. "Wait! I've just had a searing revelation of the obvious. That turd Andy guy killed Angel."

"But why would he do that if he was acting for Dean Perkins?" Iggy asks with incredulity.

"Angel must have drunk something intended for John when he was in John's office. By the time John was ready to be strung up, he wasn't interested in anything that didn't have alcohol in it, and we know that Angel would only drink something that was non-alcoholic. Also, what Angel did in John's office took time and effort, and a guy working that hard would need a drink. Alan left the poisoned drink for John and ended up killing Angel."

The room becomes quiet as this sinks in.

Finally, Aunt Isobell says, "Poor Angel," in heartfelt manner, for all us.

After another silence, Luna says, "Murder most foul," and Iggy follows with, "Oh my God, Phelim, you are probably right!"

"There was an empty bottle of some healthy sports drink on the floor in one of the photos Aunt Isobell's got from Ben. I remember then vaguely thinking it was out of place because healthy is something John would never drink."

"But if so, why didn't he die in John's office?" Luna, the queen of common sense asks.

"It depends on dosage in the drink as well as how much he actually consumed. Being a large person might also extend the time enough that he could finish up in John's office and get home," Aunt Isobell answers.

Sister Sandrine then asks, "What in the world is next?"

"There is something else," Aunt Isobell answers. "Lucy took an urgent call this afternoon from one of John's wives, not sure which one, but it doesn't matter since they have conferred, talked to the university, and there is agreement to have a celebration of life for John this coming Monday in the Great Hall."

"That soon and on Christmas Eve?"

"Yes, the university closes at noon, and then the celebration of life begins so there are no conflicting events, classes, or appointments."

"But why would they have John's celebration of life in a place that holds five hundred people, for a guy who at the time of his death had been suspended from teaching? He died persona non grata."

"The university is trying to prevent a PR disaster. Because the debate got canceled and is the newest and highest-profile example of cancel culture in the country, and of course, on the heels of the gruesome murder of the defender of free speech, they want to make sure the university is not portrayed as the enemy."

"And because to be loved, sometimes you gotta die first," I add, somberly.

"That too," Aunt Isobell says and continues, "The wives are mad at the university, and there has been talk about taking legal action. The university is trying to prevent that, especially the media circus that would ensue, so they are not only agreeing to anything the wives want, they are trying to embellish the event's importance. For example, the wives wondered if anyone, that is any of the bigwigs at the university, would attend the event. Apparently, the president responded he will personally guarantee all the significant officers of the university will be there. All directors, managers, chairs, deans, and prominent faculty, as well as members of Senate and the Board of Governors."

"I'm pretty sure that kind of attendance rule has never happened for any event in the past," I respond, with mounting incredulity.

"The wives realize that and are feeling listened to, even if they cynically understand why. But there is a but. The representative wife who called today says they want you and only you to do a substantial, no-holds-barred eulogy for John. They would like an answer soon, and anything that you want to do related to giving the eulogy they will agree to, and if they agree to it, the university will too."

I think about this. The whole thing seems odd and not quite the right way to deal with the many issues John's death raises. But then, as I always do, I have a thought. "Um, in answer to Sister Sandrine's earlier question, what in the world is next, maybe the eulogy, if done right, is what's next."

CHAPTER THIRTY-SEVEN

Friday evening, four days before Christmas,
at the decrepit colossus called Home

The picture is coming into focus, except for the part that is murkier than ever. Clear as mud being a fitting figure of speech. John committed an elaborate swan song suicide, Angel was killed by accident—but it was murder nonetheless—and the reasons for Heather's suicide have been recently revealed.

A suicide note received by a friend has come to light. It confirms that Heather killed herself because of a relationship entanglement she could not fully end. Her references to timing and events when pieced together prove that she was distraught over issues between her and Dean Perkins and not John Staffal. She lamented losing who she loved and not being able to lose who she did not love. Heather wrote she was pregnant and that the person she had been most recently involved with could not tolerate having anything to do with *his* baby. She also cited being pressured to make unfounded allegations of sexual harassment against a male faculty member, which caused her extreme guilt and distress. She recanted and expressed regret to the injured party. There was only one implicit reference to John, as "the fat old English prof who made me laugh." Her reference to Dean Perkins sharply contrasted with John's, ending with the words, "she knows less than she thinks, and didn't make me laugh." For reasons unknown, Heather never uses either John's or Dean Perkins's actual name, though implicitly their identities are clear.

Being right can be overrated. Knowing much exacerbates the disparity between what we know and what the public will never learn. Knowing the cause of death is important, but it is not the only game in town. After death persist details about life that continue to matter. People have died for reasons that could not be fully explained by their postmortem. Why they died affected the political landscape they had vacated whether or not they were political animals.

None of the dead or their deaths are forgotten or even long out of our minds, but it is the weekend before Christmas, I have a new family, and it is time to take a pause. I'm also a tad fatigued after yesterday's brush with mortality. I'm trying to conceive of a plan to resolve what we still don't know, but there are only limited possibilities circling in my mind, like a hamster on a wheel. Whatever I might conceive during my false dawn ruminations will soon be coming to a theater near you.

I also have that little matter of delivering a knock 'em dead, no-holds-barred eulogy for John on Monday, but that is a concern for Monday. It's not indifference, it's just how I work. On Monday, I will be presented with thoughts too deep for words, and the words will come. And yes, I know, to say I'm a bit quirky would be overly kind. In the meantime, I have online shopping to finalize. The last shopping mall in our fair city went bankrupt last year, just as online delivery has improved with twenty-four-hour guarantees now standard service. Amazon is bigger than the combined heft of the next three biggest companies in the world. Shopping malls are closing faster than Block-buster did two decades earlier, with the last holdout expected to be taken down somewhere in the Midwest within three years. There is a national movement to convert the graves of old shopping malls into community gardens. The concept fits the broad goals of the meatless Green New Deal, and many billions in funding is expected to be approved and allocated next year.

More important, I recently made an unexpected discovery that will enhance the celebration of Christmas. I have always had a Christmas movie–watching tradition. It's no mystery in the absence of much family. I've lived precariously through the happy endings of families from my substantial Christmas movie collection. This year has been complicated, and the Christmas movie tradition has suffered a late start. Brenda and Pearl finally and fully moved in (thank God), and so the opportunity for harmony or conflict has been heightened. For better or worse, what I want to do or watch is no longer possible without the possibility of compromise. Harmony is the goal.

Brenda, Iggy, Aunt Isobell, or Sister Sandrine (or all of them) might watch part of a Christmas movie with me, but none has the inclination to watch the entirety of my vast collection. Fools. So I've begun watching, as I have my entire life, a selection of Christmas movies, all by my lonesome.

Now Pearl is not a kid to convince or coerce or try to be cleverer than, unless your goal in life is to look foolish. And I love that her quirky brilliance has much to do with the freedom with which her highly disciplined mind is able to roam the world, looking for challenging and interesting phenomena. So what are the chances that the number-one fan of Christmas movies is going to find number two living under the same roof? But that is what happens. To my surprise and delight, I find a kindred spirit. I'm five minutes into a little-known classic with Jimmy Durante called *The Great Rupert*. I am settling into the first of my must-watch Christmas movie list, when I hear a question from Pearl. All her initial questions are from the outside of the adult world to test if she wants to come inside. I try to turn and look at Pearl hanging on to the doorway between the living and dining rooms in our big old monstrosity of a house. But between my ever-increasing bulk and decrepit neck, I'm never going to turn far enough to actually see her. I also didn't fully hear what she asked.

Pearl creeps up toward where I am sitting but still lingers behind me. She takes a deep breath and condescends to repeat the question, as if it is a question far too obvious to need repeating. "You started watching that movie alone?"

I pause so as not to overplay my hand. "Ah, well, I usually just start watching Christmas movies because most people don't want to watch a Christmas movie with me every day."

"Well, if you don't know it by now, I'm not *most* people."

"How about I just rewind it, and we start again."

"It's digital, so you can't actually rewind it, but sure, start at the beginning if you don't mind seeing the same scenes again."

"Pearl, I never mind watching Christmas movies any number of times. Not sure why, but I don't fight it either. I know what I like, and I like Christmas movies."

The movie begins again. Pearl settles into a chair beside me and simply says, "Me too."

We don't talk much while a movie is playing, though we do afterwards, often comparing the finer points from the movies we love best. Talking to the group at dinner, Pearl or I might refer to a scene we've seen in *How the Grinch Stole Christmas* or *Holiday Inn*, and although the group has probably seen the movies many times, they are almost always confused, cannot remember, or don't know what we are talking about. And that makes Pearl and me laugh. And most of all, it allows us to maintain our own little world separate from prying adult minds. If you don't know why it's funny when Max has to pull the Grinch's sled up Mount Crumpet wearing his silly antlers, or when he finally gets served the roast beast, well, don't expect us to explain it.

Our conversations aren't limited to what happens during the scene just seen. We discuss how to organize our respective schedules between now and Christmas Day to maximize viewing time. Basically, watching Christmas movies is all we want to do, after which we will not watch Christmas movies again until next Thanksgiving. We don't discuss why we agree on this, but we do agree the reasons are obvious and make perfect sense. From Thanksgiving until Christmas there are thirty days, which means the potential for thirty films, but this year we missed most of that time. We have some serious catching up to do, as well as refinement of our schedule. There is lots to talk about, and Pearl and I talk about it lots.

The others in the house have about as much enthusiasm for Christmas movies as Scrooge has for Christmas before being transformed by the three ghosts. But they cannot help being pulled into the vortex of our enthusiasm and, if I do say so, expertise. First Brenda, then Iggy, and finally the two Sisters drop by the living room just to be social, but Pearl and I are serious film connoisseurs, so no small talk. They linger, not chatting but not leaving either, until they are back with Bing waiting for snow in Vermont or cheering for Matthew Crawley and Lady Mary to finally declare their love on Christmas Eve at Downton Abbey.

They who linger with intentions to leave become hooked, and before long, our twosome of devoted Christmas movie watchers has expanded to include the entire house. Pearl and I are fine with this, but we still choose which movie, and we set the schedule. Going to bed exhausted, Brenda asks, "What's got into Pearl? I'm never seen her …."

I place fingers over her mouth and say, "Shh, my love, let's not ask. Let's just drink in the forgiveness this life has to offer." She understands, and we sleep like the dead without the necessity of staying that way.

Next day is Saturday, and Pearl and I have serious plans. We announce to the group what the day's film schedule will be. Normally, we might watch one film in the early evening, but between the need to make up for lost time and the fact that it is the weekend before Christmas, we schedule two after-noon movies for both Saturday and Sunday, with an evening film to follow. Pearl is particularly excited because her mother—in failing to provide the poor girl with a proper education—has neglected to expose her to some of the finest Christmas movies ever made. This afternoon features *The Santa Clause* (starting with the first one, of course) followed by the original *Miracle on 34th Street*, with *Elf* to close off the day. When people request that we alter the schedule to accommodate their various needs, Pearl and I—in a manner that is both cruel and fair—give a decisive no. For the sake of the greater good and the benefit of the group, the show must go on as scheduled. Pearl finds our tyrannical ways very funny, a sentiment she is not willing to concede very often.

So when Aunt Isobell approaches me with a very important request which impacts by several minutes our 1:00 p.m. scheduled screening of *The Santa Clause*, her reception from Pearl and me is justifiably icy. But when Aunt Isobell, who never asks for very much insists, I am forced to listen and must confer with Pearl.

"She is the oldest and smartest person in the house, so you better do what she says," Pearl reasons.

Aunt Isobell responds back, "Well, while I may have to surrender the title of smartest to you shortly, I doubt I'll be giving up the title as oldest for a while."

"I'll be in my room reading the chapter on transmissions in the auto mechanics book you lent me, so just call when you're done," Pearl instructs me. I agree without astonishment or doubting the veracity of what she says, being used to her quirky genius.

"This must be important," I say, turning to Aunt Isobell.

"It is," she says, serious and determined. "I want you to meet two important people, one of whom you once met but may be surprised to become reacquainted with. I'd explain more, but I only got the email they are coming over ten minutes ago, and they don't have much time. Still, they do want to talk to you and have gone to much trouble to make it happen. They'll be here any minute."

"Auntie, can't you give me some more—"

"There's the bell," Aunt Isobell says and is gone.

Fifteen seconds later she is back with two young-looking guys (you know, late fifties, so young like me). They are similarly dressed in brand-name sporting clothes, but that is where their similarity of appearance ends. One rotund—word chosen to be kind—and the other diminutive. Wendell something or other has three distinct dimensions; Craig the other something, seems to have only one. Their somethings and others are substitutes for last names I don't catch because I'm not paying attention. Pearl, or Bing Crosby, or Jimmy Stewart would understand why. My eyes scan the wall clock. With only introductions and a few words about weather exchanged, they seem to fit body type stereotypes, the round guy being what can only be described as jolly, the skinny one all nervous energy, and that voice. Something about it.

Wendell sees the pile of old Christmas DVDs on the table beside me and laughs, kind of like, well, Santa Claus, before giving us a synopsis regarding why each one is a classic. I decide I like Wendell.

Craig chirps in that it brings back memories to see DVDs again. I wonder how impressed he'd be if I brought out a book.

Aunt Isobell, never one to rush anyone, seems to be waiting for the proper moment to let me know why these guys are intruding into an inviolable house rule about our uninterrupted Christmas movie schedule. I half listen until I hear Auntie refer to the Board of Governors.

"Board of Governors?" I repeat. "Sorry, what was that?"

"Mr. Turner," Aunt Isobell says indicating the round guy, "and Mr. Del Monte," she finishes referring to the small guy, "as you know, are members of the Board of Governors and have heard you have concerns about the sale, planned renovations, and most important, where the money came from for purchase of the convent." Then with great deliberation, she adds, "And Mr. Turner and Mr. Del Monte are particularly concerned about the large sum of money that you raised for accessibility."

I have a moment to let this sink into my thick skull as our guests insist on being called by their first names.

Aunt Isobell knows I had no idea that they are members of the Board of Governors, but the question remains, how did she meet these guys, and how did she get them here into our living room on this Saturday?

"We're all ears," the small one says, encouragingly and with that distinctive voice again.

"Your incredible Aunt was so kind as to give us a sense of all your concerns, so please let's get straight to what we can do about it."

I look at Aunt Isobell, not understanding what they understand as *it*, not knowing why she didn't talk to me before they came in, and not sure whether to give her the death stare or else the Nobel Prize for Peace. It occurs to me I should be careful how many of these prizes I give out in case they are running out of them in Norway.

When I don't immediately respond, Wendell says, "We've surprised you. Sorry, but we only found out that we would have time to meet you today. Our flight to San Jose was cancelled"—as has become standard practice for almost one third of scheduled flights since the new global warming protocols came into place—"and after talking to your aunt last evening at the Board of Governors' holiday social, we felt we just had to come and meet you."

I vaguely remember Aunt Isobell and Sister Sandrine mentioning something about going to something last evening, and I remember responding to their question about whether I would like to join them instead of watching a Christmas movie with Pearl with "I'd rather put needles in my eyes." Apparently, the board has an annual holiday—once called Christmas—function I have been invited to and have failed to notice or respond to these past thirty-five years of working at St. Jude's.

"And we have to admit we have a personal reason as well professional interest," Craig says.

"Oh?" I ask.

"So you don't recognize me or my name?" Craig asks with a strange and strangely familiar laugh.

I have no idea who he is, even if his voice and laugh have irritating familiarity.

"Well, you and I both are a little different today, so easy to understand that you don't recognize me. And hey, it's been a while." Craig gives another high-pitched laugh, a little like a railway car screeching to a stop. I know and I don't know. "And—well, you're not exactly the same guy I remember either, which I feel real bad about."

Wendell's jolly face contorts into exaggerated and sympathetic expressions that mirror whatever emotion is being conveyed by his companion. I'm flummoxed, which brings Aunt Isobell to the rescue. "When we met last evening, I mentioned that you were concerned about the reputation of St. Jude's if it should come out later that the money used to buy and renovate the convent came from funds you raised, which were to go to making the campus fully accessible—"

"For people like yourself," Craig cuts in.

Glad you clarified that, I think, *just in case I forgot which one of us is in a wheelchair.* "I'm very glad you are both here, gentlemen, and I very much want to talk to you about these issues, but I'm curious about your personal connection."

"We knew each other in our first year at St. Jude's, not well, but we knew each other. My nickname then was Squeaky. Of course, you might not recognize my voice today after years of elocution and public speaking lessons."

And then it all comes tumbling back. His voice, yes his voice, and man, did I mercilessly tease him. Worse, I tried to steal his girlfriend. He wasn't special, she wasn't special, but it's what I did back then. It's why guys couldn't stand me, and women, all women liked me, but learned to get over me quickly, sometimes with a passion. Worse still, his girlfriend's name was Candice. I remember her, and I didn't just try to pick her up, I successfully did pick her and another gal the night of my accident. Though they would surely have died if left to my drunken judgment, the two girls protested, and I reluctantly took them back to the party. Thank God. Then indignant and alone, I set off in my tin can before sailing, all six foot three inches of me, through that VW Beetle windshield. I suspected, for all Aunt Isobell's good intentions and hard work, this meeting wasn't going to go well. It was time to beg forgiveness.

"Look, I'm sorry, I'm not the same—"

"Sorry?" Craig says in a high-pitched and cracking voice. "One of the reasons I wanted to meet you again was to say I'm sorry, that is, we're sorry we never visited you after the accident. Candice just felt too guilty, didn't know what to say. I kept saying if sorry is what you've got to say, then just go and say it."

My head is swimming. "And you, she …."

"Yup, married twenty-nine years, four kids, back in San Jose. Anyway, Candice will be glad, relieved even, that I was able to say sorry and thank you personally for letting her out of the car that night. You saved her life, and don't you think we don't know it."

As I contemplate the inexplicable, Wendell speaks. "Gosh, after that deep personal connection, I'm almost embarrassed to say what my very slight connection is. And it isn't to you at all, but to your friend, Professor John Staffal. Your aunt told us he was real concerned about the funding and the convent too, so that's enough for me. Back when I was a student here, I majored in computer science when absolutely nobody was doing that, but I also took Professor Staffal's first year course. I loved it and it changed my life. And as for his acting, don't get me started. I went to see him in *Cyrano* whenever it was playing, whenever I was home over the years. He was the best actor, the best Cyrano who ever lived. Gosh, I would have loved to have been an actor, though making millions in Silicon Valley hasn't been too shabby either."

LARRY J. MCCLOSKEY

"Wendell and I both graduated from St. Jude's about a million years ago," Craig says, "and we wanted to give back after making our high-tech fortune, so we joined the board. Well, you don't just join, but you do get invited to become a member after giving back millions, with the hint of millions more to come."

"So, if there is anything we can do …." Wendell reiterates, to my confused and everlasting gratitude.

"Anything at all," Craig finishes.

This tag-team extraordinaire has done it. I didn't think there was anything that could derail me from my deep focus on this afternoon's Christmas movie with Pearl, but all thoughts of *The Santa Clause* are gone. For now. Even Fred and Roma might have been temporarily distracted from their glorious mission if presented with this scenario.

"So just to be clear," I begin, "you think you can help me get back the $66 million for accessibility that I applied for that the Special Adviser to the President took for buying and renovating the convent?"

"Or die trying," Craig responds.

"And we may look like lightweights, but I can assure you that when we built our high-tech company, we were anything but," Wendell states.

I look at Wendell's shape and think the last thing I would accuse him of is looking like a lightweight, but that is not what I say. "You just gave me an idea. You've always wanted to act, right?"

"Always."

"What if I were to propose to you a way to act and a way to emulate the late, great John Staffal?"

"I'm absolutely in, even before you say what your proposal is."

"And Craig, have you ever thought about putting those elocution and public speaking lessons to a good and different use?"

"I'm all ears and enthusiasm," Crag answers.

I've touched a nerve, and our two guests are as excited as five-year-old kids at Christmas. "Before I explain, were you planning to be in town for John's celebration of life midday Christmas Eve?"

"Does this acting and John Staffal emulating depend on us being here?"

"Yes, I'm afraid it does," I say, hoping my crazy scheme is not about to be deflated. "But I can promise to make the acting gig the opportunity of a lifetime."

Regrettably, both five-year-old kids are transformed into adult nerds when confronted with my question. But then they pause, look at each other, nod, and smile. "That's only two days from now," Craig says. "So we can fly out Monday afternoon, and with the time difference we'll still get back to the coast in time for a late Christmas Eve dinner."

"Great," I say and mean it.

"And Phelim, I assume you will send us the script for our acting roles so that we can stay busy until Monday," Wendell says, like a kid who has broken into Santa's secret stash of candy canes.

I feel like the kid Wendell has shared Santa's secret stash of candy canes with. I also notice Pearl has crept back into the periphery of the living room and is waiting.

Aunt Isobell, who is a save-the-day type of gal, saves the day. "While I'm sure Phelim is anxious to supply you with your acting assignment, I do feel compelled to mention he has a very important appointment he must now attend to. Perhaps he can send your parts in about an hour forty-five, once you have settled into a hotel and scheduled your flight."

"Perfect," Wendell purrs, as I dumbly nod my grateful head.

"Love your precision," Craig adds.

Aunt Isobell continues. "One last piece of intel. My friend sent information from the Library of Congress on the establishment of St. Jude's, and it's been checked by a legal historian. It seems that the founders of St. Jude's foresaw the problems of the secular world that we face today. It is clear that the convent can only be part of St. Jude's University as a convent, and if it is no longer a convent, St. Jude's cannot buy it. I talked to Mother Superior, and clearly she was misled by a university representative who told her that at the founding of St. Jude's it was agreed that if the convent was sold, the university must get right of first refusal. Unfortunately, she never asked for any documentation to verify that claim. She was just too trusting."

"Nuns do have that terrible affliction," I say.

With smiles all around, it is a good time for the meeting to end. As the titans of Silicon Valley are gently ushered out the door, I hear Wendell exclaim, "Gosh, I'm looking forward to becoming an actor."

Craig chirps, "Can't wait to debut my elocution chops."

There are very few justifications for delaying the screening of an afternoon Christmas movie, but we have just encountered the mother-lode reason smack in the face. I feel Pearl will understand, and more to the point, our Christmas movie plans now are completely unencumbered.

Pearl comes forward and settles in her comfy chair until a thought pervades her curious, crowded brain. She gets up and picks up and examines the DVD jacket for *The Santa Clause*. "Makes sense."

"What?" I ask, truly puzzled.

"*The Santa Clause* is one hour, thirty-seven minutes long. That's why Aunt Isobell said you would send them their parts in an hour and forty-five minutes."

I realize that is exactly right. I further realize, for the millionth time, I don't know how the old gal does it. "You and Aunt Isobell are going to be such good friends."

Pearl smiles that devious knowing half-smile, the other half conceding she doesn't know everything. Yet.

John's celebration of life and the theft of our $66 mill were intractable problems a half hour ago. I am feeling some traction on the intractable. Something is percolating deep down. Best way to percolate is a blissful hour and thirty-seven minutes of film forgetfulness in the company of a precious gem called Pearl.

CHAPTER THIRTY-EIGHT

Christmas Eve noon, in the Great Hall

I've always felt the best strategy for mitigating the seriousness of life is to seriously lean on humor.

So, with only slight sleight of hand on the logic front, the antidote for corruption in life might just be to luxuriate in farce. I suspect John will approve when he sees what I've got planned for him. And I'm sure he'd agree that having a celebration of life for a dead guy, who happens to be him, attended by all the officers of the university who just happen to hate him but want to demonstrate how un-hated he was, is farcical and therefore commendable in the extreme. I checked with all three of John's ex-wives, and they gave the same response—conduct the celebration however you see fit. I said I see it as John would see fit, which might leave you fit to be tied. They all assured me that having once been married to John, they knew him.

So here I am stuffed back into the same suit that I wore a measly week ago, from celebration of wife to celebration of life. But unlike the friends upon friends who attended Edie's wedding, I wait in my chair as the seats in the Great Hall fill with a motley collection of John's loved ones, hated twos, indifferent threes, and innumerable assassins. Their faces are uniformly impassive, but whether friend or foe, there is likely consensus that John was a more potent force when celebrating life by actually living. Friends are greatly outnumbered.

The mood in the Great Hall today is vastly different than at Edie's wedding. Then, the house was electric with love and goodwill, even among people who only met that day because of their relationship with the bride or, in a few instances, the groom. Everyone was pulling in the same direction, a rarity of modern life.

Today, an acidic, rancid mood prevails with most everyone wanting to be anywhere else. Wanting to be anywhere else while wanting to maintain a mask of solemnity, people sneak glances at half-hidden devices that offer escape from present unpleasantness. At Edie's wedding I looked into a full room of smiling faces; today there are blank stares and advanced states of boredom. And hence, all the more reason for farce. If I were Persian, I'd conduct the whole farce in Farsi. I vaguely hope that in his transformed state, John can read my mind. He would howl at that one, particularly because it is *so* bad.

The president sits gamely in the front row, close to the cluster of John's exes. He looks nervous, out of place, even as he occupies the space his staff have strategically chosen. In the second row are the four vice presidents, of which there were recently three, but like mushrooms in the forest, another three sprang into existence. No one seems to know what words differentiate their new vice presidential titles, so we call them Diversity, Inclusion, and Equity, or when they appear together at a celebration of life, we refer to the four stiffs as a near DIE experience. John would enjoy the kitschy irony of DIE sitting and waiting for little ol' moi to be the life of the party. The Special Adviser to the President, Exceptional Student Experience, whose fulsome title is well known, dominates the vice presidential cluster both in terms of stature as well as being clear winner of the four Olympics.

The president rises out of his chair to begin the somber occasion. I think it's too bad the celebration is considered too serious to allow for music throughout the proceedings. It would have been fitting to have Steven Tyler belt out "Don't Want to Miss a Thing" as the president spoke. Though upon hearing the president, John might have changed the lyrics to "Don't Want to Have to Hear a Thing." I intend to address the music deficit at the end of the celebration.

The president begins by acknowledging that St. Jude's is located on the ancient unceded lands of several native American tribes. Which if true, and I don't doubt it is true, we really should give it back. All of it. And now. Really. Why acknowledge a crime with a studied, repentant, and subservient tone, only to remain criminal? I barely resist the temptation to interject.

The president speaks about Professor John Staffal's many contributions to St. Jude's and to the community at large. He is the university's all-time most popular professor after all, and he is well-known across the country for his dazzling theatrical performances. On this point, the thin-lipped, thin-skinned, do-as-you're-told president almost smiles. "Particularly for his renowned role as Cyrano de Bergerac." And on and on, but no mention of his years of pushing back against the elimination of Shakespeare and other dead, white dudes. Who cares if they and notable women writers made up a literary canon that is the foundation of Western civilization? Why would it possibly matter that many faculty members who condemn John secretly agree with him? The president has been well briefed to touch on uncontentious highlights and avoid controversy. The purveyors of avoidance have achieved the equivalent of Fred Astaire footwork to pull it off.

The chair of the English department is up next. She seems to lack both dictum and imagination, repeatedly saying John was "great" for unspecified reasons, before excitedly claiming he was an outlier because he did not have a PhD. She is almost breathless with revelation. This is passed off as a back-handed compliment that the audience is supposed to relish, for reasons only relish-loving academics will understand or care about. He was, it became known, the only non-PhD in the department. The next so-called backhanded compliment is another blatant put-down for those who give a rat's ass. She says with glee—bearing in mind this is a tribute—that despite his many theatrical accomplishments, John never did publish. If this further revelation is supposed to hush the audience with scandal, it falls short. For all her use of the word "great"—it was twelve times, I counted—the chair of the English department has taken a chainsaw to her colleague, and we are not supposed to notice.

I did notice that her area of expertise is Wiccan poetry. How nice. I wonder how she manages to have a career in literature and not understand the concept of irony.

A representative from Senate speaks. John served on Senate for six years, trying desperately to uphold academic standards, even though he hated committee work, Senate committee work most of all. The Senate guy talks about how John challenged that august body, which is code for how he was the only faculty member and only Senate member who actually spoke up for fundamental rights such as freedom of speech, which were taken away by a plethora of nonacademic meddlers who substituted ideologically correct training for academic teaching and research. What John said that was "controversial" was nothing more than reminders to Senate members of the way the university was thirty years ago, which faculty pretends has not changed. *Controversy* has become code for failure to capitulate to the demands of progressive orthodoxy. John often said to me—three Irish whiskies in, a Kilkenny on the side—it wasn't just that prescriptive ideologies undermined the academic mission, but most grievous, they offended his sense of style.

It is my turn. People expect pablum from these affairs; people expect a somber version of pablum from me. The guy in the chair has just got to be riddled with a sense of tragedy. Somber, somber, somber. But John was not somber. He took life by the horns, and this is his send-off. I don't want to put people to sleep. I don't want to put myself to sleep. I want to wake up the woke, for John, you understand. And there is something else. For all I felt about John, for all I hurt for what I felt about John and the horrible, courageous way he fell on his sword, I really do not want to expose myself to these people. That would be too much for me, for John, for us. It was not what John would have wanted. I will do what John would have wanted.

I introduce members of his family, all three wives, and his six adult kids. They all say something nice about John, but it isn't heartfelt. It is fine, it is as expected, but it is not the searing passion of the bereft.

It is now my turn; I mean really my turn. My play is to move from theatrical to indecent exposure, theirs, not mine. I begin by introducing two members of the Board of Governors by name without indicating what their contribution to John's celebration of life might be. There are murmurs in the audience which I infer as jittery concern. Who wants the perpetual fool mixing it up with people who have real power? And what in the world can this strange connection mean? So far, so good. I think a little mystery might be nice.

"Anyone who knew John, and many more who did not, knew of him in his most storied role as Cyrano de Bergerac from Edmond Rostand's play of that name. Ladies and gentlemen (two words now officially banned for use at St. Jude's for denoting the existence of traditional gender rather than the acceptable ubiquitous non-binary version), I give you Wendell as Cyrano and Craig as Roxanne, in the Board of Governors' tribute to John Staffal."

The effect is immediate and electric. Consternation and confusion are everywhere as people turn and strain to see what such an unexpected and outrageous introduction can mean. The visual effect is stunning. First Wendell as Cyrano, followed by Craig as Roxanne, sashay across the audience's view in seventeenth-century French period costume, looking both authentic and —the only other word that fits—ridiculous. In other words, the effect is picture-perfect.

Wendell, with his studied walk and pear-shaped figure, is not only a credible John Staffal understudy, but to further the illusion I loaned him the prophylactic nose and plumed hat from John's recently received package. He looks authentic. At least, that is what I tell him. Most important, it is what he believes.

While it may be true that if you smear lipstick on a pig, it is still a pig, Craig has relinquished his former self. So the result is closer to Roxanne than to Craig Del Monte, but not by much. His small stature, long flowing wig, draping gown, and strategically placed body stuffing gives him odd and bodacious curves, just not necessarily in the right places. Still, his contrived cleavage, which probably involved shaving chest hair, shows real effort. I could have hugged both of them even before they began. I heard practice versions of what they are now going to perform from our several phone calls and teleconferences over the past two days, but every rapturous word and gesture I now witness is entirely fresh. And it must be said, this rendition of what was rehearsed takes their art to a whole other level. They are—to employ sports parlance—clutch players.

Initial rustling sounds give way to absolute silence as the audience waits with bated breath for whatever in the world these two clowns and holders of prestigious office at St. Jude's are about to do. (How in the world does one actually bate one's breath?)

Wendell, after a lifetime of hoping against hope for the opportunity to act, is not about to waste it. He is determined to be passionate, audacious, and daring—but subtle, not so much. Though he has an overall cornball demeanor, he convincingly captures audience attention with an exacting use of anticipation. He also seems, for a novice, strangely comfortable. He turns and walks this way and that, with his nose in the air, taking his sweet time, before abruptly pirouetting and saying,

> A great nose may be an index
> Of a great soul.

This evokes some nervous laughter, and then Cyrano (for Wendell no longer exists) does an obviously practiced counter-pirouette, for obvious effect. *"All souls are written in our eyes."*

These initial one-liners are prelude to dramatic speech. "I have a different idea of elegance. I don't dress like a fop, it's true, but my moral grooming is impeccable. I never appear in public with a soiled conscience, a tarnished honor, threadbare scruples, or an insult that I haven't washed away. I'm always immaculately clean, adorned with independence and frankness. I may not cut a stylish figure, but I hold my soul erect. I wear my deeds as ribbons, my wit is sharper than the finest mustache, and when I walk among men I make truths ring like spurs."

By now, for all intents and purposes, Roxanne is a mute and pretty face to be loved by Cyrano from afar. Wendell and Craig know that Roxanne's tragically too-late-requited love is the gist of the play, but still, they want to give poor Roxanne a bit more airtime. In his practiced high voice, still not devoid of his trademark squeak, Craig improvises with a couple sentences outside of the play. "John Staffal was just such a man. Not a pretty boy, not on the cover of *GQ*, but he had impeccable moral grooming and held his soul erect and intact. He was a man of truth."

Use of the word *man* likely makes people cringe in their seats. I think I couldn't have scripted this better for effect, or truer to John. My grin widens, threatening to meet at the back of my head.

Craig then says, "Cyrano and John were their own men, lived by the beat of their own drum, believed in independence, in forging one's own way over the conformity of their times."

Which is cue for Wendell to strut and pivot like a practiced peacock, as he recites:

> What would you have me do?
> Seek patronage of some great man,
> And like a creeping vine on a tall tree
> Crawl upward, where I cannot stand alone?
> No thank you!
> Be a buffoon
> In the vile hope of teasing out a smile
> On some cold face? No thank you!

335

So, when I win some triumph, by some chance,
Render no share to Caesar—in a word,
I am too proud to be a parasite,
And if my nature wants the germ that grows
Towering to heaven like the mountain pine,
Or like the oak, sheltering multitudes—
I stand, not high it may be—but alone!

Without a pause for bewilderment to settle into discomfort, Craig, that is Roxanne, and Wendell, that is Cyrano, then perform a much-practiced signature duet:

Roxanne: Live, for I love you!
Cyrano: No, in fairy tales
When to the ill-starred Prince the lady says
"I love you!" All his ugliness fades fast—
But I remain the same, up to the last!
Roxanne: I have marred your life—I, I!
Cyrano: You blessed my life!
Never on me had rested woman's love.
My mother even could not find me fair:
I had no sister; and, when grown a man,
I feared the mistress who would mock at me.
But I have had your friendship —grace to you
A woman's charm has passed across my path.

And now worked up, and with a lifetime of repressed desire to act, to be an actor, Wendell, er, Cyrano, gives his last speech, and most fervent tribute to John:

My nose is a Gargantuan! You little Pig-snout,
you tiny Monkey-Nostrils, you virtually
Invisible Pekingese-Puss, don't you realize
that a nose like mine is both scepter and
orb, a monument to my superiority? A great
nose is the banner of a great man, a
generous heart, a towering spirit, an
expansive soul—such as I unmistakably am,
and such as you dare not dream of being,
with your bilious weasel's eyes and no nose
to keep them apart! With your face Asia

lacking in all distinction—as lacking, I say,
in interest, as lacking in pride, in
imagination, in honesty, in lyricism—in a
word, as lacking in nose as the other offensively bland
expanse at the opposite
end of your cringing spine—which I now
removed from my sight by stringent
application of my boot!

Roxanne, who has had few lines, has the last empathetic word: "Oh, don't take it so hard. I drove into this madness. Every woman needs a little madness in her life."

The performance ends, and it being a somber celebration of life affair, Wendell and Craig began to exit stage left without taking a bow (though Wendell later admits that bowing after a performance was also part of his lifelong dream). The audience seems too dazed and confused to know whether it is proper to applaud, and, it has to be said, many would have preferred to brandish pitchforks.

But then a single volley of loud clapping erupts from the back of the hall, followed by equally loud whistling. I can see Smokey, now standing, and when I wave, he yells, "Yeah man, great show, a little weird, but really great!" A pause follows Smokey's inspired example, then a dribble from disparate locations in the Great Hall, causing a wave, resulting in a crescendo, that peaks with all the great leaders in the Great Hall clapping, which inspires Wendell and Craig to come back to center stage and take that long and proper bow. Followed by three bowing encores, for no particular reason.

I love Smokey for that, which consolidates my hunch that I have a new bromance pal for Paddy's Pub. John will approve.

As Wendell lingers over his fourth colossal low-flung bow, I wheel over for closing remarks and quite possibly my St. Jude's swan song. I have to pause to still my still laughing silly self, and as per Edie's familiar instructions, I break the laugh by shutting my gob. I also have to wipe rapturous tears of laughter from my eyes with the back of my hand. I did invite Wendell and Craig to add relevant lines from the play to keep the audience engaged. When they showed what they had selected, I suggested they cut the program by half, thinking once we have audience attention, let's not induce boredom. But after this performance, I wish they'd quadrupled the size of the program. Hell, I wish they'd tied up the sitting stiffs for the entire afternoon and performed the whole play, twice.

With an intake of unbated breath, I begin, to reluctant and unwilling ears, what remains unsaid about John Staffal. "As Wendell, alias Cyrano de Bergerac, and his able assistant Craig, alias Roxanne, have dramatized, John and his own Cyrano alter ego forged their own path, even or especially when facing the ire of the madding mob. They were independent to a fault, and John wanted it known that his fault cost him his marriages and families, leaving him to hang with the likes of me at Paddy's Pub on a Thursday night. I won't dare list many of the invectives he used against himself in this regard. Suffice it to say, for all his extravagances and indulgences, he suffered the isolation of his choices, for as Christopher Marlowe says in Faustus, 'Hell is just a frame of mind.'

"But independence also allowed him to pursue truth with integrity, always, in a way few of us will ever have the courage to do. Still, it is important for us to know that for all his independence and eccentric ways, he was motivated to do what was right for all of us. Because 'No man is an island entirely of itself. Any man's death diminishes me, because I am involved in mankind.'"

From the back of the hall a voice screams, "Try person-kind!"

"Thank you," I respond. "John Staffal was telling John Donne just that the other day."

I'm frankly shocked at how little protest there has been so far. While the president's office communicated an expectation for the officers of the university to attend and behave at John's celebration of life, protesters may not have gotten the memo. "The thing is, in the interests of person-kind, John had a mission, which included the right to say or desist from having to say person-kind. He had an idea of the university, based on a thousand-year-old tradition, not as a safe or risk-free space, but as a cauldron of strife and disharmony that just happened to be bloody interesting; a place of constant controversy where conflicting ideas can coexist precisely because in allowing for diverse ideas and discourse, a progression from ordinary to extraordinary will percolate, ferment, and eventually come to fruition for the betterment of woman, man, or person, whether kind or not. And we, who are required to tolerate ideas good and bad, will create our own, often better ideas, which surely is the only route to greatness. At least this is what John believed.

"It used to be about the idea; that is, the idea that can rock and transform our world, even or especially if it exists outside of the self from which the idea emanates. But the Canaries Grand Telescope that we use to gaze into the universe has been turned around and inward such that we are now navel-gazing. And what we see close-up and personal is race, skin color, a kaleidoscope of gender possibilities, among many other distinguishing features, which all informs us of what, exactly? No matter how hard we navel-gaze, no matter how close up we go, we will never locate where merit, compassion, internal fortitude, and the content of character are located.

"In the safest place and the most affluent time in history, people are scared, perpetually fearful, stressed, and depressed. All day I hear, 'My life has no meaning, what should I do?' I say, 'I'm a simple guy, let me think about it.

In the meantime, go work in that soup kitchen.' Whether or not ladling soup solves the problem, turning the Grand Telescope of life around and outward again—where no person-kind is an island—surely gives some perspective on our own minutiae, and seemingly intractable problems.

"We are not our various and many birth features. Those immutable qualities do not define us. The sum of any of us is greater than our parts. I am not this wheelchair. While it limits me if I let it, it does not define me. I, wreck of a human being as I may be, am more than that. You are more than that. We are more than that. I will never recognize the you that matters, see the you that resides within by adding up your external identity features. Really seeing you requires knowing you, and that takes more than what can be seen. This is a question of what it is to be human."

I stop. I wait. I stretch, and again Smokey claps, with other scattered applause in his wake. I am being serious but fight the urge to break into a great belly laugh. Again. I think John may be playing with me.

I hold up a flaccid limb to still the crowd, which reverts from slight shuffling to absolutely still. "Thanks, Mom." I get a few giggles, Smokey most of all. "Just a few housekeeping notes, and then I want to end this celebration of life with a piece of music that has great significance for John."

There is a sense of relief that I might be winding down. "You are no doubt relieved that I haven't referred to the gruesome way that John died. That story has led to John's death receiving worldwide media coverage. There is an ongoing police investigation that will determine what actually happened. But in knowing John, I know that whatever happened to his physical body had less of murderous intent than what happened in response to what he believed in and acted on here at St. Jude's. I think it is important when someone dies, especially if that someone was devoted to truth, to set the record straight. I am setting the record straight.

"John was accused of sexual misconduct, which was often referred to, especially in university communications, as the certainty of sexual assault. These untrue accusations were deliberate and shameful. John was not a white supremacist, Islamophobe, misogynist, ableist, or whatever disparaging name you might want to call him. He was just a guy who was not afraid to offend, because his telescope was properly pointed outward into space. It's also true he wasn't always a nice guy. He once called me a gimp without a limp. He often pissed me off, by the way. Still, and emphatically, I loved this guy who could piss me off while astounding me with courage, loyalty, and such bloody interesting conversation. Most of all, he cared and went the extra mile when it mattered.

"Like for example when I got a federal grant for $66 million dollars for accessibility. It was John who let me know the university has taken it and has designs to use it in other, highly suspicious ways. His investigation of university spending, especially nonacademic spending of the last few years, was suppressed, and he was vilified. The malfeasance of our accessibility money was just more of the same. John documented over two hundred inappropriate messages and threats to his person-hood, which he passed on to me, just in case anyone is interested. Same, in about the same number, when he raised controversial issues in Senate over the years. What has crept into university functioning is the belief that threats made and money spent by the enlightened in the interests of progressive causes are immune to legal consequence. John's death and what remains of my life say otherwise. And it turns out we have friends, since no man or person is an island. Those for whom this message is intended may learn that persons and their actions cannot be isolated to an island, a safe space, or an ivory tower. You will be hearing from us. Thank you."

The look on people's faces defies description, so I won't describe it. Still, I take my sweet time, freeze the entire scene in time, take in frozen faces, one by one, into my mind's eye, grin, and think, *Hope that's the send-off you wanted, bud.*

At which point the Great Hall fills with the voice of Renata Tebaldi's rendition of Puccini's "O mio babbino caro," same music as began Edie's wedding, a different affair, with a different audience on a different and better day. Still, this day threatens to end well. Very well, indeed.

CHAPTER THIRTY-NINE

Two Christmas Eves, decades and distances apart

"Is it fair to say, in throwing a dangerous grenade, you got a nice Christmas present this afternoon?" Aunt Isobell asks, with childlike innocence and a touch of teenage mischievousness.

"Yes," I answer, and then pause while others sit down. We are about to dig into an elaborate Christmas Eve dinner, our first together, with the table fully laid and everyone accounted for, except Pearl, who is in her room finishing a book on the Egyptian pyramids. Steam rises from the various dishes, each carefully timed to be ready at this exact moment. Sister Sandrine has made a magnificent seafood casserole, Brenda serves vegetables and rice, and Iggy has frozen his ass off, barbecuing a large salmon. Luna, who we are pleased agreed to join us, prepared a series of interesting appetizers that we polished off an hour ago. Pearl was responsible for making a very special dessert, which is code for the fact that she chose it and we bought it. Still, it will be a surprise, saved for after we put up and decorate the Christmas tree. I love the togetherness of our celebration and am truly grateful that no person-hood is an island.

"I had a word with John's three exes, who were very pleased, so with the celebration of wife in the bag, I think John would have been pleased too. Craig and Wendell, and especially Wendell, were thrilled at the opportunity to show off their dormant acting chops. Craig mentioned that my reference to inappropriate spending, and especially explicit mention of the $66 million, made the president's head explode."

Iggy asks, "What about the Special Adviser to the President? How will she explain it? How did she handle your—"

"Little financial magnum opus," I finish.

"Oh Phelim," my aunt Isobell says with urgency, "it was more than that."

"A truly human moment," Sister Sandrine adds, "that some willfully will not hear."

"We inmates of the asylum always create problems when we speak up," I say, saluting the two good Sisters with my mug. "Anyway, Luna came up to me afterward and reported that our SAP was not having an exceptional experience."

"I would describe it as the world's worst experience," Luna says. "I wonder if they will have to change her job title."

"I only caught her backside as she vacated the hall as if it was the epicenter of a new corona virus. Come to think of it, I must be the virus."

"How concerned are you?" Aunt Isobell asks.

"Not nearly as concerned as I was before the celebration."

"I suspect your aunt was referring to concern for your job and the Center," Sister Sandrine offers.

"Ah," I begin. "Well, same answer. They will want to fire me, despite my protective cloak, and decimate the Center, but there was national press in the room—I know because I've been asked for a couple interviews about my closing comments—so whatever happens, it will not go unnoticed."

"You used to love it when you were able to operate just under the radar," Iggy says.

"That's true, but for different reasons. Then, nobody gave a hoot, and being under the radar allowed us to launch innovative, bold projects and seek funding without having to ask for permission. Today, being under the radar means they can have their way with us without the watchful eye of anyone who can verify what the hell just happened."

"Did you wash your hands?" Brenda asks her precocious daughter as she joins us at the dinner table.

"Yes."

"Really, because I can still see at least three marker colors on your fingers, and you weren't even using your markers today."

"You didn't ask if I washed my hands *today*," Pearl answers.

"You knew what I meant, young lady."

Pearl thinks about this, which guarantees that her answer will pierce the messy logic of adult reasoning. "What if someone is on trial for murder and the lawyer just asks if the murderer is guilty, but he forgets to ask if he is guilty of murder?"

"Okay," Brenda says passively, not really following.

"Well, the murderer might get off because the lawyer could have been asking about stealing or speeding. The lawyer has to ask the right question or else everyone is going to think the criminal is innocent."

"You've been thinking about this for a while, haven't you?" Iggy asks.

Pearl looks content with her presentation but does not respond.

"Ah, very clever. Pearl is calling for a general moratorium on the use of imprecise language," Aunt Isobell comments.

"Fine," Brenda says. "Pearl, please go and wash your hands right now, today, this Christmas Eve at 7:24 p.m."

Pearl half smiles and gets out of her chair, knowing she has been defeated by rank but not by logic.

"Will Wendell and Craig continue to pursue the $66 million debacle through the Board of Governors?" Aunt Isobell asks.

"Oh, yes," I say. "Craig is sending me an email today to look at his draft letter to all members of the board. I thanked him and said he didn't have to do that until after Christmas, but he said he has plenty of time since he and Wendell were flying to San Jose right after today's celebration. It's probably already done, but I haven't checked my emails for a while, and I don't intend to."

"It almost sounds like you may have some time to relax this Christmas," Sister Sandrine says with a wide smile.

"How about that?" I answer, "Real time in this really good company, and it really doesn't get any better, which reminds me, we didn't say grace. Auntie?"

"Thought you'd never ask," Aunt Isobell responds, quick as a whip. "How about the simple version? Dear Lord, we want to express our gratitude for this bounty, particularly these people, our family at our gathering at this time, for all time. Amen. Oh, and Merry Christmas."

"I think you nailed it," Iggy says.

"Even by Luna's bottom-line standards," I add.

"If I knew praying was that easy, I'd probably do it sometimes," Luna says, wistfully. "It's those long-winded and insincere prayers that put me off. Sorry, I don't mean to say you and Sister Sandrine shouldn't pray a lot, that is, whenever you want to." Luna, waits, a bit flustered for a moment. Then, seeing that Aunt Isobell and Sister are smiling, she asks, "What?"

"How do you know we pray for long hours, or for short minutes, or at all?" Sister Sandrine asks.

"I-I don't really, I just assumed ...."

Aunt Isobell giggles. Her normally uber pale complexion has a reddish glow whenever she indulges in a glass of wine. "Well, there are many ways to pray, actually. And I'll let you in on a little secret. I get bored by scripted long prayers, too."

"Really?" Luna exclaims. "So how else do you pray?"

"Same way you do," Aunt Isobell answers.

In answer to Luna's look of incredulity, Aunt Isobell continues. "I've seen you working with students. You care, and more to the point, you do what needs to get done to help them, even when it is difficult."

"We all do that," Luna responds.

"Not all. And it speaks to your character that you do it and don't think much of it. But you can't fool us. The truth is you pray through your work. There is a quote I've always liked by the poet Kahlil Gibran, who simply says that work is our love made visible."

A quiet, peaceful mood descends upon the table.

"Well, I hope I didn't create a somber mood," Aunt Isobell remarks.

"Quite the opposite," Brenda answers.

"Well then, will anyone mind if I tell a joke?"

We all look at Aunt Isobell and wonder, in a happy way, what has gotten into her.

No one answers and then we all do. "Sure." "Absolutely." "Good ahead."

"Good. Now let me get this right. I don't like it when I start a joke and then realize that I haven't got it right and it's too late. Okay, a new restaurant named Karma has opened downtown, but it doesn't have a menu because you get what you deserve."

She enjoys the group response and is pleased with the telling. And so our Christmas Eve progresses, a made-up family enjoying each other's company, pleasantly surprised it has ever come to be. Yes, that would accurately describe our festive time and version of home on our island of the misfits.

The sequence of events for Christmas Eve has been much anticipated and meticulously planned. Dishes are to be cleared before attending to our naked Christmas tree. Cutting real trees for Christmas has been banned for the past three years. Rather than commit acts of violence, we now purchase plastic imitations from China. We are impressed, even if confused, by the packaging that promises "real green coloring." Our festive tree is guaranteed for twenty years and has some recycled plastics. What "real green coloring" is and what percentage might be recycled is anyone's guess. Unadvertised is the fact that the "green" alternative to tree violence takes over five thousand years to break down in landfills around the world. Still, it claims to be eco-friendly, and we are comforted by the fact that we have all gone green. White Christmas is so yesterday in a world that seeks to correct the corrosive past.

After dishes are done, decorations will be laid out in designated piles according to how they are to be coordinated into the look we hope to achieve. When we are satisfied that our tree has the right Christmas look, presents will be placed underneath, and then Pearl wants photos taken of—bless her heart—her family. After our family portrait, dessert will be served with coffee, this being the most carefully guarded secret of the century as per Pearl's instructions. The architectural keystone feature of our Christmas Eve is going to be a screening of It's a Wonderful Life. By now Pearl has heard much about this Frank Capra classic, but as mentioned, Brenda has been negligent of her daughter's cultural education, and the poor girl has never seen it. We are both excited, Pearl almost as much as I am.

During these times of coordinated group effort, I do nothing except feel content and useless. Only Luna and I are left at the table, and even she says she had things to do, people to see, which doesn't include me. She brought a big bag of presents that still need wrapping, and Brenda is searching the house for scissors and wrapping paper. Luna is about to lay rubber, but she stops and says, "I've been meaning to ask you something. I saw David today and he barely said hi. What gives?"

"Did you notice who he left with today?"

"No."

"Our esteemed SAP of exceptionally disturbing experience."

"What? How is that possible?"

"I was going to save this little diddy, but since you ask, David called me yesterday morning. He beat around the bush and then not so subtly asked what I was going to say at John's celebration today."

"Why, what the hell?!"

"He was fishing, as emissary for the SAP."

"Son of a ...."

"What I didn't tell you about when my computer got hacked is that it was David who did it."

"I'll kill him! Why would he—you mean he's in league with, with the SAP?"

"I'm afraid so. Anyway, before you explode, of course I didn't tell him about the grenade I had planned for today. And as we chatted, he understood that his little fishing expedition was too fishy for me. I was going to leave it at that. But then as we passed each other in the hallway before the celebration, I just said it."

"What?"

"I said, 'I know it was you.'"

"Just like Michael Corleone to his brother Fredo on New Year's Eve in Havana?"

"I hadn't thought of it like that, but yeah, just like that, and I just left it at that. He couldn't look me in the eye, was uncomfortable as hell, but didn't deny it, and I suspect from now on will be as scarce as, well, a real Christmas tree."

"But why, why did he do this to you, to us?"

"A job, a career is the easy answer, but beyond that there are many imponderables in life, and this just gets added to that pile."

And then, swearing like a drunken sailor, Luna is gone to wrap presents with a fury. I remain grateful for a rare exit without having been so frustrating.

I'm alone. Again. I take in the scramble of bodies moving back and forth across my line of vision, in the frantic holy moment. It feels good. It is the gift I always wanted but never expected to get. A gift of men's briefs that will adorn the bottom of our tree before gracing my bottom will be my second favorite gift this Christmas. Thoughts about family—that lie too deep for tears—will remain unspoken, while expressions of thanks for my gift under the tree will be brief.

I feel a swell of gratitude that has not always been easy to conjure. Which reminds me of another place I need to be. And since these Christmas preparations might take a while, I briefly exit the site of briefs. I know, I've gone too far, far beyond brief. I have time, and it is essential I make a Christmas Eve visit to Roma and Fred. Frankly, I'm feeling sheepish for leaving them on the proverbial cliff-hanger of Hitler's dangerous digs.

We are not excited so much as resigned. Looking skyward we can no longer see pine boughs swaying across our line of vision as has been a comfort during previous nights. The sky is cloud-covered, dark, ominous. There is no bright yellow moon; there are no distractions. There is no escaping the deed we must do. I am aware of my Luger in the same way as Roma regards her vial of cyanide. I take succor in the fact it will be easier to survey Berghof activity in darkness.

I almost smile to myself, aware that in my other pocket is half of a large sausage as bribe for Blondi, should the opportunity arise. I can't help but think, even in this dark moment, of the ribald humor this sausage would elicit among old Boston friends from my former life. I look up again and see darkness as reminder that moonlight and former life are gone. The pine boughs we cannot see and the deed we must do will not reveal themselves. Clarity and comprehension will not come; desperation and determination remain.

Though we cannot be heard, we rarely talk and when we do, we whisper. Roma leans toward me, our heads touch, and she whispers hot breath into a cold ear, "Merry Christmas Eve."

"You too," I whisper back, wanting more hot breath against cold winter air.

"But we don't celebrate Christmas," she says back.

"But you might want to when you're with me."

"When I'm with you," she says simply.

It is a poignant moment, laying bare the juxtaposition between what we rarely admit to even to ourselves and the reality of our plight.

The hours pass slowly. We are used to cold and boredom but cannot get used to enduring the same within a stone's throw of Hitler's house. Though we have done surveillance past nights, we half expect German soldiers to take us captive any second. We wonder if the Goebbels family visiting at Christmas will shake up the habits of the household. We know Hitler stays up late, has a curious addiction to films that he insists others watch with him every night. But surely this habit will not remain unchanged on Christmas Eve. Surely, with children at the Berghof, what people do and when they go to bed will change. We know nothing but whispering fragments of nothingness passes time, during which nothing happens.

The side door opens, and a maid comes out for a cigarette. She is joined by someone in uniform. Neither is dressed for winter and once again can be expected to last for the duration of one cigarette. At least our familiar clandestine couple are adhering to habit on Christmas Eve. They agree to meet later. It is 9:13 p.m. I try not to check the time too often. Time moves more slowly when one checks too often.

Lying in the snow, not talking, arms and legs touching under three blankets, we are not bored, we do not mentally try to hasten whatever may come to pass. We are scared and have unspoken awareness that these will likely be our last moments together. And it is surely the unspoken nature of our many fears that compels Roma to finally whisper vignettes of her life, memories of her family and what they meant to her, into my waiting ears. I have hungered for this intimacy but did not expect it. Wounds too deep have come up against moments too few.

"I've been thinking of life, the early years before we realized what the Nazis, what their ascent to power could mean to a Polish Jewish family living in Warsaw. I mean when we were happy, there was no reason to think our happiness would not grow into more happiness. I now realize how naive I was, but what is the alternative for children, teach them to be unhappy? I know my father knew some things of another, unhappier world, but he was very protective, and I believed, we all did, that he would protect us, that his strength would save us. It was all we knew. Sometimes, he and two of my uncles on my mother's side would be whispering in the kitchen, and I knew they were worried about something, but then they would end their whispers and turn to us and play a game or make a joke.

"I knew something worried Father, but ours was still a happy home. I often asked him if he was worried about something, and he always said no. That is why I was so shocked when I called home after Kristallnacht, and he said I was never to come home. I needed to see my family; I don't regret coming back. But I can never forget the unhappiness in people's eyes when I arrived at our family apartment, where six of us had lived, to find so many people. They too were family by some connection, but they were strangers, and they were terrified.

"In her letter to me as I prepared to come back from Boston, my younger Sister Ruth wrote that they would not escape the hell that had descended upon them, that Father was dead in advance of the fact. I think my worse moment was when I first saw the look on Father's face as I walked into the crowed place that had been our home. He died thinking he had disappointed us all. He had not saved us, and in his estimation of himself he had failed even to convince me, who was safe in America, to just stay where I was."

I am aware of piercing silence once Roma pauses. I want to comfort her, reassure her, tell her sweet lies, but it is time to listen, not comment, not speak.

"Ours was the only family that had its own room, not shared by any of the other nine families that occupied our apartment. All six of us were in my youngest sister Aria's small bedroom. There were smiles, hugs, some laughing even, but most of all, what I was confronted with was defeat. My mother was broken. Ruth had lost all her vitality. My brother Asher, whose name means fortunate or happy one, was depressed and dispirited. He never had my father's strength. Aria, who alone had some life in her, was ecstatic to see me. But she was too young, even in these conditions, to fully understand.

"Because of the near starvation conditions in the ghetto, I volunteered to try to get more food from the Germans. And it worked for a while. But it also gave me a reputation for being audacious. One day when I went to the Germans, the commanding colonel came out to have a look at me, and he decided then and there that I was to be his. Two soldiers brought me back to the apartment. I was told I had fifteen minutes to pack a suitcase and say goodbye to my family. In reality I had less than five minutes. I did not pack a suitcase. I did not take anything. My thoroughly defeated family was driven down another peg, and Aria clung to me and wailed. The soldiers had to pull us apart, and the soldier who held Aria was quite rough with her. She was thrown across the room. My last sight of any member of my family was looking at Aria on the floor looking at me uncomprehendingly, and I knew she was about to join the ranks of the defeated. Our eyes locked, and the innocence and playfulness that is to be the domain of childhood was gone. I think I hate the Nazis most of all for stealing the childhood of children. All that Aria had left was terror and the horrible details that would end her life. I heard rumors, then confirmation from one of the colonel's staff members that in just ten days over 300,000 people were deported from the Warsaw ghetto and sent to Treblinka. Warsaw ghetto Jews will not survive the Treblinka gas chambers, and if any do, they would have to have more life in them than my family."

When Roma stops, I can hear her shallow breathing in the crisp night air. I say, "Thank you."

She leans into me. "So you see, for our fifteen minutes of life that remain, you're all I have."

Our cold cheeks touch. "It's enough," Roma says.

"We're enough," I simply say back. It was not, was never going to be us against the world. Rather, in our pathetic attempt at revenge and redemption, it is us against the evil that has descended upon the world. That is more than enough.

Another two hours pass. I have returned from surveying the entrance to the kitchen from the other side of the house. The kitchen door never opened. I still do not have a plan. It is almost midnight. It is hard to believe that children of all ages are becoming excited at the prospect of presents, family gatherings, and a carefully prepared goose. Who knows what kind of Christmas the children might have inside the Berghof?

My mind has been moving a hundred miles an hour. I have worked out several scenarios, and I've considered different timeframes for a desperate attempt at killing Hitler and Goebbels. I have not lost my nerve but cannot decide which scenario might make possible our wild, delusional assault. I cannot reconcile the meaning of the holiday with what I must do. I tell myself, *Think plan of action*, and I think about Christmas.

The one decorated fir tree or Christbaum on the grounds is adorned with a ridiculously large swastika. Tree lights are also shaped into a crude-looking swastika. The Nazis, by decree, have reinvented Christmas, with Santa Claus supplanted by a Germanic Odin figure. And most important, the belief in Christmas as a harbinger for the coming of Christ under the Nazis is referred to as the coming of the savior Führer. It occurs to me that the Führer is going to be busy this Christmas, between getting presents to all the children around the world and tending to the six Goebbels children. Saving Christmas is reason enough to kill the bastard. I am about to relay these deep insights to Roma as well as an update on the time of 12:02 a.m., now Christmas Day, when we hear a voice.

Figures emerge from the side door, one low-slung, moving quickly in haphazard fashion. Blondi attacks her newfound freedom and the cold night air. She stops suddenly, to our stupefied relief, presumably to relieve herself. I don't know whether to first grab my Luger in one pocket or the sausage in the other. We hear voices and can see that there are two people walking slowly behind as Blondi darts this way and that along the path. We wait, afraid to inhale, terrified to exhale. We are not close enough to be seen or heard, but we are also not fully rational. The two figures pass in front of light from a window in the house.

"Yes, a limp. See, Goebbels."

A few more steps, and Roma whispers. "And Hitler."

I turn toward Roma. She senses what I am thinking and says, "They will see you."

"No, look," I say pointing. "A little further along, and the path is completely dark."

"Surely, they will not go so far."

"They are following the dog, so maybe. Roma, look at me. Either way, I have to go."

"The dog—"

I kiss her, cup her face, and we look at each other in the semidarkness. Love, sadness, panic, regret, tenderness, resignation, and reluctance to let go sweep across her face. "I have to go."

I crouch low and creep forward, pulling both my Luger and the sausage from my pockets. The conversation between Hitler and Goebbels has become low and muted. Goebbels has been systematically answering Hitler's question regarding how to shape German public opinion about the Wehrmacht spending the winter in Russia. Goebbels says that the public will accept the campaign taking longer than expected, but the bigger issue is the number of dead German soldiers.

"I don't believe Halder," Hitler scoffs. "I agreed to send another 750,000 soldiers in spring, but that doesn't mean I agree with his estimates of casualties."

Hitler's voice grows louder, as neither stopping nor resuming walking again seems to be the ideal state for his continuing diatribe. I mentality beckon them to keep moving forward, from light into the darkness where they permanently belong.

I have cleared the last cover of trees. I was on an upward incline but am now crawling across level ground and wet snow. I have lost sight of Blondi, and so apparently have Hitler and Goebbels. Hitler begins to move again and calls for Blondi to come. His first call is gentle, but the second is impatient.

Come on, come on, come on, I beckon silently. I'm also worried about where Blondi is. Hitler and Goebbels are about ten yards from where the path darkens; I am about thirty yards from where they stand.

I am still crawling but will soon need to stand if I am to take a shot. If they start back to the house, I will need to be close, since I might slip as I try to shoot. But I will shoot.

Quite suddenly Hitler changes subjects and seems delivered from the demon of his recent diatribe. "You know, we have that Gary Cooper Western, and it is quite good. I am not in the mood for something more serious. Perhaps we should go back; we did promise the children to be up early."

"They will wait in bed until whatever time suits the Führer."

"No, no, a promise is a promise. Even with all my responsibilities, tomorrow is Christmas, and the children deserve—"

"The children do not deserve but are honored, are forever in the Führer's debt, as are Magda and I …."

They have crossed from light into darkness, and I rise quickly and silently. They show no sign of alarm, and Hitler calls once more for Blondi. Suddenly from my right side Blondi is upon me. She lunges, without barking, and I raise my arm and hold her up, standing on two legs. I instinctively raise my left hand to fire the Luger, but then I pause and shove the sausage held in my right hand into her receptive mouth. A German shepherd is among the most formidable of all guard dogs, but as large and gangly as Blondi is, she is not quite as threatening as she will become. She falls to all fours with the prized sausage in her mouth, just as Hitler and Goebbels come to realize they are not alone.

A cursory, guttural noise escapes from Goebbels. Hitler snorts and turns toward me. I approach them quickly and aim where I reason the next threat of vocal alert is most likely to come. I hit Goebbels in the middle of the chest. I then shift and aim at Hitler. A shrill noise escapes from his throat as my shot hits him on the left side just under the collar bone. I swear. This is not a decisive shot in a decisive moment. Hitler falls but threatens to get up until my left boot catches him under the jaw. He falls backward, and I shoot him in the chest. I then move to Goebbels. It is completely dark, so I reach down, locate his face and then his mouth, pull back my fingers, and shoot. I turn back to Hitler, kneel and place my right hand on his face, locating the stubble of his ridiculous mustache. I place the gun into his insolent, perverse mouth and shoot at close range. Even in darkness, even if partial guesswork, Hitler's and Goebbels's dental work, skulls, and brains are shattered, and they are dead.

I run. I slip and fall, get back up, and run again. Blondi comes bounding toward me, jumps up on my left, Luger side, thinking it is a game. After watching the Nazis with their German shepherds, I have never liked the breed, but young Blondi is okay. She is playing, not biting. If there is the prospect of more sausage, she is interested. But there is not, so she forsakes the game. And now that she might be raised by an owner other than Hitler, I suddenly have high hopes. For her, not Roma and myself.

Roma comes toward me, I stumble again, and we fall together. Through the haze of a thousand emotions, I am annoyed, for I want her to be running away from this house. But again, and inexplicably, for an infinitesimally short time that seems suspended in time, I stop and look into the face of a thousand expressions, a face I thought I'd never see again. I breathe deeply, extending the stolen gift of perhaps two perfect seconds, and I am drinking in the forgiveness this life provides. And then we run. And run.

EPILOGUE

Three months later at false dawn, ostensibly Phelim's bedroom, where his consciousness resides but cannot be located.

On Christmas Eve, Pearl's surprise dessert was a chocolate Santa village. We all enjoyed it, and the consensus is that I ate the most. By far.

The other consensus is that *It's a Wonderful Life* is the best Christmas film ever. By far. The proof being that Pearl agrees with me. Just in case that fact was not heard, seen or recorded, Pearl agrees with me!

The investigations into the deaths of Professor John Staffal and Hercules Angelopoulos are neither solved nor closed. Interviews and communications with police officers related to the case are unequivocal in their conviction that John was murdered, but questions remain unanswered. Detective Kritanta alone equivocates. We agree that Angel was murdered, especially after the good detective discovers a single strand of hair in John's office that is DNA confirmed to belong to Andy MacPherson. The same was found on an article of Angel's clothing after his death in his apartment. But about John Staffal, she of kind eyes either knows something or knows I know something. She hasn't said so, but her kind eyes have a knowing intelligence that cannot be denied. But I'm not worried. If there is too much heat in the future, I can always wear John's gargantuan nose and plumed hat and wheel around campus without anyone knowing who I am.

Though it may be hard to avoid detection from Kale. They have had their security budget doubled, with talk of more to come. A national recruitment campaign for additional security officers of the proper identity parts is under way. They have also been promoted to Dean of Security. I fear for Kale, for the impossible demands placed upon them—rolling a ball of wax uphill seems a fitting metaphor. I would hate for them to become an insecure has-dean. (If Kale falls off the dean's list, they would always be welcome among our motley crew.) The question of assigning the title *Dean*, historically the purview of academia, to a nonacademic, non–student service position is posited in Senate without answer. Kale's deanship happens within days of police disclosure that John's death was due to a gruesome medieval torture known as the "Vigils of Spain." This name is identified by a St. Jude's medieval scholar who is shocked—stumbling into sunlight from darkness seems an apt comparison—to have been able to offer expertise on anything relevant to the last couple hundred years.

Though not part of the official investigation, they have followed up on all possible leads in the Staffal case. For example, they interviewed the bewildered chair of the Spanish department about the Vigils of Spain. The chair's incredulous response was that interviewing her made as much sense as suspecting a Spanish omelet. Without expectation, but with the determination of someone who leaves no stone unturned, they inquired at the cafeteria, and sure enough, from seven until eleven each morning, Winston creates Spanish omelets. Winston howled during his interview even as he continued flipping omelets on the grille, including perfect Spanish omelets. With tears in his eyes, Winston said, "I don't know anything about the Spanish angle, but I do have a cousin whose middle name is Virgil." Kale left the cafeteria with intel on Winston's cousin but not before sitting down and eating one of Winston's delectable Spanish omelets.

John's death was not in vain. But it is also true, we won't win the culture wars engulfing university campuses these enlightened days. We just won't. Those would be the same culture wars I had no idea were in play a decade or so ago. Still, we limp on (my kingdom for the ability to limp) and do our best, one student, one appointment, one controversy, one act of kindness or meanness—depending on which student you talk to—at a time. We need each other, and none of us can solve the big problems all by our lonesome. We kid ourselves; that is, our narcissistic-induced selves have been educated to believe we can do anything, that anything is possible if we only believe enough. In ourselves. Personally, I have no idea how I got here, how anyone else got here, what I and everyone else is doing here, or what our purpose in life might be—except, maybe, for this one minor revelatory proviso: nothing makes sense, no cause, no purpose, and certainly no ambition, without other people. So the notion that I hold the keys to world change, that I can lead us, save us by belief in self, is the greatest delusion of all time. Our only context in life exists in the people who surround and bookend our sorry asses from the cradle to the grave. John made a mighty contribution, heavily flawed as he was, but his work continues. It was always just a strand in a tapestry, and we hope that in the afterlife—and most of all we hope there is an afterlife—the tapestry comes together, and we human strands remain tightly woven for all time. Weird analogy, I know. Hopefully, the strand closest to me on the tapestry will be Brenda and not

John. He can be a few threads removed. Still, the analogy stands, and who knows, maybe when I get there, I'll be standing.

The Special Adviser to the President, Exceptional Student Experience received a dusting off to be sure, but she survived, was always going to survive. If anyone is to be beheaded over the $66 million debacle, it will be our president, Brad. Rumor holds that the Board of Governors had a replacement in their sights. As is well known, the president of Harvard resigned after the Israeli–Hamas protest debacle a few years back—as if leadership requires taking an actual stand when ideological musings serve so well. Equally insulting, she was accused of academic plagiarism—as if neglecting petty citations is more important than correcting world order. Recently, it was learned that she has accepted a senior position with the World Economic Forum, so we can gratefully expect advanced reordering to follow. She is to head a new think tank dedicated to formulating enhanced DEI policy for organizations throughout the world—whether asked for or not. Apparently, her first initiative is to reimagine university plagiarism policies and to identify groups for whom recycling *duplicative language* is to be lauded. Those who leveled accusations of plagiarism will shamefully come to understand that the issue is fundamentally one of *context*. The document is called "Appropriate Cultural Appropriations for Oppressed Peoples." St. Jude's has indicated it intends to be an early adopter.

Staff and faculty at St. Jude's were disappointed that the former president of Harvard will not be available to lead our noble institution. Still, our SAP was likely glad that she will not have to share the limelight as future DEI plans are enacted. True leadership is not shared; it is special.

David has received a promotion. And why not? He demonstrated his loyalty, resilience, and sophistication regarding the subtleties of university politics to the she who matters. Both he and Tim, the SAP's ever ready Swiss army knife, have ascendant careers, despite being white hetero males. But if they thought what would be required of them has been given, they are mistaken. They will always be tested, will always be required to display their ideological stripes and corrosive loyalty. It is also true that their career perks will be many. Who they will see looking back from the mirror each day is another matter.

Alan, our tech guy, took the hint and got out of Dodge before it got him out. He landed a job in a tech start-up and reports making three times as much moola, with the same ratio applied to how much more he has to do. He's happy with the move. Arthur is still with us, for now. He continues to do essential work for us, one hour, one day at a time, which is all any of us can give. He still enthusiastically interacts with students as if it is his first day as an intern. We are considering taking the SAP, Exceptional Student Experience's suggestion and changing the name of our Center. Center for Redundancy Center comes to mind.

Dean Perkins's DNA test confirmed that she has Celtic and Northern European lineage, so she'd be best advised not to spent too much time in the sun. But the revelation that she is neither Native American nor colored lost its thunder once St. Jude's announced its intention to lead all progressive postsecondary institutions with an awe-inspiring policy that allows and even encourages people to choose their color and ethnicity. How this will square with California's reparations bill, soon to be enshrined in law as an Act of Congress, raises an interesting question. The greater question might be just how do we include all people at all times to partake of all entitlements? When affable President Brad was informally asked about St. Jude's new race and ethnicity liberating policy, the president's office issued a terse formal communication, as follows: *"It is inconceivable that students, staff or faculty members would ever claim to belong to the ethnicity of their choice for personal gain."* Inconceivable.

Andy MacPherson was found and arrested and predictably ratted out Dean Perkins. The case is still being investigated, and charges are likely. It is uncertain whether Andy, the dean, or both will be charged with murder or person-slaughter. Nor is it known if the charge will be for the death of John Staffal or Angel. The word-speak verbiage around the question of who, what, and when together communicates a very telling narrative that the police haven't got a frickin' clue. For the past three months the university's Caring and Compassionate Communications Department—in overdrive to insulate just one person—has stated its strong support for Dean Perkins to continue as dean of Racialized and Gender-Fluid Communities for Diversity, Equity and Inclusion. Reverting to my favourite acronym, dean of DIE, accused of murder, seems fitting. Several thousand students, staff, and faculty have signed a petition demanding that charges against Dean Perkins be unconditionally dropped. Evidence is fake news; proof of murder is conspiracy. How nice.

Craig and Wendell keep in touch via teleconference from Silicon Valley and visit whenever they are in town. (And yes, it's a toss-up between incredulous and ironic that St. Jude's, our $66 mil, and my sorry ass were saved by a couple of dudes from Silicon Valley.) They are still working on it, but they assure me the stolen money will be returned to my office, and our accessibility plans will get back on track, so minor victory for sure. But that will not be an end to it. The intent and resolve of assassins will only grow.

The fate of the convent has not been settled, but it is clear by its founding charter it cannot simply be lopped off and used for any purpose. Its use has to relate to either hospital care or education, the two endeavors the Gray Nuns have performed throughout their, dare I say it, illustrious history. St. Jude's did try to argue that as a postsecondary institution, it fits the bill, but the determination of suitability is adjudicated by Gray Nuns board members.

The problem is, the board was disbanded when members died—well, most of them at least. There is one remaining member who sat on the board when it last convened twenty years ago: Aunt Isobell. Wendell is working with a lawyer, and he is pretty sure it will fall to Aunt Isobell to decide the fate of the convent.

Wendell and Craig have made several proposals for convent use, any of which, with their high-tech company, they are willing to fund. Fully. Craig asked, what about The John Staffal Institute for Free Speech? Wendell was up next and proposed The John Staffal Theater for the Performing Arts, or The John Staffal Shakespearean Globe Theatre. After a moment, during which I made the appropriate oohs and ahs, Wendell mentioned that he would be willing to act in the new theater. This was clearly a bigger deal to him than the money. Craig finished by casually mentioning that there is enough space, and money for that matter, for both. I said, "I'll ask my auntie."

I still haven't and may not ever do anything about Diesel and the guys. I've stopped trying to figure what is the right thing to do. In fact, I've stopped thinking altogether, and I've gotta say, what a relief it is.

My pussyfooting will not matter. Diesel recently opened Instagram, Tik-Tok, and Gangsta-Glam (is new, makes and has billions, but no clue how) accounts displaying few clothes and eye-popping curvaceousness, which combined with her unique name has propelled her number of followers into the stratosphere. With the West on the verge of banning fossil fuels, and with diesel fuel and diesel trucks relegated to the trash heap, Diesel Axel Ford has become a sensation with, among others, nostalgic, displaced, disenfranchised, toxic male millions. Especially former owners of Ford diesel trucks. In China, where diesel and the banned fossil fuels are not synonymous, Diesel's followers number in the staggering hundreds of millions. There is even rumor that Diesel has been offered a substantial amount of money for the book and movie rights to her story. And what aspect of her story might make it into books and films? When I met with the guys for one of our periodic shoot-the-breeze sessions, I asked how they felt about it all. They surprised me and agreed, with smiles bordering on bragging, that if Diesel leaves the attendant program and tells her story, they wouldn't mind a few million or billion people knowing. Everything. If it helps Diesel, that is. Ben suggested they wear matching tuxedoes to the Academy Awards for the ensuing multi-award nominated Hollywood extravaganza.

Hogwash, you say? Wait, there's more. A former high-ranking member of the Chinese Communist Party—presently a CIA-protected asset in the US— claims that Diesel may have prevented nuclear war. The rumor—soon to be an *Atlantic* magazine feature, anticipating a book that will substantiate the rumor—is that China was about to attack Japan for its 8 percent commitment of GDP to defense spending into the foreseeable future. After Washington's weak-kneed inaction over China's takeover of Taiwan and after Japan vacated the Nuclear Non-Proliferation Treaty, the CCP was apparently willing to risk international ire and destroy Japan's newly acquired nuclear arsenal—with the intention of deflecting from their own internal dissension that threatens to explode.

There have been increasingly emboldened riots from "little emperors" (over thirty million young entitled male progeny who will never find a female partner because of China's historic gender bias exacerbated by its fifty-year one-child policy). The situation was becoming desperate until someone within the CCP hit upon an audacious and creative solution (it had to happen eventually). It occurred to this rare genius that the problem was not political so much as an abundance of testosterone in need of relief. It further occurred to said genius that the solution was obvious. It is well known that Japan makes the best, most sophisticated life-like, life-sized sex dolls. The way to quell the rioting is to facilitate the flow. Which resulted in a policy to gift all single Chinese males between the ages of fifteen and fifty-five their choice of a new Japanese sex doll, courtesy the Chinese Communist Party. The initial order of 30 million sex dolls came with one caveat: in addition to the many choices currently available in the Japanese sex arsenal, there needed to be one new creation in the form of Diesel Axel Ford. The rumor of the rumor is that Diesel's millions could become billions. The issue of China surreptitiously contributing billions to Japan's defense budget on the sex doll deal, has not been discussed.

Returning to work one Monday in January, we discovered that a university crew had painted our corridor walls. We thought okay, but with a perfectly white canvas we worried how Kevin might feel when confronted with the fact that his erratic driving is responsible for our corridor scuffing. All of it. Every inch.

We needn't have worried. Kevin proceeded to reapply his creative scuff genius extravaganza with impunity. Kevin has intelligence, sensitivity, and insight, but like us all, he has his blindside. He did not notice the reaccumulation of scuffing along our hundred feet of corridor, did not notice that a thousand or so brushes against white canvas transformed it into a continuous visual scuff installation. He just didn't notice; we who again stare at the mangled corridor as we enter or exit the Center have decided it is as it should be. The scuff lines are our version of Hansel and Gretel's dropped pebbles pointing to our Island of the Misfits. It is our way home. Proof that our Center will hold, and to hell with Yeats.

Most important, Kevin reports that this past winter in our northern scrubland has gone quite well, thank you very much. He still calls me a Papist bastard for reasons only he can explain. He and George are pals, their monthly movie ritual continues, and in my perverse way I think, to those who expect little, much is given.

Three items in the news today. First, Congress has passed legislation to create a new national holiday to replace the recently debunked Martin Luther King Jr. Day. Passage of the bill represents an emerging need for government to take responsibility for the third item from the inalienable rights in the Declaration of Independence, "Life, Liberty and *the pursuit of Happiness*." National Self-Absorption Day or SAD will be held on the third Monday of January to help offset the effects of Seasonal Affective Disorder, or SAD.

Second, recent indices in the economy and in education paint a dismal picture of American decline. Covid-induced temporary problems such as hyperinflation, supply-line problems, and inability to fill millions of entry level and service jobs have become endemic. Meanwhile, innovation and research, as well as skill and knowledge acquisition among new graduates, show a stark lack of competitiveness in a world Americans used to lead. Asked for comment on this disturbing trend, the White House responded, "We have created a new national holiday on the third Monday in January to address this issue."

Third, China says it has definitive proof the Covid-19 virus of years ago was a deliberate biological weapon created by the CIA. President for Life and Beyond, Xi, said the World Health Organization has been given the proof and agrees with China's assessment of origin. Asked if he is in receipt of such proof, the WHO director general responded, "Who, me?" Since President Xi's declaration, a new forty-one-country PEW Research Center poll indicates the percentage of people who have an unfavorable view of China, which hit historic highs during Covid, has been significantly reversed. China has decided, in the spirit of world reconciliation, not to share its proof.

Meanwhile, the Chinese economy, though in a shambles due to the West's overreaction to the virus it caused, is officially recovering nicely. An unidentified party official recently made an off-the-record comment that between "official" economic progress and decline in American universities, China may soon be liberated from its need for cyber theft of research from the corrupt Western world.

I never did locate Perry, and it haunts me. If he is holed up in some obscure place, I hope he is at least writing the Nobel Prize for Literature winner. I fear that Perry may be among a large number of decent people who never did get the memo proclaiming that no man or person-kind is an island. I feel for the Perrys of the world who feel deeply and reveal nothing. They walk as ghosts apart from us, are actually the *we*s among us, but never know it.

Even that failing, disappointment, loss—call it what you will—does not sting as much as the immediacy of Angel's tragic death. We are our brother's keeper, and the responsibility extends beyond our limits for providing care. Yes, an awesome, possibly futile, and yet necessary responsibility which helps mitigate the dilemma of what it is to be human. John would agree, borrowing from Shakespeare, Horatio to Hamlet, as the Danish prince lies dying: "And flights of angels sing thee to thy rest."

For John, I would steal the same Shakespearean send-off along with the preceding line: "Now cracks a noble heart. Good night, sweet prince." As for the Vigils of Spain, what an astonishing, grotesque, macabrely playful (in John's warped mind, and therefore to a minor extent, mine too), and theatrical exit, guaranteed to keep the enlightened lit up now and for all time. I've decided, without agreement with John's method (which is the basis of free thought, free speech, and freedom to act), to keep John's secret, to allow for his one final gesture to continue its unforeseen ripple effect in perpetuity.

What a pain in the ass it must have been to arrange for the drug-induced painless pain in the medieval tortured ass. And to many, if not most, John was considered the biggest pain in the ass of all (and to John many to most were the same). As John knew, the exit effect would be gargantuan—with increased security, commissions of inquiry, and candle vigils (John laughs at this one)—all experienced with one part fear and six parts gratuitous titillation. John's Vigils of Spain debacle did not injure (except for us few who loved him) so much as give the great unwashed, enlightened public something to think about. Maybe the next character assassin slouching toward Bethlehem will give pause before plunging the dagger. Unlikely as pause may be, what a final-curtain performance John pulled off, even if we few are the only ones who appreciate it!

And who comes up with such a caper, and then actually pulls it off? Who? Makes me think the next time I need someone extraordinary to, say, assassinate Hitler, John can be my man. I can just see him in his breeches, leather boots, and doublet, plumed hat and dangling prophylactic olfactory appendage, dueling with SS and Gestapo Nazis. And winning, of course, before plunging his rapier into Hitler's sorry-assed heart. Come to think of it, maybe he and I can go together. Yes, I'll have to give that some serious thought when I next crave flights of fancy to escape a meeting or else caress my way from false dawn into morning light.

Aunt Isobell and Sister Sandrine are fixtures at the Center, the most popular advisers with their students, the most popular staff among my longtime peeps. They are also family, my family—the one I thought I'd never have, but for the grace of God, fell on my fat and grateful lap. Apparently, they like their digs and our living arrangements in the caveman convent we call home. Most of all, they think they'll stick around for a while, be useful and have fun.

Brenda and I are an item extraordinaire. No, not quite right; we are good, very good, but all good relationships are a work in progress, and progression includes some regression. Still, the goodness of our good is that we are family. Pearl too is family, my family, my kid. She isn't quite ready to call me dad yet but did tell me that she wants to stay and live with me forever for three reasons, as follows: my Christmas movie collection, my three auto mechanics books, and the fact that I am someone who is okay—no more, but also no less—that she can talk to. I'll take it.

Roma and Fred escaped. Escaped! Big shock, I know, but they did it. After months of hardship and with newfound hope after dispensing with Hitler, they were ready for anything. But what they faced was almost as unlikely as what they had accomplished. Hiking through the Bavarian Alps in winter was an endurance test worthy of Shackleton at the South Pole. Or even the von Trapp family. We know, Pearl and I, because we just watched the von Trapps' escape through the alps in *The Sound of Music*. Much as we worry for Roma and Fred, we felt reassured after watching the movie.

Iggy is doing fine, though he could use a shot of confidence, assertiveness, all and any of the buzz words these days. In rare instances, when he meets some-one who interests him, he becomes quieter. I try, in my indiscreet way, to make him understand that his is not a formula for how the boy gets the girl. Maybe it's just as well, with Sister Sandrine living under our roof in the bliss of our manufactured family, that she doesn't know. It's also likely true that if Iggy ever declared his love, it would probably be more like a dam bursting than words spoken. Innuendo intended. Still, I'm not convinced that she doesn't know. Edie decided that she was going to take on the Iggy Project; that is, kill the shyness within and drag out a refurbished Don Juan. I applauded her determination and even noticed she'd made a wee bit of progress until she got too sick.

We lost Edie at the end of February. It was hard on all of us, though probably hardest on Edie. She'd like the way I phrased that. She went down quickly after the wedding glow dissipated. She said she had no regrets and talked about the wedding of the century, which was *her* wedding, every time any of us saw her right up to the very end.

She was a fighter and went out hard, like a prize fighter who kidded her-self about the outcome until the last knockout punch. Still, for all she said to the contrary, she knew. She just didn't want us, her peeps, to worry, to be down, to not joke. We are worried about the peep she married, but a number of us will do our best to keep an eye on Joey.

We have to, because Edie said so.

The firemen who attended her wedding turned up in their formal uniforms for her funeral. She would have liked that. Again, I had to deliver a eulogy for someone I loved, and again I had to pull it off as if I didn't care as much as I did, to please the dead person who would never forgive me if I was all weepy and jokeless. I threw in something about her jumping from her coffin into the waiting arms of the firemen in attendance. Shocking, in bad taste, very inap-propriate, all true, but exactly as Edie would have wanted—no, would have insisted. I dealt with her plenty in life and don't want to have her mad at me when I die.

I went to see her the afternoon of the evening that she died. She had had legions of people most days, but for this one last visit, Joey and I were the only ones with her. She was in and out of consciousness, mostly out. She did not recognize me and no longer recognized Joey, who had sat by her bedside and tried to comfort her for over three weeks. I stroked her forearm and said useless things, looked down a final time for a final goodbye. I then wheeled to the foot of her bed and heard Joey say, "Would you look at that?"

Edie, who had not gained consciousness or sat up in bed for any of her three-week stay in hospital, sat bolt upright and smiled. Then, miraculously and yet in strangely fitting fashion, she laughed, that full, surround-sound, all-encompassing laugh, enough to drag any depressive mood out of anyone and demand jolly camaraderie. I had been feeling low, very low, and this was Edie's gift by way of a lesson to and for me. It was exactly what I needed, even though the supposed purpose of the visit was for me to give comfort to her. I was and am grateful. I do and will always remember that laugh.

Rumor has it that, before his assassination, Vladimir Putin applied to teach Shakespeare at St. Jude's. Not having the proper identity parts, much like oppressor Shakespeare, eliminated any chance for this happy occasion. The fact that I started the rumor has to be considered.

This just in, courtesy of a major news outlet: "Diversity Training Increases Prejudice and 'Activates Bigotry' Among Participants, New Study Says." Who knew? St. Jude's progressives will slouch and scheme over this with murderous intent, whereas I will ignore the headline, ignore the prospect of murder, and joke with known assassins as they cross my naive and grateful path. In my inclusive way.

Luna continues to find me so frustrating. I continue to be so frustrating.

And when not being so frustrating, I'm channeling from Springsteen's "Book of Dreams":

> *Tonight, I'm drinkin' in the forgiveness*
> *This life provides*
> *The scars we carry remain but the pain slips away it seems.*

LARRY J. MCCLOSKEY
Foreword by John Weston, Former MP

INARTICULATE
SPEECH
OF THE
Heart

CASTLE QUAY BOOKS

Lament for Spilt Porter

LONGING FOR FAMILY AND HOME

Larry J. McCloskey

CASTLE QUAY BOOKS

WE ARE THE SOLUTION
TO POVERTY

JUST ACT

ANGIE PETERS

CASTLE QUAY BOOKS